# ABERCROMBIE TRAIL

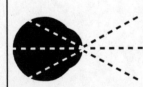

This Large Print Book carries the
Seal of Approval of N.A.V.H.

ABERCROMBIE TRAIL SERIES

# ABERCROMBIE TRAIL

## A NOVEL OF THE 1862 UPRISING

# CANDACE SIMAR

**THORNDIKE PRESS**

*A part of Gale, Cengage Learning*

GALE
CENGAGE Learning·

Detroit • New York • San Francisco • New Haven, Conn • Waterville, Maine • London

Copyright © 2009 by Candace Simar.
Map by Rick Jaskowiak.
Thorndike Press, a part of Gale, Cengage Learning.

Thorndike Press® Large Print Western.
The text of this Large Print edition is unabridged.
Other aspects of the book may vary from the original edition.
Set in 16 pt. Plantin.

LIBRARY OF CONGRESS CATALOGING-IN-PUBLICATION DATA

Simar, Candace.
   Abercrombie Trail : a novel of the 1862 Uprising / by Candace Simar. — Large Print edition.
      pages cm. — (Thorndike Press Large Print Western)
   ISBN-13: 978-1-4104-6124-7 (hardcover)
   ISBN-10: 1-4104-6124-6 (hardcover)
   1. United States—History—1783–1865—Fiction. 2. Great Plains fiction. 3. Large type books. I. Title.
   PS3619.I5565A64 2013
   813'.6—dc23                                              2013016651

Published in 2013 by arrangement with North Star Press of St. Cloud, Inc.

Printed in the United States of America
1 2 3 4 5 6 7 17 16 15 14 13

# ACKNOWLEDGMENTS

I owe a debt of gratitude to Diana Ossana for her encouragement and help along the way. Also a special thanks to the many friends and fellow-writers who helped me with editing, critique, encouragement and good advice. You know who you are — Thanks! Thanks to the good people at North Star Press. And most of all, thanks to my husband who endured countless trips to museums, historical sites, and writing conferences to let me follow my dream. Keith, I couldn't have done it without you.

# AUTHOR'S NOTE

Minnesota history is one of my passions. Since childhood, I've daydreamed about life in the earliest days of Minnesota and wondered how historical events impacted the lives of ordinary people.

One sultry Fourth of July, I was shocked to learn how little our adult children knew about the 1862 Sioux Uprising. Our children, all born and educated in Minnesota schools, thought it a minor skirmish in New Ulm, not realizing how it affected the entire state.

"You ought to write a book," my son said.

As a result, I started researching primary and secondary sources about 1862 Minnesota. I didn't have far to go. My great-grandfather drove the stagecoach from St. Cloud to Fort Abercrombie in the years directly after the uprising. I became entranced with the idea of what he might have experienced had he arrived in Minnesota one year sooner. *Abercrombie Trail* is the story of Evan Jacobson — the story that might have been my great-grandfather's.

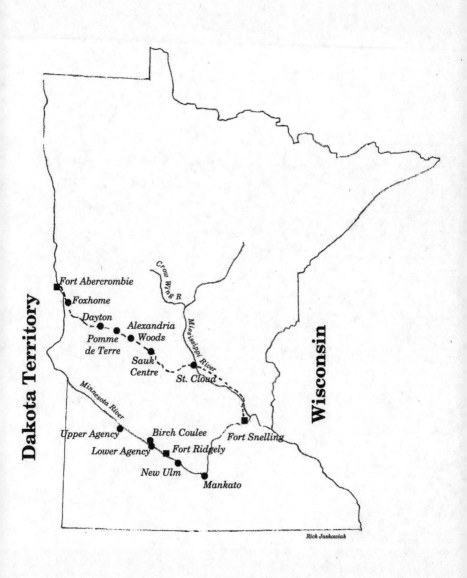

# 1

*1859*

Hatred did not drive me from Norway.

I was angry, angrier than I had ever been in my life, but I did not hate Ole. How could I hate my only brother? Perhaps he spoke from pain, not cruelty. Whatever the reason, his voice echoed in the room where Christina died, where her body lay still warm on the bed.

"We're lucky it is only our sister who died." He looked me full in the face, tears floating in the blue sea of his eyes. "We live to carry on Far's, our father's, name."

A sudden rage blinded me and I raised my fist, but Mor, Mother, stepped between us.

"Evan!" Her voice shrilled, and the tilt of her chin proved she would tolerate no argument. Mor stood only as tall as my armpits, but fire sparked in her eyes, making her loom large as a giant. "She's gone." Her voice dropped to a whisper. "Words and fighting will not bring her back."

I dropped my fist, ashamed of the fury still roaring in my chest. Ole stepped away and stood by the door. I looked at Christina's cooling form, her pale skin, blonde curls around her thin face. Bitter tears choked my throat, and my body quivered with grief and rage though I pushed it down with all my strength and willed my limbs to stillness, my lips to quiet.

Mor's face blanched white but set dry and hard as solid stone. She fumbled for scissors, always carried on her large key ring, and clipped handfuls of Christina's curls. One tendril fell between her fingers and I bent to retrieve it, fighting the urge to bury my face in its softness, swallowing the sobs that threatened to overwhelm me, fearing that if I gave way to weeping I would never stop.

"Shall I fetch Hansa Trygg?" Ole's voice sounded hesitant and far away. "For the coffin?"

*"Ja, ja."* Mor's knees wobbled. I pulled the bench from the long table, and she sank onto it. When Far died the year before, Mor said there were no tears left for him — they had all been used when her boys died. If she wept for Christina, I didn't see it. Her

face locked into an expression I could not fathom.

The room darkened quickly once the sun set behind our mountain, spreading shadows first in the yard and then down the slope of our pastures, our fields, so steep that we bound ourselves with ropes to scythe the hay. The house, always dark with its ancient logs and single window, became as night though the hour was early, and it was still September, the day before Michaelmas. The room stifled from the stove stoked for Christina's dying, a slow ordeal that had lasted through yesterday and today. Mor made no move to light the lamp. Nor did I.

I could not bear the stillness. Silence roared in my ears until I thought I would explode. Grabbing the axe by the doorsill, I headed toward the woodpile behind the stable. Cold air filled my lungs, and I kicked a hissing gander out of the path. The axe bit into the pine logs, releasing a fragrance sweet enough to cover the smell of death lingering in my nostrils. Unspent fury churned within, and I could have chopped wood all night, my strength stoked by anger. Why Christina? Why not the moony-eyed Borgetta engaged to Ole? Why not the half-witted Saatre, who herded goats in the mountain pastures?

I dragged an ancient linden tree felled by a recent storm to the center of the clearing. My strength seemed endless, my body fired by strong emotion. I hacked the tree into pieces small enough for Mor's stove. Then hacked them again until they were the size of kindling.

My future looked bleak indeed. Only my brother and I left of our family of eight children. Ole, the older, inherited the farm. Its five acres would barely support him, especially with his plans to marry. Working as a laborer for our upperclass neighbor with meager wages meant a life of dependence and drudgery. I would forever be someone's hired man, unable to own land or choose my own way.

Norway was a dead end, a place without future. A graveyard. Anger boiled and tormented until I finally threw down the axe and lifted a heavy rock from the edge of the path and flung it as far as my strength allowed. Then, and only then, did my anger quiet to gasping breaths and hot tears.

Slumped to the ground behind the wood-shed, I vented my grief. Although it was my sister who died, I felt dead as well. And though hatred did not drive me away from my homeland, dreams of America did. There behind the stable in the midst of the

14

meandering geese and the scattered wood chips, I focused my mind on America.

It's what Christina would have wanted.

Cleng Peterson, a young man from our village of Sonmorgaard, immigrated to a place called Minnesota. His brother once showed me a letter from that distant land. It said, ". . . come and join me in this place of opportunity. The soil is black and rich with hardly a stone to pick. There are no nobles. Every man stands equal on his own merit."

Ole was skeptical. "You should stay here, work with me on the farm." His vision was clouded by love for his soon-to-be bride. "Far was out of his head. He didn't know what he was saying."

As a young man, Far had served in the king's bodyguard and received a silver watch at the end of his service along with the five-acre farm. Being a second son, it was wealth beyond expectation. As Far lay dying, gored by the neighbor's bull, he pressed the watch into my hands.

"You're eighteen," he said. "Same age as when I served the king."

I held the treasure, the silver cool to touch, and heard the gentle *tick-tick* that measured Far's final minutes on earth.

Strong emotion choked me, and although I wanted to tell him my heart, I stood mute before him, helpless as a child.

"Sell it and go to America." His breath came in short panting bursts that smelled of blood and death. He pulled my face to his. His eyes were dull and his voice was weak, but I saw the love in his eyes, felt it envelop me in its sweetness. "It's your only chance."

But I stayed because of Christina. She was unwell and hoped to emigrate with me when she regained her health. We were always more like twins than just brother and sister, she being only fourteen months younger than I. Perhaps we both knew that day would never come, but we spent her last year dreaming of a better life in America. Her health rallied around St. Botlov's Day, during the peak of the midnight sun, but by St. Olaf's Day, while we were harvesting the wheat, her bouts of coughing worsened. By the end of summer her body shriveled to bones and courage. Clearly her days were numbered though we spoke only in hopeful terms.

But even when she spat red into her handkerchief with every fit of coughing, and when strangled breathing made her speech difficult, Christina continued the dream.

How we would own a farm together and a team of horses. When we each married, we would build another house on the same property and live side by side as neighbors, working the land together. We would send passage to Mor, and she would spend her old age with us in the new land. Each would stand godparent for the other's children.

"Just think," Christina whispered on St. Matthew's Day, when the days were shortened and the dreaded night of winter loomed before us. "In America there is daylight every day of the year." Her eyes burned in sunken sockets. "Light." She coughed a red splotch into her crumpled handkerchief edged with the fine Hardanger lace of our mother's people. "Every day. Not just in summer."

I thought she slept but she spoke again as I turned to leave. "I'm afraid of the darkness, Brother."

"But the northern lights." My throat tightened so I could hardly speak. "You'd miss the colors of the long winter."

*"Nei,"* she fastened her eyes on the windowpane as if trying to gather the weakening sun into her eyes as we gathered cloudberries for the winter supply of jam. "I'd rather have sun."

On the day of her death, a sickening dread

haunted my thoughts of America. Christina had been part of every dream. I'd have to dream a new dream. One where I traveled to America alone.

The watch, although valuable, would not purchase my entire passage. I had nothing, could expect nothing. I must find a way to earn the needed gold.

One day in March, just after St. Gertrud's Day, Ole carved a new axe handle while I sharpened the iron plowshare. We worked in the house to share the light and warmth of the kitchen. Ole shaved long curls of wood from an oak branch. The shavings heaped on the floor, scented the room with their sweetness. I gripped the plowshares between my knees and polished with a small whetstone. It was tedious work but warm in the kitchen with Mor baking *lefse* at the stove.

"I could work on a fishing boat." I carefully spat on the whetstone and rubbed it over the iron edge of the blade, scraping the rust down to a dull shine.

*"Nei!"* Mor slammed the stove door shut with a bang. This rare burst of temper shocked me. Ole looked up from his work. "No son of mine will die a watery death on a boat!" She poked the flat *lefse* stick under

the paper-thin bread and expertly flipped it over on the stovetop, brown spots bubbling on the finished side. "I forbid it." Her eyes flashed, and she lowered her voice to near whisper. "It's bad enough you travel so far across the ocean, never to be seen again. I'll not have you drowning in the North Sea."

It was foolish. I knew it and Ole knew it. Our eyes met across the table. The only hope of gathering enough *kroner* to purchase passage to America was in hiring out on a fishing boat. Everyone did it.

"You don't want him living the life of our ancestors?" Ole's voice held a hint of teasing, his way of easing the tension in the little room that held the long table where we worked, the stove, and the box bed in the corner. "Evan could sail like Ketil the Flat-Nose, protecting Eric the Red, Viking King."

A smile curled the corners of Mor's lips, and she flipped the *lefse* onto a clean cloth lying on the table.

"Don't you think Evan would be a great Viking?" Ole pulled a fresh *lefse* from the cloth and stuffed it into his mouth. "Or maybe even a berserk?"

"Leave alone!" Mor rapped his knuckle with the *lefse* stick. "It's for dinner!"

"A Viking raider who brings enough booty to pay his way to America and buy a

19

hundred-acre farm in the heart of Minnesota!"

"Evan is hardly a berserk," Mor said,
"though he lets his temper get the best of
him sometimes."

"But we've not seen him in battle," Ole
picked up the axe handle again and shaved
another curl onto the floor. "Maybe he has
the gift . . . like Far."

"Hush, now!" Mor scooped up the shavings off her clean floor and dropped them
into the stove. "Evan is not a berserk.
Heaven knows that was in the old days.
Don't speak of it."

"Bestefar told us the stories," Ole said and
just the thought of Bestefar, with Christina
on his lap, telling us the old tales brought a
lump to my throat. "Of the poets, Bard the
Strong and Auden the Uninspired."

"Unn the Deep-Minded." I watched Mor
roll another sheet of dough.

"And Egil the Wild," Ole said. "Though
he was a berserk." He held the axe handle
up and measured it against the length of his
arm. "Fearless and indestructible in battle."

Later that day, I sorted through potatoes
in the root cellar, pulling off the white
sprouts growing from each eye to prevent
them from spoiling. The root cellar was a
hollowed out cave in the side of the moun-

tain with a heavy wooden door. We needed every bit of food to keep us alive until the next harvest. The potatoes lay limp and scant. Six head of cabbage rested on a bed of straw. Salted fish hung from the rafters. A fat bag of rutabagas was the only abundance left in the cellar.

As I worked, I thought of my grandfather. Bestefar's white beard collected crumbs and his rheumy eyes watered and dripped. He smelled of urine and old flesh and died the year before diphtheria took my oldest brothers. His stories boasted of Vikings' exploits and fierce battles. We were descendants of mighty warriors, even of the berserks who were fierce in battle. Uncontrollable rages overwhelmed them to where iron could not bite their skin. Bestefar claimed every man in our family carried the trait, that he had experienced such rages himself when fighting wolves attacking his sheep, that my far had distinguished himself in service to the king by the same virtue. He looked us over carefully as if searching to see if we small boys were berserks as well. But of course, berserks lived long before St. Olaf brought Christianity to Norway.

I heard a sound at the trapdoor. Ole and Mor entered with a blast of cold wind behind them that flickered the candle in its holder. Ole bent over to avoid hitting his head on the low ceiling but Mor stood upright with room to spare. Her face carried a strange look of triumph. Or maybe despair.

"Here," Ole shoved a small purse into my hands. "It's enough to pay your passage." Ole looked surly, obviously forced to contribute. "There's nothing left. You'll have to make your own way once you get there."

I held the leather bag in my hand, fingering the coins that held my future. "But how?" My hands shook. With a start, I realized it was his bride's dowry. I pushed it back toward him. "I can't take it."

Relief showed in his eyes but Mor stepped between us and shoved the purse into my pocket.

"Of course, you'll take it." Her eyes glowed like embers beneath their hooded lids. "Brothers help each other."

I stood helpless between the two of them, wanting desperately to both take the money and refuse it. Ole would hold it over me for the rest of his life. He would blame me if his children hungered, thinking how I had taken what was rightfully his. As I would often think how unfair it was for the oldest son to inherit the farm.

"*Mange takk,* Brother." I reached for his

hand and he slowly took mine. "*Tussen takk,* A thousand thanks. I will not forget this."

"*Ja, ja.*" His voice sounded steel-edged and cold. "You're making a big mistake."

"Someday I will repay you."

"I'm sure." He turned but not before I saw the tears. "When you gather gold in America's streets."

# 2

*Spring Day, April 14, 1860*

Mor wept when I left, pressing the back of her chapped hand against her mouth and leaning against the doorframe of our little house with its thatched roof. This show of emotion frightened me. The ship would leave Trondhjem in three weeks, and I must leave if I hoped to arrive in time.

"Don't forget the Commandments." Her words strangled and her voice carried no strength. "I have taught you the best I could and now wonder if you are old enough to make your way in the world." She gulped her tears and fumbled for a handkerchief from her apron pocket, rattling the keys around her neck. "You are still a boy."

"I've worked a man's job for five years." I pushed emotion back as I spoke, swallowing hard. The April sun shone down on our farm, the only home I had ever known. Black and white lambs frolicked in the tiny pasture behind our house. I jerked my thoughts back to the conversation. "How could I forget the Commandments? You've drummed them into my head."

"Mind your manners and stay out of trouble." The tilt of her chin spoke louder than her words. Her voice strengthened and the tears left her voice. "Stay away from women unless you find a nice Lutheran girl from a good Norwegian family."

"I will."

"Stay away from liquor. It will impoverish you."

"*Ja, ja.*"

"And don't harbor ill feelings towards Ole. He's the only brother you have left." She adjusted my collar and brushed a stray hair from my jacket. "Don't leave with anger in your heart."

"I don't. I promise."

"I'll pray for you, son."

The lump in my throat put an end to my words and I grabbed her and hugged her as if I would never see her again. In truth, I never would.

I caught a ride with a merchant traveling to Storen, a surly man carrying a load of wool. He allowed me to ride on top of the wagon after I promised I would leave the bundles undisturbed and keep quiet. He didn't wish to be bothered by conversation, and I was happy to oblige.

We traveled in silence past the country church yard where Christina, Far, and my six brothers slept. Indeed there were graves of my ancestors back to the time of the plague, although the markers had crumbled with time and decay. Lilac bushes budded against the backdrop of the steepled church. In truth more of my family slept in the graveyard than walked alive on the earth.

Before I left, Mor and I had traveled to the Lutheran priest and filed my intentions to move away from our village. The priest gave me a copy of my baptismal and confirmation certificates along with a stern warning of the need for a young man to join another Lutheran congregation as soon as possible.

"Above all," he said and shook a long finger in my face. "Stay away from the Roman Papists who would rob you of the grace of God."

"Yes, sir." I kept my eyes on his cowl. He held my future in his hands and it would not do to anger him and perhaps make him change his mind. A word from him could stop my emigration. "I will."

"You will by the Grace of God," he corrected, "and the power of the Holy Ghost."

I swallowed hard at the memory and grabbed the sides of the wagon as it jolted over a rut. Was it so hard to walk in righteousness? Surely the catechism prepared a man to live. Mentally I rolled the words of the Lord's Prayer over my tongue as we left the little church behind.

Before us rose the steep slope of the mountain. Snow still clung to the highest peaks and a waterfall drained the spring rains into a lake as blue as Christina's eyes. Surely America would hold no beauty as great as my homeland. I removed my hat, strong emotion cutting off any words I might have said if I were allowed to speak.

Once in Storen, I watched the train leave for Trondhjem, wishing I had the *kroner* for passage. I imagined what it might feel like to ride in the smoke-billowing carriage and feel the rumble of the tracks beneath me.

Instead, I hoisted my pack and set out walking. One of my ancestors had walked barefoot all the way from Tolga to the Nidaros Cathedral as penance for his sins. Of course, that was long ago, before Martin Luther brought Lutheranism to Norway. Such penance was no longer necessary to find salvation, but I breathed a prayer to St. Olaf all the same, asking for his protection and strength. The weather was fair and I walked, catching rides whenever I could, traveling the mountain roads toward my destination on the northwest coast of Norway.

I imagined myself on a Viking ship sailing for Iceland with Eric the Red, ready to serve my chieftain, willing to fight as a berserk in battle against the king's enemies. It was a foolish pastime, but better than thinking of Mor's tears or remembering Christina's death. Truly if I were a Viking, I'd spin a poem about my family's troubles. It would be a poem greater than any written by Audin the Uninspired or Unn the Deep-Minded.

Once in Trondhjem, I found the *Hvid Farne* at dock and bought my passage. My heart beat almost out of my chest when I learned the price. It left me with nothing but a few coins and I needed food for the journey. While the ship rested in the peaceful harbor and my ticket lay secure in an inner pocket, I prepared as best I could, buying hardtack and black bread, turning away from a small jar of cloudberry jam. Then I entered the ship and found a corner in the dank hold, deep in the belly of the giant, claiming a stale bunk for my own.

Knute Iverson, slept beside me. Knute, a

tow-headed youth from Hammer, wore ancient leather leggings, new wooden shoes, and a hand-knitted sweater and cap. His bright eyes reminded me of a squirrel eyeing a nut, and he hunched his shoulders and thrust his head forward as if he couldn't wait for what might happen next. During the tedious voyage, Knute bragged he would live with his rich aunt and uncle who had been in America for five years and held good jobs in a Chicago bakery.

"I'll have all the bread I can eat." He rubbed his belly.

The lie popped out of my mouth before I knew it. I concocted a fine story about my cousin, Cleng Peterson, who waited for me in Minnesota, with land that would be my own when I arrived. I forgot the seasickness that roiled my stomach and made me despair of living throughout the thirty-two days aboard the *White Dove.* I told and retold my story until even I believed it.

When I awoke in the morning to the restless rising and falling of the ship, the story made the trip bearable. It distracted me from both sickness and hunger, once the hardtack was gone and I subsisted on moldy bread. When darkness descended at the beginning of another long night, the story merged with my dreams and lulled me to sleep with its beauty. Cleng waited for me in America. I would own land in Minnesota.

We sailed through the Great Lakes and landed first in Sault Ste. Marie, Canada, and then south by a smaller boat to the city of Chicago, across the choppy waters of Lake Michigan. Knute and I stood on the deck and watched the waves bounce the little vessel that carried us forward to our future. White tinged waves slapped against the shore, and we laughed at our trembling legs when we stepped onto the long dock that was America.

Knute's family met him with hugs and kisses all around. His aunt handed us fresh bread, and we stuffed our mouths as fast as we could, the seasickness finally gone, leaving only desperate hunger in its wake.

"Where are you headed?" Knute's uncle said.

"He's got family waiting in Minnesota." Knute spoke around a mouth filled with bread. "He's in a hurry to get there to help with the crops."

Too late, I realized the gravity of my sins. My own lies choked me. Who did I think I was? I made up stories that made me seem grand and important when all I had in the world were the ten American pennies in my pocket, changed from the *kroner* I carried by Knute's kind uncle. I thought to confess all, admit that I had no one waiting, had no money and no prospects, throw myself upon their mercy and beg for help. But in the end, my pride silenced the truth. I gathered my bundle and started west.

I turned to wave good-bye, but I saw only the thronging crowd. It was too late. The Commandments forbade lying and though I had promised Mor to follow them, I had so soon broken my word. *St. Olaf, stand by me in this strange land and help me both speak and walk in truth.* If St. Olaf truly saw the hearts of petitioners, he knew the remorse and desperation I felt.

It seemed I had stepped into an anthill. Everyone milled around in total confusion. I joined the others, wishing I knew the language, feeling as insignificant as a grain of sand. In truth, terror gripped me until I could hardly breathe. Chicago was filthy with sewage flowing in the streets, its stench rancid and bitter, far different from the golden streets talked about back home. I hoped to ask someone for directions, but I didn't know who to trust or where to find someone who spoke Norwegian.

In the end, I just wandered west toward the setting sun and soon came upon a railway station. Cars of bawling cattle and squealing hogs sat by the stockyards. The heat stifled me, so different from the cool land of my birth. The farther I walked away from the water, the worse the heat. How could I live in such oppressive heat?

The railroad tracks pointed straight west out of the city and I followed them, knowing in the end they would lead me to Minnesota. As I left the city, the air cleared and I felt a cooling breeze at my back. Farms lined the tracks with their fields of wheat and barley, hay and oats. Sometimes I passed farmers driving horse-drawn plows or hay knives. I had never before seen a field of corn but recognized it from a picture in a newspaper, with the tall plants each standing in little hills. Wheat and oats stretched in fields, one after the other, as far as the eye could see, unlike the small fields of my homeland. No mountains limited my vision. How flat and open America was!

In spite of my lack of language and insufficient money, hope sprouted within me. I would find a job and earn money for my own place. The dream Christina had helped me envision would come to pass. It lay before me with endless possibilities, within my grasp. But as night fell I realized that although America could boast of daylight every day of the year, it also had night as well. At home everyone would be enjoying the midnight sun.

On my second day of travel, hope turned to despair.

It had been a long day and I was hungry. Walking on the tracks proved faster than hiking on uneven terrain. My head was in the clouds, worrying how many pennies I needed for bread.

Suddenly someone yelled. I turned my head just in time to see a train roaring toward me. It seemed impossible I had blotted out the sound. I leapt from the tracks and rolled into the ditch as the train whistled by.

I looked to see who had warned me but no one was in sight. Perhaps St. Olaf himself had called to me. But surely, St. Olaf would have called me by name and spoken in Norwegian. The voice I heard spoke in a strange tongue.

A man walked up to me as I gathered my scattered possessions. He wore a tattered hat and an overcoat several sizes too large for him. About the age of my far, his hair was white and he carried a bundle wrapped in a red handkerchief.

"Are you the one who warned me?" I asked in Norwegian. *"Mange takk."*

He shook his head to indicate he couldn't

understand me and muttered something about "damn Norskie." I felt the heat rise in my cheeks and instinctively reached for my bundle.

The man pointed to his chest and said in the too-loud voice Americans used with foreigners, "I'm Robert."

"Robert," I said and the man roared with laughter.

"Damn Norskie." He pointed to a small campsite in the trees.

*"Ja."* I had no other words to offer. He might be ill mannered, but he had saved my life and for that I owed him my gratitude.

We drank coffee boiled in a rusty tin can. Then he pulled out a hat filled with fresh eggs and fried them in an old skillet greased with a bacon rind. A full belly, the first good meal I had eaten since leaving home, heavied my eyes. I hoped to converse with the man, maybe learn a few English words, but sleep overcame me. Stretched out beside the small fire, I slept like a stone.

The next morning when I awakened, the fire was cold and the man gone. I reached into my jacket pocket. My pennies were gone. The man who saved my life had robbed me as I slept.

I had made a mistake. A terrible mistake. America was an awful place with its noise and confusion, its heat and humidity. What a fool I had been to think I could make my own way. Ole was right. If by some miracle a boat ticket fell from heaven, I would have leapt at the chance to return to mucking stalls as his hired man. I thought of the story of the prodigal son, realizing how lonely he must have felt, wondering if Ole would prepare a feast for me if I returned home, knowing that he wouldn't, and remembering his cold words.

I had no choice but to gather my things and continue west, this time more wary of both trains and strangers.

My possessions were small in number and light in weight. I carried a blanket, frying pan, knife, spoon, tin cup, clean shirt, and a watch fob braided from Christina's blonde curls. At times of loneliness, the touch of her hair brought comfort. I clutched it in my hand when I slept.

The vastness of the land amazed me. The cities sprawled with room to grow. The farms were large and prosperous in some places, less prosperous in others. People were varied, not at all like the light skinned, blond people from home. Rivers were bigger, the roads dustier and voices louder.

The Rock River barred my path. I had no money to pay the ferry and searched for an alternate way to cross. The water swirled with the spring meltdown and I feared the churning current. Surely, I had not come this far to die in a watery grave after all.

A lone railroad trestle spanned the river. If a train would suddenly appear while I was still on the trestle, I would be killed. But I had little choice. I knelt on the damp ground and pressed my ear to the track. No rumble met my ear. I gathered my courage and ran with all my might across the track, watching the roaring water below the bridge, knowing I would never survive a swim in such current. After the crossing, my heart pounded for hours. Surely, St. Olaf guided my steps.

The Fox River loomed impassable in its wildness. Once again, I listened at the rail and ran across, foolish with the confidence of youth. When a train roared across the trestle only minutes after my crossing, I gave fervent thanks. Surely, Mor prayed for me that day.

When I could, I chopped wood for a meal, helped farmers pick stones from their fields and cleaned chicken coops or calf pens. Sometimes they gave me a penny in addition to cold potatoes or bread. My boots shredded and my clothes tattered and ripped. My slight frame, although six feet tall, resembled a skeleton. I grew a wispy red beard to hide the hunger in my face. The days seemed to pass but I made little progress, my travel slowed by my need to work for food. As the summer came into its fullness, the dread of coming winter haunted me. *St. Olaf, pray for me.*

Worst of all was my ignorance of the English language and inability to communicate. Folks talked too fast. The sounds and rhythms of the words were unlike those of my homeland speech. Lucky for me, there were Scandinavian people to be found in almost all my travels. Their languages were similar to Norwegian and we could communicate.

At a farmhouse near Denton, Illinois, I spied a large woodpile next to a log cabin and hoped to split some of it into kitchen wood in exchange for food. A burly man smoking a long necked pipe opened the door when I knocked.

"Can I help you?" he said in broken English, looking me over from top to bottom. I cringed, aware of my ragged filth.

"I'm in need of food. I will chop your wood or clean your barn in exchange for supper." I held my breath along with my hat.

He removed the pipe from his mouth.

"You look near starvation," he answered in Norwegian. Smiling, he held out his hand. "Anyone from the Old Country is a welcome guest."

Potato dumplings simmered on the stove while his missus set the plates. I felt moisture in my eyes and wiped them with my shirtsleeve while he said the table prayer. The missus, a plump woman about the age of my mother, gave me a bowl of dumplings and nodded for me to eat.

"What is your name, young man, and what are you doing so far from home?" he asked.

"Peter, let the boy eat!" the missus said. "Talk can wait."

The mister chuckled and slurped down a mountain of dumplings with amazing speed. The missus stood to the side, waiting on the men as was good manners, adding dumplings to my bowl as quickly as I emptied it and refilling my cup with fresh milk too many times to count.

Finally when I could not eat another spoonful, I looked up and said, "*Takk fer mat.* Thank you for the meal, Mr. . . ."

"No mister or missus in this house," he said. "We are not of the upper class, just ordinary folks. My name is Peter Anderson and this is my wife, Signe."

"I am Evan Jacobson, from Sonmorgaard."

"I know it well!" He seemed pleased with the recollection. "My far sold wool in Sonmorgaard."

"To Per Hansel?"

"To the Hansel family. It was years ago though I recall a small boy named Per." He lit his pipe and took a long pull on the stem. "To think you are from Sonmorgaard. We lived in Tolga."

We drank our coffee in silence. Sleep heavied my eyelids after such a meal, and I could not help but marvel at finding someone from home.

"Where are you headed?"

I shrugged my shoulders, embarrassed. In truth I was lost in both spirit and body. In my struggle to stay alive, I had no plan. I swirled the last drops of coffee in my cup and before I could speak the missus refilled it once again.

"A young man from our village emigrated to Minnesota." I took a small spoon of sugar and stirred it into my cup along with a splash of thick cream, trembling with the luxury of hot food at a real table.

"It is north and west of here," Peter said, "a long walk."

He smoked his pipe, deep in thought.

39

Finally he spoke in a careful voice.

"I have need of a hired man to help me with farm chores and the coming harvest. I cannot pay but I'll put a roof over your head and feed you through the winter."

It was surely an answer to Mor's prayers.

After supper, the missus trimmed my hair and beard with a sharp knife. She offered a small gourd of soft soap that smelled faintly of lavender.

"And now you shall have a bath."

I carried water to fill the iron tub beside the kitchen fire and afterwards dumped the dirty water outside, as Mor had taught me. It shamed me to see the filth left in the tub. The missus bustled while I stood by the stove, wrapped in my blanket. I hated touching the dirty cloth to my clean body.

"These are old, but clean. I don't think it possible to repair your clothes." Signe handed me a folded pile of Peter's old clothing.

"Do you have family here in America?" I asked.

"*Ja*, Bettina, our daughter, is married and lives in town with her man, a storekeeper. They have no children and we have no sons to help with the farm. Only the old ones live in Norway."

I felt ashamed, as if I had asked her a

question too personal for comfort. Mor had taught me better than to pry into the affairs of others.

"*Mange takk!* I will work hard to repay you."

Later over more coffee and with my eyes nodding, Peter told me all he knew about the young State of Minnesota. He found a map in an old newspaper that showed the place. Land was available to those willing to work for it.

I traced my fingers around the outline of the state. Cleng Peterson lived there somewhere. It was a comfort to know at least one person there, even if he wasn't my cousin.

# 3

"South Carolina, Georgia, Florida,
Alabama, Mississippi and Louisiana
Secede after Lincoln Inaugurated"
~ St. Paul Journal

Peter directed me to a one-room country schoolhouse where a Mr. Aaronson taught anyone desiring to learn, regardless of age. I hurried through the morning chores and attended school as many days as possible after the harvest was done. The school was a log structure with a fireplace on one end of the room and rows of small desks filling the center. The master's desk stood on the wall opposite the fireplace and a picture of George Washington hung on the wall behind the teacher, facing the students.

At first I was ashamed to sit with the young ones, reluctant to admit I was more ignorant and less educated than they were. But I knew that to survive in America I needed both to read and speak the language. The master found a larger chair and small table for me to use since I was too big to fit into the desks. I sat at the back of the room, looking over the heads of the other students.

Reading and understanding came easy, but the strange sounds strangled in my throat when I tried to speak. The little ones laughed until they caught the stern eye of Mr. Aaronson. I learned the alphabet and the basics of the written language. For this I am grateful. I have yet to master the speech without stuttering, though I stayed in during recess and had extra tutoring from Mr. Aaronson.

One late afternoon in mid-winter, just before Candlemas, Mr. Aaronson stopped me as I hurried home for chores. The sun was almost behind the western horizon though it was not yet suppertime. What luxury to enjoy such long days in the dead of winter. Christina would have loved it. Back home in Sonmorgaard, there would be only a few hours of twilight in the middle of the day, nothing like the extravagant light of America where even the houses were lighted by the sun during the daytime hours.

"What are your plans?" he asked in Norwegian. "Will you be moving west?"

His question surprised me. He had reason

to think me stupid and usually demanded I speak only in English. It was a relief to answer without stuttering.

"I know someone in Minnesota," I said. "I've thought of traveling there in the spring."

Mr. Aaronson put on a fur-lined coat and hat and tied a muffler around his neck. "Do you mind if I walk with you a ways?"

I was most flattered by his attention. The west wind rustled dried corn stalks in the field by the school and a red squirrel chattered in an oak tree. The smell of burning wood lingered in the air, and smoke spiraled upward from every chimney. It was cold, and I pulled my collar up, grateful for the mittens and scarf Signe had knitted for me.

"It seems as there might be a war in the South," he said. "Have you thought of signing up in the army?"

It was a thought foreign to my mind. All I wanted was to find a farm of my own. I said as much to the good teacher. Snow crunched beneath our feet and the cold air seared our lungs.

"The country is at a crisis," he said. "There will be a war unless God intervenes."

The political situation seemed far away and unimportant. I wanted only to mind my own business.

"If I were you," his words made short bursts of cloud on his beard that soon froze to icicles. "I would find land in Minnesota."

"Have you been there?" My heart beat double quick at his words.

"*Nei,* but I have a brother in the army who was stationed at Fort Snelling. He transferred south but wrote a letter telling about the railroad selling land to settlers." He rubbed his hands and pumped his arms to keep warm. "The treaty opened up land."

"Any trouble with the Red Men?"

"*Nei,*" he said. "Chippewa dwell in the north and Sioux in the south. There is no trouble."

"Would you let me read your letters?"

"I will bring the letters tomorrow," he said. "And I have old newspapers that tell of the treaties. It will be good practice for your English."

With a brief handshake, we parted at the crossroads. I walked west toward the Anderson's and he headed south toward his lodging. My sense of duty knew I had to be home in time for chores, but I would have much preferred to ask Mr. Aaronson more questions. However, I owed Peter and Signe for my food and lodging and I must do what they wished.

How wonderful it would be to run my own life. The Andersons were good people but too much like parents. In spite of all my travels and struggles, I was still no better off than I would have been back home. I was not a landowner, only a hired man working for his room and board.

That night I wrote my first letter home. I had been putting it off for weeks, not having any news to tell. The pen refused to co-operate, and I started the page with an ugly blot. Not having another sheet of paper, I continued anyway.

Denton, Illinois
January 30, 1861

Dear Mor

A kind man and his missus have given me shelter for the winter in exchange for chores. They are from Tolga and know Per Hansel. Their names are Peter and Signe Anderson. They send greetings to Per Hansel if you see him.

America is a land of opportunity. I attend school and learn the language. When the snow melts and spring arrives, I will travel to Minnesota and become a farmer. It would take many years to become a landowner in Denton, Illinois.

In Minnesota, the railroad sells rich land suitable for farming. I will seek Cleng Peterson for advice on starting out. The Red Men are no trouble since the 1858 Treaty. Do not worry about your son. He still remembers the Commandments.

Your faithful son, Evan

Good food and warm housing restored my strength. My body grew, stretching out the seams of Peter's old clothes. The wrists were too short, the pants legs above my worn boots. My shoulders filled out, and I felt I had the strength to tackle any job in the world.

Every night I read and reread the old newspapers. They told great things about Minnesota but also mentioned unrest among the Sioux, late government payments and unscrupulous traders. The newspapers contradicted themselves. While speaking of peace with the Sioux, they also hinted at great dissatisfaction among them. I devoured every word I could find about the place and its people.

The winter passed quickly.

Mr. Aaronson seemed pleased when I told him my decision. He sat at his desk and pulled out a sheet of fine linen paper from a slim drawer. Carefully blotting his pen, he wrote in beautiful script the color of summer grass.

April 2, 1861

To Whom it May Concern,
Evan Jacobson is a young man of fine moral character. He has disciplined work habits and will make a fine employee for any establishment. He reads and writes English and can tally figures.

Sincerely,<br>
Aaron Aaronson<br>
Teacher of Public School,<br>
Denton, Illinois

"*Mange takk,* Mr. Aaronson." Blowing to dry the ink, I rolled the paper and placed it carefully inside my coat sleeve. It was my ticket to freedom.

It was difficult to tell the Andersons my decision to leave. Peter needed help to plant the crops. I was leaving at a bad time.

"*Mange takk* for everything." I shook their hands repeatedly.

Signe kissed my cheek, weeping openly.

"Don't leave now." Peter said. "Stay on and work for me. I'll pay you a wage. Maybe you could save up to buy this place when my years are over. Bettina and her man don't want the farm. All they can think of is buying and selling."

I pushed down strong emotion in my throat before I spoke. I could have stayed in Norway to work as a servant, and Bettina and her man might think differently when the time came. I couldn't take the risk. "*Mange takk,* Peter and Signe. You have been most helpful to me but I must now find my own place in this land."

I didn't look back as I journeyed down the oak-lined lane, heading west along the railroad track toward the Mississippi River.

# 4

"Attack on Fort Sumter Is
Attack Against Freedom"
~ St. Paul Journal

People had told me Minnesota looked like
Norway. It didn't. My Norwegian homeland
was filled with cold mountain streams,
towering snow-capped mountains and icy
blue fjords the same color as my eyes.

Fort Snelling sat high on a hill. The blue
waters of the Mississippi and Minnesota rivers were in view but Indian villages surrounded the fort instead of mountain peaks,
and I could see for miles in any direction.
The fort was an enclosed structure the size
of a small village. Soldiers guarded the
gates. Inside were barracks for the enlisted
men and a two-story painted house for the
commanding officer. A huge barn housed
the fort's horses and two milk cows. A
round stone building stored ammunition

and weapons.

A small store sold snuff, tobacco similar to our *snus* in Norway, clothes, medicine, boots, knives, and anything else a person might want. Married soldiers lived with their families in small dwellings built inside the fort. Indians and civilians had tents and cabins around the outside of the fort's perimeter.

I couldn't help but stare.

A young white man gambled with an Indian outside the gates of the fort. They threw painted bones onto a blanket; the resulting patterns determined the winner and loser.

He was about my age and dressed in baggy pants, a dirty shirt and wooden shoes. His right hand was twisted as if he had been in an accident.

The young man threw the bones and his face reddened. He started to leave but the Indian's dog growled and bared his teeth. The Indian pulled a knife. The white man paused, looked at the knife, and reluctantly pulled a coin from his pocket. He threw it at the Indian's feet, said something I couldn't understand, and walked away.

The Indian picked up the coin and gestured for me to play. I shook my head and backed away. Although there may not have been a commandment against gambling, I knew what Mor would say about it. I needed the few pennies in my pocket to survive and couldn't risk losing them. Besides, the Indian still held his big knife.

The Indian stood erect and looked at me with an air of defiance, or maybe disgust. He was shorter than I and wore stained buckskin leggings. His dark greasy hair was thonged off his face and adorned with colorful feathers. An unfamiliar odor was about him, a musky scent that may have been from his clothing. I felt helpless before him, unable to communicate, almost as I had felt before my upper-class neighbors back home.

I looked away first and squeezed through the partially ajar gates.

The letter of reference from Mr. Aaronson helped me secure a job with the army. At first I worked as a hostler. I'd learned to care for horses in Norway and always felt at home with them. A chaw of snuff or a carrot in my pocket bought their undying friendship. The horses did not care if I spoke Norwegian or English. With them I could be myself.

Ashamed of my poor speech, I kept my mouth shut and said little to anyone. I understood most of what was said to me and answered with a nod or short reply. Ted, the young man I had seen gambling, also worked as a hostler.

One day Ted came up to me in the barn with a taunting smirk on his face. He lounged against the horse stall while I shoveled manure. Perhaps it bothered his injured hand to use the pitchfork.

"Norskie, you gonna sign up?"

The War of Rebellion rumbled in the south. The newspapers churned with news and rumors. People said it was because of the Negro slaves. War might be a big adventure, something I could tell my grandchildren about someday. I chewed my lip and bent my back to muck a stall.

"A-are you?" I finally stuttered, hating the halting voice that showed him my ignorance.

Ted laughed and abruptly left the stable leading a team to be hitched to the stage scheduled to leave for Fort Abercrombie, Dakota Territory. He jerked the bit of a horse named Betty, trying to hurry her along.

"Damn you!" The great beast reared up, and Ted jerked her halter and beat her around her head and back with the ends of the reins until she snorted and pulled away, her eyes rolling white with fear. "I'll show you who's boss!"

The sergeant walked by and cranked his

head toward the quivering horse. Ted quickly released Betty and returned to the manure pile.

Surely, a slave didn't work any harder for his bread than we had in Norway. I pitched a forkful of manure into a steamy pile, angry with Ted and frustrated with life in general. Far's death left half-grown sons and a grieving widow to try to scratch enough wheat and potatoes from the stony soil to keep the family alive. Even the backbreaking labor of the whole family hadn't been enough to keep Christina alive. *Nei,* slavery couldn't be any worse than that.

Ted said neither the black man nor the red man were human. He said it was God's will for the black men to serve as slaves, said he'd heard it in church. The Norwegian priest had said the same about the class system, preached at Christina's funeral that her death had been the will of God. I shoveled faster and shot a stream of brown snuff into the manure pile, disrupting a swarm of blue-tailed flies.

It almost made me want to sign up to fight against slavery, but Far told me time and again not to be caught up in a rich man's war.

"Fight your own battles," he warned, "you'll have enough of your own."

I knew the Commandments. I decided to honor my father and his words to me. *Nei,* I would stay in Minnesota, far from the danger of war. I hoped the slaves would find freedom without my help, and hoped that I, too, would find it. Mor taught me to keep my mouth shut and stay out of trouble. That's what I would do.

The fort paid regular money, enough to feel like a person instead of a slave. The food was plain, but good, and I could eat all I wanted in the mess hall, just like an American citizen or a real soldier. I tried my best to make inquiries about Cleng Peterson. Either I communicated too poorly to make others understand my question or else Cleng lived in a different part of the state. It was disappointing to come so far and not find him.

When I tried to sleep in the dirty, cramped cabin with the other hostlers, the mosquitoes kept me awake with their vicious stingers. We set smudge fires outside the cabin walls in a futile attempt to drive them away, their whining drone a steady hum surrounding the cabin.

I listened to the loons calling from the river and my thoughts drifted homeward to Sonmorgaard. I knew it was just a dot on the map, but it was still the center of the universe to me.

Christina and I had been each other's only playmates. Ole was older and already working. During the darkness of Norway's winter, Christina and I played cat's cradle using string from an old fish net, practicing over and over the intricate web designs and the story that went along with each pattern. We made pictures in the frosty window glass with Mor's silver thimble. As children, we slept side by side in the family bed, and whispered stories to each other in the cold darkness, to keep away fears of trolls and bears.

My thoughts drifted to the future. I would make Christina proud of me. Far and my brothers would look down from heaven and see me carve a place for myself in the Minnesota wilderness. I would have a house with two rooms and a good team of horses. My land would have black soil that produced more wheat than I could ever eat. I would send Ole his money with interest. A pretty blue-eyed Norwegian girl would be my wife. She would be sweet in temperament and a good hand with cattle. Our blond, blue-eyed children would grow up without knowing hunger or class. American citizens and landowners, they would know of Norway only through my words.

They would know the stories, I vowed. About how hard we tried. I fell asleep holding the watch fob braided from my sister's blonde curls. Only with her hair in my hand could I sleep.

Most able-bodied men went to war and workers were in short supply. Sometimes I rode along on the stage as shotgun rider with one of the drivers, Hjalmer Thoreson, though I was a poor hand with a gun. The army might not have trusted me had they known I never so much as held a gun in my hand until the day they handed me the 1831 Danzig muzzle-loading shotgun.

The Danzig was an ancient relic that could do great damage at close range. It felt heavy in my hands and sent a thrill of power through my body. I acted as if I knew what I was doing and gradually caught on, target shooting outside the fort in my spare time.

Hjalmer and I drove the long trip out to Fort Abercrombie and back again. I was entertained by his dry sense of humor, listening to his never-ending stories about people he had known in his lifetime, his experiences as a Norwegian seaman. He had a jovial laugh and a hidden bottle of aquavit in his coat pocket. The entire trip lasted twenty days, but it was possible to do it in nineteen days if all went well.

The trip rarely went well. The roads were bad, following the ruts of the Red River Ox Cart Trail. The mud weighted the stage wheels in the wet season, and the ruts rattled our bones in the dry season.

We ferried the stage across impassable rivers. The waystations were houses of settlers with a contract to care for the replacement teams and feed the drivers and passengers. At night we slept by their fires. We ate whatever they set before us. The schedule was unpredictable, though. We might drive the same team for two days until we reached a scheduled stop or we might change twice in one day. It all depended on roads and weather.

Many were the homes of Scandinavian immigrants. I was able to converse with them and get to know them. Sometimes I pretended they were friends or relatives when I stopped for the noon meal and a change of teams. Other places were foreign, the food and language impossible to understand. These places welcomed me with veiled hostility. I pretended not to notice and spent most of my time in their barns. The work suited me. I dreamed of my own place and kept a watchful eye for just the right spot.

My savings grew.

Ted confronted me in the stable after my first trip.

"I'll bet you thinks you're something special, getting to ride on them stages and all." He clenched and unclenched his injured hand while he spoke. "I wonder if them sojers would be so quick to give you the job if theys knews you a scalp hunter."

His remarks caught me off guard. I was exhausted and hungry after the long day of fighting the spring mud. "What do you mean?"

"I've seen them scalp you carry."

"Scalp?"

"Them braid of hair on your fob. Funny you have one with nary a timepiece." He leered and pressed his face closer to mine. "Her must have been special, all right."

A wave of white anger enveloped me. My fingers clenched into a fist but Mor's words echoed in my head. With sheer determination, I walked away to the mess hall where fish stew awaited.

It was late and I took my dish to the farthest corner, wanting to avoid everyone. Never had I felt so lonely as I did at that moment. Another man ate his supper in the dim corner. I had never seen an African before and he must have noticed me staring. His face was as dark as the blackboard in the Illinois schoolhouse. His eyes were warm brown and the whites around them were clear and white.

"I'm starved," I said, curious about the man and wishing to talk with him if I could.

"It's burned but still tastes almighty good," he said.

"I could eat a horse — burned or not burned." The words came out of my mouth in strangled sentences.

He looked down at his plate and I wondered if he was afraid he had overstepped, been too friendly. Perhaps he mocked my speech.

"My-my name is Evan Jacobson."

"Gabriel," he said. "Gabriel Timmers."

I struggled to form the words in English that would communicate the thoughts in my mind.

"Are you-all new here at the fort?" he said. "I haven't seen you around."

"*Nei,* I spend most of the time on the stage."

We both chewed and swallowed and looked up at exactly the same instant, seeing the other starting to speak. I could not help but smile.

"Do you work here?"

"Yes, sir," he said. "I'm a free Negro and

work for the Commander as his servant."

I had never heard of a free Negro and my mind was filled with questions. He obviously was educated, speaking English with ease although in a strange lilt unlike any other men I knew. I wondered if all Negroes spoke in such a manner. While I could understand most of what was spoken, I still could not put my Norwegian thoughts into American words. Instead, I smiled and nodded as I left the table.

Gabriel, once a slave, worked for himself. The similarity to my own life comforted me. Once I was a working slave to a rich man without hope of improving my condition. Next I worked as a free man for the army, saving for my own place. *Nei,* we had much in common. I decided then and there to talk to Gabriel Timmers again and ask him about his slavery. Maybe I would tell him about mine.

I made several trips to Fort Abercrombie the fall of 1861 and I made friends among the Scandinavian settlers on the stage route. Lars Larson and his family lived in a log house between Alexandria Woods and Pomme de Terre. Lars and I had much in common. He urged me to find land nearby and settle in as his neighbor. It was some-

61

thing to think about. Another young Norwegian, Rasmuss Rognaldson, farmed near Fort Abercrombie by a small prairie settlement called Foxhome. We spent many an evening sharing our common dreams of making it big as landowners. Everyone knew a man couldn't get ahead by working for someone else.

It was a lonely feeling when winter stopped travel. There was little to do at the fort other than cut firewood. Ted taunted and teased me, called me names and played practical jokes on me from dawn to dusk.

Bishop Whipple, a missionary, invited me and several others to attend winter classes at the mission to improve our English. We were homesick and bored and thrilled to have something to do. He wasn't Lutheran, but Bishop Whipple was a good person and had spent his life working with the Sioux. Several Indians attended the classes as well.

It was at the mission where I met Crooked Lightning. He was the Indian who had gambled with Ted my first day at the fort, the one who pulled a knife when Ted tried to cheat him.

"Mr. Jacobson," Bishop Whipple said, "please repeat this sentence after me. 'In the beginning, God created the heavens and the earth.' "

"In da be-be-beginning, Got create da heavens and de-de-de-de-ert."

"Earth, earth, Mr. Jacobson, the word is earth with a t-h on the end. Th-th-th."

"Ert, er-er-ert, ta, ta," I stammered back.

While I stuttered and stammered and failed miserably at saying the strange words, Crooked Lightning learned quickly. He did not laugh at my mistakes like some of the others. After class one day he stopped by my bench and offered to help me. What a strange scene it must have been! To see a Sioux brave teaching English to a redheaded Norwegian Lutheran at an Episcopalian mission. That was the way of America; everything blended.

Crooked Lightning lived in one of the Indian villages around Fort Snelling. His wife, Many Beavers, was related to the famous chief, Wabasha. Crooked Lightning wore long black hair, shiny from bear grease and decorated with pretty feathers and shells. A brilliant red and white striped blanket draped across his shoulders, which he wore with the air of a royal cloak. Because of Ted's teasing, I visited Crooked Lightning almost every day through the coldest weather. His bark house was snug and warm, and I much preferred his company.

We communicated using gestures and drawings in the dirt, when our speech failed. I gave him snuff and taught him how to chew and spit tobacco. Many Beavers fed me stews made from small animals and dried berries. One time we feasted on buffalo steaks grilled over the fire. It was the best meat I had ever eaten, better even than the reindeer meat Mor had fixed back home.

"You are from a different tribe," he said as we sat around the cooking fire.

"*Ja,* from Norway. Far across the ocean."

"Did you cross the great water on a fire-boat?"

I chewed my mustache as I pondered this question. The ship on which I traveled didn't have a steam engine that spouted fire.

"*Nei,* it was a clipper I came on," I said. "With sails." I raised my arms in a poor imitation of the sails of the *White Dove.*

We sat in silence, pondering the mysteries of a boat traveling by steam or sails.

"And did you travel by the fire-boat-walks-on-mountains?" He made a chugging sound while churning his hands like a loco-motive.

"*Nei,* I had no money for such things." I slapped my boots. "I walked."

Crooked Lightning chewed and spit expertly into the fire causing a long satisfying hiss. "A horse is better. It does not need a . . ." His hands motioned two parallel lines.

"A track," I said. "A horse can go where there is no track."

He nodded solemnly, digesting the information along with his squirrel stew. "A horse can chase a war party."

"*Ja, ja,*" I said. "A train cannot leave the track." A sudden worry filled me. I wondered if I had somehow betrayed the white people, said too much.

"It is good to know these things."

After a long silence, Crooked Lightning spoke again, "Come."

We left the fire and walked up to the top of the hill beside the fort walls with his dog following at our heels. I could not keep the shiver off my lips but Crooked Lightning did not display any evidence of feeling the frigid cold other than pulling his blanket tighter around his shoulders. I scrambled to keep up with his long stride through the deep snow. I wondered what Crooked Lightning would think of skiers, gliding over the snow like flying birds, as they did in my homeland.

We finally reached the top of the hill with the panorama of the countryside before us.

Trees stretched as far as we could see on all sides. A low fog huddled over the open waters of the Mississippi and Minnesota rivers.

"The Big Knives want to own the whole world." Crooked Lightning spat the words from his mouth. "Even each other. They paint their slaves black and now they must serve the Washichu, the Big Knives, forever. Their Great Chief has said all places cannot have slaves and now they fight each other in jealousy."

"They fight far to the south."

"The Dakota people know of this war," he said. "Our chiefs read the words that tell of the battles."

It was true. Crooked Lightning often asked for war news, and I had seen him reading the newspapers posted at the fort.

"Warriors are driven forward to battle like antelope and forced to fight," he said. "Their chiefs are women and hide in the rear, out of danger."

A recent newspaper told how the generals watched from the hillsides with spyglasses. I listened, astonished at his interpretation.

"The Great Father may lose the war." Crooked Lightning adjusted his blanket and tossed his head back so that his hair fell behind his shoulders. "The Dakota Chiefs fear the generals in the south will try to enslave our people, paint us black as well."

"The Great Father is strong," I said. "I do not think he will lose the war."

I hoped I spoke the truth. I had been in America too short of time to understand politics. Newspaper reports were grim.

"But his braves die, too many to count. He cannot win if his braves are dead."

We trudged back to Crooked Lightning's lodge and Many Beavers ladled more stew onto our plates. Crooked Lightning tossed a bone to the dog at his feet.

"The Big Knives are a strange people," Crooked Lightning said. "Perhaps the Great Father forgets the Dakota people — his eyes are fastened to the south where his braves fight. Last year the payments were late and our children cried for food. This year the payments are late again — maybe will not come at all."

The rumor at the fort was that Washington wanted to send the payment in paper money rather than gold. Chief Little Crow went to the commander of the fort and demanded the payment in gold as promised by the treaty. He carried his copy of the treaty into the commander's office and read him the promise line by line. Soldiers at the fort muttered that if Washington didn't send the gold soon, there would be real trouble.

"The Dakota people will not become slaves," he said firmly. "They will not allow themselves to be painted black or their land stolen without payment."

I did not answer.

"We are not 'Sioux.' That is a name given to us by our enemies and means 'snake.' " He spit again. "We are the Dakota. Do not call us the name given by our enemies."

Every white man I knew except Bishop Whipple called them the "Sioux." It showed how little we understood them, how much we needed to learn. I decided to write Mor and tell her the thoughts of this Indian brave, how he had become my closest friend in America.

"Don't eat they's dog meat!" Ted tossed a fork full of wet straw over his shoulder into the manure pile. His crippled hand didn't seem to hinder his work when he set his mind to it.

"Dog meat?" I was caught off guard. Ted always seemed to say things beyond my understanding, making me feel ignorant and stupid.

"Don't eat them Injuns' dogs. Theys make you sick."

I kept shoveling, pondering his statement.

Many Beavers' stews sometimes tasted foreign, but I never sickened after eating them. Besides, Crooked Lightning's dog was his faithful companion, not to be lightly thrown into the cooking pot.

"Folks'll say you're an Injun-lover," Ted said.

"Injun-lover?"

"Decent white folks won't like yous if you's too friendly with them Injuns, especially Crooked Lightning." Ted threw another fork of manure into the pile and wiped his forehead on his shirtsleeve. "You saw him pulls his knife on me that time. He's a bad Injun, cheats at gambling and wouldn't care a lick if he stabbed yous in the gullet."

I had no answer for Ted. The decent white folks he talked about hadn't seemed too interested in welcoming me to Minnesota. Certainly not with the warmth Crooked Lightning had shown me.

# 5

"Battle of Shiloh at
Pittsburgh Landing, Tennessee"
~ St. Paul Journal

One day in late April the sergeant came into the barn and barked an order. I didn't understand one word he said.

"What's the matter, Jacobson?" he said. "You deaf? I said get on the stage and take over the driving. The driver enlisted and left us high and dry."

I had never driven the stage before but it didn't look too hard. I knew all the horses and thought I could find my way on the trail. With a nod I threw down my pitchfork and headed for the stage. Ted glared at me as I passed and shook his fist in my direction. I watched him stomp over to the sergeant and argue with him, nose to nose.

"You're letting them damn Norskie drive?" Ted yelled loud enough that I could hear every word. "That's a job for Americans."

"Shut your trap," the sergeant said. "He knows more about horses than you'll ever know."

I was hardly out of the gates before I encountered my first crisis. One of the big mares, Betty, pulled to the left and the front wheel slipped off the trail. It took all my strength to keep the stage upright in the mud. The sergeant came running with Ted close behind. The sergeant cussed me out while Ted smirked. They helped push the stage back on the track while I steered the horses.

"Watch Betty," the sergeant said. "She'll drag you off course if you don't keep a tight line."

"I will, sir." My mouth tasted like copper, and I waited for him to fire me on the spot. I had a little money saved up, but if he fired me, I figured to join the army. It didn't seem I had any other choice.

"Take it easy and follow the trail. You'll be all right."

Ted climbed up on the box and whispered into my face. His breath reeked of onions and beer. "You'd better watch your back, Norskie. There's some don't like foreigners taking American jobs." Then he jumped down.

"Tell it to the sergeant." I slapped the reins on the horses' backs and hurried down the trail. For once my speech had been without stammer. Maybe the lessons with the bishop had helped after all.

And so I took over driving the stage because I was familiar with the route and a good hand with horses. Besides, there was no one else.

It was the best of jobs. Sometimes I transported officers or settlers. Mail and orders traveled in a leather pouch that had to be guarded with my life. When I carried payroll, a shotgun rider was provided for extra protection. With the manpower short-age of the war, though, they often sent me alone. I didn't mind. The wildness of the trails, the Indians along the way, the sheer joy of driving a matched team of six horses made me think I was asleep and dreaming.

The settlers cheered me as a hero when I stopped with a piece of mail or a newspaper from home. I visited Lars Larson and Ras-muss Rognaldson each trip and midway I met Hjalmer Thoreson driving the other stage from the opposite direction.

We would stop and visit a little, taking a much-needed break from the solitude of the trail, catching up on the news, warning about bad ruts and river crossings. I came to America from Norway hoping to improve my situation. My life was improved already.

On my second trip out, I met Ingvald Ericson. Only one couple waited at Fort Snelling that early spring morning, just before Holy Cross Day. He was a big-shot Swede, just the type of man I left Norway to get away from. He wore a fine suit of clothes, finer than I have ever worn in my life. Middle aged and balding, his boots were shiny in spite of the steamboat ride to Minnesota from where the railroad ended in southern Wisconsin.

Behind him a woman clamored to gather packages and bundles from the rented wagon. She wore an inexpensive garment such as Mor had worn. Her shoes were torn and scuffed. She was very young, the age of Christina had she lived, and too thin. Tired brown eyes glanced at me from underneath a calico bonnet. Something in her eyes reminded me of Mor, and I reached to assist her with the bags while the man glowered at us both.

"Leave her be," he said in English that held a strong Swedish accent. "She's small but strong as an ox."

He looked at his watch and said over his

shoulder, "Woman, stack them on the platform and don't let them out of your sight." The man straightened his jacket and directed a question toward a soldier standing nearby. "Where can a man find a hot cup of coffee?"

I recognized the tone of someone in the upper class, used to commanding attention and respect.

"The mess hall is next door, Mr. Ericson." The soldier tipped his hat. "There's always coffee cooking."

Mr. Ericson walked toward the mess hall without so much as a backward glance at the woman struggling with the baggage in the chilly dawn.

I helped her stack the bags and trunks on the boardwalk.

"*Takk skal du ha!* Thank you very much," said the woman in Norwegian with a shy smile. She straightened up to remove the kinks from the journey and rubbed the small of her back with both fists. I was so relieved to hear my native tongue that I forgot my manners.

"You're Norwegian!" I said. "I, too, am from Norway."

She seemed reluctant to speak further, as if she suddenly recalled orders to remain silent. She looked down at her feet.

"My name is Evan Jacobson," I said. "Who are you?"

"Inga." She hesitated a moment, "My name is Inga Ericson."

With a start, I realized she was married to the Swede. I had assumed she was his servant. My face reddened, and I remembered to remove my hat. Inga turned away and sat on the trunk. Almost as an afterthought I brought her a dipper filled with cold water from the pail by the trough. She accepted it and drank. *Mange takk!* she said.

I hurried to ready for the journey. I checked each horse's mouth for sore spots and lifted each shaggy foot to examine the hoof for cracks or loose shoes. I used a small penknife from my pocket to remove a pebble lodged under one shoe. The horse snorted and shook his head in gratitude then swished his tail in my face in an attempt to chase the flies away. I led the team to the watering trough.

Mr. Ericson shouted orders to his missus and then stood in the barn door, watching the horses drink.

"I'm looking for stock," he directed the question at me in English. "Do you know any for sale?"

I managed to mumble a negative reply and

continued working on the harness.

"I'm on my way to buy a farm northwest of here. There's a Scandinavian community already established," he said. "Too many Norwegians there, I'm afraid, but at least they are Lutherans."

In a preachy voice he intoned the many virtues of living in Minnesota and the quality and quantity of land available for a rich man such as himself. He droned on about the need for educated, well-bred citizens to move to the area and assume a leadership role in the church and community. He seemed to know a lot about Minnesota, more than I did after being here a whole year. I held my tongue. Leave it to a Swede to be pompous even in the wilderness.

"Your-your missus is Norwegian," I stammered in English, hating my own voice in its weakness, but not wanting to give him the satisfaction of making me speak Norwegian.

"I married her in New York after we landed," he said. "Her man died on the ship coming over, fool that he was, and she was desperate for someone to take care of her. Not a penny to her name and completely ignorant of the English language. I felt it my Christian duty to help her out."

Mr. Ericson walked closer and confided

in a quiet voice, "She's a stout little heifer and will be a sturdy hand on the farm. She knows how to lie on her back," he said with a sour laugh. "You can see she's nothing to look at but she's built to breed."

He kicked the dirt with his shiny shoes, making small swirls with his foot. "I'll need sons to run the farm," he said. "Did you notice the spread of her hips?"

I looked at him in disbelief. Wordlessly I turned and walked away. It was breakfast time, and I needed to eat before getting the stage on the road.

"Are you sure you don't know of any stock for sale around here?" Mr. Ericson called after me, "I'm looking for stock."

I kept walking and did not answer.

# 6

"Grant Forces Beauregard to Withdraw
from Shiloh"
~ St. Paul Journal

After breakfast we loaded up the baggage
and passengers, hitched the animals and
started our journey west as the sun was
coming up. My anger at Ericson simmered.
I had known his kind in Norway. He was
used to quick answers but I wouldn't respond. Mr. High and Mighty could find his
own horses to beat and abuse, if he treated
his animals as he treated his missus. Men
who mistreated their women deserve to be
horsewhipped — or worse.

My thoughts drifted to that poor woman,
losing her husband, then forced to marry
that swine to survive. She might as well be
a Negro slave in the south. She would work
for him until she died without a kind word
or wages. Life for her would have been

easier in Norway.

I chewed my lip and tried to forget those brown eyes that reminded me of my mor. Their eyes were both brown, but it was more than just the color. Then I remembered Mor's eyes after Christina died. Inga's looked the same.

I thought the journey would never end. At each stop I saw first hand the misery of Ericson's woman. He insisted she stand to the side of the table and serve him, even when the meal was ready and time limited. She never replied or complained, but I noticed her chin tilt upward from time to time, a slight clenching in her jaw. After the men finished, he graciously allowed her to finish the leftovers while he hurried and bullied her the whole time.

"Hurry up, woman! Can't you see the stage is waiting?"

Watching that poor woman gulp down cold greasy venison was more than I could stand. Finally I spoke, "The stage isn't ready to leave yet, Missus. Take your time." Which was a bald-faced lie; we were behind already.

I left the cabin and climbed up on the stage. That particular team of geldings was my favorite. The pair of bays and two pair of blacks were agreeable and compliant. I had named them after my brothers back home — Sven, Ole, Emil, Nels, Carl, and Martin. Of course, only Ole lived past childhood, but they were still my brothers even if they slept in the graveyard by the Norwegian Church. I spoke to them softly as we traveled, trying to take my mind off the couple in the stage. I told these silent brothers about my life in America, about my trouble with Ted, the cruelty of Ingvald Ericson, the war in the South, the plight of the Dakota. If they had opinions, they kept them to themselves and plodded along the wilderness trail.

It was just outside of Beanpres Ferry that I noticed the screech in the right rear wheel. Damn Ted! He hadn't greased the wheel, undoubtedly to cause me trouble. If the hubs weren't packed tight with grease, the wooden wheels screeched from friction. If it got dry enough, it could spark a fire.

I pulled over to the side of the road and examined the wheel. It was warm to the touch. Damn him! Why did Ted hate me? I only wanted to be left alone and do my job in peace. I could just imagine his angelic innocence if I confronted him on it.

Ericson and his wife got out of the stage as I searched the boot for a supply of grease. I found a hammer and a piece of rope, but no grease. Hjalmer always toted an extra bucket in case of such emergencies. Why hadn't I thought to do the same?

I thought I might have to ride one of the horses back to the ferry to scrounge some grease when Inga pulled a piece of brown cheese from her basket.

"My far once packed a wheel hub with *gjetost,*" she said. "There's enough fat in the cheese to grease the wheel, at least for a little while."

Ericson sputtered about the stage company owing him money for his lunch, but to my relief, Inga pared enough cheese into the hub to pack it tight, and we made it to the next stop without trouble. I drove a little slower than usual, just in case, and pondered the wisdom in that Norwegian girl's head to think of such a thing. I'd have to be sure and tell Hjalmer about it.

We were late pulling into the station that night. I couldn't stand to see the Ericsons' bed together on the floor pallets. Of course, there was nothing wrong about them being together. They were married, after all, but I kept thinking of his boast to breed sons for the farm. It bothered me so much that I slept in the barn with the horses every night, not wanting to see them together or hear him command Inga as lord and master.

They traveled as far as Pomme de Terre. I

helped unload the heavy trunks and bags while Ericson berated and chided both Inga and me for slowness. He pulled a heavy watch chain and snapped open an ornate timepiece. I basked in the knowledge that the watch my far had received from the king was much nicer. It was a petty thought, and I admit it was spiteful. I left as soon as the horses were changed, not even bothering to eat the meal prepared at the station. I forced my face forward, refusing to look back and see what direction they went.

She must have been desperate to marry such a man. But married they were, and Mor had taught me the Commandments: I would not covet another man's wife.

The soldiers at Fort Abercrombie cheered when I rolled into the fort and gathered around me as if I were Abe Lincoln himself. The stage was their only source of news, supplies, and mail. They begged for news. Sven, the Norwegian cook, translated as I spoke of the headlines from the newspapers posted at the fort as well as small gossip learned along the way.

I told them about a bloody battle at Shiloh, how the Union was victorious in spite of staggering casualties on both sides. The soldiers heard the news soberly, wondering aloud when the casualty lists would be published, if anyone they knew had been killed.

Fort Abercrombie was a green outpost in the wilderness, only a few years old. In fact, it was the farthest west of all northern military outposts. It did not have a stockade around it, just a cluster of buildings. A ragged, lonely bunch of soldiers called it home. The purpose of Fort Abercrombie was to defend against the Dakota Indians in case of an uprising. I couldn't imagine the seventy-eight soldiers would be able to do so.

"Bring us a whole paper next time you come!" I made promises such as I thought I could keep and after a night's rest, headed east toward Fort Snelling.

At Pomme de Terre, Ingvald Ericson waited at the station.

"I need to send an urgent message to the Commander at Fort Snelling," he said. "It is of the utmost importance." He spoke in Swedish, for once laying down his textbook English.

"*Ja,* I'll take a message," I said. "I'll be there in about a week."

"This message is urgent. It must get to him at once. Is there no telegraph in this state?"

"*Nei,* there is no telegraph this side of St. Paul. No newspaper west of St. Cloud either. You are looking at the fastest means of getting a message to the fort unless you want to ride horseback yourself for 200 miles. Only a man on horseback will be faster than this stage."

Mr. Ericson paced back and forth on the dirt road while I plotted how to get away from his demands. With luck I'd be at the fort in another week. It might take longer. There were no guarantees in the wilderness.

"Mr. . . . Mr. . . ." he looked at me with a question in his face.

"Jacobson. My name is Mr. Jacobson." The unfamiliar title sounded foreign on my tongue and I sat up straighter on the seat.

"Mr. Jacobson," he said. "I demand you leave the stage and take this urgent message on horseback to the commander at Fort Snelling."

The heat rose in my cheeks and my heart lurched in my chest. The nerve of that man! "I take my orders from the fort," I said in my coldest voice. "It is my job to get the stage back to Fort Snelling. I cannot and will not leave the stage here. You will have to make other arrangements."

"You don't understand, Mr. Jacobson," he said. "There have been Indians at my shelter. They walk right up to the door and ask for food and water. Something must be done!"

"Have they harmed you?"

"*Nei,* but I don't want them on my property. They are ferocious and dangerous. The army must do something about it at once."

"Mr. Ericson," I said. "The Indians around here are Chippewa. They are friendly. If you give them water or food, they will be your friends. If they were hostile, you would not be alive to tell about it. You have to expect contact with Indians when you move into the frontier."

As I drove away, he stayed on the edge of the trail, hollering about how he would report me to the governor and I would lose my job. That fool! It would serve him right if the Indians did kill him. But then I thought about his wife. *Nei,* I did not wish them any harm.

I dreamed of having my farm somewhere between Alexandria Woods and Pomme de Terre. It was prime country, between the Big Woods and the prairie, rolling land with small lakes and sloughs scattered everywhere. There were enough trees to build a house and barn and yet not too many to clear for fields. There would be no lack of water for stock. Fishing and hunting could supplement my food supply. Living near Lars would be an added benefit. I started to picture a little log house with two rooms and a sweet-tempered Norwegian wife with blue eyes underneath a calico bonnet.

Only the eyes were brown.

Shaking myself back to reality, I ran the team a little harder than necessary, just to leave Ericson and the brown eyes behind.

The Larsons welcomed me when I stopped for the night. The pickled herring was a taste of home. The missus was big with child. Lars and I chewed snuff on the front porch, spitting into the flowerbeds around the cabin, watching the fireflies dart in and out. The little girls, Ragna and Borghilde, played on a swing made from a sack of straw hanging from a stout ash tree. Their laughter added to the feeling of home. Best of all was the freedom of using the Norwegian language.

"What do you hear of the Indian annuities?" asked Lars. "They were late last year and the year before."

"Crooked Lightning says some of the Indians are hungry already." Borghilde pushed Ragna on the swing until she squealed with delight. "The 'blanket

Indians' are feeling the loss of their hunting lands."

Lars took another chaw from his snuff plug and nodded his head.

"Game is about scared off," he agreed. "I haven't seen a buffalo or an elk for months."

"Besides, the crops failed last fall for the Indians who tried farming," I said. "Crooked Lightning calls them 'cut-hairs' since they were forced to accept white man haircuts and clothing as well as houses and farms."

"What difference does it make if their hair is long or short?" asked Lars. "The cattle and corn don't care."

"Some rich man thought that one up, that's for sure," I said. "The cut-hairs need the annuities to survive just as much as the blanket Indians." I stopped to spit into the peony bush. "Besides the payments of trade goods and food, they get $71,000 in gold every year for fifty years."

We sat in the darkness, spitting and chewing and swatting mosquitoes.

"At least the Chippewa are friendly," said Lars. "We should have no Indian problems here."

"Have you ever worried about the Indians turning hostile?" Borghilde climbed up beside Ragna on the swing and called for their far to give them a push.

"*Nei,* the treaties and armies can worry about that. We are friendly to the natives, like the Good Book says." He pushed the swing until both girls were sailing through the sky clutching the sack swing and squealing like little piglets. "Still I'm glad we live farther north, away from the Sioux."

I pondered the situation as I drove out of their place the next morning. It was a mystery how the United States government treated the Indians. They were willing to fight a war to free the Negro slaves in the south while turning their back on the Indians at home who were waiting for legal payment for their land. Crooked Lightning complained that even when the annuities came, dishonest white traders demanded huge payment for goods they never sold to the Indians and tricked them out of their money. Because they were white, their word was never questioned. Crooked Lightning told of a Dakota Indian who swallowed his gold coins from the annuity payment. He said, "They will not get my money for things I did not buy." It made no sense to me.

Another army stage route went through the Upper and Lower Sioux reservations, farther south. My route traveled north along the north edge of the big woods, the dividing line between the Dakota and Chippewa nations. The Dakota and Chippewa were always at each other. If Indian trouble developed along this road, it would most likely be between the two tribes and I could just stay out of their way. I was lucky to drive the northern route. Army or no army, I would hate to be on the southern route if trouble cropped up with the Dakota.

# 7

"McClellan Halts Union Army 6 Miles from Richmond in Spite of Superior Forces"
~ St. Paul Journal

Bishop Whipple understood Norwegian well enough to converse. Purposely I hunted him out to ask a question. The Indians called him "Straight Tongue" and I knew to trust him. "Bishop, can I bother you for some information?"

"Why not come to the mission, and I'll fix you supper," he replied.

We walked out the fort gates, nodding to the sentry on guard, and strolled down the hill toward the log mission. The sunset was red and pink against the western sky, a perfect backdrop for the wooden cross on the church that also served as school for the Dakota Indians. It was peaceful. Croaking frogs and the call of geese from the river enhanced the feeling of serenity. Over coffee and fried panfish, I asked him about the Dakota Indians.

"I wrote a letter to President Buchanan in 1860," he said. "I complained about the ill treatment of the Dakotas by the government agents and dishonest traders — the government promised to investigate."

I remembered reading about the investigations in Mr. Aaronson's newspaper, amazed I was sitting at table with the man responsible for them.

"And I wrote another letter to President Lincoln this past March because nothing has changed," he continued. "I had hoped the new administration would do something about the problem, but then the rebellion started and once again the Dakota are pushed aside." He lit his pipe and leaned back in his chair. "Meanwhile, the government demands they take up farming."

"The cut-hairs." I put a stray fishbone on my plate.

"In theory it would work," he said. "The treaty has given them enough acres of good land to provide for all the Dakotas. They number only six thousand."

He reached for the plate of fish and pushed it in my direction.

*"Mange takk."* I heaped another mound of the tasty fillets onto my plate and reached

91

for the salt.

"The bands taking up farming are scorned by the others for being womanish."

"Why?"

"Braves are supposed to hunt and fight; women do planting and manual labor."

I could understand that. In Norway, the women always did the milking and making of cheese and butter.

"The crops failed last year between the drought and the grasshoppers. The cut-hairs are having second thoughts." He poured another cup of coffee and slid the cream pitcher over to me. "But the treaties have already taken away their ancestral hunting grounds. New settlements and immigrants have driven the game further north and west of here. It's too late to turn back, too late to change their minds with all the new settlers moving in. Then there are the Chippewa."

"They are enemies?"

"Always at war. Back in '58 there was a battle at Shakopee's village, just south of here. If they don't avenge the deaths of their relatives, they believe they won't rest in the spirit world. Farmers won't achieve status in the tribe unless they fight the Chippewa. It's a hopeless circle."

Bishop Whipple kept me spellbound late into the night with his explanation of

Dakota ways. He lived with them most of his life and knew them well, probably better than any other white man. Several chiefs of different bands converted to Christianity under his teaching.

"Little Crow of the Kaposia band now lives in a brick house and farms. He still has twelve wives," Bishop Whipple said sadly, "but he attends church every Sunday. I pray the day will come when the Dakota people will see God's plan for all people, that war and vengeance will never bring peace."

I asked him how the Dakota government worked, who was the main chief. He told me about the different bands making up the Dakota Nation. The Mdewakantons, Wahpeton, Sisseton, and Wahpekutes constitute the Santee Dakota and live to the east. The Yankton, Teton, and Yanktonai make up the Western Dakota."

"Yet they are all Dakotas?"

"Without a single leader. The various chiefs need to agree before action of the whole tribe is taken." Bishop Whipple sighed. "That is probably the reason there has not been more bloodshed against the whites. The tribes don't agree."

"What if they come to agreement?"

"Then it is 'over the earth I come.' " It

seemed his face turned pale but it may have been the candle burning down.

"Over the earth I come?"

"It is a Dakota phrase that means all out war, an uprising like has never been seen in this country, a desperate fight to the end."

"Could they succeed?" My voice sounded small and flat and a knot clenched in my stomach. "Are they strong enough to fight us all?"

"The men are gone to war and the forts are weakened by lack of soldiers," he said. "The Dakota are not unaware of this."

I nodded. Of course, they would be aware of the white man's vulnerability. Crooked Lightning said the chiefs were keeping up with the war news from the south.

"If they would ever persuade the Chippewa to swoop down from the north and the Winnebago to come up from the south and fight with them, there would be no hope civilization could continue in Minnesota." He calmly tamped tobacco into his pipe. "In that case, we'd all be either killed or driven out."

A newspaper was always posted in the commissary window, and I went there to learn the news. Men were gathered around it, and a young private read aloud. A thick silence settled over the group when he finished. Such numbers of dead and wounded! There must be a mistake.

The soldiers backed away from the paper like backing away from a poisonous snake. They turned and left, one by one, without the usual banter. When I stood alone by the newspaper, I scanned the lists of dead. It was folly. I knew so few people in this country, but something drove me to read the names one by one. Near the middle of the column, I discovered where Cleng Peterson lived in America.

He slept forever at Shiloh.

# 8

"13,000 Union and 11,000 Confederate
Killed or Wounded at Shiloh"
~ St. Paul Journal

The route was burned in my mind. I could
travel it in the dark. I left Fort Snelling at
daybreak, traveling north to St. Anthony
Falls and then veered northwest. The stage
could make two miles an hour if the roads
were fair. On a good day, traveling from
sunup to sundown, we could expect thirty
miles or better.

The first stop was at Joe Sullivan's. It was
only a cabin on the old Red River Ox Cart
trail a half day's journey from the fort, just
past St. Anthony Falls. To my surprise, his
missus came out to help with the team
instead of his son.

"Good day, Missus." I tipped my hat.
"Where's Adam?"

"He's planting corn in the back forty."

"Have you heard from your man?"

"Says it's too hot in the south," she said. "Hopes the war is over by the time the corn is ready to harvest."

What I knew about the war was not promising. It seemed doubtful Joe Sullivan would be home in time to pick the corn. I kept my thoughts to myself and hurriedly ate the side pork and biscuits she'd prepared. I dared not linger if I would make the Elk River crossing by nighttime.

I was exhausted by the time we made the crossing. The horses dragged. I helped Anders Johnson rub them down, making sure they had enough feed and water. Those horses were like family to me; their care came first. Then I straggled into the house for a meal of milk and cornmeal mush.

Gustav, their oldest son, served in the Union Army, and they pleaded for news from the front. The house was crowded with all the children bedded down on pallets. I rolled up in my blanket and slept in the barn. Not even mosquitoes kept me awake.

The next morning, I hitched the replacement team and crossed the river before dawn, aiming for Beanpres Ferry by St. Cloud before dark. It was a good level stretch of prairie, and I made good time before stopping at John Sanger's homestead for nooning and a fresh team. John Sanger had enlisted last fall, and his oldest son, William, cared for the horses. William must have been about twelve or thirteen years old. He carried a heavy load with his far gone.

We crossed over the Mississippi River at Beanpres Ferry and slept at Sauk Rapids at the home of John Filmore. We had traveled thirty-four miles.

After Beanpres Ferry, the road became more difficult. I headed in a direct line to Fort Abercrombie, but the road was incomplete in places since I traveled north of the Red River Ox Cart Trail to avoid bothering the Dakota.

Ole Swenson welcomed us to his homestead twelve miles out of St. Cloud. He, his wife, and eight children lived in a small shelter, half log and half dug out. A straw roof such as was common in Norway covered them. The children stood like stair steps around the table, watching me eat rutabaga soup. The soup was thin, and I was conscious of their eyes on me, wondering if they would get enough to fill their bellies.

After I'd climbed up onto my seat on the stage, I handed down a shriveled carrot I had along to treat the horses. Their eyes lit up. I watched as they carefully cut it into ten round slices. *"Mange takk!"* they called as I drove away.

It was sobering to see first hand how the families fared in the wilderness. The houses were handmade structures of log or sod in areas bereft of trees. These isolated dwellings offered no protection from illness or injury. Often the meal was a thin gruel made of hand-ground corn or wheat. Sometimes there was meat on the table, hunted by the father or older boys, but most Scandinavians did not come to America with knowledge of hunting or the use of firearms. They fished if near a lake or river and trapped small rabbits or other game to supplement the meager diets. The children picked chokecherries, wild strawberries, blueberries in some areas, and a variety of nuts. Sometimes they ate wild mushrooms. Most lived on salt pork and flour. All lived more on hope than substance.

That night I pulled into the Brorson farm in Cold Spring. It was an isolated spot on the Sauk River. I made only twenty-eight miles that day due to bad roads and several streams. Spring flooding made the crossings treacherous.

Bror Brorson was a Norwegian bachelor, and we ate fried squirrel off greasy plates.

The coffee was hot and thick, the house a filthy hovel. Bror smelled of sweat and manure and his hair was a dust-covered mass of dark curls. Mice scurried around the cabin, their eyes bright reflections of the firelight, and a bat swooped across the table while we ate. Bror swatted at it with his hat but made no effort to chase it out of the house. I was glad my own hat was firmly on my head, protecting my hair.

"Do you know of any single Norwegian women in the state?" He lit a long-necked pipe like the one Peter Anderson had smoked in Illinois.

"*Nei,* they are all married or engaged when they come to this country."

"Do you know of any single women of any kind?" he said. "I'm thinking I need a woman to help me out here."

He needed help, I could see that, but I knew of no single women.

"There may be widows with so many men off fighting in the south," I said after thinking a bit and taking a chew of snuff. "There were lots of casualties at Shiloh. The lists were just published."

Bror nodded and drew on his pipe, letting out the smoke in round O's that drifted between table and roof.

"I hadn't thought of widows. It'd be good

to have sons old enough to help with the fields," he said. "Would you let me know of any you might meet?"

"I'll keep my eyes open."

If Christina had lived, I would not have wished for her to marry such a slovenly man in that lonely place. But widows were another matter. They sometimes had to choose less than their dreams. My thoughts drifted to Inga, forced to marry Ericson to survive. I stood up abruptly and started for the stable. I would sleep with the horses.

The fourth day started before daybreak. Bror fixed coffee and served the cold fried squirrel from the night before using the same greasy plate. But food was food, and I couldn't afford to be picky. I veered slightly north and traveled to the edge of the Big Woods. The roads were good most of the way and I pushed the team, traveling to Carl Evenson's cabin, twenty-two miles from Brorson's.

Carl was in his field, planting corn behind a long-eared mule. He turned and waved when he saw the stage drive into his place and hurried the mule to finish his row before coming in for dinner.

"Hot enough for you today?" I called as he came up to the stoop.

"*Ja,* it's good weather for the corn."

We unhitched the team and led them to a watering trough by the barn. Carl's twelve-year-old son, Arvid, carried the water from a spring behind the house.

"It's good water," I said as I took a dipper full from Arvid's bucket.

"Let's eat."

The entire cabin smelled fresh and clean. The food was good, too. Carl's woman knew how to bake bread. It was fresh and soft from the oven, still warm. She had fresh butter and poured thick cream into our coffee cups. Carl, Arvid, and I ate the whole loaf along with a pot of coffee. Carl's woman stood off to the side, serving us. Two little girls peeked out from behind her skirts, eyeing me with suspicion.

"We don't get many visitors here," Carl said. "The Indians come to our spring for water sometimes. Other than the stage, the girls are not used to company."

I reached into my shirt pocket and took out a long string I had saved. Their eyes were glued on my hands. I tied a knot connecting the two ends. Casually I looped the string on fingers of each hand and started weaving the string back and forth. My eyes caught a sparkle in Arvid's eyes.

"I see you know how to do the cat's

cradle," Carl said. "Have you ever seen the lovers' kiss?"

I handed the string to Carl and watched him knit and weave from hand-to-hand, telling stories from our homeland with each new design. The girls could not stay behind their mother's skirts and were soon at his knee, staring up in wonder.

As I got up to leave, I saw the disappointment in their faces.

*"Mange takk for mat,"* I said. "You may keep the cat's cradle and all the other games this string can provide."

As I left, Carl went back to the fields with his mule. The new team was restless, anxious to be on the road. I whistled a Norwegian tune to calm them, waving good-bye to the girls in the doorway, comforted.

I made it to Sauk Centre by the time the sun dropped below the horizon in the west. I knew it was risky; there were so few places to stop for help if I lost a wheel or broke a harness. But I wanted to make time when I could. Thirty-five miles were behind me.

Wilhelm Schwarz, a thickset German, had a clean house and a quiet wife. She never spoke one word in my presence. Perhaps that was good manners, but it set strange with me. She cowered away from Wilhelm when she set the plates on the table. The food was unlike that of my homeland, sausages and cabbage, but very tasty. Schwarz drank his coffee from a fine china teacup with a matching saucer. He poured cream and stirred sugar into the cup of scalding coffee and then poured some into the saucer. Slurping loudly, he drank the cooled coffee from the saucer and repeated the process. I had never before seen anyone drink from a cup and saucer and was aware once again of his wealth and power. I gazed down at the cup and saucer before me and could almost hear Mor's voice reminding me not to think I was better than anyone else was. Instead, I picked up the china cup with my awkward hands and drank from the cup as if it had been a plain tin cup or a dried gourd. *Nei,* I was no better than anyone else was.

German is enough like Norwegian that we were able to communicate a little over supper. The mister did all of the talking while I listened and the missus cleaned up the dishes. I understood most of what he said. Before I left in the morning, the missus served crisp potato pancakes. Wordlessly she pressed a leftover pancake wrapped in a cloth into my hands to take along on the journey.

*"Mange takk,"* I said.

She did not smile or answer.

The road was good between Sauk Centre and Alexandria Woods, with only a few deviations around marshy areas. At noon, I stopped at the home of a Dane, Jens Jensen, and enjoyed a meal of milk soup and cheese. His missus was a good hand with cattle as was proven by the quality of cheese. We conversed easily, the Danish language being similar to Norwegian.

I admired the large barn built into a hillside, all logs with hand-hewn cedar shingles. The Danes were an ambitious people; a Norwegian would have put on a thatch roof and called it good enough. The house was noticeably smaller and less fancy than the barn although neat and clean. A small herd of brown cows grazed peacefully in the meadow. I wondered if his missus minded living less fancy than the cows. Hjalmer Thoreson had talked about "Big Barn Jensen" and I understood why he carried the name.

By the time I reached the cabin of Lars Larson, I had gone thirty-four miles. The team was exhausted. I rubbed them down, crooning to each of the horses in Norwegian. I fed them small nibbles of oats and carrots. After supper, we sat on the porch, talking later than was common sense. His woman had just birthed a son. A neighbor woman, Missus Spitsberg, cared for them and did the cooking.

"Now then, I have some news for you," Lars said.

"*Ja,* and what can that be?"

"The littlest one is a strong, healthy son, the first American citizen. He could grow up to be president some day," he said proudly. "We are naming him Evan, after you, our Norwegian-American friend."

The news came as a complete surprise. I had not given the infant much thought but suddenly had a keen desire to look at him.

"Will you Godfather our son? We hope to baptize him when the Lutheran priest comes around."

"Surely you could find someone more worthy of the honor," I said. "I am not much of a churchgoer since coming to America and who knows when I will save up enough money for a place of my own. It would be hard to care for a child while driving stage."

"You are our choice," he said. "Please say you'll sponsor this new one."

Lars was the closest thing to a brother I had in America. It would be disrespectful to refuse such a great honor. The thought occurred to me that someday when I found a

woman and settled down, Lars could Godfather our first child, too. Crooked Lightning was a good friend, but not Lutheran
and certainly not a candidate for Godfather.

"I will," I said at last. "*Mange takk* for such
an honor."

We shook hands and I felt the sudden
weight of responsibility on my shoulders. To
be responsible for this little one in case of
the parents' death was not to be taken
lightly. To promise before God that I would
do all in my power to keep him loyal to God
and the Commandments seemed more than
I could deliver. But above all the worry, I
felt a sweet fellowship knowing I would once
again be part of a family. I would have those
to care for and who would care for me. I
would no longer be alone in America.

That night I slept in the barn. It would
have been awkward sleeping on the floor
next to the bed of Lars and his missus with
the new baby and all. *Nei,* I knew my place.
It was with the horses.

The sixth day out of Fort Snelling I left
Lars Larson's place while it was still dark,
the road open and easy to follow. I peeked
at the sleeping babe before I left, coffee cup
in hand.

"Good-bye, Lille Guten," I said.

"*Ja,* he is indeed a good little boy." The

107

missus smiled at me. "Have a safe trip. We look forward to seeing you again on your next journey."

"Good-bye, Uncle Evan!" the little girls said.

It startled me, being called uncle. But it was to be expected since I was Godfather to their little brother. It meant I would be part of the family. That was a very good feeling.

The morning sunrise was beautiful, colored pink and lavender. It was at my back and I turned my head to watch it, letting the horses follow the trail themselves for a minute. Robins and meadowlarks serenaded me. How peaceful were Minnesota mornings and how breathtaking the sunrises and sunsets. Hemmed in by mountains, I had rarely glimpsed them in Norway. In Minnesota, a man could see as far as a flying bird.

The noon stop came none too soon, this being the worst stretch of road on the trip. The lead horse had a loose shoe, and I lacked the tools to fix it on the trail. The roads were swampy and rutted, and I felt my bones jarred from their sockets. Olaus Reierson's homestead had a small forge, and I was able to fix the shoe and get it back on the horse for the next driver. I lost time doing so and had several mail deliveries along the way. It was dark when I pulled into Pomme de Terre at the home of Anton Estvold. I had covered thirty miles.

My eyes drooped while I shoveled in cold mush. Anton was a talkative man, one of the original settlers in the area with two sons in the army. A letter from his son, Emil, was in my pouch, and he grasped it eagerly, reading it aloud by the dim light of the lamp while his missus stood to one side, hands clasped before her as if in prayer.

April 8, 1862

Dear Far and Mor

It is with great relief I write this letter to you, as I never thought I would survive the two-day battle of Shiloh. The fighting was centered on a small log church in a peaceful field. Never were so many prayers said at that church and God heard us and gave us victory although at a cost too dear to tally. When there seemed no relief from the torturous heat and hatred of battle, a gentle rain fell during the night and revived us. I hope and pray the war will end soon. I wish to be home in time to help with the harvest. How are the crops doing this year? I hope you have had enough rain.

I pray you are both well. Have you heard from Ole?

Your loving son,<br>Emil Estvold

The missus wiped tears from her eyes, and I must admit to feeling a little choked up myself. I vowed to write Mor a letter and tell her about the stage route, becoming Godfather to Lars' son, and the death of Cleng Peterson. Anton went outside to care for the animals and ready things for the night. I sat at the table almost sleeping, thinking about the horrors of battle and the words of my far to stay out of a rich man's war.

Anton joined me for more coffee. He talked about newcomers to the area. I became wide-awake when he mentioned the name of Ingvald Ericson.

"The fool thinks he is the King of Sweden," Anton said. "He wants to run the church and township both."

"I believe it," I said.

"He works that poor woman of his like a Negro slave."

"I knew his kind in Norway." I knew I talked too much but was unable to stop the words from my heart. "They are all alike, think they are better than everyone else.

Someone forgot to tell him there is no upper class in America."

"You'll go right by his place when you leave," Anton said. "It is a mile west and then a short quarter mile to his cabin."

It was tempting. If I stopped by, I could see for myself how Inga was faring. The next morning I saw the trail west of Pomme de Terre and turned the team into the lane. The cabin was not quite completed, but they were making good headway. Leave it to Ingvald to get things done. Inga was in the pasture, calling the cows in her contralto voice, "Come, Boss! Come, Boss!" I could see Ericson through the window, sitting at the table.

*This is madness!* I turned the stage around in an open place alongside the lane and kept going. By the time I reached Dayton, I had calmed myself. Lewis Peterson owned the small homestead.

"Any news of the war?" he asked.

"Nothing good. McClellan is waiting outside of Richmond. Some say he should have pressed ahead and secured a victory. There's a stalemate and no one knows what to expect except that more soldiers are needed."

Lewis leaned back in his chair and stuffed a wad of snuff into his mouth. His blond moustache was stained with tobacco, as were his teeth and hands. He chewed and spit into the bucket at his feet.

"I've thought of it," he said. "I've no wife or children to hold me back."

He spit again and I finished my coffee to join him. *Snus* was a great comfort, the only comfort I allowed myself in the wilderness. It gave a satisfying feeling. Somehow, it calmed me and helped me collect my thoughts, and that helped with my stuttering.

"My far told me to not fight another man's war." I rolled the wad under my tongue.

"It's not bad advice," Lewis added. "Besides, they haven't asked me to fight, so maybe they don't need me all that bad."

We chewed and spit together without saying anything, and Lewis trimmed his fingernails with a small penknife.

"I think I'll stay here in Minnesota and mind my own business," I said at last as I climbed up on the stage, ready to get back on the trail.

"*Ja,* surely the fighting will not come this far north."

I pulled into Foxhome that night to the farm of Rasmuss Rognaldson. It had been a grueling day and I had only traveled twenty-five miles. The swamps, wet and boggy, had slowed the team. I was weary of talking at every stop but Rasmuss was starved for news, news of any kind. He did most of the talking and I listened into the night, about the war in the south, the late Indian payments, and the peculiarities of the Americans, the price of wheat, and the need for more Norwegian girls to immigrate.

"I've noticed something here in America," he said to me.

"*Ja,* what is that?"

"There are no old people. Everyone in Minnesota is young," he said. "The farmers are young, the families are young, and there are no old people at all."

He was right, I realized with a start, at least on the frontier. The commander at Fort Snelling was past middle age, but everyone else was younger. The only old people I had met in Minnesota were at the Indian village where Crooked Lightning lived.

"It is not a country for old people," I said. "I'm glad Mor is in Norway and not battling the wilderness."

The soldiers cheered as I drove into Fort Abercrombie. They pressed in, as always, hungry for mail and news of the war in the south. I climbed down off the stage, weary beyond description. I had traveled twenty-five miles that day to reach my destination. The entire trip had lasted eight days, covering two hundred and fifty-one miles. The soldiers asked question after question, and I answered as best I could.

I don't mean to brag but I made fair time. By carefully starting before dawn and continuing until the dusk was almost black, I shaved off more than a whole day of travel each way. It meant quicker dispatches to Fort Abercrombie and quicker responses to Fort Snelling, which brought praise from the sergeant.

Minnesota summer days were long; starting early in the morning and lasting late into the evening. Of course, they were nothing like the midnight sun in Norway but the hours were there for work.

I meant to use every minute of light available to keep the stage rolling.

# 9

"Rebels Awaiting McClellan's Army, Now
Five Miles from Richmond"
~ St. Paul Journal

When I stopped at the Larson's on the way
back to Fort Snelling, it seemed that Baby
Evan had grown stronger. He cried lustily
until the missus settled him to her breast. I
averted my eyes, wondering where to look,
but Lars and the missus acted as if it was
nothing out of the ordinary, and I guess they
were right. It was the start we all had and
no shame in it.

Ragna sidled up to the table and whispered something into her far's ear. He
reached toward the sugar bowl, handed her
a small lump of loafsugar, and watched as
she carefully dipped it into his coffee cup.
When the coffee stained the sugar light
brown, she popped it into her mouth, smiling at the coffee flavored sweetness.

Borghilde came for her treat as well, and I watched Lars repeat the process. It brought back a sharp memory of me doing the same with my far; I could almost taste the sweet flavor and smell the scent of his coat and beard. I fought down a quick surge of home-sickness.

The scene of such happiness left me unexpectedly hollow. Would I roam the wilderness trails forever, sleeping in the homes of strangers, without a place to call home? I did not want to be another lonely bachelor, living in solitude and longing. I was ready for something of my own, some-one to be my own.

The commander of Fort Snelling decided to travel to Fort Abercrombie to inspect the fort readiness. He was waiting at the stage my next trip out. Gabriel, his servant, climbed up on the stage box with me.

"Hello, Gabriel," I said.

"Good mornin, sir." His eyes were guarded, as if he expected me to make him ride in the boot with the baggage.

"Just call me Evan."

"Heya, Evan." His entire body relaxed and his teeth glowed white.

"You can ride sh-shotgun for me."

His laugh was like molasses melting on hot cornbread.

Throughout the trip, we had ample time to discuss the topics of the world. He was anxious to hear about my trip over the ocean, why I left Norway, if I had family still there.

"I would only be a burden to my brother and his family if I stayed."

"Do you write to them?"

"*Ja*, but I'm not much of a writer."

The mourning doves cooed their sweet music and pink roses bloomed along the trail. The earthy smell of damp earth and growing things surrounded us.

"Do you write your family?"

A look of such grief crossed his face that I at once regretted my question. Surely, Mor had taught me better than to get too personal with strangers.

"Slaves can't get mail," he said. "My mother might still be in Georgia but by now my brothers are dead or sold down river. They're dead to me, I guess."

Gabriel told me how the system worked, how families were often sold apart. He told me of his great luck to be sold to a family whose daughter did not believe in slavery. When the master died, the daughter emancipated the slaves.

"She taught me to read and write and cipher though it was against the law," he said. "She found work for all of us, helped us get a new start in the North. She did right by us, every one."

The trail became more difficult — trees and branches blocked the way. Gabriel and I jumped down and dragged the debris from last night's storm away from the road.

It was good to move our muscles, to change the topic to something less personal. The rest of the day, we talked only of the weather, the birds of Minnesota, and crops.

At the waystations along the way, Gabriel ate his food outside and slept in the barn at night. I joined him, knowing I would feel foolish eating at the table with the commander or sleeping beside him at night. It wasn't as if the folks were unkind to Gabriel; mainly they ignored him. His presence was unexpected. Many had friends or relatives fighting to end slavery. Fighting a war is different than sitting at table with an ex-slave.

Slowly we made our way across the state, bouncing with each rut and pothole.

"Have you ever heard of Dredd Scott?" Gabriel asked.

"*Nei,* I think not." I tried to steer the team around a nasty hole in the trail.

"Dredd Scott was a slave to the commander who used to be there," Gabriel said.

"He didn't want to return to slavery when the commander left Fort Snelling and took his case all the way to the Supreme Court."

"Wh-what happened?"

"He lost. The court said he was property of his master to be bought and sold at will."

My mind was astonished. If a Negro person had the brains to take his case all the way to the highest court in the land, surely it showed beyond any doubt his human intelligence. Ted said Negroes were slaves because they were not human. I wished the words in my brain would leave my mouth, to share this thought with my Negro friend. But the words refused to come and I kept silent.

Storms plagued the last part of our trip. We sat in the driver's box in drizzling rain, too cold for June. It came down in sheets, leaving the trail a muddy rut.

"I'm thinkin' of joining up," Gabriel said toward the end of the journey, just as Fort Abercrombie came into view.

"You-you are?" I did not know the Union Army would accept Negro recruits.

"There's a regiment of colored soldiers. I might join up and fight to free my people."

At first, I was speechless. I spit a wad of snuff to the side of the trail. It splashed in a muddy puddle along with the raindrops.

"I would do the same," I finally said. "Good luck to you, Gabriel." I offered my hand and he shook it solemnly. "May God grant you reunion with your mother and brothers."

It was my last meeting with Gabriel. He joined the Federals and left for the South before I saw him again. I often wonder if he survived the war, if he ever found his mother or brothers.

I resolved to write Mor a letter and tell her about the evils of slavery in America. Negro slavery was worse than working for the upper class in Norway! At least we had not been sold and separated against our will. If later I decided to join the war, she would understand why.

For once, the soldiers at Fort Abercrombie did not surround me with questions. When we arrived with the commander, they stood at attention with such looks of utter despair on their faces that I felt pity for them. Surely, the fort was in poor condition. I could have told the commander that and saved him the long trip out. At least he could report the news of the war. I was getting tired of being a walking newspaper.

"I have news for you this time, Evan," Sven said. "The circuit minister stopped at

Breckenridge and held services. He just come from New Ulm and spoke of trouble among the Sioux. One of the Indian agents has refused to give them their supplies. Says he wants to wait until the money comes and give the supplies together with the payment."

"Why?" I said. "That makes no sense."

"Just lazy, I guess. The worst is that he insulted the Sioux chiefs," Sven said. "He told them to feed their families grass if they were hungry."

"That fool!" I said. "Doesn't he know the danger of the situation?"

My mind tossed this new information back and forth. Of course, it might be rumor. Preacher or not, rumors were rampant in the wilderness. I decided to ask Bishop Whipple about it when I reached the fort. He could be trusted for the truth.

The commander decided to stay a few days and come back with the next stage later in the week. Of course, Gabriel stayed with him. The stage box was too quiet on the return trip.

That night I pulled into Foxhome and saw Rasmuss Rognaldson milking his cow in the lean-to barn. He was short and stocky in build, his dark hair a contrast to his sky-blue eyes.

"Hello, Rasmuss!"

"Come down and help me, Evan!" he said. "Can't you see there is work to do?"

I climbed down and walked over to the barn made of sod blocks. It was the building material of choice there on the flat lands. Rasmuss sat on a three-legged stool beside the brown cow. Rich milk flowed into the bucket with each squeeze of his strong hands. The sound and smell reminded me of home. I quickly turned my head and changed the subject.

"I see you have not found a woman yet."

*"Nei,"* he said, "and I'm tired of women's chores and sleeping alone."

"I'll keep looking for an available woman for you."

"I'm not picky," he said. "Any one will do at this point!"

We drank the warm milk and ate stale biscuits for supper while we slapped at the flies and mosquitoes. Rasmuss was a likeable fellow. His shelter was clean and neat. I knew if I had my own place, I would keep it the same. I shared the news heard at the fort. His expression turned immediately serious.

"I've had some bad dreams lately," he said. "About Indian troubles."

A sudden dread settled in the pit of my

stomach.

"I dreamed the Sioux swooped down upon me while I has picking corn," he said. "They were painted and fierce. They killed my cow and were coming at me with spears." He shook his head as if to displace the memory. "I can't shake the dread. I think I'm spending too much time alone."

"*Ja,* it is not good to be alone so much of the time."

"I'm tempted to go back with you and look for a woman in Pig's Eye," he said. "Last time the minister was here, he spoke of several single women there."

"I have not heard of them," I answered carefully. It would not do to contradict a man of the cloth.

"Nevertheless, I think I'll return with you next trip and find out. I'll leave the cow with a neighbor. There's not much work to do on the fields until harvest."

"You're welcome, Rasmuss. I'll enjoy your company."

"To be truthful, Evan, I can't bear the thought of another winter alone. If I can't find a woman, I may join the army or look for work as a hired hand further east. I'd rather keep my hair than become a rich farmer."

Who could blame the man? The country

was flat beyond belief with hardly a tree to break the emptiness. I could not stand to live alone in such a barren place either. But the land was rich and black with no trees to cut or stumps to pull. What wheat grew on those fertile prairies! A man could do worse than own a farm in Foxhome, Minnesota.

The next morning I left Rasmuss. A man could imagine all sorts of calamities in such solitude. We arranged that he would go east with me on my next trip back.

Lewis Peterson was in the field pulling weeds, and I waved to him as I drove into his yard. I watered the horses and loosed them into the shady fenced pasture by the barn. They rolled in the green grass, neighing and whinnying, greeting the other team.

"They are beautiful animals," Lewis said.

"*Ja,* the best of all God's creatures," I said and meant it.

We drank coffee and ate cold pancakes slathered with butter and sugar. Of all the bachelors on the route, Lewis ate the best. Often he ate summer sausage or sardines, delicacies to be savored.

Our talk switched to the report from the Lower Sioux Agency.

"He really told them to eat grass if they were hungry?" asked Lewis.

"That's the story, if it can be believed."

"They're asking for bloodshed with such remarks. The Sioux are a proud race. They won't turn their heads at insults."

"It is a good thing you live further north."

Lewis washed down his pancake with a swallow of coffee and looked at me.

"There you're wrong, Evan," he said. "If the Sioux go to war, they won't spare those of us on the outskirts. In fact, we may be the first to go. This area is their favorite hunting land. They still come and hunt a little now and then. *Nei,* we will not be spared."

I left Lewis' cabin with a heavy heart. Of course, he was right. No one would be safe if the Dakota sought revenge. The men were gone to war. No one was left to defend the scattered families.

It was late when the stage passed Ingvald Ericson's cabin. I couldn't help turning my head to look down the lane but I saw no one. At another place, I may have stopped to water the animals that were laboring in the heat. But I would not stop at the Ericson cabin. I didn't need water that badly.

"Nice crop," I said to Anton Estvold later that night. His fields were lined with stones picked off the fields. He leaned over, picked up a small rock at his feet, and pitched it onto the pile already there. The mosquitoes whined and I could hear the frogs chirping in a nearby pond.

"*Ja,* it is fair," he said. "The wheat and oats are coming on well."

"*Ja,* I would think so."

"Come in. Dagmar will have food ready."

We feasted on greens and side pork. His missus made buns that were light and fresh and smelled like home. They melted in my mouth, and I ate more than my share.

"Go ahead, eat," she said. "You're too thin."

They didn't have any other children that I could see besides the two off to war. We spoke of the news from the south and the difficulty in getting letters back and forth.

"What was it like when you first came to this country?" I asked after we pushed back from the table.

"It was a dangerous place to live until the treaty was signed," he said. "Since then, it has been much better."

"Did you have any trouble with the Dakota?"

"*Nei,* but we had reason to take precautions," he said. "Their actions were unpredictable. I plowed that first year with my rifle at my side, and we built the fort on the hill for protection."

A mounded area of fortifications could still be seen on top of a small hill.

"The payments are late again this year," I said. "The war in the south has slowed up the money even later than last year."

"It'll work out." He patted his pockets, looking for his snuff plug. "Things always work out in the end."

I didn't share the gossip I'd learned at Fort Abercrombie about the Indian agent's words to the Dakota. Somehow, I couldn't bring myself to speak of it.

After supper at the Larson's the next night, I held little Evan and bounced him on my knee. He looked at me soberly and almost smiled for a brief second. "Did you see the president smile?" I asked.

"*Ja*, he smiles for his Godfather."

I told them about the trouble on the Lower Reservation, about the foolish remarks of the Indian Agents.

"Surely the Indian Agents would have more sense than to antagonize the Sioux," said the missus.

"*Nei*, they have no sense at all, according to Crooked Lightning and Bishop Whipple," I said.

"Do you think there'll be trouble?" Lars asked.

"Who can tell? It's best to be alert in any case."

"Evan, get word to us if something develops." Lars looked at his baby son. "We would want to know."

"I will, Lars. I plan to speak to Bishop Whipple and find out for sure as soon as I get back."

It was always a highlight to meet the other stage midway along the trail. Hjalmer would take out the small flask of aquavit and take a nip while we shared the news. I heeded Mor's warning and refused his offer for a drink but the snuff flowed as we chewed and spit.

"I heard the agents insulted the chiefs at the Lower Agency," I said.

"How did you hear that news way out here?"

"You know how fast it travels, good or bad."

"*Ja,* it is true," he said. "The fool told the chiefs to feed their families grass if they were hungry. Just because they were too lazy to make the dole twice — once for the food and then later for the gold annuity payment which is late again."

128

We sat in silence digesting the many implications. It was hot. The mosquitoes and deer flies swarmed around our heads. We swatted and slapped without relief and finally decided to get back on the road.

"I'll see you next trip out," I said.

"Maybe we can share some good news then."

"What about the war?"

"They're still bleeding in the Shenandoah Valley. Who knows what will come of it all," he said.

"Are they getting recruits?"

"*Ja,* there is another bunch ready to march this way."

"This way?"

"The big shots decided the men need training before going off to be killed. They're going to march a bunch of them to Fort Abercrombie and then march them back to Fort Snelling. Another group will march to Fort Ripley and back."

I couldn't decide if Hjalmer was pulling my leg or telling the truth. What a ridiculous idea, to march the men more than 500 miles and wear them out before sending them to battle. Far was right. I'd best stay away from a rich man's war.

"Will I meet them on my way back?"

"*Ja,* they are making poor time. The

129

sergeants bawl and beller like muleskinners," he said. "Trying to make them march in a pretty line. You'll most likely hear them before you meet them."

Sure enough, I did meet them west of Beanpres Ferry. They were hot and bedraggled in their blue wool uniforms, almost eaten alive by mosquitoes and surely the most miserable of all God's creation.

I searched their faces, looking for someone I might know. One of the men had been living in Pig's Eye; I had seen him before but did not know his name. I tipped my hat as I passed through their ranks, breathing a prayer of thanks I had listened to Far.

# 10

"McClellan Poised to Attack Richmond,
Robert E. Lee Leads Confederates"
~ St. Paul Journal

"Did you meet them recruits?" Ted yanked a harness causing a skittish black to kick against the singletree.

"*Ja,* I met them." I reached out and stroked the horse's mane, shushing it and pushing my nose against its soft lips. "By Beanpres Ferry."

"Maybe they'll fight Sioux instead of Rebels." He coiled the reins around his elbow and hooked thumb and looped it over a nail on the barn wall.

"You've heard about the trouble at the agency?"

"I'd like to kill the red devils," he said. "I'd sign up if I could fight them. It's too hot in the South."

The weather seemed like a poor reason to

either fight or not fight a war. I wondered
about Ted and his way of thinking, so
foreign to me. I wondered if his far had
ever told him to stay away from a rich man's
war or if his mor taught him the Commandments.

A new servant girl at the mission said
Bishop Whipple was called to the Lower
Sioux Agency. She didn't know when he'd
return. Uncomfortable around a female, I
kept my eyes on my feet, scuffing the toe of
my boot in the dust. The rumors must be
true. If Bishop Whipple could not work it
out, there would be no working it out.

"Would you care for some coffee?"

She was pleasant, not the most beautiful
girl I had ever seen, with a large nose and
buckteeth, but surely capable. Four loaves
of fresh bread cooled on the table. She
wiped her hands on her apron and straightened her crown of blonde braids.

"*Ja,* coffee would hit the spot, miss."

"Just call me Solveig."

I drank the coffee and hatched a plan of
my own.

"Solveig, may I ask you a personal question?"

"Perhaps." Her face turned bright pink
and she fingered her apron.

"Are you married?"

"*Nei,* I just came here from Norway," she said. "I have to work off my passage."

That was a difficult problem. Indentured servants worked seven years to pay off their passage. It was not all bad, especially for a female. It allowed them safe passage and a place to go when they arrived. They could learn the language and make plans of their own while they worked off their debt. Sometimes a man would pay off the debt for a woman willing to be his bride.

"Would you consider being a farmer's wife out in the frontier?"

"I do not know your name, sir," she said. "How could I answer such a question?"

How stupid and ignorant was I in the ways of women. She thought I wanted to marry her myself!

"*Nei,* it is not I who seeks a wife," I said, "but a friend who has a farm on the prairie."

Her disappointment was fleeting, to my chagrin.

"Does he have a nice house?"

"It will do for a start."

"Is he good looking?"

I had never before considered such a question. I chewed my lip and thought about my answer. "He has a healthy cow and keeps himself clean."

It was enough. We visited and finally agreed I would tell Rasmuss Rognaldson about Solveig and invite him to ride back with me to meet her himself.

The news at the fort was not good. Besides the dismal news from the Shenandoah Valley, Corporal Tom Murphy had died from an infected dog bite. His wife worked as laundress at the fort and had done my washing a time or two. She sat crying on the step, holding her six-year-old son and small baby in her lap. She was a young woman, dark hair pulled back in a single braid and covered with a kerchief. Her dress was faded brown and the patches sewn in several places were almost covered by an apron.

The soldiers were angry about the incident. Tom was a favorite of all the soldiers stationed at the fort. He was quick tempered but friendly and jolly. His death was a blow to their already low morale.

"What will happen to the missus?" I asked a soldier currying his horse in the stable.

"She'll have to leave the fort," he said. "Only married women are allowed to live here."

"Where will she-she go?"

"Maybe to Pig's Eye or somewhere else," he said. "Maybe back home to her family."

Mor had grown sons to help her after Far died. Surely, the world stopped when a young boy lost his far; I remembered all too clearly the helpless place of grief.

"A better question'd be to ask what'll happen to the dirty Injun that didn't watch his dog," said the soldier. "We shot it after it bit Tom; should have killed the Injun, too, and would've if we'd known Tom'd end up dying."

"What happened to the Indian?"

"That Injun disappeared right quick," he said. "If he knows what's good for him, he'll never come back."

Later that evening, I summoned all my matchmaking courage and approached the grieving woman. Her eyes were almost swollen shut with weeping.

"Missus, what-what are your plans?" I fingered my hat in my hands and tried with all my might not to stutter.

"I have no plans yet," she said. "I need to think."

"There is a Norwegian farmer west of here looking for a wife."

"What kind of man is he?" she said.

"He needs a woman to help him. Said he would welcome a son to help with the farm."

It seemed like a long time but probably was only a few minutes before she answered in a flat voice. "Will you take us to him?"

"*Ja,* I leave in the morning."

It was strange having a woman and children riding out with me. Along the way, I stopped and invited the boy to sit with me on the driver's seat.

"Can I, Ma?"

"You be good, Billy. Don't talk the poor man to death."

It was good to have company. Billy talked continually, although in English. He talked about every tree and bird he could see. I understood most of what he said. Every other sentence was a question.

"What kind of bird is that, mister?"

"Call me Evan."

"Mister Evan, what kind of bird is that?"

"What bird?"

"The one over there. Oh, no, now it flew away. It was a black bird with a red spot on its breast and a white spot on his head."

"I didn't see it."

"Maybe it will fly back and you can tell me then."

The stage rocked on in the summer heat. He slapped at mosquitoes and deer flies.

"You talk funny."

"*Ja,* I must learn the English."

"Where are you from?"

"Far away . . . Norway."

"Why did you come here?"

It was a hard question but one I thought I needed to answer.

"My far died."

"Your father?"

"*Ja,* I needed to leave my homeland to help my mor."

This he digested slowly without comment.

"My dad died."

"I know."

"A mad dog bit him. It was a vicious, mad dog owned by a dirty rotten Injun. That Injun deserves to be shot for letting his dog kill my dad."

The stage hit a rut in the road and instinctively I placed my hand out toward Billy, holding him in place during the bounce.

"I want to kill him myself. Someday I'll take a gun and find old Crooked Lightning and kill him myself."

The name leapt at me. Crooked Lightning's dog traveled with him most places. It was protective of him, had growled at me once when I walked up to his dwelling unannounced.

"Was it a dark-brown dog that looked part wolf?"

"That's the one! Hey, mister, how do you know about that dog? Did it bite you, too?"

"Crooked Lightning is a friend of mine.

I've seen that dog before."

"Are you an Injun-lover?"

I didn't answer right away. The deer flies buzzed around my head and I spit a stream of snuff over the side of the stage.

"I don't hate Indians," I said. "They have a right to live, too."

"No, they don't!" he said. "I'm going to kill Crooked Lightning when I get bigger. I hate him! The soldiers at the fort said they'd help me get him. He's a bad Indian. He killed my dad!" His face contorted and tears squeezed out of his eyes.

"I don't want to ride up here anymore. I want my mama."

I pulled up on the reins and helped the sniffling Billy into the stage. I could hear him telling his mother that I was a dirty Indian-lover.

"Don't worry, Billy," she said. "He's a foreigner and doesn't understand."

"I hate that foreigner!" said Billy. "What's a foreigner, Mama?"

I was glad when the noise of the team and the squeak of the stage wheels drowned out his voice. By the time we reached Bror Brorson's place, I wished I had never agreed to help him look for a woman at all.

Bror perched on a grindstone in the shade of his yard, working on his plowshare. He

138

stood up quickly when he saw the woman and her two children get out of the stage. He lifted a filthy hand to push back stringy locks of dark hair.

"Bror, here is a widow woman willing to be your wife. She brings two healthy children," I said in Norwegian.

Bror stood looking them over, reminding me of a farmer examining stock before making a bid. "Come in," he finally said in English.

The place was even greasier and dirtier than I remembered. The woman looked around and said, "My name is Sadie."

I left them, relieved to be able to go to the barn and care for the horses. If I ever married, I hoped to have at least a time of courtship — we could learn to care for each other before the vows were said. I also hoped I would find someone who spoke Norwegian so I wouldn't have to stutter for the rest of my life when I talked.

Bror called me in for supper about an hour later. The house looked cleaner already. The coffee cup was clean, and the pancakes were light and tasty. The woman spent her time caring for the fussy baby. Billy ate his food in abject misery, not looking at Bror or me.

"Will you be my pa now?" he finally

asked, looking at Bror.

"*Ja,* I will be your pa," said Bror. "I can teach you to be a farmer."

Even Bror, a man I almost despised for his slovenly ways, spoke English better than I did. I slept in the barn with the horses. I wanted no part of whatever happened in the house that night. No talk of finding a minister was mentioned in my hearing. It was their business and not mine, no matter what the Commandments said.

The next morning the woman made coffee and biscuits. I had never before enjoyed such tasty food at the Brorson table. Maybe it was worth all the trouble of matchmaking to get decent food every trip. She didn't look at me, only served me silently.

As I climbed up on the stage box, I heard Billy asking questions.

"Pa, are you a foreigner like Evan?"

Ignoring the boy, Brorson came over to the stage and reached up to shake my hand. His hands were washed and his hair combed.

"*Mange takk,* Evan," he said. "You are a true friend to me, and I will never forget what I owe you."

"It is nothing, Bror," I said.

"In the fall when I butcher my pig, I will save you a ham for your Christmas dinner."

"*Mange takk,* Bror, but it is not necessary."

"And in the spring when my horses foal," he said, "I will give you one of the colts for your very own."

I was speechless. My dream of owning my own horse was happening. Strong emotion choked my throat and I looked down at my boots to hide it from him. Surely America was a land of opportunity. Who would have known a matchmaker's lot was so prosperous?

"*Mange takk,* Bror," I looked up and met his eye. "*Mange takk.*"

He turned to leave, heading for the barn with Billy at his side.

"Are you an Injun-lover like Mister Evan?" said Billy. "He's a dirty Injun-lover."

I was glad to leave.

# 11

"Confederates Force McClellan's Army of
the Potomac to Retreat"
~ St. Paul Journal

The missus of Wilhelm Schwarz carried a
nasty bruise on her face. Without thinking,
I asked how it happened when we sat down
to table. "She the savages wants to feed."
Schwarz said. "She again will not do it."

The woman cowered away from him, carrying the plate of food. She turned toward
the stove, and I noticed a slight limp.

"The Indian payments are late and many
starve," I said.

"Let them." he said. "Their lazy bellies
will not I fill."

"Most settlers keep peace with the Indians
by giving them a little food once in a while."
I knew I was saying too much. "It keeps
away trouble."

"I've guns for trouble," he said. "Waste I

will not tolerate."

We ate in silence. The food was good. The company was not. I had never before considered that a man might beat his wife for doing a kind deed. I hoped the Indians would not judge all white men by the actions of this German. Although the bed was clean, I headed for the barn. What would Mor think of such a thing?

Baby Evan was growing.

"My woman has plenty of milk," Lars bragged. "She is a prize heifer!"

I could not blame him for boasting of his healthy son. The baby had fat rolls around his legs and feet. He smiled from at least six chins. Never had a little one been so healthy and hearty.

"Let me hold the president," I said.

We ate the bounty of the early garden. Dandelion greens, strawberries, rhubarb and radishes. The fresh food tasted wonderful after months of side pork.

"Missus, you are a wonderful hand in the kitchen."

"*Mange takk,* Evan," she said. "You are too kind."

"When will the minister be around?" I asked. "I need to be sure and be on time for the baptism."

We discussed the possibilities of the minister's timing. It might be later in the summer or it might be any day.

I reached into my pocket and pulled out two pieces of peppermint candy.

"I wonder if there are some little girls here who would be interested in having this candy."

"There might be one or two." Lars' eyes twinkled.

"I think I'll leave it on the table and see if anyone wants it."

I laid the sweets on the table and laughed when Ragna and Borghilde sidled up to retrieve them.

"What do you say, girls?" their mother reminded.

*"Mange takk,"* they chimed. Giggling they ran out to play.

"You shouldn't spoil them," Lars said. "But maybe they need spoiling once in a while. It's not easy getting started. Sometimes I think maybe it would have been easier back home."

"But you're making progress." I looked around his cabin and the single window that overlooked his field of oats. He was so far ahead of me that I swallowed hard with the sadness of it. I had nothing to show for my time in America. "You've done well."

"So much can happen so far from family and neighbors." He reached for his woman's hand. "Accidents, sickness — it frightens me how fragile our life is from day to day."

"*Ja,* it can be fragile," I said. "A soldier at the fort died from a dog bite gone bad. His widow and two children traveled with me this trip as far as Cold Spring."

"On the Sauk River?" he said.

"Did they have family there?" the missus asked.

"*Nei,* I knew a Norwegian farmer tired of living alone," I said. "He asked me to keep look-out for any single women or widows willing to live in the wilderness."

"So thanks to you he now has a woman and two children," Lars said.

"*Ja,* Bror Brorson has an overnight family."

They questioned whether the new woman was Scandinavian, Lutheran, the age and condition of the children and the details of the gruesome death of her husband. Any news was welcome conversation. I gave them every detail I could muster but it was far short of what they wanted to know.

"So now you are matchmaker," said the missus with a laugh. She reached for her knitting. "You should look for a wife for yourself."

145

The heat rose in my neck. I was too young to marry. Besides I had nothing to offer a woman.

Quickly I changed the subject. "Did you hear about the army recruits marching to Fort Abercrombie? They will be passing by within the week."

When I was in the wagon box and ready to leave, Lars reached up and shook my hand. "I shouldn't have talked so . . . our troubles are not your concern."

"Don't be foolish," I said. "I want you to know that if anything were to happen to you, I would do what I could to help your missus and children."

*"Tussen takk,"* he said. "I wasn't asking for your help."

"I know," I swallowed hard, embarrassed that my eyes moistened. "But I have no family here either — I would help out where I could."

Rasmuss wasn't in his cabin or in the barn. Finally I spied him in the cornfield south from the house. I hailed him and he came jogging from the field carrying a rifle. The dreams must still be bad.

"You'll kill yourself, running in this heat."

*"Nei,* I hope only you bring good news."

*"Ja,* and I have the news you seek."

146

We watered the animals together and went into the soddy to cook coffee. The room was dark and dreary but much cooler than outside. He lit a lamp and filled the gray enamel coffee pot from a bucket on the floor.

"I found a woman."

"Don't fool with me."

"*Nei,* it is no joke," I said. "Bishop Whipple has a new servant girl from Norway. She's young and strong and makes good coffee, certainly better coffee than this swill."

Rasmuss punched me in the arm, grinning from ear to ear. I had never seen him in such animated state.

"What did you tell her?"

I stuffed a wad of snuff into my lip. "I told her you had a nice cow."

"A cow! Surely you could think of something better than that! Did you not mention my charm and good looks?"

"*Nei,* only the cow."

"What is she like?"

"She has beautiful blue eyes, like the blue flags that grow in your slough, underneath a crown of golden hair." I thought not to mention the buckteeth and large nose. A man cannot be too choosey in the wilderness and it seemed wiser to dwell on her good points.

"I'll leave the cow with neighbors and return with you," he said. He paced back and forth across the room, running his fingers through his dusty hair in a frantic manner. "I can't wait to meet her."

"There's a problem — she is indentured and must work seven years to pay off her debt."

"Oh, my God!" he said. "Seven years!"

He dropped on his chair and we sat in silence. Once again I had not handled the situation well. Of course, I should have kept the cow out of it. And it was cruel to raise a man's hopes when he did not have money to free her from servitude. Mor taught me better.

"I know Bishop Whipple," I said. "He is a kind and fair man. Surely there must be a way to work this out for the satisfaction of all."

"Every cent I have is tied up in this parcel of land," he said. "If I could pay it in dirt, I would do it."

It was the plight of every farmer. They sat on potential wealth but often did not have the cash needed to produce a harvest. Those starting out had the least money of all. Plows, seed, labor all cost money. Only a well-established farmer with many sons could expect to do well and even then had to contend with uncertain weather, insect damage, and a hundred other complications.

"You are a friend," I said with great care, knowing I walked on thin ice. "I have a small savings. Perhaps I could loan you enough to pay off Solveig's debt."

"Solveig! Her name is Solveig?"

"*Ja,* Solveig is her name."

"A sign from God." He looked at me with wide eyes. "My mor's name was Solveig." He grabbed my shoulders and slapped my back, laughing as if the wedding had already taken place. "I cannot believe how good you are. You are a true friend! I will pay you back every cent out of my next crop." He shook my hand up and down, almost jerking my shoulder from its socket and crushing my fingers in his enthusiasm.

"You'll stand Godfather to our first child."

I wondered how much responsibility I could bear.

True to his word, Rasmuss was anxiously waiting to return with me to Fort Snelling. He scarcely slept the night before we left and kept me awake with questions.

"Is she sweet tempered, Evan?"

"I hardly talked to her."

149

"But was she patient and mannerly when she gave you coffee?"

"*Ja,* she was like any other woman." His disappointed expression caused me to think of an addition to my first answer. "She is wonderful," I said. "You're lucky to find her."

The next morning he was bathed and dressed in his best coat, far too hot for traveling in the summer heat.

"You'll cook in that get-up," I told him. "You'll be as hot as the recruits marching to Fort Abercrombie."

"*Nei,* I won't feel a thing but love," he said. "I need to look my best."

"Then look your best the last day of the voyage, man, not for almost a week of travel!"

His face fell, but he cheerfully pulled off the clean shirt and wool coat, folding them carefully in his knapsack.

"Of course," he said. "I'm too excited to think."

He climbed up on the driver's seat with me and talked of only Solveig and how happy he would make her, how thankful he was to me for finding her and loaning him the money, how lonely he had been and how blessed to find a mate at last.

We pulled into Dayton, and Rasmuss immediately told Lewis about Solveig and how I had found her for him. Lewis looked at me with surprise.

"I am not turning into a matchmaker," I said. "It just worked out this time, that's all."

"You can look for me, too," he said. "By God, I didn't know you had it in you!"

"It is the quiet ones you have to watch for," said Rasmuss. "Still waters run deep."

Rasmuss and Lewis turned their attention on me, teasing and having a good time. Rasmuss decided to sleep in the stage for a while, and it was a relief to travel east again. Too many questions this trip — both going and coming.

At Pomme de Terre we found Anton Estvold busy in his hay field although it was almost dark. "Hello, Evan! What's the news?" Rasmuss did most of the talking. He was glad for the task since he was lonely for conversation. The hardest part of my job was the need to repeat the news at every stop. Mor would say I was turning into a gossip.

"Did you see Ericson when you passed by?" Anton washed up in the horse trough.

"*Nei,* I saw no one on the trail," I said.

We went into the cabin and sat down to eat cream and bread.

"He is determined to be involved in the county government," Anton said. "He is going from place to place asking for their vote in this fall's election."

"Do you think he has a chance?" I asked between mouthfuls of the sweet cream and fresh bread.

*"Nei,"* Anton said. "His going from place to place, but revealing his ambition and arrogance will squelch any chance for winning."

"I would think so," I said. "Who's running against him?"

"You're talking to the man!"

We laughed over the joke and the foolishness of the Swede to act like the upper class in Minnesota where there was no class.

"He'll find folks are different here in America," I said.

"More independent in our thinking," Rasmuss said. "And anyone can vote, not just the upper class."

"The best part is there will be no vote this fall," Anton said. "Governor Ramsey himself will appoint the county commissioners for the first term. He has already spoken to me about an appointment, although it is not official."

"Why?" asked Rasmuss.

"It's done in new counties in order for the

county government to get off to a good start," Anton said. "After the first term, the voting will start."

"Have you told Ericson about the appointments by the governor?" I asked.

*"Nei,"* Anton said, a slight smile playing around his lips. "He never asked."

We laughed to think of Ericson's prideful foolishness.

"His woman is left with the farm work since he is out campaigning."

"How convenient to be gone during such a busy time." I tried to push down the quick worry his statement stirred.

"*Ja,* he knows how to stay away from work," Anton said. "But he runs a nice farm. He'll do well if he doesn't go to Washington to become president."

Sleep came slowly that night in the Estvold barn. Rasmuss talked about his plans for Solveig while I worried about Inga. I would never leave a sweet wife defenseless in the wilderness. I would care for her, work as hard as I could to provide for her and love her as the Bible said. When the mosquitoes and worry finally let up enough for sleep, I dreamed of Ingvald Ericson preaching from a pulpit, his voice like the whine of a million mosquitoes, telling me to mind my own business.

I kept my eyes open, hoping to spy the first hint of the marching recruits. In truth, I expected to meet them earlier. Steady marching eats the miles. But as much as I watched, I never saw a hint of dust or smoke that would indicate their approach.

Big Barn Jensen and his missus met us at their stoop.

"Come in! Come in! What's the news?"

Rasmuss made quick work of telling the scraps of news we had gleaned along the way. The missus fixed open-faced sandwiches made of cold sliced potatoes and raw onions with salt and pepper. She stood by the table, pouring coffee and pressing food upon us until I thought I might burst. Rasmuss had no such reservations and ate until the plate was empty.

We left as soon as the meal was over, many miles to travel. That night we pulled into the Schwarz's farm just as darkness settled.

"Have you seen any recruits from Fort Snelling march by?" I asked.

"Nein," he said. "Warum do you ask?"

I told him then about the plan to train the new soldiers by marching them off to Fort Abercrombie and back again.

"Dumb *Kopf* army," he said.

"I thought they would be here by now."

"Watch we will," he said. "Maybe new potatoes they buy."

The next morning we left at daybreak with potato pancakes in our pockets.

"The missus there knows how to cook," Rasmuss said.

"*Ja,* and gets little thanks from her man."

"It sounds like you don't like him."

"*Nei,* I care not for men who beat either their women or their horses."

We traveled in silence. The foliage of the trees offered shade along the trail. Most likely Rasmuss dreamed of Solveig as he slept; his chin bounced on his chest with each jolt of the stage. My mind was quiet, wondering how Mor and my brother were doing in Norway, hoping their crops would be enough to feed them through the winter. Ole would be married by now. I daydreamed of sending money home to them, enough to buy a ticket for one of them to join me. It was a foolish thought. My brother would never leave, and Mor was too old for the journey. *Nei,* I had best settle on being the only one of my family in Minnesota.

Carl Evenson struggled with a fence post in the pasture with Arvid at his side. The little girls stirred mud pies behind the cabin.

"Hello, Evan!"

"Carl!" I said. "Your corn is doing well."

"You're just in time for dinner!"

We unhitched the horses and led them to the watering trough. They snorted and drank with great zeal. We washed our hands and faces in the same trough and headed toward the cabin to eat.

"What's the news from the war?" asked Carl.

Rasmuss again took over the chore of repeating the news. I may have imagined it but it seemed he was less enthusiastic about this rendition, as if he had been asked the same question once too often. I ate the fresh bread with butter and slabs of side pork set before me. The coffee was hot and good. The missus poured cream into it, and I felt like a king, eating such good food and being served in a clean kitchen while being spared the burden of being the newspaper.

The little girls peeked around their mother's skirts, their hands and faces dirty and soiled.

"Rasmuss here is seeking a wife," I said. "Do you have any daughters interested in getting married?"

Carl looked at me in surprise, spied the girls peeking at us and played along with the game.

"Why yes, I have two daughters," he said. "Maybe one of them would care to marry such a nice young man."

The girls stared in horror.

"Kersten! Thea!" he said. "Which one wants a bridegroom?"

The girls ran shrieking out of the house while the rest of us laughed.

"In truth, Rasmuss thinks he has found a wife," I said.

Rasmuss did all the talking, and I was able to rest. Before we left, the Missus pointed out a patch of purple delphiniums growing by the step.

"These are from the seeds you delivered earlier this spring. They were tucked in the letter from Norway," she said. "See the beautiful color and sniff the scent of home."

She glowed while she spoke of the flowers. *Ja,* it was a good job I had, to bring mail to these folks in the wilderness. I resolved to write Mor and tell her about it.

We slept at Cold Spring. Bror greeted us at the door. He was bathed and his hair was clean and trimmed. His clothes were clean and his face shaven. Somehow he looked younger. Maybe it was the hopeful air about him.

"Greetings to you, my friend!" he said

"Your crops look good."

"*Ja,* the corn tassels," he said. "If I can just keep away the critters I may harvest a crop."

The house was markedly cleaner, and the place smelled of soap and home cooking. Billy eyed me suspiciously from the corner but soon could not resist the opportunity to ask questions.

"Mister Evan, are you still an Injun-lover?"

"Billy, mind your manners!" his mother said.

"This is my friend, Rasmuss Rognaldson, from Foxhome, Minnesota, out on the prairies west of here."

Introductions and handshakes were exchanged.

"What brings you to Cold Spring?" asked Bror.

It was the wrong question. Over tasty stew, Rasmuss told the story of how I found him a woman at Fort Snelling. Bror's eyes lit up with interest and I could see the missus listening to our conversation.

"I had no idea you were such a successful matchmaker." Bror smiled with his dark eyes.

"Things work out sometimes."

It was an awkward moment. Bror's missus looked down at the baby in her lap. I didn't want to talk about their situation. It was no one else's business.

Billy's questions spared further embarrassment. Bror motioned for me to go with him outside and leave Rasmuss at the mercy of Billy's curiosity. The night air was sweet. A whippoorwill sang in the willows by the river. A coyote howled in the distance.

"You have a nice place."

"*Ja,* now that I have family to share it with," he said. "Thanks to you my days are no longer lonely."

I looked down at my feet and rolled a wad of snuff in my mouth.

"Come, I will show you the mare that will drop your colt."

We walked in the stillness to the barn where several horses stood patiently in their stalls. One was a medium-sized brown mare with black mane and tail. A white spot splashed across her face. She nickered softly as we entered the barn, and I reached into my pocket for a carrot top, watching her eat it slowly, showing manners proper for a lady, her lips soft against my hand. She smelled as if she had just finished rolling in the pasture. I rubbed her neck and back with both hands, hardly restraining my emotions.

"She's bred to this stallion." Bror pointed

to a horse in a separate stall. He stood tall with a dark brown coat and white spots across his back. The horse seemed spirited and strong. "He's a fine animal and the two of them should produce a fine colt for you."

It was almost too good to be true. I said as much to Bror.

"Evan, to have Sadie and the boys here with me is almost too good to be true also." He patted the face of the mare and said slowly, "I'm taking instruction at the Roman Church in the settlement. When I am finished, we will get married in the church."

I was speechless. No self-respecting Lutheran would dream of turning Catholic. He did not seem the type to embrace papism.

"I wish you and your new family well," I said at last though my throat turned to dust. My actions had turned someone away from the Lutheran Church. A dark wave of guilt washed over me. Far always said what's done was done and a person needed to forget it. It would be hard for me to forget such a sin.

Rasmuss' constant talk wore me down before we reached Fort Snelling. We ate a thin soup and hardtack at Ole Swenson's. The children looked just as hungry as last time although they were brown from being out in the sun, their hair bleached white. When the harvest began coming in there would be more food. I had started carrying a few oats for the horses, wanting to make sure they had energy for the journey. Before we left, I called one of the older children to the stage.

"I have some extra grain. It isn't much but it might be of some use to your mother."

His eyes were round in surprise as I measured out almost a peck of oats and gave to him.

*"Mange takk!"* His face lit up with a smile. *"Mange takk!"*

He waved good-bye. I left quickly before there might be a protest from the adults. The settlers were a proud people and would do without before accepting charity. Soon their potatoes would be big enough to use. That would get them through until the corn and wheat were harvested.

The fields grew lush and green and smelled of damp earth. Cicadas flew past with their noisy drone. The air was heavy and hot. Deer grazed in the shade of the oak trees along the trail. They lifted their heads to watch us pass.

"I don't know how you do it, Evan," Rasmuss said.

"What do you mean?"

"You are such a quiet man and yet you have to answer so many questions. It would wear me out!"

We crossed the Mississippi River at Beanpres Ferry and Rasmuss repeated the same news at the Filmore's.

Sanger's missus sat on the doorstep, weeping. The children gathered round, silently watching, the least one holding her mother's apron.

"What's wrong, missus?" I asked.

It took her a few minutes to blow her nose into a soggy handkerchief and finally meet my eyes. Her face was like dough, blotched and puffy; her eyes rimmed with red.

"He's dead," she said. "Killed at Shiloh."

"Your man?" I asked in disbelief, not remembering his name on the casualty list.

"I begged him not to go, but he went anyways and now he's dead. Killed at Shiloh," she said. "I just got the news."

She was in no condition to fix a meal. We cared for the animals ourselves, not allowing her to help. After drinking from the bucket by the trough, we headed on.

The miles crept by, and soon we were at Elk River and finally on the home stretch through St. Anthony Falls and then the familiar trail to the fort. Rasmuss was like a

162

small boy on a long journey.

"Are we there yet?"

"*Nei,* we have a few miles to go."

I pointed out the rivers and the Indian villages around the fort. Rasmuss insisted I stop the stage so he could wash up and change clothes. He did look handsome. The heat made him red in the face and sweaty before we reached the mission.

"What will I say? How can I make a good impression?"

"She is a pleasant girl. You have nothing to fear."

"Will you come with me to talk to her?"

"I have chores to attend at the fort."

Bishop Whipple answered the door. If he was surprised to see me, still carrying my leather dispatch pouch, and a young man sweating in a wool coat, he gave no indication.

"Evan! How good to see you!" he said. "Solveig told me of your visit while I was gone."

"I wanted to ask you about the Indian problems."

"Yes, I would enjoy a visit."

"I bring a friend, Rasmuss Rognaldson."

"How do you do Mr. Rognaldson," Bishop Whipple said. "And what is your business here?"

"I am seeking a wife, and Evan tells me there is a single woman at this place."

The Bishop screwed up his face in a puzzled frown. He looked at me with blame in his eyes and Rasmuss' face turned even redder.

"News travels quickly," Bishop Whipple said. "Perhaps we could discuss this over coffee."

We sat in his kitchen, and Solveig served coffee. Rasmuss' eyes darted to the place where she stood but I noticed he quickly looked down at the table. Solveig's face flamed, possibly from the heat of the stove. She served deftly, calmly, without hint of embarrassment other than the color of her cheeks.

"It is hard to find capable help," Bishop Whipple said.

"*Ja,* women are scarce." I was anxious to leave.

"I paid good money for her passage, and she has a contract to serve seven years in return."

The twinkle in his eye did not escape me. I let out a sigh of relief, knowing the details could be worked out. Rasmuss had no such assurances and twisted and squirmed on his chair, sometimes attempting to scratch his upper back beneath the thick wool jacket.

He looked almost as miserable as the recruits marching to Fort Abercrombie. The thought jogged my memory.

"Bishop, have you heard of recruits marching to Fort Abercrombie?" While we spoke, Rasmuss and Solveig blushed bright red, looking at each other, smiling and then looking away. "I passed them on my way out but did not meet them again on my way back."

"They were called back. The Union needs replacements after the blood-letting in the Shenandoah." It was if the lovebirds didn't hear a word he said. "They left by steamboat for the south."

"Who fetched them?"

"They sent a rider. The hostler named Ted," he said. "They won't let him join up because of his crippled hand, no trigger finger."

No wonder Ted hadn't enlisted. What fool had chosen Ted? He was not sensible when it came to the care of animals. No doubt he'd abused the poor horse. I'd hear all about it when I got back to the fort.

While we talked, Solveig and Rasmuss had somehow communicated. I didn't see them speak but being ignorant in the way of women perhaps would not notice a signal if I saw it. Rasmuss excused himself from the table and left the mission, speaking to Solveig on the front step in the hot sunshine. I needed to return to the fort and care for the horses but hesitated to interrupt them.

"They'll make a fine match." Bishop Whipple looked their way. "He seems like a sensible young man."

"*Ja,* he has a good farm but in a lonely place. Unless he finds a wife before winter he will give up altogether."

"Solveig is afraid of nothing. She will be a good wife."

We drank our cooled coffee. I thought of the questions I had about the Red Men but knew I had little time to spare. It would have to wait.

"I will write another letter to the man who arranged the agreement with Solveig." Bishop Whipple sighed heavily. "I'll need to find another girl willing to come to Minnesota."

"Have you thought about taking a wife instead?" I asked.

"I heard you were matchmaker to the widow at the fort and I've seen with my own eyes how you stole my servant girl. Now you encourage me to tie the knot."

"I did not mean to be impolite." I wondered quickly if I had offended him by my brash question. Mor taught me better manners!

"I'm teasing. You are such a quiet one, so serious," he said. "You should look for yourself and forget the rest of us."

"I have not met the right one yet, Bishop," I said. "Solveig is a nice girl but she is not for me." It was hard for me to reveal my inner fears to someone else. I felt naked before the good bishop and stuttered over the words. "Maybe I'll never find the right one. Maybe she's already taken."

"Don't worry, you'll find her when the time is right." He thought a minute and added in a confidential tone. "You know, I've met a young teacher. Maybe I will seek a wife." He clapped me on the back and shook my hand.

Solveig and Rasmuss walked toward the river as I drove away. Rasmuss never looked away from Solveig. I guessed he would find his way to the fort later.

# 12

"Poor Generalship Reason for Staggering
Losses of Seven-Days Battle"
~ St. Paul Journal

Ted swaggered into the stable, his cap at a
jaunty angle, his mouth twisted into a smirk.
"Well, Norskie," he said, "try and guess
what thems had me do whiles you was
gone."

I said nothing. It would be of no benefit
to tell him I already knew about the trip to
fetch the green recruits west of Beanpres
Ferry.

"I's carried them dispatches for the commander," he bragged.

"Which horse did you take?" I asked, unable to stand the suspense.

"Betty." He rocked back on his heels and
stuck out his chest. "Real important it were.
Wild Injuns and fierce animals. Why the war
might be won from whats I did, fetching

them sojers."

"Where did the soldiers go?"

"Left by them steamboats. Real important it were."

His smugness and self-importance could not hide the gravity of the situation. Things must be bad in the south for such a change of plans. Betty seemed no worse for the journey. She nickered a greeting when I carefully rubbed her legs and mouth, looking for bruises or injuries.

I hurried through the chores, glad I had already delivered the pouch to the commander, and rushed toward the posted newspaper, unable to comprehend the dead and wounded, the loss of life for the futile battle near Richmond.

"Sixteen hundred Federals killed!" A private said. "I can't even count that high!"

"But 20,000 Rebs met their maker," another soldier said. "That's the best part. Twenty thousand less for us to kill."

"McClellan's a dang fool!" said an older soldier with corporal stripes on his sleeve. "He hesitated when he had them in a corner, and now he's drove back." He spit snuff into a brass spittoon in the corner, causing it to ring like a bell. "Old Abe best find someone who can win the war."

He seemed to know what he was talking

about. Far used to say a man needed to shit or get off the pot. There was truth to it.

Rasmuss met me at the hostler's cabin. His coat was thrown over one shoulder and his buttons loose at the neck of his shirt. His face had a dazed look, as if he were still asleep and dreaming.

"Evan, you'll not believe my good luck." He threw his coat down on the bunk.

"What?"

"The wedding will be tomorrow!"

"Tomorrow!" I sat down on the bed. Things were moving too fast. Maybe I did not have enough savings to pay off the indentured fee.

"How much money will you need?" Once again my own foolishness astounded me. That I'd offer to loan an undetermined amount of money was ridiculous. It might leave me penniless. What if Rasmuss's crops failed and he couldn't repay me?

"Not a penny of your money will I need," he said. "Although I am forever grateful for your kind offer."

"You don't need my money?"

"*Nei,* Bishop Whipple will take shares of my next seven crops. He figures he'll regain what he paid for Solveig's passage by that time." Rasmuss looped his thumbs around his suspenders "Heck, I'm such a good farmer and the land is so rich, he might make money on the deal!"

"*Ja,* he might at that." I knew Bishop Whipple could be counted on to do the right and just thing. He truly was a man of God although not a Lutheran. I breathed a sigh of relief. In truth, it would have been painful to part with my small savings.

"And Solveig!" Emotion overwhelmed poor Rasmuss. "Have you ever met such a beautiful and gracious woman?" His voice squeaked and his eyes welled with tears. I worried he might actually weep.

Solveig seemed quite ordinary to me, but then I hadn't really talked to her that much. She did have eyes the color of the Norwegian Sea and her golden hair would be a sight to see fanned out on a pillow.

"*Ja,*" I said. "She's a lovely woman, a fit queen for the King of Foxhome!"

Rasmuss picked me up right out of the chair and whirled me around the cabin, even though I was a good twenty pounds heavier than he. He laughed and twirled me around until the other hostlers came in to see what the commotion was about.

"What's going on?" Ted asked in English.

"To-tonight we celebrate. Rasmuss has found a wife." It felt good to think about something other than war and killing.

"How come I didn't know about a woman at the Mission?" asked Ted after he figured out our conversation. "I'm looking for women all the time."

"Well this one is taken." Rasmuss began telling how he found his precious Solveig. His embellishments would have made Un the Deepminded proud.

A puzzled frown troubled Ted's face. He looked at me almost with respect. It was an awkward moment and I hoped to change the focus.

"Hail to the King of Foxhome!" I said. "Tomorrow he takes a queen!"

# 13

"Lincoln Replaces McClellan with Henry
Halleck as General-In-Chief"
~ St. Paul Journal

As best man, I scrubbed and washed, trimmed my hair and beard and wore the best clothes I could borrow. Rasmuss was most handsome in spite of sweat stains on his shirt, but I assured him that no one would notice if he kept his jacket on. A little honest sweat was unavoidable in such heat and humidity.

Bishop Whipple preformed the ceremony at the Mission, there being no Lutheran priest at the fort. Solveig was beautiful with her golden crown in place, holding blue flags picked by the river. The flowers a perfect match to her clear blue eyes. She wore a plain cotton dress the color of the gray chinking between the mission logs. Solveig stood shoulder to shoulder next to

Rasmuss, almost equal in height. She was indeed a strong, capable woman with large hands and feet.

"Isn't she beautiful?" breathed Rasmuss at my side.

"*Sot,*" I agreed.

The ceremony was short and then we sat down to cake and small glasses of elderberry wine, the cake baked by the bride earlier in the morning.

"I propose a toast." I lifted my glass. "*Skal* to Foxhome's king and queen!"

"*Gratulerer!*" Bishop Whipple added. "May your troubles be few, your joys many, and may God bless you with sons to work the farm."

"And *lykke til,*" added Rasmuss, "good luck the next seven years!"

Conversation lagged. The bridegroom had eyes only for his bride and for once had little to say. We finished the crumbs remaining on our plates, and Bishop Whipple stood to his feet and reached for a straw hat with a wide brim.

"Evan," Bishop Whipple said. "Walk with me. Let's leave these love birds."

I feared I had offended him in some way. Perhaps he had changed his mind about the money. I worried a strategy, a defense in case he demanded cash. But he had agreed to take shares of Rasmuss's harvests. Maybe he needed more.

Solveig's face blazed red as the feathers in Crooked Lightning's hair. "*Mange takk,* Mrs. Rognaldson, the cake was fit for a king." I had thought to lighten the mood but no one noticed. Rasmuss stared at her with such a level of devotion it was a relief to leave the kitchen.

At the door I turned, "Will you be on the stage in the morning?"

"Tomorrow?"

"*Ja,* daybreak."

"We'll be there." They said no good-byes, so wrapped up in each other's eyes.

Bishop Whipple and I walked the river path and commented on the flock of passenger pigeons flying overhead. There were thousands of them, enough to darken the sun for a short time while they flew over.

"They're good eating," Bishop Whipple said.

"Makes even a poor man rich. A club on the head will do if you find them roosting." We headed toward a shaded spot and took a seat on the grass.

"I don't think I've ever seen a face so red as when Solveig first met Rasmuss," Bishop Whipple said with a smile.

There was nothing more to say about it.

They were wed and that was that. We sat in silence for a few minutes, Bishop Whipple chewing on a fresh blade of grass, putting two blades together and blowing a duck-like whistle.

"There are problems on the reservation."

"I've heard." The cloud of doves had flown almost out of view. I hoped they would roost where some of the settlers could catch enough for a few good meals. Just enough to get them through until harvest, not enough to do crop damage.

"Payments even later than last year and there's rumor it's coming in paper instead of gold."

"Why doesn't Lincoln do something about it?"

"It's not simple. The rebellion is all consuming; he leaves it to his agents."

"They do a piss-poor job of it." I played with a stone by my feet, picked it up, and looked at it closer. It was an agate, lined and beautiful. I slipped it in my pocket.

"The agents are in over their heads. I'm worried."

"What can I do?"

"Keep your eyes and ears open. If trouble breaks out, I will try to get word to you, and you to me." The grief on his face startled me, it was unlike him to sound so

hopeless. "Someone needs to warn the settlers in the outlying areas."

"What would I say?"

"Tell them to gather together in defense.
A family alone out on their farm has no
chance. Strength in numbers, you know."

It seemed so unlikely, as far away as the
rebellion in the south. "I'm sure it will all
blow over."

Rasmuss and his bride were at the stage on
time the next morning. They barely greeted
me, having eyes only for each other. They
climbed in the coach and I reflected on how
things had changed since the trip east when
Rasmuss sat by me on the box and chatted
nonstop. In truth I felt like I had lost a
friend.

The night before I had stayed up late writing a letter to Mor. The letter was long
overdue. In the letter I told her about Cleng
Peterson's death. It left me out of sorts,
despondent. After more than a year in
America I had little to show for myself. I
wondered if I would ever meet a woman I
would love and marry. In all my travels
I had met only one girl who interested me
and she was taken.

A letter addressed to Ingvald Ericson
burned in my pouch. I could stop and

deliver it in person. I often delivered mail to farmers living close to the trail. It would be a chance to see for myself how Inga was doing.

At the Sullivan place, Adam came to help with the stage. "Do you have any letters for us from Pa?"

"*Nei,* I'm sorry to say," I said. "Any news lately?"

His face worked. "He's captured, sir. Captured at Shiloh. Our neighbors down the road told us. Their son slipped away from the Hornet's Nest but Pa was captured." He lifted the harness from the team and led the horses to a nearby pond to drink. "The dirty Rebs took the prisoners to Georgia. One newspaper says Oglethorpe Prison in Macon, another says Andersonville."

"Is he wounded?"

"No mention of wounding — just capturing."

"It's a good sign then, without a wound he'll make it fine and be home before you know it." I sounded more cheerful than I felt. "I've read of prisoner exchanges between Federals and Rebs."

"Really? Mister, will you let me know if you hear anything?"

"That I will."

The missus was sullen and distant. Adam told her about the prisoner exchange while we ate cornbread with molasses. Solveig and Rasmuss spoke quietly together in Norwegian and didn't help with the conversation.

"Evan promised to tell us if he hears about a prisoner exchange," Adam said.

"How would he know about such things?" Her lips pressed to a thin line and the tightness of her hair pulled back from her face added to the severity of her features. Her whole appearance conveyed distinct disapproval.

"The soldiers at the fort tell news from the war," I said in a calm voice, trying hard not to stutter. "Besides, there is always a news-newspaper hung up for all to read."

She didn't look convinced. It would be a waste of time to explain that I knew how to read and write. Instead, I pushed away from the table. *"Takk* for *mat."* I readied to leave for the hot afternoon ride. Who knew if the exchange would take place? As I left she pressed two letters into my hands. One was addressed to Private Joe Sullivan, Oglethorpe Prison, Macon, Georgia, and the other addressed to Private Joe Sullivan, Andersonville, Georgia.

"Maybe one will find him." Her skirts

dragged in the dust as she returned to the cabin. The corn had sprouted weeds and the garden looked unkempt. War was hard on the women at home, that I had learned.

That night I slept in the house with the Johnson family although I had never done so before. Bedbugs kept me awake half the night. Rasmuss and Solveig had the barn to themselves. Things had certainly changed. I was glad I hadn't loaned him the money to buy his bride's freedom. It would have been like paying to give away a friend.

I dreaded seeing Widow Sanger. Her man was dead and nothing could bring him back.

"He was killed at Shiloh," she said. Her face was like stone and she looked thinner. "He's dead."

There was no pleasant small talk around the table, just army beans with cold water to drink. Rasmuss and Solveig ate quietly, but I noticed them look at each other from time to time. The children pulled weeds in the fields. Overhead the sun blazed hard enough to make a grown man falter.

As I climbed up into the box, the missus said in a strange voice, "Killed at Shiloh, he was."

"Missus, it's time for your children to

come in for dinner. It's too hot for them in the fields at midday."

She looked up at me and grasped my hand, "He was killed at Shiloh, at a spot called the Hornet's Nest. I begged him not to go, but he went anyways and now he's dead.

As we drove away in a choking cloud of dust, I thought of the thousands dead from the war, about their families receiving the news one by one, how their man was killed, wounded or captured. Thousands of families grieving. It was a depressing thought and one that suited my mood.

Rasmuss called out to me and asked to sit up on the box. It was the first time he had spoken to me the entire trip and I was glad to oblige.

"She's crazy, Evan," he said. "Did you see her eyes?"

"Crazy with grief."

"We can't leave the children with a crazy person. Something must be done."

"And what would that be?"

"Solveig says something must be done."

*Uffda feedah!* So that was the way of it. Now Solveig would tell us what to do. It made me glad to avoid marriage altogether.

"I have a letter for William Jenkins down the road, a near neighbor," I said. "We can

181

explain the situation to him when we stop and let him worry about it."

Far had told me to fight my own battles. Right then I didn't have the strength to fight anyone else's. Rasmuss crawled back into the coach, and I drove on, scratching bed-bug bites and swatting the never-ending deer flies.

The trail was hardly a path. Two ruts stretched before me, sometimes in open prairie, other times beneath a canopy of trees so thick the sun was hidden. Bass-woods bloomed and filled the air with sweet fragrance. Bees buzzed among the flowers and I daydreamed about having my own place, finding a honey tree and bringing enough sweetness home to last through the winter. A streak of red flashed before my eyes, a bright red little bird nesting along the trail. The air was heavy and thick, like my own brain in the afternoon heat. Morn-ings were better, the air fresh, cool, and welcoming. But by afternoon it was as if the troubles of the world descended, leaving a hopeless feeling.

The horses plodded on while I dozed in the box. No matter, the horses would follow the trail. The brush and trees along each side made it impossible for them to go anywhere else. Rasmuss snored in the coach. Solveig called to me from the coach, waking me from my nap.

"Evan, can I sit with you?" she said. "I need some air."

I tightened the reigns and slowed to a stop. Solveig stepped out as I climbed down from the box and helped her up to the seat though she needed little help from me. Rasmuss stirred but did not awaken. We soon plodded along again.

*"Tussen takk!"* she said. "I was starting to feel a little seasick in there — like I felt on the boat coming over. Too much up and down for me."

I smiled to think of my own bout of seasickness coming over. There were indeed similarities between the ship and the rocking of the stage.

"I could use the company to keep awake," I said.

It was pleasant to have Solveig seated beside me. She did not chatter or intrude in any way, just sat and looked over the dense foliage.

"It is beautiful country," she said.

"*Vakker* indeed."

"These trees remind me of home. Leafy trees were everywhere, always my favorite."

"What made you leave Norway?"

"My parents died and my brother married," she said. "It was either strike out on my own or live as an old maid with family the rest of my life."

"Surely there were men in Norway who would seek you for their wife."

"*Nei,* I was without dowry or beauty. I have you and Bishop Whipple to thank for my marriage."

"It was nothing." Such talk made me squirm on the seat. I had merely told Rasmuss and Solveig about each other; anyone would have done it.

She did not seem so bossy in person. I decided to forget about the incident with Widow Sanger.

"What made you think to act as matchmaker between Rasmuss and me?"

I chewed and spit snuff over the side of the coach, covering a hazelnut bush with brown juice. I couldn't understand it myself, let alone try to explain it to an almost stranger.

"I think the world of Rasmuss," I said. "I could see he wouldn't last in Foxhome alone."

She seemed to digest this, listening to the frogs sing in the nearby slough, watching for the glint of color in the trees that were the trails of canaries and bluebirds.

"Tell me about Foxhome," she said at last.

I chewed my lip, thinking. What could I say about such an empty place? She favored trees but would not find any there. I pulled the stage to a stop and tied the reins to the seat. Grabbing my spade from behind the seat, I jumped down and found a basswood sapling about a foot high. I carefully dug around the roots and placed the young tree at the edge of the trail. Pulling an old gunnysack from behind the seat, I dipped it into a small pool of standing water. I wrapped the roots of the small tree in the wet sacking, enjoying the smell of the damp earth, pulling it snug and then securing it on the seat between us.

"Here is a wedding present for you. Every summer you will see the lovely blossoms and smell the sweet fragrance in your own home in Foxhome. It will be shade and beauty."

Solveig looked at the trees around us and at the sapling wrapped in cloth. Finally she raised her eyes to mine.

"Is it that bad?"

"It is flat and barren and lonesome as a frozen lake but with the blackest, richest soil God ever made." I nudged the team forward. "You and Rasmuss will grow wheat and corn and raise your children in wealth and safety. It is a land of milk and honey."

"Solveig, where are you?" called Rasmuss.

"I'm riding with Evan," she said. "I needed some air."

"We're almost to Beanpres Ferry." I flicked the reins and started the team down the trail. "You go back to your snoring — I'll wake you when we get there."

It occurred to me that Christina would have liked Solveig, enjoyed her pleasant ways and strong determination. From that moment on, I felt the same.

The farm families greeted Solveig with great interest and curiosity. Rasmuss had told his story at every stop going east and now they could judge for themselves if the happy ending he had boasted would happen. Ole Swenson's missus shyly handed Solveig a bit of handmade lace.

"*Jeg skal hilse fra,* you might edge a pillow case," she said. Her dress was immaculate although threadbare and patched, her face haggard and worn. The bulge around her belly hinted of another Swenson on the way.

"*Takk skal du ha!*" Solveig said. "It's lovely for a pillow case or a table scarf. I'll work on it when winter sets in."

Solveig picked up Halvor, their youngest, and held him in her lap while she ate the meager meal. The boy was thin, and his nose ran constantly. I noticed Solveig fed him bits of bread and wiped his nose with her own handkerchief.

The missus clasped Solveig's hand when it was time to leave, as if she were reluctant to let her go. "Come again. It's nice to see another woman."

"And you, too, come to Foxhome if you get a chance," Solveig said. "You would be a welcome guest in our prairie home."

At Cold Spring, Sadie chatted non-stop with Solveig about everything from the price of saleratus to the need for more schools in the frontier. I was dumbfounded. Never before had Sadie said more than a few words in my presence. Of course, it should not have surprised me knowing how Billy could talk. An apple doesn't fall far from the tree, Far always said. She spoke in English and I could catch most of what was said; I wondered how Solveig was doing with it. By the look on her face, she seemed to understand everything. Luckily, she had no time to reply, Sadie spoke so quickly and about so many different topics.

Bror was neatly shaven and clean, down to his fingernails. I tried to remember the filthy hovel of the past but it seemed a distant memory. Now everything was scrubbed and clean. He smiled and picked up the baby and set her on his shoulder.

"Why don't we go out and look at the horses?" he said and headed for the door, Billy at his heels. "What are we going to do, Pa?" he asked. "Are we going to show them the horses? Will you show them the new calf, too? Pa, will you show them the chicks?"

Rasmuss and I followed. Later we enjoyed a special meal of fried chicken and new potatoes. Bror filled his plate repeatedly, laughing and joking. Marriage seemed to agree with that one.

In truth, there was a wedding celebration for Solveig and Rasmuss at each place. The missus would fix something special to eat for the occasion and sometimes there would be a small gift as well. It wasn't everyday the settlers were able to entertain newly-weds.

At Carl Evenson's cabin, Kersten and Thea brought a small mewing handful of gray fluff and handed it to Solveig with care. It was a baby kitten, just old enough to leave its mother.

"You'll need it," said the missus. "The mice and rats almost drove us out our first year. After we got our cat, things were much better."

*"Mange takk!"* Solveig and Rasmuss said together. "What a wonderful present!"

The kitten took its place on Solveig's lap and quit mewing. It stretched out its legs and wrinkled its face.

"What shall we name it?" Solveig said.

Thea and Kersten looked at each other shyly and Kersten said, "We named it Fisk — because it's gray like a fish."

"Then Fisk it will be!" Solveig lifted the kitten and looked into its face. "A perfect name for a beautiful kitty."

Fisk slept on Solveig's lap in the stage. The missus had sent a gourd half filled with milk from their fresh heifer.

"Fisk, Royal Cat for the Queen of Fox-home," Rasmuss said from the stage and then it became very quiet.

# 14

"General Pope to Defend Washington
from Robert E. Lee's Army"
~ St. Paul Journal

The heat oppressed, the air heavy and wearing. It was too hot for work, too hot for
thought. Clouds in the west darkened and
threatened. Thunderheads swirled into
shapes and pictures that kept me entertained all afternoon. At times I saw the
mountains of home, snow capped peaks and
valleys. A slight switch of wind brought a
band of angels, standing guard over the
earth. Then a ceiling of lighter-colored
clouds settled overhead with round protru-
sions hanging down, reminding me of a
precious glass bowl owned by my mor, every
orb symmetrical and dainty. The clouds
grew darker, greener, and the circular
clouds stretched out like the teats of a nursing cat. Suddenly one of these orbs changed

into the face of an Indian complete with war paint and feathers in his hair. From his face dropped another vision so frightening the horses reared back and I jerked the reins with all my strength to hold them.

A huge cone-shaped cloud undulated before me in the southwestern sky, the tip of the cone dipping toward the earth, almost touching down. It grew larger as I watched it move toward us. A roaring sound, like a speeding train, filled the open air though we were hundreds of miles from the nearest railroad track.

"Rasmuss! Solveig!" I fought the horses with all my might, almost pulling my arms from their sockets. The noise roared and dust and debris blew around the stage, blinding and confusing me even more.

"What is it?" Rasmuss leaned out the window of the coach door. "Good Lord! It's a twister!" He and Solveig jumped out of the stage and knelt behind a fallen oak alongside the trail. I huddled against the horses, calming them as best I could, helpless before the great snake-like beast. I watched it writhe up into the sky again where it veered to the north of us. The air was so still it seemed time had stopped. We stood motionless in the quiet, no birds singing, and no frogs chirping in the sloughs.

"It missed us," Rasmuss said in a weak voice with his arm around Solveig. "We were lucky."

My knees felt weak as jelly. I staggered to a boulder at the side of the trail and sat down, hoping to hide the quiver in my legs. Either the air had cooled or I was so frightened I had turned cold. Solveig looked at me with a white face and I knew mine looked the same.

"Twisters are common," Rasmuss said. "They drop out of the sky, unexpected, and if they touch the ground will tear up everything in its path. They uproot trees, make kindling from the strongest houses and rearrange huge boulders."

"Do you have twisters in Foxhome?" asked Solveig in a worried voice.

"*Nei,* not since I've been there."

"How can a person protect himself?" I asked.

"It's best to go below ground, in a cellar or dugout," Rasmuss said. "It's flying debris that'll kill a person or maybe being blown away. I heard of a man by Alexandria Woods who was plowing when a twister came. It picked him up and let him down ten miles away. The strange thing is that he was dropped down naked, even to his laced-up boots. He ran hysterical until he came to someone's cabin. Not a scratch on him nor a stitch of clothes, every inch of his body bruised beyond belief."

Solveig looked at Rasmuss in horror. She clutched Fisk to her chest.

I looked around. The ground was flat without ditch or gully. Surely Mor prayed for me today. The sky was still dark and thunder rumbled in the distance, lightning sparked bright streaks in the skies to our west. I went to the team and fed them bits of carrots from my pockets, petting and stroking each one, crooning to them my love and gratitude. They were such good horses, so trusting and faithful and true to me in every way, my best friends in the whole world.

"It's time to get back on the trail. We have a few miles to go before we stop." I held the door while Rasmuss and Solveig climbed back in the coach. Solveig leaned down and kissed Fisk's head.

"Don't waste kisses on a cat!" Rasmuss grabbed her and kissed her cheeks, laughing and teasing. "Three more days and we'll be home."

I climbed back on the box and pretended not to feel the stab of loneliness in my chest.

The letter addressed to Ingvald Ericson burned in the mail pouch. Maybe I would deliver it in person. It would be good to know Inga was well, that she was surviving in the wilderness. Besides there could be no hint of impropriety with Rasmuss and Solveig along, even if the Swede wasn't home.

The horses drove into the storm, hunching forward in a sheet of cold rain with stinging pelts of hail. There was no refuge; we could only plod onward, hoping it would soon be over. Carl Evenson's crops had looked promising — I hoped they hadn't been hit by hail. It would be a shame after all his hard work.

Wilhelm Schwarz was overjoyed by the storm. He insisted on taking us out to a backfield to show us how the twister had cleared a field for him. We splashed through puddles of rainwater, walked over fallen branches, and downed trees.

"Mother Nature, she worked all this in *drei minuten*," he bragged. "Look, firewood. Ready for the clearing. My pockets lined with gold will be. Even the stumps they are pulled."

I gazed at the field in awe. Huge oaks pulled up by their very roots and tumbled together like so much kindling, grooves in the soil where the twister gouged and plowed huge furrows, rocks tossed here and there. The question came to me why God would clear this field for such a cruel man and yet allow the Sanger family to lose their man at Shiloh or let Inga marry such a bastard. If Christina were alive, I would have asked her. She was wise about such matters. Far always said life wasn't fair; once again, he was right.

The next day I thought the same question when we came upon a huge windfall across the trail about a mile before Lars Larson's farm. Why directly on the trail? Rasmuss and I chopped and dragged; even Solveig set the kitten down and pulled branches off the trail. When we reached Lars' cabin, we were exhausted and starved. Solveig's hair had fallen down and her face was dirty. She wrapped a clean handkerchief around Rasmuss' thumb where a branch had smashed it.

"We thought you weren't coming." Lars greeted us on the stoop. "You've never been this late before."

"We had bad luck; well, really, good luck first and then bad luck," I said while shaking his hand.

"How is that?" Lars asked.

"We saw a twister but it passed us by. That was our good luck. Then we came upon the place where it had touched down, ripping up the trail and dumping trees and branches, blocking the trail altogether. That was our bad luck."

Over cold cornbread and milk, we talked about twisters. Rasmuss told about the field cleared by the tornado for Wilhelm Schulz and then the tale of the man from Alexandria Woods found naked on the prairie. Solveig and the missus did the dishes while the men moved to the porch to chew snuff. Ragna and Borghilde played with Fisk, carrying the little kitten everywhere.

"Mor, can we get a kitten?" Ragna called through the door.

"A kitten would be nice but there are none to be had in this place," she answered while stepping onto the porch. "Maybe we can find one in the fall."

"The Evensons' might have more kittens. I could ask," I said. Cats were valuable on the frontier and brought a good price. Mice and rats would ruin a crop stored over the winter.

"Maybe we could trade for one."

The talk changed to the crops and weather. Rasmuss talked about farming on the open prairies, about the gopher problems and the richness of the soil.

"*Nei,* we don't grub trees in Foxhome,"

he said. "But we will plant one when we get home. Evan gave us a basswood sapling for a wedding gift."

"Basswood is the best for making shoes," Lars said.

"And the best honey," said the missus. "A basswood tree is a sight to behold when it blooms. You will enjoy your wedding gift for years to come."

"Thanks to Evan, there was a wedding," Rasmuss said.

Once again he went over the story, detail by detail. He made me bolder and wiser than I was and described Solveig in such glowing terms that her cheeks flamed.

"I told Evan to forget about finding women for others and look for himself," Lars said with a teasing look on his face. "He's the most eligible bachelor around. Our neighbor girl, Tilla Spitsberg, is of marrying age. We'll have to invite her to the baptism."

I suddenly remembered chores that needed attention in the barn. As I left, the room erupted into laughter.

The following day lasted forever. The weather cooled after the storm and the air was not as heavy, making life more bearable. We found more trees over the trail and took time to drag them off and fill in at least a few ruts and holes while we were at it. Part of my job was to keep the trail open. When we bedded down at Anton Estvold's, I could hardly sleep, thinking about the morning mail delivery.

We were up and on the trail as the first light bloomed pink in the east. The horses were fresh and anxious to move. Anton waved good-bye from the yard and we splashed through puddles leftover from the storm.

The stage turned into the Ericson's west of Pomme de Terre and drove up to the cabin. I pulled the horses to a stop and jumped down with the mail pouch.

"What are you doing?" asked Rasmuss from the coach. "Why are we stopping?"

"It's nothing," I said. "I have a letter to deliver."

I didn't invite them to go in with me. It would, no doubt, be a brief stop and the day was just beginning.

"Who's there?" a voice called from the cabin.

"Missus, I have a letter."

The door opened and Inga stood before me, clean and fresh in a gingham dress. Her hair was neatly braided into two brown braids that reached her waist. Her eyes flashed recognition and she invited me in.

"Mr. Jacobson, *Velkommen!* You could have left it at Pomme de Terre and saved yourself the trouble." She looked at me and added in a quieter voice, "Please call me Inga. I'm only Inga."

I looked around and saw no sign of Ericson. The cabin was tidy and sweet smelling, biscuits baked in the oven and a pot of coffee on the stove. A pan of milk was set to strain on a small table. Everything was in order, as Mor's kitchen would be.

"Will you have breakfast?" She bustled toward the stove and took biscuits out of the oven. "I would enjoy the company. My man is away on business and it gets quiet here."

"I'll stay for breakfast if you sit at the table with me and forget about manners."

Inga's laugh was like the low notes on a fiddle. She looked healthier than the last time I saw her. Her cheeks were pink and her eyes did not have that look of agony. Maybe she had even put on a little weight. Overall, she made a most pleasing picture. I did not mention I had just eaten a full breakfast at Pomme de Terre. I sat in a chair by the table and felt totally tongue-tied.

"What kind of letter is it?" Inga set the biscuit pan on the table with a small bowl of butter.

The letter! I almost forgot to get it out! I removed it from the pouch and set it next to her plate. She wiped her hands on her apron, picked it up with great care, and sat down at the table. She scanned the address. A look of disappointed crossed her face.

"Were you expecting a letter from your parents?"

"*Nei,* my mor is passed on, also my far. I had hoped it was a letter from my brother in the Norwegian army. He's all the close family I have left."

Her words caused a surge of happiness. Her brother was all the close family she had left; she didn't consider Ericson her family.

"*Kvar kjem du fra?*" I sought neutral ground that would keep her voice speaking. "Where are you from?"

"Verdahl. Have you ever been there?"

"*Nei,* I've heard of it but have not been there myself. *Eg kjem fra* Sonmorgaard."

She poured the coffee and added a splash of thick cream. She cut a thick slab of brown cheese, *gjetost.* No doubt about it, Inga was a good hand with dairy. I pondered a question that had bothered me since the first day I met her. Rude or not, I decided to ask; *A ga som katta rundt den varme grauten,* not pace around hot porridge like a cat.

"Was your first man from Trondheim, too?"

"How do you know I was married before?" She tilted her chin.

"Ericson told me the day we met," I said.

She seemed to be considering whether she should answer my question. I waited, ashamed of my poor manners.

"*Ja,* my man died on the boat coming over." Her hands fingered the butter knife. "We were both from Trondheim, grew up together. *Eg heiter* was Gunnar, Gunnar Thormondson."

She spoke his name with quietness, respect. It cheered me knowing she chose not to speak the name of Ingvald Ericson, let alone with such loving tones.

"What happened to him?"

"A fever. He was ill only a few days but didn't make it." She made circles on the table with her finger. Her hands were worn and chapped. "He'd never been sick a day in his life and we kept thinking he'd get better. He was as surprised as I when it took him."

"What happened next?" I needed to know the circumstances, to understand why she had married Ericson.

"They wouldn't let me off the boat unless I was married or had proof of engagement."

Her face twisted at the memory. Mor taught me better than to pry into other people's business.

"So you married the Swede."

"*Ja,* we were wed." Her voice was flat and her brown eyes looked into mine. I wanted to tell her that had I been on the boat, I would have married her first, before Ericson could put his dirty paws on her. But of course it would do no good to make such declarations now. It was too late.

It was almost dark when we reached the Foxhome soddy. The sun was a red rim on the western prairie, a perfect background for the corn waving in the breeze. There was a smell of earth and growing things about the place. The night was filled with the serenade of frogs and crickets.

"I hope Bossy isn't causing the neighbors any problems," Rasmuss said. "I'll fetch her first thing in the morning so we can have fresh milk again."

He seemed anxious, maybe worried that Solveig would be unappreciative of the stark surroundings. We lingered by a slough, watching the horses drink their fill. Solveig stood apart, looking around. Finally she turned and faced Rasmuss.

"I have never seen such a beautiful sunset,

Rasmuss," she said. "You never told me how lovely it is out here."

With a grin from one ear to another, Rasmuss pointed out the distant twinkle of their nearest neighbor's light. Only one pinpoint of brightness could be seen in any direction. As we finished caring for the horses, the stars came out. It seemed they took turns, one after another, friendly dots of light to comfort us in the darkness. A huge moon began its climb in the sky, making the pathway to the soddy a golden road. It was a good sign.

When we reached the door, Rasmuss swept Solveig up in his arms and carried her and the cat over the threshold. If Solveig was disappointed, she didn't show it. She laughed breathlessly and set Fisk on the floor while Rasmuss lit a small hurricane lamp. The flame brought to life the shadows and rustling of small animals in the corners. She bustled around, cooking coffee and a bite of supper. After the meager meal of cornmeal mush without milk, I headed for the barn. It would not do to share the soddy with the King and Queen of Foxhome their first night home.

I laid in the barn next to the horses' stall, listening to the call of wolves in the far distance, and the restlessness of the horses in response. Maybe it was good Solveig had visited farm after farm on her way to Fox-home. It gave her a true picture what pioneer life meant for a woman; there were few surprises when she arrived.

I tried to keep my mind away from Inga but I couldn't do it. My thoughts kept wandering back to how she looked, the brown of her eyes, the way her finger drew a pattern on the table when she spoke of her first husband. It was easy to imagine living with Inga in that cabin, laughing over coffee every morning. She would introduce herself to strangers, "I'm Inga Jacobson." She wouldn't hesitate or call herself 'only Inga' but say the full name with pride. And she would refer to me, "my husband, Evan Jacobson," with loving respect. I would be her 'close family' and she mine.

Sleep was slow that night. The last thing I remember was reciting the Commandments over and over.

After breakfast of the same corn meal mush and coffee, I harnessed the team and made ready for the final stretch to Fort Abercrombie. My mind gathered the bits of gossip I had gleaned from the settlers along the way and rehearsed once again the news of the war. The soldiers would ply me for details and I wanted to be ready.

Rasmuss and Solveig walked me to the stage to bid me good-bye. They stood hand in hand in the dew, a glow of happiness and hope about them.

*"Tussen takk!"* said Rasmuss, reaching to shake my hand. *"God tur."* Rasmuss pumped my hand firmly. "Good journey."

Solveig hugged me, then kissed me on my cheek. I could feel the wetness of tears on her face and the smell of coffee.

*"Mange takk,"* she said. "If you ever have need of our help, just call out and we'll do what we can."

This frank show of emotion overwhelmed me. I thought of how Christina would react to the tears and kisses and with an impulse strong and unleashed, I reached out and hugged them both, then quickly turned and climbed up on the box.

*"Ha det bra,"* they said. "See you tomorrow night on your return trip."

*Ja,* I would see them tomorrow. I didn't trust my voice to answer and instead snapped the reins, tipped my hat and started west. Rasmuss walked briskly in the direction of his neighbor, no doubt to bring Bossy home so they would have milk for their porridge. Solveig carried the basswood sapling into the shade of the soddy and returned inside.

How good it must feel to be home.

# 15

"More Recruits Needed to Defend
Washington from the Traitors"
~ St. Paul Journal

Fort Abercrombie bustled with activity.
Soldiers sawed trees along the riverbank and
another group split firewood. Still another
group stacked the wood into neat columns
called ricks. How lucky they were to have
cooler weather for such a job. Usually
woodcutters worked in the winter when the
mosquitoes and temperatures were more
compatible with hard labor. No doubt the
commander saw the need for more firewood
during his last visit; the wood growing along
the riverbed was too gnarled for anything
else.

The men waved as I drove in and rushed
for mail call. They pressed around the
stagecoach, and I waited on the seat to
answer the rush of questions I knew would

be coming. If only I knew the language better.

"What's the news? What's happening in the south?"

I cleared my throat and carefully quoted the memorized headlines from the newspaper posted at Fort Snelling.

"You must have read it wrong!" someone called from the crowd. "There can't be that many dead from one battle."

My cheeks flushed and I looked for Sven to interpret. The men didn't trust me, thought me stupid and ignorant. Sven was nowhere to be seen. "*Nei,* there are thousands dead," I said in what I hoped was a confident voice. "The families are just now getting word. John Sanger from Beanpres Ferry was killed."

"Not John!" another voice cried. "He's married to my second cousin."

"And Joe Sullivan was captured and sent to a Georgia prison," I continued. "They've sent the captives to either Oglethorpe Prison in Macon or further south to Andersonville. There's talk of an exchange."

The crowd grew silent. I climbed down and pulled the mail pouch from behind the seat. The letters were silently delivered. One of the men got a letter containing a newspaper clipping with the lists of dead and captured from Shiloh. The others crowded around, pushing to read the lists.

"Damn Rebs!"

"We'll get back at 'em!"

"They'll regret they ever started this mess!"

I led the horses to the stable, removed their harness and rubbed them down. The horses were the best to be found. They'd pull for me until their hearts gave out if I asked them. A soldier carried water to the trough, and we watched as the horses drank their fill, snorting and flicking water with their massive heads. I could hear singing in the distance and cocked my head to listen, trying to understand the words. It was an unfamiliar tune, a lilting cheerful melody.

"What's the name of that song?" I asked the soldier.

" 'Rally Round the Flag'. Lately it's all they sing around here." He began to sing along with the distant voices:

"Yes, we'll rally round the flag, boys, we'll rally once again. Sounding the trumpet call of freedom. The Union forever, hurrah boys, hurrah! Down with the traitors and up with the stars. Yes, we'll rally round the flag, boys, we'll rally once again. Sounding the trumpet call of freedom."

I liked the tune and whistled it while I

finished with the horses. *Ja,* the sight of the stars and stripes was enough to rally the faint of heart. But it would take more than a song to win the fight against the Rebs. They needed soldiers.

Before I left the next morning, I sought out the second cousin of John Sanger's widow.

"She was in a bad w-way with grief. A passenger was worried about how the children might fare with their mother so upset," I said to him. "If you know of kin who might be able to help her out, I'd deliver a letter when I get back to Fort Snelling."

My journey east had hardly started when I met a band of recruits marching to Fort Abercrombie. I heard them before I saw them, just as Hjalmer Thoreson had said. The sergeants bawled like muleskinners, and the soldiers struggled to keep in step. They must have been behind me all the way west and I never knew it. I thought how convenient it would have been to have them near when the trees were blown across the road after the storm. Such was my luck; they were behind by one day's journey. With red faces they dragged muskets and packs westward. I tipped my hat and pulled up the stage to let them by. Their sergeant stopped by the stage and wiped his face with a red handkerchief.

"Are we almost there?" he asked.

"*Ja,* the crossing is a few miles west."

"Will we have any trouble with it?"

"*Nei,* the water is down, and you'll get across with nothing worse than wet feet."

"Good! Enough trouble already, running into the storm and eaten alive by the skeeters."

I thought of the miles from Fort Snelling to Dakota Territory and how terrible it would be to walk all the way in the heat and humidity. At least a man could rest his feet riding in a stage and save on his boot leather.

"Good-bye then." I tipped my hat. "Enjoy your stay at the fort."

"I wouldn't bet money on it," said the sergeant.

Solveig had supper ready when I pulled into Foxhome that afternoon. Rasmuss made a fuss about the quality of the butter and the tastiness of the cornbread. Her cheeks pinked, maybe from the heat of the stove. I told the news I learned at the fort, about the new song and the recruits marching westward.

Rasmuss said, "*Ja,* I saw them when I got

Bossy from the neighbor. They marched a little north to avoid the slough."

Solveig had cleaned and straightened the soddy. Fisk slept on a bit of rug in the corner, purring contentedly.

"How is the royal cat?"

"He is concentrating on growing bigger than the mice so he can clean them out of here," Solveig said. "He has a big job ahead of him."

"I met a man related to the Widow Sanger," I said. "He sends a letter back to relatives in St. Paul. Maybe they can help her."

The smile on Solveig's face was thanks enough.

When I went out to the barn, the stars were out and the moon coming up. I could hear nighthawks squealing in the sky as they hunted mosquitoes. Frogs croaked from the nearby slough, and somewhere an owl hooted. I planned the route I would take the next day, to Lewis Peterson's by noon and then to Anton Estvold's for the night. I would travel right by Inga's cabin. As I fell asleep, I dreamed there was another letter to deliver.

Big Barn Jensen was in the far field, cutting

the hay. I could see the rhythmic movements of his scythe. I pulled the stage to a stop in front of their cabin and his missus came out, wiping her hands on her apron before she tucked strands of hair back into her braids. I couldn't help but notice her rounding belly. Soon there would be a Little Barn Jensen. Quickly I averted my eyes and tipped my hat.

She fed me thin slices of bread topped with cold potatoes and sliced onion. She pushed the salt and pepper toward me and I sprinkled each piece generously before eating. A large cup of coffee with cream and sugar was pressed toward me and I ate without speaking.

As I stood to leave, the missus took a letter from a drawer in the end of the table and handed it to me. Spidery script covered the envelope.

"Will you mail this letter at the fort?" she asked. "It's to my mother in Copenhagen. I want her to know about our crops and . . . family." Her face colored cherry red and I realized she had come close to telling me about the baby, a serious breach of manners. Breathing a sigh of relief, we were spared the embarrassment, I took the letter and went out to the team. She must be lonely, I thought, to make such a slip.

I wondered what the letter said, if she told of the big barn and the small cabin, mentioned the loneliness of life in the wilderness, if she longed for home. The missus didn't look much older than I, married to a slightly older man. *Ja,* it could be lonely.

Bror Brorson and his missus hung curtains at the window when I stopped for the night. I could hear them laughing before they knew I was there. The yard was neat and orderly, weeds pulled and a patch of flowers had sprouted by the door. I think they were poppies, brilliant red and orange.

"Anybody home?" I called and Billy ran out the door.

"Hello Mister Evan," he said, "are you still an Injun-lover?"

"Billy! Mind your manners!" said the missus.

Bror helped with the team, and I couldn't help but notice he was wearing a different shirt, it was cleaner and in better repair. We watched the horses roll in the cool grass, freed from their burden for another day.

"Nice corn," I said,

"*Ja,* it is a fair crop this year. I've been keeping watch at night to keep the 'coons and black bear out of it. I'm hoping to find a dog to stand guard. Another three weeks until harvest."

We looked at the mare and I dreamed of the colt I would have in the spring, my own start of a team of horses, the fulfillment of a dream. The pigs squealed in a pen made from split rails. It was hard to keep pigs in such a pen; they were forever rooting their way out from underneath.

"I'll be glad to butcher that one," said Bror. "He is nothing but trouble but will be a Christmas ham for both of us."

What would I do with a Christmas ham? Maybe give it to Lars and his family to enjoy. I could join them in the fall before the weather got bad and we could feast early.

I wondered what commandment I had broken in making Bror leave the Lutheran Church. How could he turn to popishness and idol worship after knowing the truth from Martin Luther's Catechism? I cautiously looked around, half expecting to see a plaster saint or other such nonsense. But I couldn't deny his happiness.

John Sanger's widow helped with the team in silence. Her eyes looked at the floor and her lips refused to answer my questions about the children or the crops. Solveig was right; she was in a bad way. I breathed a silent prayer of thanks for the letter from her second cousin.

# 16

"Congress Passes Law to Free
Slaves of all Rebels"
~ St. Paul Journal

"It was Crooked Lightning did it," Ted said with a leer. "That dirty injun raided the storehouse at the reservation and took what he wanted."

The name caught my full attention, and I looked up from currying Betty.

"Crooked Lightning?" I said. "Are you sure?"

"It was Crooked Lightning all right!" Ted hung the harness on a nail in a slap hazard fashion, the ends dragging in the dirt. "The men from C Company just got back from patrol. It's too bad they didn't kill him when his dog bit Tom — it would have saved a lot of trouble now."

If Crooked Lightning raided the store-house, it was only out of desperation, I was sure. The payment still had not arrived.

"Was anyone hurt?"

Ted shook his head. Maybe there was hope then. Without violence the fence might be mended. I finished the care of the horses and headed straight for the Episcopal Mission and Bishop Whipple.

Whipple cleaned sunfish and crappies at a bench outside the mission, throwing the scales and entrails into a bucket. A neighborhood cat ate from the bucket and hissed at me as I approached him.

"Five thousand Dakota gathered and demanded the goods." Bishop Whipple flipped a cleaned fillet into a bowl beside him. "Said their people were hungry, that it wasn't their fault the gold was late."

"What happened?"

"Galbraith gave out a partial dole; he was backed in a corner and had no other choice," Bishop Whipple said. "The Indians promised to go home and wait in peace for the gold."

"Ted said Crooked Lightning was the cause of it," I said. "Said he heard it from the soldiers."

"Crooked Lightning was there, but I doubt he was responsible. He doesn't have enough authority to influence other braves in the presence of the great chiefs."

"I haven't seen him since the dog bite," I said. "Where has he been anyway?"

"Crooked Lightning drew a knife on the soldier who killed his dog. It could have been worse." The bishop dumped the fish scraps under some rosebushes and picked up the bowl with the cleaned fish. "I expect Crooked Lightning is on the Lower Reservation, waiting for the annuity like all the others."

We started into the mission and the bishop turned and said, "Evan, how are you at frying fish? Somehow I lost my cook and could use a hand."

It was dusk when I left the mission and headed for the hostler's cabin. It wasn't exactly home, and I almost dreaded going in the cabin. I knew there would be filth and noise, no wife to laugh with over curtains, no future president to greet me.

I was surprised to find two letters waiting for me on my crude bunk. One was addressed to Evan, Stage Driver, Fort Snelling, Minnesota. The script was plain and clear, almost childlike. It said:

July 1, 1862

Dear Mr. Stagecoach Driver,

I heard you helped my sister-in-law after my brother died at the hand of that injun. Thank you for doing this even though you ain't kin. Please give this letter to her next time you see her and ask her to write and tell me where she is. She can send the letter to me at Mankato, I got wounded at Shiloh and won't be fighting no more.

Yours truly,
Jack Murphy


I pondered these words, remembering the curtains. Maybe this letter would put an end to their laughter. I could lose it, pretend I never got it. But I knew the commandment; I wouldn't bear false witness to my neighbor. Billy deserved to know his Uncle Jack lived through Shiloh. I folded the envelope carefully and slipped it into my pocket, next to the watch fob of Christina's hair. Bror's missus would get the letter the next time the stage stopped.

My eyes then scanned the second letter. The stamp was blue with the face of Norwegian royalty. The script did not belong to Mor. My heart raced.

June 29, 1862

Dear Evan,

It is with a sad heart I send news of Mor's death. She complained of a sharp headache the morning of June 27 and died later that same day. She did not suffer and was of sound mind until the end. We held her funeral today and the text was from John 11:25 "I am the resurrection and the life: He that believeth in me, though he were dead, yet shall he live." She was a good woman and her memory will live forever in our hearts. Before she died she asked me to remember I had a brother in America and to include him always in my prayers.

Borgetta and the children are well. A son, Emil Daniel, was born to us last winter. He is a healthy boy and lives to carry on the family name.

Write soon and remember your old home in Sonmorgaard.

Your brother,
Ole Jacobson

I read it again and again, trying to digest the words. All was quiet around me, but grief roared through my inner self. When Christina died, my childhood died with her.

At Far's death, my world was shaken. With Mor's passing, the cord to Norway snapped. I was without roots, homeless in the world, no one left.

I walked by the river in the late twilight and a pair of gray foxes frisked in front of me, startling me out of my thoughts. They scurried into the hazelnut bushes, their long tails disappearing into the leaves. A pair of eagles screeched as they dove for fish. Even the eagles had each other. Truly I could join the war with an easy heart; no one would mourn if I were killed. The tears started and I wiped them with my sleeve, leaving smudges of dirt with each swipe. I thought of how Mor comforted me when Far died, how she held me in her arms and wiped my tears, reminding me of the glad reunion someday in heaven. It seemed distant and far away. Now I comforted myself with the glad thought that Christina was with her once again.

I hadn't realized until her death that my focus in living had been hinged on telling Mor about it. Such a quiet, gentle person, it seemed impossible she could be so important to me. But from Mor I had known unconditional love and now it was gone. I should have written more letters filled with the words I should have said. Surely she must have known the great love I carried for her. She knew.

It was time to join the army. As I returned to the cabin, I stumbled over a root in the darkness and fell to the ground. Mor would not wish me to make a hasty decision when my heart was hurting. It wouldn't hurt to wait for a while. Perhaps I would think differently when I got used to being both motherless and fatherless. I lay on the ground for a few minutes, just looking up at the stars.

This must be how Inga felt when she lost her man. In her helpless crisis of grief she married that bastard, Ericson. For the first time, I almost understood.

The Lutheran priest came to baptize Evan Larson. On my next trip to Fort Abercrombie, arrangements were made as to the exact date of my return trip. I hoped and prayed no storm or mishap would prevent me from arriving on time. For once the weather cooperated.

Reverend Hultgren was an older man, clothed in white cowl and stern countenance. He scrutinized me up and down and I felt his disapproval. Of course I was dressed in my stinky driving clothes and he had no way of knowing if I kept the Commandments or not. He probably thought a Godfather should be more mature and better situated. Although correct in his thinking, we had to make do with what we had at hand.

Lars' neighbors, Sophus Spitsberg and his missus and five children were there for the celebration. Their oldest daughter, Tilla, was beautiful with her blonde hair and sparkling blue eyes. She must have been about sixteen, close to marrying age. Lars was prompt to introduce us and her handshake was most enjoyable, causing my face to flush and my lips to stammer out a greeting. I turned and picked up the baby, hoping to avoid further embarrassment.

The future president greeted me with happy coos and gurgles, then promptly spit up on my shirt and filled his diaper with a soggy wetness that wet my hands down to my wrists. Lars' missus whisked the child away to clean him up and put him in the family baptismal gown. I went out to the water trough and tried to wash away the filth and grime of the trail as well as the baby mess.

"Are you all right then?" asked Lars as he followed me out to the trough.

"*Ja*," I said, "It takes a powerful stomach to be a *far*."

He laughed as if I had spoken the funniest joke in the whole world.

"You'll get used to it when the time comes," he said with a grin. "That is the least of a *far*'s worries."

We went back into the cabin, and the missus poured a pitcher of water for the minister to use in the ceremony. A clean cloth was placed on the kitchen table, and the priest opened his Bible and prayer book. We crowded around while the young president protested the unexpected sprinkle with great vigor. Vows were said and I promised God to watch over this young life, care for him in case the parents died and make certain he was educated in the ways of the Lord and Martin Luther's Catechism. Ragna and Borghilde stood to the side with wide eyes. The Spitsbergs watched in strict attention, but I noticed Tilla glancing at me out of the corner of her eye. The minister said, "Amen," and Evan Gustav Larson's name was written in the Book of Life.

We sat down to fried chicken, fresh peas, and new potatoes. Tilla's face was crimson as she passed the heaping platters of chicken around. When she stood beside me to place a drumstick on my plate, I smelled a clean soapy fragrance. There was lefse with sugar and for dessert a plate of crispy rosettes.

The men ate until they could not eat another bite and retired to the porch to let the women and children take their turn.

Reverend Hultgren and Sophus lit long-necked pipes and the fragrance of tobacco wafted in the air. Lars and I chewed, spitting into the flowerbeds as we watched the darting lights of fireflies. A whippoorwill sang from the trees next to the cabin. All was at peace.

"What's the news from the war?" asked Lars.

"Nothing good, that's for sure." I hated to go back to that hopeless subject, wishing instead to enjoy the baptism and the celebration.

"Rebellion is as the sin of witchcraft," Reverend Hultgren said in a serious voice. "It is never the will of God for people to rebel against authority."

I bit my lip to keep from asking about the cotter system of Norway. Surely it would be a just war to fight against that. *Nei,* I kept my thoughts to myself.

"And what about the Indian annuities?" Sophus drew a deep breath from his pipe. He was a tall man and his legs stretched out before him seemed longer than any I had ever seen.

"There was a partial payment of food and

supplies last week." I tried to keep the tone positive. "The gold will come soon."

From the corner of my eye I could see Tilla laughing at the table, the lamplight framing her face against the shadows. Her voice reminded me of Norway, of the bells we tied on our cows when we loosed them on the mountain to feed on summer grass.

"Did you hear what I said, Evan?" Lars said.

"Excuse me, my mind wandered." I flushed and all but the priest laughed.

"I asked you if you had heard about the prisoner exchange, if it really would happen," he repeated.

"There's talk at the fort — that the Confederates don't trust the soldiers who swear they'll not fight again," I said. "They might just keep the prisoners 'til the end of the war to make sure."

"Surely they don't want the bother and expense of feeding all those men," Lars said. "It only makes sense to have an exchange like they've done before."

"I'll try to keep my ears open for any more news."

"I heard the Rebs might be behind the delayed annuity payment to the Sioux," Reverend Hultgren said. "Heard they are plotting to steal the gold for themselves and turn the Sioux against us as well."

We sat in stunned silence. England had used the Indians, convinced them to fight with them against the Patriots in the Revolution and in the War of 1812 as well. The French had done the same during the French and Indian Wars.

"Even the Rebs wouldn't stoop that low!" Lars said. "Even they wouldn't turn Indians against helpless civilians!"

"It's what I heard." Reverend Hultgren tapped the side of his pipe with his finger and removed a stray piece of tobacco from the stem. "In a cold-blooded way, it makes perfect sense. If they could convince the Indians across the northern states to rise up, the soldiers would have to stay home to defend their own. It would weaken the war effort."

"Lincoln has his hands full," Sophus said, "blacks, generals, Injuns, and all of us to worry about."

"I've heard there are Confederate rabble rousers up north, trying to make the trappers sympathetic to their cause," Reverend Hultgren said. "I heard about it from a trapper in Breckenridge."

"That brings it pretty close to home," Lars said in an even voice

We smoked and chewed in silence. Bats

dipped and swooped across the yard, eating mosquitoes. The little ones caught fireflies and held them in their cupped hands, peeking in between their fingers to see the glow. Dishes clattered in the kitchen, almost drowning out the chatter of the women. I wished a desperate wish, almost a prayer. Please let it stay this way, peaceful, unafraid. We've risked so much to move to Minnesota, all of us, please let it be worth it.

Sophus stood and stretched his long arms above his head, his big hands reaching for the stars. "Morning comes too soon, and there's much to do tomorrow. The hay is ready to cut if the weather cooperates."

"Do you need help?" Lars asked. "I could come over tomorrow afternoon with my scythe and help out."

"I won't turn it down." Sophus laughed a booming laugh that rang out over the yard. "I thought you'd never offer!"

We shook hands all around. Reverend Hultgren would stay the night at the Larson cabin, and I would bunk in the barn. Sophus' missus gathered the children, and I saw Tilla picking up Thor to carry home.

"Let me walk you home," I said, "and carry the littlest one for you."

I was surprised at myself. It was an unbidden thought unexpectedly spoken.

"*Ja,* that would be good," Sophus said. "Let the younger men carry the load a while."

I scooped up the little boy who nestled his sweaty head under my chin, sleeping already, worn out from the party and playing. He smelled of sweat and fried chicken and was heavier than I expected, dead weight. I fell in line behind the family, walking north in the direction of their farm. They lived about a mile away and the moon gave enough light to see the trail. Tilla walked at my side.

"He's heavy," she said. *"Mange takk."*

"It's nothing," I answered, embarrassed and surprised by my actions. There's not a man alive who wouldn't notice a beautiful girl, but I've never been bold or talkative around them. She was remarkably similar to my daydreams of a future wife with her blonde braids around her head and eyes as blue as a Norwegian fjord.

"It was a wonderful baptism," she said. "You'll make a good Godfather to little Evan."

I could think of nothing to answer such a statement. In truth, I was unsure exactly how a Godfather should act.

"It was the best meal I've had since leaving home," I said at last.

230

"They went all out for this one, this first son and citizen."

"Were you born here?"

"*Nei,* I was born in Norway, but my parents brought me over when I was still a baby," she said. "I cannot remember our homeland."

She was lucky to carry no memory. At least she didn't remember the famine years or the cotter system. I realized she had spoken and shook myself back to the present.

"What was that you said?" I felt foolish and preoccupied.

"I asked if you were confirmed before you came to America."

"*Ja, ja,*" I said. "Have you read for the minister yet?"

"*Nei,* Reverend Hultgren is starting confirmation classes soon. I expect to be confirmed in the fall."

I wondered aloud where he would have his classes, there being no church.

"We'll meet in homes," she said, "for both classes and services. Come to church if you are here over a Sunday."

"I'll do that." I spoke the polite words but thought the opposite. I'd heard enough of Reverend Hultgren to last a lifetime.

Sophus shook my hand, and Tilla whispered good-bye in her child-like, tinkling laugh. She was petite and pretty and knew it. Somehow I got the feeling Christina wouldn't have liked her.

Lars fussed with the team the next morning, more talkative than usual. "We could invite them for supper again," he said.

His words surprised me, doubtless prodded on by his missus.

"*Mange takk,* Lars, but I think not," I answered. "She's too young."

I thought then as I have since how it was more than just the age difference. She hadn't been through what I went through. She never lived through a famine, nor understood what it meant to be crushed down by the cotter system, never lost her parents or wandered alone in a strange land without knowing the language. *Nei,* there was a gulf between us too wide to travel.

"Rally Round the Flag" echoed in my brain as I hit the trail again. I whistled it softly to the horses. They liked the lilting melody.

Hjalmer Thoreson hailed me from the other stage as I neared the Evenson's.

"*God ettermiddag!* Good afternoon!"

"You, too, Hjalmer!" I pulled the stage

232

into a shady spot in the trail, a good resting place.

"What's the news of the prisoner exchange? Any progress?"

"Doesn't look like there will be an exchange." He spit into a pile of bear scat and disrupted a swarm of blue-tailed flies.

"Any other news?"

"Reb agitators are up among the trappers of northern Minnesota, trying to gain sympathy for the South."

"Are there that many trappers?"

"They must think it worthwhile."

"I met a man who thinks the Rebs are behind the delay of gold to the Indians," I said. "Thinks the Rebs want to steal it and turn the Dakota against us."

"Even the Rebs couldn't be that low," he said with a careful cadence to his voice.

"Happened in the last two or three wars," I said. "Would make sense the Rebs might try it in this one."

We chewed and spit, glad for the rest and the company.

"You might want to stop by and tell your story to the commander of the fort," he said at last. "It might be gossip, but he should know. It might be important."

"Maybe." I dreaded the thought of speaking to the commander. "I'll do my best but it's probably nothing." My poor English was a constant embarrassment.

We continued our opposite journeys as I thought of the war, how we couldn't get away from it even in far off Minnesota. It dragged men away from their families, killed or imprisoned them, threatened our fragile relationship with the Dakota, and tormented those of us who didn't enlist with guilty consciences. Like a living, breathing thing it affected everything in our lives, like a twister dropping from the sky and plowing furrows in the earth.

Near Beanpres Ferry a lone figure stood alongside the road as if waiting for the stage. When I came nearer, I saw it was Crooked Lightning.

"Crooked Lightning, how good to see you!" I pulled the stage to a stop next to where he stood. The horses needed a rest anyway in the heat. I jumped down from the box to speak with him. He looked thinner than he had last winter and I saw gray streaks in his long dark hair. His dog was not with him, of course, and it gave me a sad feeling to realize his loss.

We sat in the shade of a walnut tree along the trail. Pulling out my plug of snuff I offered him a chew.

"What are you doing way out here?" I asked.

He seemed to compose his thoughts and said after a brief silence, "There will be trouble unless the gold comes. The people are impatient and hungry."

He still hadn't answered my question but we both knew the answer. It wasn't safe for him at the fort.

"The people demand what is promised them." His face was like a stone sculpture, impassive and grim. "The young men are anxious to prove their worth in battle and will not listen to reason. There is talk of war."

I looked at him in silence, not able to summon words to my lips.

"When?" I heard my voice quaver and break.

He looked at me as if sizing me up, wondering if I could really be trusted. When he was satisfied in his mind he answered, "Soon."

"What can I do?"

He did not answer, gazing at me with a silent look. We sat without talking, chewing and spitting in the weeds. I stood up to leave, and reached to shake his hand. He accepted the white man's farewell with awkwardness.

"*Mange takk,* Crooked Lightning, for tell-ing me."

"Watch."

"*Ja,* that I will."

I hated saying it but took a deep breath anyway and said, "Is there anything you can do to stop it?"

The words stung, as I knew they would. It put him in a bad place; to admit he was without power and prestige in his tribe and wasn't able to dissuade them or else to ap-pear disloyal to his people.

"My words are like water in the river," he spoke after what seemed hours of silence. "The young men will not be turned back. They will not listen even to the great chief Little Crow."

An eagle flew overhead, its white head reflected in the sun. It swooped down and picked up a small rabbit from a nearby meadow and gracefully flew away, doubtless bringing food to its young.

"Over the earth I come," said Crooked Lightning.

I had never known August to feel so cold.

The commander was busy when I brought the pouch, but I asked the soldier on duty if I could speak to him. He gave me an un-comfortable straight-backed chair, made for someone much smaller than I. In the afternoon heat I waited, twisting in the chair, fidgeting, trying to get comfortable, remembering the spots where the bedbugs had bitten and feeling them start to itch again. A brass spittoon sat at the edge of the soldier's desk, and I chewed and spit, trying to hit the spittoon from different angles, feeling like a boy playing games in school. Finally the commander came out of his office.

"Evan, that is your name, isn't it?" he said. "Come in and tell me your business."

We went into a smaller room, even more stifling than the outer office had been. The fact that he still had his jacket neatly buttoned to his neck amazed me. He must be near boiling point in the heat.

"I just got b-back from Fort Abercrombie." I prayed I wouldn't stutter. "I met a Lutheran priest who fears the Rebs might be after the Indian gold. Thinks the Rebs will try to stir up the Dakota to their advantage. And I heard the Rebs are up north already, trying to get the trappers on their side."

The commander listened silently and gazed out through the small window that looked over the parade grounds. The guards were changing, and we could hear the drum beat as they marched to their places. A wasp fought the corner of the windowpane, fighting it as if it were a mortal enemy. I felt like a complete fool, bringing gossip to the commander when he was busy with other matters. Surely Mor had taught me not to think myself better than I was.

"On August 4th, five hundred Dakota surrounded two companies of the Fifth Minnesota Regiment led by Lieutenant Timothy Sheehan at the Lower Reservation," he said as if addressing a large audience. "Indians broke into the warehouse and carried out sacks of flour to feed their people."

"Was anyone killed?" The war had already started.

"The Indians promised to go back to their villages if another partial payment was made and the army persuaded Galbraith to do so," the commander said. "No one was hurt, but Galbraith's pride might be a little wounded."

"A Sioux friend warns there will be war unless the gold comes soon."

"It has to come," he said with a weary look on his sweating face. "It has to come."

He thanked me for the information I brought and dismissed me. I left the dispatch pouch on his desk and headed for the cabin. If he thought the gossip I brought about the Rebs was valid, he didn't let on, didn't even comment on the trapper situation to the north. I could have kicked myself. Hjalmer was quick to tell me to report it. I should have made him be the one to go to the commander.

One thought consumed me, to go to the river and jump in. I needed to wash the sweat and grime away and feel the coolness of the water. Maybe I could wash away the fear of an Indian war and the worry about the Rebs interfering with the Dakota.

The water was lukewarm and stank of vegetation and fish. Deep down I knew it was useless. If Crooked Lightning said war was imminent, it meant war was coming. Only a miracle could save us. I stopped by the mission on my way back from the river but Bishop Whipple wasn't there. Slowly I headed back to the cabin. It was too hot to sleep, too worrisome to rest. I dreaded the long night ahead.

"Can yous keeps a secret?" Ted pushed his face so close that I smelled the reek of onions on his breath. "I knows something big, something only I knows."

"*Ja,* I can keep a secret, but maybe you should, too."

Whoever entrusted Ted with a secret of any kind was a fool. His mouth blabbered as soon as his brain thought of a thing, large or small.

Ted pressed closer and whispered, "I seen them wagonload of gold leave this here fort today heading out for them Injun Reservation."

He was a liar, didn't know truth when he saw it. "How do you know it was gold?"

"It were the ruts them sank deeper than them other wagons. Had guards stood around but I snuck over and lifted them canvas when the men et breakfast. Weren't notice me one bit. It were gold all right, a wagon full." He held up a single five-dollar gold piece he had filched from the wagon and grinned an open-mouthed leer that showed rotten teeth sprouting in all directions of his mouth. "Pure gold, I tell you, pretty and shiny were the sun."

Stealing was against the Commandments but for once Ted had done right. A great sigh escaped my lips. I hadn't realized I had been holding my breath since hearing the words from Reverend Hultgren about the Rebs.

The gold was on its way to the Lower Reservation. The crisis had been avoided, at least for this year. I laid on my dirty bunk, not minding the shifting straw tick that fit in all the wrong places or the scratchy wool blanket. I slept like a baby.

# 17

"Poor Generalship Blamed
for Recent Defeats"
~ St. Paul Journal

Singing orioles woke me the next morning,
singing from the trees around the hostler's
cabin. I dreaded reading the news, but knew
I would be questioned by everyone I met
and could not disappoint them. The men
were already out on patrol or at their duties, so I stood by the window reading the
news alone. The building stank of horses
and sweat. Dust filled my nostrils as I read
of desperate fighting in a place called
Richmond. The Federals were forced back
when they thought they were winning. They
called it the Seven Days' War and the dead
and wounded were terrible in number. The
Federals lost 16,000 men in one week.
President Lincoln called for more volun-
teers.

Would it never end? In truth, it mattered little to me if the South stayed in the Union or not. There was plenty of room for everyone to my way of thinking. But slavery was another matter.

Adam Sullivan talked of joining up while he helped me with the team later in the day. He couldn't have been more than fourteen years old.

"I'm going to go fight those Rebs myself!" His eyes were red, as if he had been crying. "They're not going to keep my father penned up for the rest of his life. Who knows how they're treating him."

He was as grieved for his far as I had been for mine. It must have been worse knowing his far was kept out of his reach, beyond his help.

"What were your far's last words to you before he left?"

Adam looked up and his gullet bobbed in his neck. "He said to watch over Ma and the young'uns."

"Hard to do if you joined up," I said.

We led the horses to shade and walked into the cabin together. The missus had pancakes frying in a cast-iron skillet on the stove. The heat straggled her hair and caused sweat to drip down her face while she served the pancakes with molasses and butter.

"Adam!" she said. "The stove is dying down. Get some more kitchen wood. Not oak, that's too lasty. Just bring in some small pieces of that birch out there, just enough to finish the frying."

The missus looked at me with a stern face as Adam left the room.

"Don't be talking that young'un into joining up, you hear?" she scolded. "He's only fourteen and needed at home."

Her accusation stunned me. Once again, I was put in the situation where if I tried to defend myself, it would only make me look worse. I swiped the last of the pancakes into a pool of molasses and filled my mouth with the sticky sweetness.

"You do need the boy on the farm." I got up to leave.

"There's more pancakes," she called after me.

Adam and I hitched the fresh team. "Why not write a letter to your far and ask him for permission before you sign up. That way you'll know his mind on the matter."

He brightened at my words. "I'll do it. I'll have a letter ready next stage."

At Elk River I steered clear of the bedbugs in the house. Mosquitoes would torment a person but bedbugs were worse, they ate a man alive and reminded him of it for days. *Nei,* I'd chance it with the mosquitoes.

An elderly woman greeted me silently at the Sanger's door the next day. She motioned me to the table with a crooked finger before her lips and pointed to the Widow Sanger sleeping in a bed in the corner. I ate in silence and left quickly, glad to escape the heaviness of the room, glad someone had come to help her, wondering where the children could be. The woman walked with me to the stage and introduced herself as the mother of William Jenkins.

"I can't stay here forever, you know," she said. "We've got work of our own. There's blueberries to pick and jam to be made."

"I sent a letter to her kin," I answered. "Maybe someone will come soon."

"I sent the young'uns to William's house," she whispered. "The missus is in a bad way and not getting better."

Betty stumbled in an uneven place in the road. I stopped the stage and checked her legs and hooves. It wouldn't do to have a lame horse on the team. Betty seemed fine, but I had noticed before she was prone to stumbles. She was a sturdy beast, shiny black and agreeable, but a little smaller than the other horses on this team.

There was nothing I wanted more at that moment than to forget about the plight of John Sanger's widow. I whistled "Rally Round the Flag" to cheer myself and continued down the trail, reminding myself that the gold was on its way to the Dakota. The crisis was averted.

A barking black dog met the stage at Brorson's.

"Prince!" Bror stepped from his doorway and the barking ceased. I jumped down and unhitched the team, leading them to drink at the trough in the shade. White fluff from a cottonwood drifted across the top of the water. The horses seemed not to mind, burying their noses deeper into the water and drinking their fill. I reached in and skimmed a handful of the cottony wetness from the water and tossed it to the ground.

"Nice dog," I said.

"We'll see if he can keep the bear and deer out of the corn," he said. "It's tasseled out but no silk put on that I can see."

"Bears like corn?" I had never considered bears a threat to crops.

"*Ja,* they'll destroy the whole patch, sitting on the rows while they grab everything within their reach, pulling the roots right out of the ground."

"I'd think Prince could watch it for you," I said.

"*Ja,* at least give me warning so I can bring the gun."

"Any other critters bothering you?"

"A weasel in the hen house caused some trouble," Bror said. "Sucked the eggs dry and killed two hens before I got there. Prince's bark woke me before he got the whole flock. A few deer and a stray elk once in a while."

Sure enough, the dog barked loud and long in the middle of the night. I got up from my bed in the hayloft, looking out in the darkness to see what kind of critter it might be. A lamp glowed in the house.

"Go back to bed," Bror said. "I'll sit up for a while with my gun. Maybe I'll have fresh meat for the table."

A rifle shot woke me from just before dawn.

"Any luck?"

"We'll have fresh venison for breakfast."

His missus fried the heart along with a dozen eggs. She spoke of salting and smoking the meat, putting some away for the winter. As I got up to leave she went to the cupboard and took out a letter with a Mankato address.

"Would you post this for me?" she said. "I want my brother-in-law to know we're doing good."

"Did you tell him about my new pa?" Billy asked.

"Sure did," she said and looked at me and smiled. It lifted my heart.

We ate roasting ears, green corn from the fields not quite ready for harvest, at every stop on that trip to Fort Abercrombie. It tasted good, not sweet like some I'd had, but fresh and dripping with butter, sprinkled with salt. There were new potatoes and fresh green beans, too. At Big Barn Jensen's the missus fixed a kettle full of tasty beet greens. There was an air of expectancy, high hopes for a good harvest. Talk of the war was secondary to talk of weather and crops.

"What about the Indians?" asked Lars as we walked to the fence to watch the corn sway in the breeze. "Did they ever get paid?"

I thought about whether or not I should confide in him about the wagon of gold on the way to the Lower Reservation. News traveled fast, even in the frontier, and it might mean my job.

"Looks hopeful," I said. "The commander

at the fort said it should be coming any time."

The Minnesota evening embraced us as we stood at the fence, watching the sunset behind the waving corn tassels. The wheat field was a golden blanket spread over the side of a hill. Loons laughed from a nearby lake and nighthawks swooped and dived at the mosquitoes. Already there was a hint of fall in the air, just a little nip to remind us of the coming winter. Along with the relief from the heat was the release of the worry about the Dakota.

"I love it here." Lars chewed on a blade of grass. "Did you know that if you listen on a hot night you can actually hear the corn growing? It makes a gentle stretching sound all its own."

"The black dirt of Minnesota," I said, "better than all the soil of Norway."

"The dirt called out to me," he laughed, "all the way across the ocean, urging me to come and get rich."

We smiled at the simple thought. As if anything was simple anymore. We leaned on the fence with both arms and soaked in the quiet of the moment.

"Did I tell you my mor died?"

"*Nei,* when did this happen?" he asked.

"Earlier in the spring," I said. "I got a letter from my brother, Ole, with the sad news. She didn't suffer; just had a sharp headache in the morning and gone by night."

Lars rolled the snuff in his mouth and spit a brown stream over the fence into the cornfield. He seemed to weigh his words. "It's hard to be so far away."

"*Ja,* it's hard." No doubt flowers bloomed on her grave in the Norwegian churchyard.

It felt good to share the news. His mor lived across the water, too. He understood. I wished I could share how I felt about her death, how I felt rootless and cut off. But such things were not discussed. Good manners did not allow me to impose my grief on a friend.

"Any mail?" Anton Estvold hurried from the barn wiping his hands on the back of his trousers.

"A letter from one of your sons."

"Dagmar!" he called. "A letter!"

They took the letter and I unhitched the horses and led them to a shady spot at the edge of the yard. We sat in the shade of an oak tree and Anton read aloud.

July 3, 1862

Dear Mor and Far,

The battle is not going well. Just when we thought we had Richmond, Robert E. Lee counterattacked and outflanked us, pushing us back again. They're calling it the Seven Days' Battle since it lasted a whole week, night and day of bitter fighting. McClellan's army is in a bad way, needing more troops to replace the 16,000 dead from our side alone. The paper says the Rebs lost 20,000 men and I believe it. The dead were heaped in great piles, rotting in the hot sun, horrible beyond description. I fear the stench of rotting flesh will never leave me. I had thought the war would last only a short time, that I would be home by harvest to help get in the crops, but now I see that it is only just beginning and will be a long hard fight before we crush the rebels.

I am well. Last time I saw Ole he was well, too. No injuries or sickness to speak of although many in the outfit suffer with the "Virginia Trots." I keep with what Grandfather said about drinking only coffee and leaving the plain water alone. For some reason it has agreed with me and I have not been afflicted as the others. Ole has been sent with a different outfit. They left in the direction of Washington after the Battle of Shiloh. At least he was spared this last horrible battle. I hope he gets a good rest and can stay out of the heavy fighting for a good long time. This heat does not agree with him and he says he cannot wait for winter and a good snowstorm to cool down.

The gun is working well and I have all the ammunition I need. Last week we were issued new boots that were sorely needed. Mine were shredded to rags from walking. We are so often in swamps that the boots never have time to dry.

We have learned a new song written for the Federal soldiers. It is called, "The Battle Hymn of the Republic," and goes like this:

"Mine eyes have seen the glory of the coming of the Lord; He is trampling out the vintage where the grapes of wrath are stored; He has loosed the fateful lightning of his terrible swift sword; His truth is marching on. Glory, Glory, Hallelujah, His truth is marching on."

Mor, when we sing around the campfire at night, I remember home and family. If anything happens to me, remember my love. If I live through this war, I will name my first daughter after you in honor of my affection for you. Please keep praying for us. Only God can see us through this ordeal.

Your son,<br>Emil Estvold

Such grim news dampened conversation that night. I felt embarrassed to have heard such deep emotion from their son. Anton was unusually quiet and I knew he was filled with dread and worry for his sons so far away. At least they were still alive, or had been at the time the letter was written. Information from the front traveled so slowly it took weeks or months for the news about death or wounding to reach families.

The fresh straw in the haymow made a comfortable bed although the scurrying mice kept me awake for a little while. I wondered the tune for the song he had written about. All I could remember of the words was "glory, glory hallelujah." When I got to Fort Abercrombie, I would ask the soldiers to sing it for me.

# 18

"More Recruits Needed, General Pope
Guards Washington"
~ St. Paul Journal

Inga stood by the trail waiting for the stage. She wore a heavy shawl wrapped around her against the cool morning air. Her hair hung in two neat braids, almost to her waist, strands the color of new rope. My heart beat a little faster, and I pulled the stage to a stop beside her.

"Inga!" I felt like a complete fool and my face flushed.

I wanted to ask if Ericson was home. If he wasn't, I could stop and visit for a short while.

"I have a letter." She handed me a letter neatly addressed. "To my brother."

"It goes in the mail right now."

The horses startled, and I crooned to them in Norwegian. Inga looked at her shoes, then said in a halting voice, "Please don't speak of the letter to anyone. It might cause trouble for me." She fingered the corner of her shawl and pulled the fringe. "Mr. Ericson fears family in the old country might ask for money."

That blackheart! Stingy miser. Dirty dog. I forced my voice to be even. "It's no one else's business."

Her face relaxed. "I knew you'd understand."

I needed to be on my way. The horses were restless, and I was pressed for time. One thought demanded to be spoken.

"My mor died," I said. "My brother wrote me the news."

"I'm sorry to hear it."

"He said she didn't suffer."

Her eyes were liquid brown, soft with understanding. She reached up and touched my hand for a brief second, then turned and walked back to the house.

*"God dag!"*

She did not look back but waved over her shoulder, her shawl pulled tightly around her.

Lewis Peterson shoed a horse in the shade of an elm tree. Sweat poured down his back and made wet rivulets down his chambray shirt. Curse words streamed from his mouth as he struggled with the horse's hoof.

"Need some help?"

"*Ja,* before I shoot the beast."

I leaned my shoulder into the horse's flank on the opposite side of where Lewis struggled with a sweet yearling with gray spots and a white mane.

"She's a stout little filly," I said, "valuable with the war on."

"But stubborn as a Swede."

"Like all females." Lewis hooted and pounded a final nail into the hoof. He dropped the hoof and jumped out of the way as the horse crow hopped back into the barnyard.

"Have you found me a woman yet?" Lewis plopped down into the shade and wiped his face with a dry shirttail.

"Maybe," I said. "There's a nice girl who lives near Alexandria Woods, a neighbor to Lars Larson."

"Is she pretty?"

"Tilla Spitsberg is both pretty and from a good Norwegian family."

"If she's so pretty, why don't you want her?"

I chewed my lip. It was a risk to speak so plainly about how I felt but Lewis was a good friend and I decided to trust him.

"I will probably never marry." He looked at me strangely and I swallowed hard before speaking again. "I am in love with someone already taken."

Lewis said nothing. There was no answer to such a hopeless situation.

Over dinner, Lewis brought up the subject again. "How can I meet this Tilla Spitsberg?"

Solveig and Rasmuss met me at the barn door, Solveig's face crimson red and her hair littered with fresh straw. Rasmuss came out to care for the team.

"Any news?" said Rasmuss as he tucked in his shirt. He glanced at Solveig as she strode toward the house, still preoccupied with his bride by all indications.

"I heard a rumor about the Dakota payment, that it's coming soon."

"I've heard that before."

"This time it's more promising."

The horses drank long and deep. I petted and rubbed them with strands of fresh hay newly mounded by the barn. Rasmuss had been busy. We led them to the fenced corral where they rolled in the green grass. Rasmuss measured out a small portion of oats and dumped it in the feed trough. Only then did we turn toward the house.

Solveig fixed roasting ears from the field. The soddy was neat and orderly. Fisk slept calmly on a rug in the corner.

"How's the royal cat?"

"Caught his first mouse yesterday," Solveig said with pride. "It was almost as big as he is."

"He will be a good mouser," Rasmuss said and reached down to pet the sleeping cat.

The butter was excellent, and Solveig blushed when I mentioned it.

"I have a good woman to stand with me in the wilderness," Rasmuss said.

"Have you seen Bishop Whipple?" Solveig asked.

"*Nei,* he has been to the Lower Sioux Reservation, trying to smooth out the problems there."

"Be sure to greet Bishop Whipple from us and tell him we are doing well," Solveig said as she poured coffee from the gray pot.

"And tell him the wheat looks promising," added Rasmuss. "Our wheat, that is."

New recruits sweating in the August sun hardly looked up when I drove the stage into Fort Abercrombie. Of course, without a stockade around the buildings, it wasn't a very grand entrance.

"What's the news?"

"Lincoln fired McClellan as head of the federal troops." I tried to speak clearly without stuttering. "The newspaper said it took God seven days to create the earth and Robert E. Lee only seven days to push George McClellan out of Virginia."

"McClellan should be hung for treason!" called out a soldier in the crowd. "He had Lee cornered at Richmond. What was he waiting around for?"

"Who's taking over?"

"Lincoln promoted Henry Halleck," I said.

"Old Brains Halleck!" a soldier said. "It's a lost cause with him at the helm. He's worse than McClellan!"

"And General Pope defends Washington," I said. It was all I could remember from the newspaper.

I pushed through the muttering soldiers. Lord knows they had reason to complain. It was their necks being stretched. I brought the dispatch pouch into the office of Captain John Van Der Horck, the commander of the fort.

"Looks like you'll have plenty of wood for the winter," I said

"It keeps them busy and we can always use the wood. Maybe I'll have them build a stockade when the weather gets cooler." He sat in his chair and opened the pouch. "Any news on the Sioux payment?"

"It looks promising, sir."

He read the message from the pouch and I turned to leave.

"Looks like the gold will be there today or tomorrow," he said.

He took off his reading glasses and wiped his face with a clean handkerchief. His eyes met mine with a look of pure relief. Captain Van Der Horck looked more like a professor than commander of a frontier fort. He spoke with a German inflection that spoke of his European heritage. I wondered how he ended up in this desolate corner of the earth but didn't dare ask.

"Mr. Jacobson, there is to be a new treaty with the Pembina and Red Lake Chippewa bands. You can expect to meet thirty wagons and two hundred cattle heading west to Fort Abercrombie. I am to provide them escort to the treaty site, further north at the forks of the Red and Red Lake Rivers."

I thought of Crooked Lightning's opinion that the white people wanted to own the whole world. "You must be joking! What are they doing making more treaties when they can't keep the ones they've already made?" My voice was too loud and I knew I was out of line. The words hung on the sultry air.

Captain Van Der Horck looked up and words left his mouth, too. "It's madness."

We looked at each other in silence, helpless before the decisions of more powerful men, duty-bound to go along with it and keep our mouths shut. Captain Van Der Horck stood and stretched out a sweaty palm. We shook hands, an unspoken agreement to keep our conversation private.

"I'll pick up the courier pouch in the morning." I walked out into the blistering August heat cursing the federal government in spite of the Commandments.

The first hundred miles of the trip back to Fort Snelling was uneventful and I dozed in the box as I contemplated a hard truth. If there were no Indian treaties, there would be no land available for settlers. It was a cold fact and one I had to accept. I may not have wanted to own the whole world but I definitely wanted a piece of it. Maybe the new treaty was needed. Maybe it wasn't pure foolishness after all.

I met the cattle and wagons heading to Fort Abercrombie just as Van Der Horck said, met them just west of Pomme de Terre. The cattle were made gaunt by the heat, tongues hanging out of the corners of their mouths, hides covered with cockleburs. I wondered how they would ever make it so far north; Fort Abercrombie was only half way to their intended treaty spot. The men driving the cattle were a surly lot, no doubt plagued by the heat and mosquitoes and the herd of unruly cows. A cow is a dumb animal, as any farm boy could tell you, always looking for escape and often finding it.

I asked them for news of the Rebellion but got little more than a nod and a grunt. There was no clear leader that I could tell. I swerved off the trail to go around them rather than waste time waiting for them to pass. The trail was filled with cow pies and mud holes from the cattle's hooves. A curse slipped past my lips. Mor wouldn't have liked it, and I vowed to quit swearing.

Minnesota was in full harvest. Meals along the route became sparse and haphazard because the men, women and children were busy in the fields. Wheat shone golden in the August sun, heads bowing down under the weight of grain. There would be flour and grain to feed families and livestock, and garden produce to fill root cellars and winter bellies. It was a happy labor, their reward for work and worry.

Hjalmer Thoreson was jovial when we met

west of Sauk Centre. We pulled up beside each other on the trail. The teams chewed tall grass within their reach.

"How is the world treating you, my friend?"

"Not so bad. And you?"

"Couldn't be better," he said. "Had a letter from my brother in Norway. He's coming to join me after fall harvest."

A stab of quick envy pierced me but I shoved it down. Of course I would rejoice in my friend's good news. "You lucky dog!"

"Luck didn't have much to do with it," he said. "I sent him the ticket and he's glad to leave the fishing boat."

The horses stomped and flexed their ears to shoo pesky flies, stomped their feet and swished long tails. We loosed the reign to allow them to reach more grass and continued our conversation. I told him about the soldiers and cattle heading toward Pembina.

"No wonder the trail is full of flies and manure." He spit a stream of brown tobacco juice into a swarm of flies on a cow pie. If he disapproved of the treaty, he didn't mention it.

"You heard about the Sioux payments?"

"*Ja*, the army rests easy. I figured the gold must be on the way."

"I heard it from Captain Van Der Horck

in Abercrombie," I said. "The gold should be there by now."

"Thank God. All we needed was another war."

"The settlers can harvest in peace."

Talk turned to weather and crops and prices in St. Paul. Without even a good-bye, we both started back on the trail, the horses anxious to be on their way, mail to be delivered and a schedule to keep.

# 19

"Serious Outbreak of the Sioux Indians"
~ St. Paul Journal

The first hint of trouble came at Cold Spring. Bror Brorson pulled me aside after the horses were watered. I noticed his fidgety hands and troubled eyes but I also noticed something else. His hair, clothes, fingernails, and everything about him was clean. Marriage suited the man, that's for sure.

"Prince barked during the early morning, just before the sunup. Thinking it was a bear, I came out with the gun." There was a look of fear on his face and he spoke rapidly in Norwegian. "It wasn't a varmint but two Indians slinking around the horse pen." He picked up the harness from the ground and carefully wound it around his arm into a neat spiral before hanging it on the fence post. "There may have been more but I saw only two of them."

"Sioux?"

"I couldn't tell in the dark, but it's too far south for the Chippewa unless they're on a raiding party."

Crooked Lightning's words jolted back to memory, how I needed to keep alert.

"I pretended it was a bear and called to the dog and shot the gun up in the air, hoping it would scare them away. It did. I stayed close by the barn the rest of the night keeping watch."

"That was smart. If you had challenged them, who knows what might have happened."

"All I could think of was Sadie and the young ones. I didn't care about the horses or anything else." His voice cracked. "I haven't told them — don't want to frighten them."

"Good thing you have the dog."

"Prince is worthy of a meaty bone." He bent over and rubbed the dog's head, patting it's neck. "Good boy."

My mind swirled with questions. The trouble should be over. What if the gold had been stolen or delayed?

"I'm worried," he said. "I'll have to keep watch."

"How can you stay awake all night and

work your harvest during the day?"

"Billy ran to the neighbors for one of their boys to come and help," he said. "We'll have to take turns keeping watch."

It would be disastrous if the Indians were to steal the stage teams. I'd heard they abused horses, ran them to the ground and ate them. The responsibility of their value staggered me. Surely the army couldn't expect me to protect them from the Dakota.

We had just started eating when Billy rushed in and collapsed in a heap on the kitchen floor. He was pale and for once, speechless.

"Billy!" demanded his mother. "What's wrong?"

Billy gulped and gasped, unable to say a word. Tears flowed down his face and his nose ran, choking him even more.

"It's all right, Billy," said Bror and scooped him up into his arms and held him like a baby. "You're home now."

Billy quieted and between gulps and sobs told of finding the neighbors' house burned down.

"Fire's still warm. No one around. Chickens hacked to pieces and left in the grass, and an arrow through the milk cow."

Bror's face hardened. "Are you sure it was an arrow?"

"An arrow with blue and green feathers. It's legs stuck out funny," he said. "Flies crawled on her eyes."

Bishop Whipple's words echoed in my brain and I spoke aloud.

"Gather your family and livestock and head for shelter until we find out what is going on." I spoke in Norwegian so as not to alarm the missus. "It's not safe here."

Bror looked up in surprise but didn't question my command. I could almost hear him measuring his crop in the field, weighing the risk.

"Where is the strongest building?"

"I guess it would be the Roman Church."

"Then go there and spread the word. We need to find out what happened."

I pushed away from the table. It didn't matter the food was left untouched. All I could think of was Crooked Lightning's warning.

"It's war."

"What makes you say that?" Bror stared dumbly, unable to grasp the situation.

"Let's hope I'm wrong," I said. "We should err on the side of caution. If nothing comes of it we can laugh about it later."

Bror looked at his family around the table. "I have too much at stake to risk it."

We heard the church bells ringing before

we reached the church.

"It's not time for mass," said the missus. "Why are they ringing the bells?"

I drove the stage with the extra team tied to the back of the coach. I couldn't leave the horses to the mercy of the Indians. Bror brought his horses and brindle milk cow.

Other families were there, milling around the yard amongst children, cattle, and horses. A rooster and three hens scratched in the dirt. A cluster of people stood on the top step going into the church, one pulling the rope and ringing the bell. Two were dressed in clerical robes.

"It's trouble," Bror said. "Good God."

The older priest's robes ruffled in the breeze as he clapped his hands for attention. The bells grew silent. "Father Michaels comes with a warning of Indian trouble."

A younger priest stood beside him with muddy vestments and a face haggard and worn. "Brothers and Sisters," Father Michaels said. "God spared my life and gave me strength to bring warning of an Indian uprising."

A murmur of voices almost drowned his words and the local priest rang the bell once more to restore order. "Let him speak!"

"Acton. In Meeker County." His voice barely a hoarse whisper. "Near Grove City, not far from Kandiyohi County."

A woman brought him a gourd of water, and he paused to drink before speaking again. "The Sioux raided two farms, killing five people. Children. One woman survived by hiding in the basement with her baby. Said they walked in friendly and without warning began killing."

Father Michaels's voice broke and he struggled to regain his composure, steadying himself on the railing, "I knew the victims. I baptized the children."

We stood, stunned at his words. Had the rebels stolen the gold? What part did Crooked Lightning have in the raids? Surely he couldn't hurt innocent women and children.

"We thought it a renegade raid, an isolated fluke," he said. "But a large war party attacked the Lower Agency. Led by Chief Little Crow."

"When did it happen?" Bror's voice startled me, so close beside me.

"August 18th," said Father Michaels, "they slaughtered every man they could get their hands on and took the women and children captive. They cleaned out the storehouse. I was lucky to escape with my life."

"Where's the army?"

"I ran to Fort Ridgley with warning," he said. "Captain Marsh tried to rescue the captives." The priest took a deep breath before he continued. "Over half of his command was killed. More than 200 soldiers."

Low murmurings swept through the crowd. A baby cried and a calf bawled for his mother. *My God. What could we do?*

"John Other Day, a Christian Dakota, rescued many whites. He told me the Dakota are raiding all along the Minnesota and Cottonwood rivers. He says they will not stop until every white has left Minnesota," said Father Michaels, "or is killed."

"They'll scalp us all!" a woman shrieked and small children wailed in terror. I quieted the team, rubbing their noses and crooning to them in whispers.

"God sent me with this warning," Father Michael said. "Gather together to defend yourselves. It is not safe on your farms." He clutched the hitching rail, wobbling as if he might faint.

"But our crops!"

"We'll lose everything."

We all stood there, anxious and afraid, not knowing what to do next.

"Come pray for the souls of the dead and for those taken captive," Father Nagel, the local priest said. "We will ask God for protection and guidance." His face was grim. "The Holy Angels will defend us."

One by one the people entered the church until only a few of us remained outside.

"We will go to the Ingalls' cabin and see for ourselves," Bror spoke in English, taking charge in a firm voice.

Several of us mounted horses and rode warily out to the homestead. It was getting later in the afternoon, and I worried we would be left in the dark, that the Indians would still be around. I carried the cumbersome Danzig shotgun and was thankful for its heft as I rode on Betty's broad back. The cabin still smoked and the cow laid on its side with arrows in it. Billy was right; the feathers were blue and green. A sickening smell filled the air, the smell of death.

Bror stepped into in the smoldering ruins of their cabin and exited with a grim look. "It's Ingalls, scalped and with an arrow in his back." Bror leaned to the side and puked in the bushes. Not a man blamed him. I breathed a silent prayer of thanks for the good dog who saved Bror and his family from the same fate.

Another man returned from the stable. Made of green timber, it only partially burned. "Come," he said grimly and led us into the barn where the bodies of the missus and two girls lay on the floor. Their clothes were ripped off and scattered around them. I kicked away an apron lying in my path, revealing blood and gore swarming with flies. I stifled a scream. Their scalps were gone and their faces grotesquely carved leaving their mouths slit from ear to ear. The girls were no older than Christina had been. No older than Tilla Spitsberg. My stomach turned over to realize what they had endured.

"Good God!" said Bror. "To think Billy might have seen this."

No one answered. We continued our search in silence, knowing the family had two boys. We found them in the grove beyond the cornfield. Both dead and mutilated, their privates stuffed in their mouths. They couldn't have been more than fifteen or sixteen years old.

As if reading my mind, one of the men said, "Their father thought they were too young to go to war, said they would stay home where it was safe."

We carried their broken bodies back to the barn. Bror took a shovel from the ashes and began digging graves in the cow yard. We all pitched in and buried those poor folks where we found them, the stench of burning flesh choking us, the bile rising in our throats.

"We'll ask the priest to come out later and say prayers over them," Bror said and leaned the shovel up against a post in the yard. We mounted our horses and began our journey back to the Roman Church in the deepening twilight. "I was a fool to send Billy alone," Bror said as we rode. "He could have come upon them, could have been killed."

Maybe Indians were still around, maybe they watched from across the field hoping to ambush us along the road. Others in the group must have feared the same for I noticed them probing the bushes and trees with anxious eyes. Our ride took forever, but in truth it couldn't have been more than thirty minutes. More settlers were at the church when we arrived. Bror spoke to Father Nagel, telling him the news about the Ingalls family.

Another fear plagued me. All my life I had been warned of the danger of entering a Roman Church where people prayed to idols and blindly obeyed the pope. Fear rose up within me as I entered the doors of the church, almost as great as my terror of the Indians. Sure enough, there was a fount of Holy Water by the door, something labeled pure superstition by Martin Luther. Plaster saints graced the walls and kneeling benches were there for folks to pray for the souls of the dead. It was all I had been warned against. But in spite of my fears, I couldn't help but recognize a calming presence in the building. Maybe it was the hum of people praying; maybe it was the Holy Angels. Whatever the reason, I found a spot near the door beneath the urn of Holy Water where I couldn't see the idols, and leaned my head against the wall.

My duty to Fort Snelling was clear. It was my job to return the dispatch pouch as soon as possible. But the settlers on the frontier were helpless. Who would warn them? I pictured Lars' daughters chasing fireflies and his missus gathering eggs. Solveig and Rasmuss would be harvesting their oats. My throat closed when I thought of Inga alone so much of the time.

Near exhaustion, I drifted into a fitful sleep. I dreamed of picking loudberries with Christina back home on our mountain. In my dream Mor came toward us, laughing and telling us that we needn't be afraid of either bears or trolls.

# 20

"The Indian Disturbance,
Rumors or Fact?"
~ St. Paul Journal

I made my decision. Common sense told me head to Fort Snelling as fast as the team could go. But I felt a responsibility to the settlers on the frontier. Bishop Whipple had urged me to warn the settlers if something happened. Mor was gone, Inga was married, and nothing held me to this world. I would risk the danger for my friends. If I lost my job, so be it. I could always enlist.

Father Nagel prayed a blessing over me before I left. He didn't ask my permission, just began praying, asking God to keep me safe and to guide me to those who needed my help. Tears blinded my eyes and I looked away so he wouldn't see them. It was probably the first prayer said for me since Mor's death. Maybe it would be the last prayer said for me.

Bror grasped my hand. "I'll go with you."

"*Nei,* your family has need of you. I'll make a quick trip of it." I climbed the stage box and gathered the reins. "Maybe the alarm is exaggerated. Perhaps we worry for nothing."

"We'll send one of the single men to St. Cloud with the news of the Ingalls massacre," Father Nagel said. "They will pass the word to Fort Snelling."

"Tell them I have returned to warn Fort Abercrombie."

My favorite team was hitched to the stage, the ones named after my brothers. I had great confidence in their ability and devotion but had less confidence in the team tied behind the stage — the one I had driven yesterday. It included Betty, the mare prone to stumbles. I could only hope I wouldn't need to use her, that the way stations would be untouched by the Indians, and I could switch teams as usual.

The land seemed untroubled. As I traveled the well-worn trail, I tried to remember prayers or verses from Catechism and recited them aloud. The team did not object and the words pushed the faces of the Ingalls family out of my mind.

Carl Evenson's corn was lush and beautiful and wheat the color of Solveig's hair leaned so heavy to it almost rested on the ground.

"Carl! Anyone home?" I looked toward the grove of trees behind the house, half expecting a horde of Indians to come shrieking out at my call. No one answered my knock at the door. A quick inspection showed the house empty. Breakfast was left half eaten on the table. The gun usually hanging on pegs over the door was gone. I forced myself to check the barn, remembering too vividly the day before. The animals were gone and the replacement team was nowhere in sight.

They must have been warned. There were no mutilated bodies, no dead animals, and no burned buildings. The Dakota had not been there — at least not yet.

A sudden chill traveled my spine, and my face dripped sweat. I ran to the stage and climbed the box, placing the Danzig in the empty seat at my side. The horses responded, and we flew down the trail. This team could go further, would go as far as I asked. "I believe in God the Father Almighty, maker of heaven and earth," I recited in a quiet voice interrupted only by the need to spit over the side of the stage. "And in Jesus Christ His only Son our

Lord . . ."

I abused the team, running them hard in my panic. Sanity returned a few miles down the trail, and I slowed to a walk. The horses puffed and blowed, exhausted by the harsh treatment.

"Forgive me, brothers, the faces of those girls torment me. In a different circumstance, one of them could have been our sister, Christina. No woman should be forced to endure such violence. For the first time I thank God she is dead. It is better she sleeps with you in the churchyard, waiting for the trumpet call to raise the quick and the dead."

The horses accepted my apology quietly and continued to pull. A horse tied to the back of the stage whinnied a complaint.

"*Ja,* and the same to you. You deserve better than a lunatic driver racing away from trolls."

The Schwarz cabin was burned to the ground. The sickening sweet smell of burning flesh caused me to investigate further. My heart beat so loudly I was afraid any Indians lurking nearby could hear it, but I forced myself to walk among the smoldering frame. A charred body lay among the timbers but I did not try to identify it or

278

stop to bury it. Nobody else, living or dead, was found on the place. All the animals were missing, including the replacement team.

Lost. Too late. I watered the horses at the watering trough. They were skittish, smelling the smoky ruins, the smell of death. Their eyes looked wildly side-to-side as they tossed their heads snorted and stomped.

"Whoa, whoa," I crooned. "It's all right. They're gone now."

It was late but I couldn't stay there. The horses needed rest, and darkness would soon make the trail even more treacherous. The small settlement of Sauk Centre was only a few miles away. Hopefully I could find it in the dark.

My mind raced. Perhaps I was incapable of making good decisions in my terror. Maybe the Indians were watching, hoping I'd turn on the Sauk Centre road so they could ambush me. The smell of the burning body helped me make the decision. I could not sleep in its presence. It was too dark to go much farther. I would find Sauk Centre.

How foolish to leave a burning candle in the window. Scarcely a mile from the Schwarz farm, I found a small cabin nestled in a hillside. I pulled the reins and stopped as close to the house as I could get and called out in English.

"Anybody here?"

A woman's voice replied in Norwegian, "Who is it?"

"Evan Jacobson." What a relief to speak the language of my homeland. "I'm the stagecoach driver. Just looking for shelter."

Something heavy was dragged away from the door before it opened to reveal a woman dressed in a ragged dress clutching a small baby. She looked near collapse, and I jumped down to assist her with the child.

"Thank God you've come. I've been praying all day someone would come." Sobs overwhelmed her and she wept uncontrollably.

The situation was critical. I swept my eyes around the yard. No sign of Indians. A small barn stood close to the cabin, built into the hillside.

"Missus, we need to get inside and blow out the light. I saw it from a distance and it isn't safe."

She took the baby and went into the cabin where she blew out the candle.

"I'll put the horses in your barn."

She nodded numbly without speaking, standing with the baby in her arms.

The barn was close to the house and without windows. It stood empty of any animals and was as good a place as any to hide the horses overnight. I pushed the stage behind some bushes beside the house. It was a perfect place to conceal the coach; also a perfect place for Indians to wait in ambush. With the Danzig in one hand I threw the horses some grain and rubbed them down with a dry sack found in the barn. There was water in the trough, thank God.

The missus wasn't alone, as I had first thought. Dragged into the kitchen were the bodies of her man and oldest son. She had carefully laid them out, side by side, next to the wall on the dirt floor. They were covered with a wool blanket and flies buzzed around them.

"Yesterday, just as night was falling, I heard some commotion outside the cabin," she said in a flat voice, still standing by the table holding the baby. "It sounded like the shrieks of devils." The darkness was thick and I could no longer see her face. "I peeked through the shutter and saw my man fall on his face with an arrow in his back. A savage with a face painted half black and half green came out of the bushes with a hatchet and took his scalp." She shifted the baby in her arms and patted its back. "He and the boys had been out harvesting the back forty. The girls picked hazelnuts behind the pigpen. It was almost time for supper and I had potato soup ready on the stove." Her voice drifted away and I asked her to sit down, to put the baby in the cradle. She obeyed.

"I dragged all the furniture in front of the door to keep the heathen out." She rocked the cradle with her foot while she talked. "When the commotion ended, I left the baby and crawled out the window to find my children. I stumbled onto Olaf's body by the barn. I dragged him inside, but it was too late."

I willed myself to listen. All I wanted was to get away, to run as fast as I could away from this nightmare that was real. My breath came in great gulps, and my heart pounded a steady tattoo in my ribs. *Dear God, help me.*

"I couldn't find my other boy, didn't dare go as far as the field. The girls were gone. I called for them but heard the baby crying." Her voice had a keening edge that reminded me of the arctic wind howling around the eaves of our Sonmorgaard house. A shiver went through me and I hunched my shoulders against it. "The Indians might come back if they heard him cry. I nursed the baby then dragged my man into the house. There was nothing else I could do."

Only the crickets outside the window made noise as we sat in silence. My heart still pounded and I hoped with all my might that Inga wasn't alone in her cabin, hoped she was still alive.

"Olaf's only fifteen, too young to join the army though he's had nothing else on his mind for months. Why would they kill a boy?" She abruptly stood up and rocked the cradle back and forth though the baby slept.

I mumbled something about being sorry for her loss. It seemed to satisfy her and she continued her story.

"I took the baby and left the cabin, thinking to search for Emil and the girls on my way to Sauk Centre. Maybe they got away. Maybe someone had driven by in a carriage and picked them up." She rocked the cradle so hard I feared she'd wake the baby. Rocked it back and forth — if it were a butter churn she'd have butter by now. "I knew the way and walked all night. The mosquitoes were bad, and my skirts kept catching on brush and branches. I was afraid I might hurt the baby if I fell and tried to be careful. Kept going as best I could; feeling my way in the darkness, praying with every step."

She left the cradle and paced back and forth in the small cabin and then went back to the cradle to adjust the blankets covering her son. "It shouldn't have taken me that long and I was glad to see smoke coming out of a chimney just as morning broke. But the hand of God was heavy on me. I must have gone in a big circle for I was back here at my own cabin, seeing the wisps of smoke left from cooking the potato soup." Her voice grew hysterical, and I strained to hear her words. "Then I knew I was being punished for my sins. I can't escape the judgment of God. My man and son are dead. The others lost." The sobs started again, "I prayed all day."

The dead were beginning to outnumber the living. I begged her to lie down and rest but she refused, saying her children might call for her. We dragged the furniture back in front of the door. She stood watch while I lay down to sleep. I was too tired to eat although my stomach rumbled. The potato soup would still be on the stove in the morning.

"Wake me if you hear anything," I told her. "Keep an eye on the barn. If they get the horses I don't know what we'll do."

The sunshine streaming in the east window woke me in the morning.

"Come with me." I wanted to take advantage of every ray of light.

"*Nei,* I cannot leave. What if the girls come back? What if Emil needs me?"

She was near the end of her rope. She couldn't continue in this state. Somehow the few hours of sleep had refreshed me and I felt hungry. I ate cold potato soup greedily, ashamed of my appetite in the presence of the dead.

"We'll look for Emil and the girls," I said carefully. "What if I find them and it's too far for them to walk back to you? It would be better to have you with me."

"Maybe you're right," she said and reluctantly pulled a shawl from behind the door and wrapped it around the baby. "But what of Oscar and Olaf? They'll feel cold here on the floor without a fire in the stove."

Her eyes had a hollow look to them. Maybe she was mad. Maybe she would become violent.

"I will help you bury them before we go," I said reluctantly. I'm ashamed to admit I had hoped to leave them there on the cabin floor. They deserved better.

We dug a shallow grave in the garden where the soil was softer. I steeled myself, dragging the bodies from the house. I tried not to look at them, to hold my breath until it was over but I failed at both attempts.

They reeked of death and blood. The blanket slipped away, and once again I faced the horror. How blessed Christina had been to die quietly in bed — I never realized the blessing of it before. I thanked God for letting Mor die quietly in her homeland, without seeing the heathen faces painted for war. My heart started its wild beating again. "Our Father, which art in heaven. Hallowed be Thy name." The first scoop of earth covered their faces and hid the worst. "Thy kingdom come. Thy will be done." The dirt rained upon the bodies in a steady stream. "On earth as it is in heaven . . ."

She helped me hitch the team. Against my better judgment I harnessed the replacement team. The other team needed a reprieve from the heavy haul.

Although no Indians were in sight I felt their eyes upon me. I felt them looking at me, lusting after my team, my scalp. "I believe in the Holy Ghost, the Holy Christian Church, the Communion of Saints, the resurrection of the body . . ."

I hoped to leave the woman, I never asked her name, with Big Barn Jensen. His missus would care for them. A continuous litany was on my tongue. "Oh, God. Oh, God." I felt He understood and heard me for we reached Big Barn's place without incident.

I saw the small cabin standing before I noticed the barn was gone. Only the stone foundation remained built into the hillside. It was too quiet. I led the horses to the watering trough and looked around, relieved to find no sign of Indians. The woman waited beside the trough with her young one, and I took the Danzig and headed to the house. I had reason to dread such investigations.

"Anyone home?" I called.

There was no answer. I boldly opened the door. The house was vandalized. Feather beds and pillows ripped and scattered, tables chopped and broken, books ripped to shreds, clothing torn. The wooden butter bowl broken into pieces. I blew a feather away from my nose and searched the loft. I let out a sigh of relief. They must have gotten warning.

There was no sign of horses or animals. I hoped Big Barn was able to save his herd. Next to his barn, they were his most valued possession.

I drank from the trough with the horses and watched the woman go back into the coach to nurse her baby. If she didn't eat soon, there would be no milk for the baby. It was as if I could feel my body aging, my hair turning gray. Numbness settled in. I couldn't recall Mor's face or Christina's middle name. I tried to remember what Bror said about sending a messenger to Fort Snelling. As I climbed back into the box I began again, "from thence He shall come to judge the quick and the dead . . ."

We hardly left Big Barn's when we met a wagon coming toward us on the trail. I strained my eyes to see if it was Indians or whites. The driver was a man dressed in the crude homespun of the settlers, wearing a straw hat. There were a dozen children, two or three exhausted women and one older man sitting in dazed confusion. I pulled the stage to a stop and waited for him to draw up beside me.

"Hey, there!" he said. "Have you heard about the Injun raids?"

"*Ja,*" I said. "I'm trying to warn the settlers. A priest from the Minnesota River Valley brings word of a widespread Dakota uprising. I saw for myself a family murdered by the Dakota not far from Cold Spring."

The man got down from the wagon and came over to the stage. His hands trembled and his eyes kept darting from side to side as if he were afraid the Indians would attack at any moment.

"The Indians have gone crazy," he said in a quiet voice so as not to alarm his passengers. "Killing, burning, butchering. I have a woman here whose little baby was burned alive by the savages. Just threw the baby in the oven and listened to the screams. Made the mother watch."

"My God," I thought of Baby Evan.

"She was baking bread and offered them a slice. Instead they grabbed her baby and threw it in the oven. It makes no sense."

"Dear God." I had no other words.

"I've been picking up survivors, heading toward Sauk Centre." He dipped his head toward the wagon box.

I wondered which woman had lost her baby.

"The raids are patchy around here, some places left untouched. Every horse stolen by the bastards, though. They're great on horse stealing."

"There's a woman and baby in the coach from near Sauk Centre, not too far away from the river crossing," I said.

Betty was straining away from the team, trying to nip the horses pulling the other wagon. I pulled her rein and spoke to her sharply.

"Could they travel with you to Sauk Centre?" I said. "She's looking for lost children."

His wagon was full; I could see him hesitate. Suddenly from the coach came a shriek. I grabbed my Danzig, ready to fight.

"Katrina! Marit!" the woman from the stage called and fumbled with the door before falling out onto the ground. She still held the baby and scrambled to her feet, running to the other wagon.

"Thank God it is you! Katrina! Marit! Thank God, thank God!"

Two little girls with matted hair and torn clothes crawled out of the wagon box.

"Mor! We thought we'd never find you!" the oldest said.

"The Indians took our hazelnuts," said the younger.

They hugged over and over until the poor baby crushed between their embraces finally let out a howl that squelched the reunion.

The woman looked in the wagon. "Where's Emil? Have you seen your brother?"

The girls looked at each other and shook their heads.

"The Indians dragged us away. Said if we didn't run, they'd kill us." The older girl's lip quivered. "They camped by a stream and built a fire. Had a bottle of whiskey. We ran away when they got drunk and sleepy. This man found us."

"Thank God! Thank God!" The woman clutched her children. "But where is Emil?"

The girls started crying again and soon they all sobbed, even the others in the wagon. I felt like crying myself.

"I'll take them with me," the other driver said with a loud sniff as he wiped his nose on his sleeve. "Someone will know how to help them."

*"Mange takk!"* I said. "It's a dangerous ride I have ahead of me and I'd rather do it alone." I lowered my voice so as not to alarm the others. "I found a body at Wilhelm Schwarz's, neighbor to this woman. Needs burying. Could you pass the word on to the settlers at Sauk Centre?"

"Consider it done. Any white person deserves a decent funeral. As for the Injuns, they should be killed like rats in a corncrib."

I couldn't blame him for his hatred. We talked a little more about where the raids had taken place, where the roads were safe.

"Nowhere is safe," he said. "Where's the army? Don't they know how it is out here?"

"They should know by now. A messenger left Cold Spring yesterday."

"There'll be hell to pay if they don't come soon."

It felt like the day would never end. I tried to hurry the horses, but they were spent. Betty stumbled once, and I worried she might have damaged herself for good. The thought passed through my mind that I should cut her loose from the other horses and travel without her.

There seemed to be less damage as I headed into Douglas County. Thank God, I found no dazed survivors or burning buildings. I let myself think about reaching the home of Lars and his missus, how there would be decent food to eat and a clean bed, a fresh team. I saw a column of dark smoke in the distance and quickened the pace of the team.

Smoke billowed against the summer sunset. I left the stage at the end of their lane and ran blindly up to the burning cabin, not thinking to use caution. The body of the missus lay in a pool of blood, her scalped head several feet away. Blank eyes stared beneath the folds of skin, her mouth open in a silent scream. The least one, only a few months old and named for me, was nailed to the cabin door, his head flat on the right side. Lars's body lay face down in the grass, seven arrows in his back. Though I called their names, Ragna and Borghilde were not to be found.

"Oh God! Oh God!" I chanted over and over, as I ran from one corpse to the other. I searched the barn, or what was left of it, dreading the thought of finding the missing girls, worried I wouldn't find them. "Oh God, oh God! Spare the girls, oh God, spare the girls." There was no sign of anyone.

Common sense pulled me to a halt. The Indians might come back, might still be in the area. The fire was burning hard; I needed to get out.

But I couldn't leave the bodies where they lay. Lars was like a brother to me. He and his missus asked me to Godfather their son. There was no one else to do it.

I dragged Lars to the grave first, breaking off the arrows so he would sleep in peace. I choked back the nausea, tried to fix my mind on something else but when I picked up the head of the missus, I couldn't help but puke my guts out. It felt so light in my hands, so empty. To this day I feel the weight of her head in my hands just thinking about it.

Try as I might, I couldn't force myself to pry little Evan off the door of the house. Of all of them, he was the most innocent, most worthy of a decent burial but I failed miserably, leaving him nailed to the burning door.

"Forgive me, Lars, for failing your son. I am a coward, unworthy of being his God-father. I promise before God that if I find your girls, I will help them." I covered Lars and his missus with the good black dirt of

Minnesota. The same dirt attracted them like a magnet from across the ocean to this place where dreams were possible. I cursed the Dakota who did such a cruel thing. I cursed the good black dirt of Minnesota. Then I cursed the dream that brought them here, falling on the fresh grave and crying as if I'd never stop.

# 21

"Frontier Devastated, Inhabitants
Murdered, Shocking Barbarities"
~ St. Paul Journal

The Indians couldn't be far away. The trail was too dangerous to navigate in the darkness. I couldn't stay there and I couldn't leave. Hysteria rose in my chest and I began again, "Our Father . . ." When I stopped the prayers, the smells and faces of the dead overwhelmed me. "Who art in heaven. Hallowed be Thy Name. Thy kingdom come."

Suddenly I remembered a turn in the trail, not far from Lars's cornfield. There was a small slough and a sheltered place behind a grove of trees. The horses could drink from the slough and I could hide in the grove until daybreak. The horses were exhausted and skittish, needing care and rest. I crooned to them in Norwegian, urging them on, promising them the world if they would pull the stage to the hiding place. Somehow we made it, although clouds darkened the moon and a million far away stars did little to guide us.

I hoped to warn settlers, to spare them from massacre. Instead I was a burial party of one, warning no one, arriving too late. How foolish I felt, charging off across the frontier trying to be a hero. Far always warned me not to think myself better than anyone else. Maybe that was my sin; I thought myself better than others, more capable, more heroic. So far I had failed miserably.

Olaus Reierson sat at his treadle grinding stone, sharpening his scythe. The tears flowed when I saw him alive in his normal routine, the buildings intact.

Words escaped me. I stopped the stage and almost fell out of the box, landing on the ground where I sat, dazed and starving, giddy with relief.

"Good God, Evan!" he said. "What's wrong? Are you sick?"

*"Nei,"* I pulled his face down to mine. "Indians." My parched lips barely formed the words. "Indians raising hell all over."

He helped me to his cabin and gave me a hot cup of coffee. The scalding brew revived

me, and I gobbled bread and milk while
Olaus cared for the team. They deserved
royal treatment after their long journey and
I hoped he had oats for them. I was afraid
to take my eyes off the horses, fearing
Indians might snatch them away.

"Are you feeling better?"

"I need to be on my way again . . . to warn
the settlers."

Quickly I told him about the raids, the
violence I had witnessed. If he was shocked
or alarmed, he didn't show it.

"You need rest. You'll be safe here in the
soddy — it don't burn so easy as cabins,
you know. We have no babies to bake or
women to rape. If they want us they'll have
to face our guns."

"Have you seen any Indians?"

"The dirty devils stole every horse on the
place. I spied them as they rode off, took a
shot but missed." He spat tobacco juice out
the door. "I couldn't give chase without a
horse to ride."

"When was that?"

"Night before last. The rooster crowed
and it was still dark. Knew something was
wrong so took my gun for a look."

"You're a lucky man."

"No red devil will chase me off this place."
He pounded his fist on the table, causing

my spoon to bounce to the floor. "I've worked too hard to give it up because of them bastards."

"Come with me to the fort where it is safe," I said.

"I won't give up!"

"Not forever, Olaus, just until the trouble is over."

He finally agreed it was the sensible thing to do. I was relieved. In truth, I was afraid to go alone. We decided to stay in the soddy until morning.

As I drifted off to sleep that sunny afternoon, I thought about Inga. She was probably harvesting the grain. I imagined her hair hanging down in two braids like a young girl.

The next thing I knew Olaus shook me awake and told me it was time to get up. We drank coffee and boiled up the last of the eggs. He had a kettle filled with clean water to bring along.

"Good thing you have that iron cover for it," I said, "otherwise the stage would jolt every drop out before we could drink it."

"I won't be left without food or drink." He picked up the basket of eggs.

We hitched the team named after my brothers to the stage and tied Betty's team behind it. Olaus sat beside me in the box, gun in hand.

"I'm glad I didn't get around to building a better cabin," he said as we started down the road. "That soddy will still be standing when I come back in spite of the Red Men."

Sleeping at Reierson's, usually a noon stop, set me off sequence. In my mind I planned how I would stop at Pomme de Terre for noon break and stay with Lewis Peterson that night. I hoped there would be a fresh team somewhere. The horses weren't quite as peppy, a little slower to respond to my commands. But God! What horses! Tears welled in my eyes when I considered their devotion, and I shook my head so Olaus wouldn't see. I was turning into a sissy, tears and emotion overwhelming my better judgment.

Olaus wanted to talk. I didn't. He prattled on about the Indians, how he heard drums in the woods one night.

"The Chippewa sometimes drum and dance in the woods," he said. "I've heard drums before but none like the other night. My skin crawled."

"What makes the Indians so brutal? So violent?" I asked. "Why would they target innocent women and children?"

"They're inhuman."

"Even if their cause is just," I said, "they

have no reason to harm innocents. Their argument is with the government; they should fight the army — not women and children."

There was no answer.

"We can stay in the fortifications if trouble comes," Anton Estvold said later that day as we ate our dinner.

I urged him and his missus to come with us to Fort Abercrombie. Like at Reierson's, the horses had been driven off a few days ago.

"The old fortifications still stand, and we can bolster them if need be."

"But there's safety at the fort," I said.

Anton looked at me with disbelief. "Do you think those few green soldiers can stop the Sioux Nation?"

He was right. I was on a wild goose chase from which I couldn't hope to return. It was insanity to think the fort would hold.

When it was time to go, Olaus pulled me aside. "I'm not going with you. I'll stay here at Pomme de Terre and take my chances closer to home."

I'll admit it was a blow. Just his presence soothed my terror, helped hold down the hysteria that welled up inside of me when I least expected it.

"It's up to you." I shook his burly hand. "I wish you luck."

The stagecoach turned into her homestead almost without my help, as if it knew the way on its own. Maybe she hadn't heard the news, didn't know the Dakota were at war. I couldn't live with myself if she ended up like the Larson woman, lying dead on the grass with her brains bashed in.

I flicked the reins and pulled up by the house. The window sparkled in the sunshine. Cattle grazed next to the barn. How peaceful it looked. I shook my head to be rid of the image of the Larson's cabin on fire and jumped down from the driver's seat. Softly whistling, I soothed the lead horse and myself, tied the reins to a tree stump in front of the stoop.

Inga's face appeared first at the window and then at the door. A look of pure relief flooded her face. My palms started to sweat.

"Come in, come in!" She pushed back wisps of hair from her face with both hands. The gesture pulled her dress up tight against her, showing the form of a woman in advanced pregnancy.

I was a fool, stopping in and expecting who knows what. She was married to Ericson, carrying his baby. It was his job to care for her, not mine. He was nowhere in sight.

"Missus Ericson," I tipped my hat and felt the heat rise to my cheeks.

"Please don't call me that," she said. "I'm only Inga."

I looked at her, straight into those brown eyes that reminded me so much of my mor. She didn't flinch away but stared right back, her chin up in defiance. The reason was plainly spoken in her eyes.

"Inga," I said. I knew the commandment. I would not covet another man's wife. But, oh, how I longed to covet, just for one sweet moment. I fixed my eyes on the wall above her head and followed her into the tidy, sweet smelling room. I turned to face her once more.

"There's Indian trouble."

"It can't be true," she said. "The Indians around here are friendly. They come to the door every so often begging bread or well water."

"Those are the Chippewa. The ones causing the commotion are Dakota, from farther south."

I looked at her again, trying to break the news without alarming her. She looked so alone, so helpless with her big belly beneath her cotton apron. Her cheeks paled and she grasped a chair for support.

"But it can't be true," she said. "We've never harmed anyone."

How could I tell her the things I had witnessed? She wouldn't believe it, couldn't believe it. I could hardly believe it myself; the smell of death and fire, the brutality and violence, children hacked to pieces, women dead-eyed and broken. It was too horrible, like a bad dream I couldn't forget. Her brown eyes pleaded with me to tell her it wasn't so. But she had a right to know, a right to protect her unborn baby and her own scalp. I wouldn't dishonor her by lying.

"It's true. And probably not the half of it. They raided fifty miles east of here and they're stealing horses all along the trail. You must come with me to the fort."

"But I can't leave! My man is gone on business. There's no one to milk the cows or feed the young stock."

"He left you alone? My God, woman! To hell with his stock!" I said. "Get your wrap, take what you can carry and let's get going. Fort Abercrombie is our only hope. The soldiers are there to protect us."

She placed a protective hand on her belly, then went to the cupboard and lifted a sugar bowl from the shelf. She took out some coins and tied them in her petticoat hem, modestly turning away as she did so. She wrapped a shawl around her shoulders and took a loaf of fresh bread from the table, covered with a clean cloth.

"Do you have a gun?"

"A gun?"

"Any weapons?"

She set the bread on the table, went to the corner and gathered up an old fashioned fowling piece along with powder horn and bag of shot. She handed them to me. It felt awkward in my hands, even heavier than the Danzig. She retrieved the loaf of bread and picked up a butcher knife from the table. She looked at me with such confidence that my courage wavered. I was a very poor shot in the best of circumstances. How could I shoot the savages and drive the stage at the same time? I prayed to God it wouldn't come to that.

We were almost ready to leave when she stopped again and with great determination turned to me.

"There's something else."

Inga set the bread and knife back on the table and went to the iron cook stove and pulled a stone from the hearth. She removed a small sack, replaced the stone and tucked the bag down the front of her dress, picked up the knife and bread again.

"I'm ready now," she said.

I opened the coach door for her but she shook her head.

"I'm afraid to be alone," she said. "Can I sit with you?"

The sweetness of the moment brought tears to my eyes. To my shame, I admit that I longed for her to be with me on the box, to sit beside me until we reached the fort, that I was afraid, too.

"It would be safer in the coach," I said after an awkward moment.

"I'd feel safer with you," she answered and tilted her chin.

I knew I was beaten.

"I'll help you up, then." She sat like a mother bird on her nest, the loaf of bread and butcher knife in her lap. We didn't talk much during our journey. The thought came to me that the sensible thing would have been to take her back to Pomme de Terre to stay with her neighbors at the fortifications. Instead I was driving her through open danger in an effort to reach the fort. I thought to ask her opinion, to let her choose. But I didn't. It was too sweet to have her with me. Besides, there had been no Indian attacks other than horse thieving for fifty miles. Maybe the worst was behind us.

Against my better judgment, I hitched the

team named after my brothers again. They had been sorely abused and needed a long rest but I didn't trust Betty's team and kept them tied to the back of the stage for emergency use only.

I was saying the Lord's Prayer under my breath when we drove into Lewis Peterson's farm. No one greeted us. It was too quiet. I took the Danzig in hand and stepped into the cabin. Lewis lay on his bed. Flies buzzed around him. There was the stench of blood.

*"Nei!"* I cried. "Lewis, wake up!"

I turned him over, blood staining my arms and hands. A hatchet was buried into his chest and his scalp was gone. Sobs overwhelmed me. When I finally looked up, Inga stood beside me. She placed a gentle hand on my shoulder.

"We'll bury him."

I looked at her blankly and wiped my nose on my sleeve. She was right, of course. I found a spade by the barn. No animals, not even chickens, were in sight. Hurriedly I dug a shallow grave and dragged Lewis to it, leaving a red trail across the cabin floor. When he was buried, I stood awkwardly, not knowing what to do next. Inga started praying the Lord's Prayer and with relief, I joined her. The words, a cooling comfort, pushed the terror back again.

"He must have been a good friend."

"We spent many an evening together, talking about farming, sharing our dreams."

"I'm sorry."

I looked up and saw those liquid brown eyes, the ones that reminded me of Mor, the eyes of grief. Knowing she grieved for me brought a sweet comfort.

It was Inga who led the horses, still hitched to the stage, to the watering trough. I was supposed to be caring for her and she showed more sense. I jerked myself back to reality and went to the barn to find oats to feed the horses. There was no time for weakness. I needed to think clearly. It was getting late and the Indians might come back to finish looting the place. It was too dark to keep traveling and the horses were exhausted. It was at least twenty-five miles to Foxhome, and I was unfamiliar with other places in this frontier area.

The barn was part soddy, part logs, with a thatched roof. There would be just enough room to have the coach and horses enclosed for the night but it would be a tight fit. We might be better off staying there in spite of the Indian danger. Inga and I could climb to the hayloft. Perhaps we could defend ourselves if need be.

Inga looked at the barn and then at me

after I presented my plan.

"It might work," she said at last. "We can take turns keeping watch."

"At least we'll have a place to spend the night," I said. "And the horses can rest."

We unhitched the horses and led them into the barn. It was cramped, dusty and smothery. Inga and I pushed the coach into the remaining space. The horses whinnied and stomped. We pulled the door closed and barred it from the inside. It was dark, the only light from between the logs and one small window to the rear. I helped Inga climb the crude ladder to the hayloft. She had the loaf of bread and butcher knife wrapped in her apron. Added to the awkwardness of the baby, she needed help. I handed the two rifles up to Inga, and she dragged them into the hay beside her. Looking around once more, I climbed the ladder and pulled it into the loft.

A small opening, just large enough to let in a small stream of moonlight, looked out upon the yard and house. I could see Lewis's grave and the spade flung carelessly to the side. I could have kicked myself for being so careless. If the Indians came back they would know someone had been there.

"I'll keep first watch," said Inga. "You must be exhausted."

"But too worked up to sleep."

The hay was scratchy but made a fair bed. I tried to push together a pile for Inga to sit on. She chuckled and sat down beside me, still holding the bread and butcher knife in her apron. She took out the loaf and sliced me a piece. It was fresh and good.

A glimmer of light shone across her face. Soft in the moonlight, Inga's face was more beautiful than I remembered. A wild notion entered my mind that it was worth going through the Indian raids to have this time alone with Inga, but the thought quickly passed. Nothing was worth the death of my friends and godchild, the violent butchering of innocents.

"Perhaps this is our last supper," I said lightly and could have kicked myself as soon as the words were out of my mouth.

"*Ja,* it could be our last."

The rustling of mice in the hay, the restless movements of the horses below were the only sounds. I peeked out the small opening and could see nothing amiss. Of course, I'd heard Indians were seldom visible before they attacked.

"*Mange takk* for rescuing me." Inga's voice startled me from my thoughts. "It could have been me killed in my bed."

It was the very thought I had been pushing back all day. It could have been Inga I found stiff and butchered, her long braids decorating some warrior's dwelling. God knows I couldn't have stood it.

"If it is to be my last night on earth," she said, "I am glad to spend it with a friend." She wrapped the bread in the cloth and carefully set it to one side. "I have needed one."

She picked up her gun and ammunition. I helped her prime and load the ancient relic. She carefully put the barrel in the wall opening.

"What could Ericson be thinking, to leave you alone at such a time," I spoke at last.

"Said it was foolishness and rumor," she said. "He couldn't believe the Indians would raid without his permission."

"Where do you think he is?"

"It's hard telling. He often goes about, trying to win votes for the fall election."

I lay back on the hay and stretched a hand out until I found the hem of her dress in the darkness. The cloth was smooth in my hand. Sleep was closing in when she spoke again.

"In truth, I'm glad whenever he leaves the farm. It's a relief to have him gone."

I've tried a thousand times to recall exactly

what awakened me but I can't remember. I just know that something awakened me from a sound sleep. Inga dozed at her post. I nudged her and she became instantly alert. I placed my fingers to her lips to quiet her and carefully positioned myself to look out the opening. All was still. There were no frog sounds, no crickets, no whippoorwills, and no loons calling from the lake.

With Danzig in hand, I scooted to the edge of the loft. The horses were quiet. There was a small rattle at the barn door but it was barred from the inside. A shadow darkened the window below but vanished in an instant. Maybe it was a cloud passing in front of the full moon. Another rattle and a shaft of light appeared as the barn door opened. I raised the Danzig and looked down from the loft into the face of Crooked Lightning.

His face was painted half green and half black and he carried a hatchet. Our eyes met and it seemed the world stopped. It must have been only a minute but it felt like we looked at each other for an eternity without moving. Finally he put the hatchet in his britches. Wordlessly, he left the barn and closed the doors behind him.

I let out my breath — I hadn't realized I had been holding it until that moment. My hands shook and I lowered the ladder and climbed down with the Danzig in hand, found the bar and replaced it at the door.

"Darn!" What a fool I was to leave the spade outside. What an idiot to think us safe with only a piece of wood across the barn doors. How ignorant to hardly notice the window that could have been our death. I should have never chanced staying at the barn in the first place. Suddenly I thought of the thatched roof — how easy it would burn if Crooked Lightning so desired.

"Evan!" Inga called in a hoarse whisper. "What are you doing?"

"Keep watch! Indians!"

I maneuvered around the horses as they whinnied and stomped. They made no sound at all when Crooked Lightning passed around them. There was nothing to see from the small window at the rear. It was small; too small for a man to climb through although Crooked Lightning had done just that.

We pulled the ladder up into the loft behind me. My hands trembled and my breath came in irregular gulps.

"Why didn't you shoot?"

Of course she was right. Why didn't I shoot? I was a coward, pure and simple. I could have easily shot him. But then why didn't he steal the horses? Why didn't he set the barn on fire or come back with others and kill us?

"I know him," I said. "He's a friend."

When the sun came up, I summoned all my courage and opened the barn doors. My hands trembled so I could hardly manage the bar. No one in sight. Cautiously I called Inga to help roll the stage out. Then I went back for the horses.

I was fastening the harness when Inga screamed. The horses reared up and I rushed out with the gun. Someone had dragged Lewis from his grave, mutilated his body and driven a stake through his heart.

We stood in silent horror. Crooked Lightning may have spared us but his message was clear. It was "over the earth I come."

# 22

"Five Hundred Whites Killed, 2000
Indians Surround Fort Ridgely"
~ St. Paul Journal

Inga dozed while holding the loaf of bread
and clutching the knife in her other hand. A
timid mouse climbed onto her apron and
nibbled on the heel of the loaf. Straw stuck
to her disheveled hair and she breathed a
quiet snore. How beautiful she looked. How
lovely even though she was married to
another man and pregnant with his child. I
almost laughed out loud at the irony. The
woman I loved was married to another, I
was killing my favorite horses with this
journey to a place I couldn't hope to survive, the friends I found in this country were
mostly dead, I could expect nothing but
trouble for not returning to the fort, and
dreams of my own place seemed farther
away than ever. Somehow I had made a

mess of my entire life.

We left the trees and traveled across open prairie. I felt naked, exposed. The Indians could see us for miles, and there was no place to hide if they gave chase. I was glad Inga slept, glad to ride in silence without hearing questions I could not answer.

The miles stretched before us. The horses were sluggish, weary. I prayed no Indian would see us, that we'd make it to Foxhome without incident. Then I prayed for Rasmuss and Solveig, that I would find them alive and unharmed.

When I saw their soddy ahead, I began my litany. "Our Father, which art in heaven . . ."

My prayers woke Inga, and I heard her low voice join me, "Hallowed be thy name, thy kingdom come, thy will be done on earth as it is in heaven."

Strength poured into me as we said the words together. "Deliver us from evil for thine is the kingdom, and the power and the glory, forever and ever. Amen."

Rasmuss and Solveig met us at the gate.

"Thank God!" I said. "Are you all right?"

"*Ja,* we are unharmed but the team is gone." Rasmuss held his rifle in hand. "What's happening?"

"The Sioux. We must go to the fort without delay."

"Solveig, get your shawl," Rasmuss said.

We watered the horses and gave them a little grain. I kicked myself for hitching the best team that morning. It might kill them but they would have to keep pulling, even with the weight of extra passengers. I couldn't risk our lives with an unreliable team.

Solveig came out with her shawl, a bundle of food and the royal cat. Inga reached out to pet Fisk, fat from mice and rats. She laughed when he purred.

"I'm Solveig."

"I'm Inga."

"We have to leave right now," I said.

Rasmuss looked toward the barn, his face twisted in anger. "If those savages kill Bossy," he shook his fist, "I'll teach them a lesson they'll never forget."

Although it seemed unlikely I tried to assuage his fears. "In a day or two when things quiet down again, we'll come back and get her."

The women crawled into the coach. Rasmuss climbed up on the box.

"I heard a commotion at dawn," Rasmuss said in a low voice, "I tried to listen but it was too far away. Maybe a gunshot . . . some screeching." His face looked drawn and pale. "I was so scared I stayed in the soddy all day, wouldn't even let Solveig out to milk Bossy."

"You did good," I said. "Folks have been hit all across the state."

I was telling him about the raids when I spotted a piece of paper on the road. I pulled the horses to a stop, and Rasmuss jumped down to pick it up. It was a letter addressed to someone in Pennsylvania. It hadn't been opened.

"What's wrong?" asked Solveig from the stage. "Why did we stop?"

"Nothing's wrong," Rasmuss said. "We just found something on the road."

We started again but found more letters scattered along the trail.

"My God!" The other stage came into view, tipped over on the side of the trail. Not a horse in sight but letters fluttered across the prairie like a flock of birds. We raced closer to the stage, and Rasmuss jumped down while I wrestled the horses to a stop. The stage had been hacked to pieces and slightly burned on one side. While Rasmuss investigated I spotted what looked like a pile of clothes lying next to the trail. I thought to climb down but the team was skittish and it took all my strength to hold them back.

"Over there," I said and motioned for Rasmuss to check it out. It was Hjalmer. He lay crumpled on the ground. When Rasmuss turned him over even from where I sat on the box I could see that he had been scalped. His face was a bloody mess.

Solveig and Inga opened the stage door and called out to see what was wrong. Rasmuss leapt up and blocked their exit from the coach.

"It's the stage driver," he said in a voice high and reedy, "he's dead."

The hair on the back of my neck stood up. "Rasmuss, get back in the stage! We've no time to waste."

"Shouldn't we bury the poor man?" Solveig said.

*"Nei,"* I said. "We have to leave right now."

There was no further discussion. We all felt it. Danger lurked and we needed to get to the fort. I thought to pick up the mail, to bring it in as my job demanded but decided against it. The mail would have to wait.

The horses stomped and kicked before settling into their traces. I crooned to them in Norwegian, trying to push Hjalmer's face from my mind.

"His eyes," Rasmuss said. "My God they took out his eyes." He looked down and took deep gulping breaths. "And his hands."

He stretched out his two hands before him. "Chopped off." He choked back a sob and put his face down into his hands. "Why would they do such a thing? My God, his hands."

We traveled about a half-mile. We were quiet and the horses seemed to sense our fear. They pulled with a steady gait. Rasmuss looked back and pointed to several black dots behind us.

"Indians," he said.

"How can you be sure?" I looked over my shoulder, straining to bring the dots into focus.

"It's Indians," he said. "We've ten miles left before the fort. Can we make it?"

"It might kill the horses," I said and my heart sank with the grief of it.

Rasmuss pulled out his pocket watch. "It's three o'clock. If we hurry we'll be there in time for supper."

We flew across the prairie. The horses were magnificent. They mustered every drop of reserve strength and poured it out for me. I could feel how much they loved me, and it grieved me to abuse them. But abuse them I must.

"They're closing in," Rasmuss said.

"Thank God you're here. At least you can shoot while I drive."

"I'm not much of a shot," Rasmuss said over the noise of the team, "and they're still too far away."

I hurried the horses even faster. We jostled over ruts and weeds. It was uneven ground although it looked flat as a pancake. The horses lathered and blew. I couldn't slow even for a minute but pushed them even more. They caught their second wind and ran toward Fort Abercrombie. Maybe patrolling soldiers would meet us, escort us safely to the fort. But I doubted they even knew about the uprising. Captain Van Der Horck thought the gold arrived in time, thought the crisis over.

From the coach came the sound of the women singing a Norwegian hymn, "I Know of a Sleep in Jesus' Name." The song, not quite on pitch, floated up to us on the box. It was a hymn usually sung at funerals and I realized with a start that they were singing it for Hjalmer.

"I know of a sleep in Jesus' name, a rest from all toil and sorrow; earth folds in her arms my weary frame, and shelters it till the morrow; my soul is at home with God in heaven, her sorrows are past and over."

The thought came to me that Hjalmer's brother would find no one to greet him when he arrived. I forced my mind to focus only on the horses, the trail, the need to get to the fort. It was a desperate, reckless ride.

"They're getting closer," Rasmuss said. "I can almost see their faces."

"Are you ready to shoot?"

"*Ja,* I'll shoot the red devils, every one."

Suddenly the stage careened to the right and I strained to keep it upright.

"You've got a horse down!"

"Betty!" I muttered feeling the force nearly pull my shoulders from their sockets. "Get Inga's knife. You'll have to cut the extra team loose."

It was a last ditch effort. The stage lurched and swayed. He climbed on top of the stage and Solveig handed Inga's knife to him through the window. I prayed to the Holy Angels to help him, to keep the stage smooth enough to prevent him from being bounced off as he crawled to the boot, stretched out his arm and cut the other team loose.

The stage lurched ahead. I didn't dare look back but Rasmuss was soon by my side on the box telling me what was happening.

"The Indians are chasing the other team. It should keep them busy for a while," he said.

"Are they following us?" The sweat rolled down my back and face, my arms almost pulled from their sockets in my effort to keep the stage upright.

"*Nei,* they are staying with the horses for now."

The fort grew visible on the horizon. I almost dared to hope we would make it, escape the butchers after all. Maybe Inga would live to give birth to her child.

"They're coming," Rasmuss said in a desperate voice.

"Shoot! Shoot as many times as you can," I said. "Maybe the fort will hear and send help."

The loud shots caused the horses to lurch and lose stride. They were in bad shape, tongues hanging out and sides heaving.

"Oh, God, please keep these brothers of mine on their legs and moving forward," I prayed. "Sweet Savior, spare us."

Tears welled in my eyes when a detachment of soldiers rode out to escort us to the fort. Never had a place looked so beautiful. Never had a soldier looked so strong.

"Thank God, thank God," I said.

Like Daniel in the lion's den, we had escaped the jaws of death.

Rasmuss looked at his pocket watch and then at me when we finally got to the fort.

"Good God, Evan," he said. "You made

ten miles in thirty minutes."

"But the team." I wiped out the horses' mouths with a wet handkerchief before letting them drink from the trough. "I've ruined them." The foam in their mouths was flecked with blood, and the one I called Martin hobbled on three legs. He would have to be destroyed. The others could barely walk to the barn, their wind broken, sides still heaving and tongues hanging out. I went to each one, stroking and thanking them for their efforts. The team had given its all for me. Then I took my Danzig and led Martin out to the corner of the manure pile behind the stable and shot him dead. The look in his eyes before I killed him was one of love and devotion. Out of sight of the others, I hid in the barn and bawled like a girl.

# 23

"People Rally to New Ulm's Defense,
Murders at Green Lake"
~ St. Paul Journal

When I looked up, Inga stood beside me.

"Don't be ashamed of your tears," she said. "It takes a strong man to do what you've done. We're grateful." She hesitated and added in a small voice, "I'm grateful."

I wondered at her speech. Of course it was a shame for a grown man to weep. Tears were for babies and weak women.

"The horses," I said as if in explanation. "Ruined."

"*Ja,* I see that," she said and placed a warm hand on my shoulder. "But they saved our lives and maybe the entire fort." She twisted the corner of her apron that covered the mound of her belly. "And saved the life of my baby."

She spoke of the baby outright, breaking

all the rules. I didn't care. What difference did it make if I saw she was having a baby or if she told me so. She looked so sweet, so vulnerable in her bulging apron and her braids coming loose from the pins. Something in me wanted to reach out and embrace her, tell her that I did it for her because I loved her, ruined my favorite team in exchange for her safety. But I held back. Instead I took out a dirty blue handkerchief and blew my nose in a loud honk. The mood was broken.

"What's this?" She picked up my watch fob that had fallen from my pocket when I took out the handkerchief.

"It's made from my sister's hair."

"How beautiful," she said. "She must have had curly hair."

"*Ja,*" I answered. "It curled."

"Do you miss her?"

"*Ja,*" I said, "every day. She died when she was only thirteen. This is all I have left of her."

She placed the watch fob carefully in my hand and our fingers touched. She didn't pull away and I didn't either. Although the commandment echoed in my head, we stood in the dim light of the barn and held our hands together, not really holding each other's hands but touching all the same. She looked into my eyes, and I saw the unspoken message there for me. At that moment I knew she loved me, too.

Inga was the first to pull away. She slowly drew back her hand and with determined effort stepped back a whole step.

"Captain Van Der Horck wants to speak to you," she said.

She turned on her heel and left the barn without another word.

"But the gold was delivered," Captain Van Der Horck said.

"Something must have gone wrong."

"Do you think the Confederates could have interfered? Used it against us?"

I told him about the raid near Cold Spring and the warning brought by the priest. Then I told him my decision to return and warn the settlers and the fort.

"It was few I found," I said. "Mainly I buried the dead."

"We would have been an easy target."

"That's what I thought."

"You're sure it's the Sioux?"

"*Ja,* I know one of the braves." I told him about Crooked Lightning, how he left us alone with the horses when he recognized me. I didn't tell him about the mutilation of Lewis' body. Maybe some things were better left unsaid, and I still felt a loyalty to my friend in spite of his deeds.

He asked detailed questions about the location of each raid, the number of dead and missing, the horses stolen. Captain Van Der Horck was an intelligent man. He was also worried.

"A detail of my men left two days ago with a herd of cattle, heading north to the treaty site by the Canadian border." He looked at me from behind thick glasses. "We are short in strength and ill prepared for an attack."

"Send a messenger. Have your men return." I was overstepping, thinking myself better than I ought. "Prepare the fort for attack and bring civilians here for protection."

Captain Van Der Horck digested my words then snapped into action. "Corporal! Double the guards! Send Private Edson in at once. I want him to take a dispatch to the Georgetown expedition. Have Private Bridger warn nearby settlements and have them to come to the fort."

"I sent word to Fort Snelling. I'm not sure if the messenger got through or if they even know what's happening. I think another messenger needs to be sent," I said. "I know it's dangerous but we need reinforcements."

"You're right," Captain Van Der Horck said. "I'll send a dispatch at once."

"Captain," I hated to ask favors, knowing I had already said too much. "Hjalmer Thoreson, the stage driver, lies dead on the trail near Foxhome. There's mail scattered across the prairie." I shifted my weight and considered my next sentence. "Could a burial detail care for him? We didn't have time to do it ourselves."

"It'll be done at once. Get some rest. That was quite a race you ran today."

"*Ja,* but I paid a price," I said. "I ruined the best team there ever was."

They put us up the best they could. Solveig and Inga were housed in the Commander's residence. Rasmuss and I were sent to the soldiers' barracks. I collapsed into a bunk and didn't wake until morning. My growling belly woke me.

Rasmuss and I found the mess hall where Solveig and Inga were drinking coffee from gray enamel cups. From the looks of it, they had become good friends, talking and smiling over the hot brew.

"Did you miss me?" Rasmuss pecked a kiss on Solveig's cheek that flamed red as the sumac along the river.

"Oh, you!" She pushed him away.

"And how is the royal cat?"

"Putting all the rats and mice on alert that

they are no longer welcome here," she said.

I looked at Inga and found her staring at me. She hurriedly lifted her cup and took a swallow. Her face was sunburned after sitting on the box yesterday. I tried to recall if she wore a bonnet but couldn't remember. It all seemed a blur. I searched for something to say.

"I hope you slept well last night."

"*Ja*, I slept," she said.

Rasmuss and I collected our plates of food and came back to sit with the women. I thought to sit somewhere else but followed Rasmuss.

"How are the horses today?" asked Solveig with a concerned look.

"Five of the six are still alive but good for nothing. Their wind is broken after the abuse I gave them yesterday." I swallowed the emotion that made my voice quiver. "They'll never pull a load again."

"They're heroes," said Inga.

"*Skaal* to the team named after Evan's brothers!" Rasmuss raised his cup.

Solemnly, we raised our cups of bitter coffee served without cream and toasted the team. They were indeed heroes.

"They are named after your brothers?" asked Inga.

"*Ja*, they have been my favorite team right

along and I named them after my brothers, living and dead, in Norway."

We ate a few minutes in silence. The food was plain but good, and I tried to recall the last meal I had eaten.

"A messenger came from the Lower Agency," said Solveig.

"When?"

"Just this morning," Solveig said. "His name is Frank Kent and he brings news of a widespread uprising. He has a newspaper clipping telling of it."

"There's a meeting right after breakfast," Inga said, "so everyone can hear what's going on."

It was sobering. A newspaper clipping meant it was really happening. Inga sat across from me, and I found it distracting, confusing. I dropped my spoon with a loud clatter and bumped heads with Rasmuss as we both stooped to pick it up.

"Have you heard anything about your man, Inga?" Rasmuss said, rubbing his head from the blow.

I could have punched him. There was no reason to bring up the Swede at such a time. The entire group turned silent. Solveig looked at me.

"*Nei,* not a word," Inga said.

I suddenly remembered she was carrying

his child. She wore a thin gold band on her wedding finger. She belonged to him and would never be mine. I knew the commandment and abruptly stood to my feet.

"It's time for the meeting."

Frank Kent was a thin man with balding hair. He stood on a stump by the Commander's house as the men and women at the fort gathered round.

"It's bad, folks," he said. "I won't lie to you. Minnesota stands in the balance and could tip either way."

The crowd muttered.

"The Sioux gave up on the gold shipment and overran the Lower Agency, killing or capturing every white. They murdered Andrew Myrick and stuffed grass in his mouth. He's the man who insulted the chiefs by telling them to feed their children grass if they were hungry."

A low exclamation went through the crowd. I thought of how Myrick got what he deserved for being so foolish, then felt guilty for thinking such.

"Yellow Medicine is looted and destroyed. About 40,000 settlers are fleeing from all parts of the valley. Some went to Fort Ridgely, but the Sioux attacked them on August 19. Fort Ridgely is under siege; the paper says two thousand Sioux surround it."

We listened, stunned and silent. It was far worse than I had thought. The smells and the faces of the dead began to swirl before my eyes. I willed myself back to reality.

"They slaughtered everyone at Lake Shetek and almost overran New Ulm." Frank Kent clenched and unclenched his fists as he spoke and his jaw muscles worked. "The people held them off by the skins of their teeth. A third of the town was destroyed."

"Where's the army in all this?" Sven said.

"Sibley is bringing relief but is almighty slow about it. All over the frontier the Sioux are raiding and butchering, stealing horses, burning crops and houses. People are flocking toward Mankato or St. Peter or anywhere where there are other folks to fend them off. It's an all out Sioux effort to rid the state of whites once and for all, and it looks like they're doing it."

Captain Van Der Horck stood up. "There is much to do. We need to get barricades of some kind around the fort. I've called the Georgetown expedition back. Messengers are calling settlers to come to the fort." He rocked back and forth on the balls of his feet with his hands clenched together behind him. "With the help of God we'll hold them off."

Settlers from the surrounding area trickled into the fort all day. About eighty people were added to the fort population. Some were unaware of any Indian problems at all and complained loudly of crops in the field needing their attention. Others brought news of more atrocities, more violence. A woman who lived fifteen miles east of Breckenridge arrived with a bullet wound to her chest and a story so horrific some refused to believe it.

"They came to my door saying they needed something to eat," said the Widow Scott. She wore a ragged, blood-stained dress hardly covering her emaciated body and her hair was wild around her face, matching her frantic eyes. "Said they were 'good Sioux.' I was a fool to believe them."

She wept and we all waited for her to get on with her story. After what seemed an eternity, she continued.

"My son and eight-year-old grandson were home with me. While I fed the Injuns victuals, my son went upstairs to change his clothes. When he came back down they took a gun and shot him dead. He never said one word but they killed him."

She dissolved into more tears. Again we waited.

"Then they turned and shot me. After I had just given them a nice meal."

It was hard to understand her at times because of her wild weeping. Inga went over to her and put an arm around her, comforting her the best she could.

"I lay there, pretending to be dead. They pilfered through the house and took what they could carry. Under my eyelids I saw one Injun with a face painted half black and half green take my grandmother's wedding dress and wrap it around his shoulders. He pulled my shawl off me where I laid. I didn't dare move a muscle. They didn't touch my grandson at all. He just sat there watching. They heard a wagon drive by and ran off to do more deviltry. I whispered to Billy to do what they said and he'd be all right. I crawled outside to a hiding place, worried they might come back to scalp us or burn the house." Her voice was flat, her eyes vacant. She had the appearance of the woman at Sauk Centre.

"I crawled out of my hidey hole when it got dark and crawled to Breckenridge where I had kin. My chest hurt something terrible and I lost a lot of blood. But I crawled all the way to town and knocked on the door of my kin."

She took a sip of water from an enamel cup. The water dribbled down her face, leaving a streak of bloody dirt. "No one answered. I used every bit of my strength and pushed it open, calling their names real quiet. I didn't know if there were Injuns around and was afraid they'd hear me."

She wiped her mouth with the back of her arm. The flesh had peeled away from her elbows and forearms. "It was dark in the house, I was crawling when I touched my nephew. He was butchered — they was all butchered." She began a keening wail that raised the hair on the back of my neck. Solveig and Inga tried to lead her away, but she pulled back from them. "I screamed for hours, went crazy out of my mind."

"Come now," Solveig said.

"You've got to find Billy!" Inga took her by the arm and led her into the women's quarters still wailing. Inga would be good for her, would help her clean up and settle down.

"She doesn't know what she's talking about," said a woman from the crowd. "I don't believe a word of it."

Others in the crowd muttered either agreement or disagreement with the statement. Jack Tarbel, the man who brought her in from Breckenridge, spoke up. "We found her hiding in the sawmill. She was crazy. Fought us and slapped us, calling us dirty devils and every kind of name. We pieced together the bits of her story and went back to the house. They were dead all right." He worked his jaw and was silent for a short minute. "Baby killed. The man and missus with their heads cut off. The other children were cleaved in half with the axe."

"My God," Rasmuss said.

"We should kill every one of the dirty devils," someone said.

"What will they do to us if they take over the fort?" a woman yelled. "We'll all be killed."

There were murmuring assents and comments.

The faces started pressing in again. I smelled burning flesh, felt the weight of Missus Larson's head in my hands. The world began to spin and the next I knew I was lying on a cot in Captain Van Der Horck's quarters with a cool rag on my forehead. Inga and Solveig fluttered round like butterflies.

"Are you all right?" asked Solveig. "You scared us to death." The tone of her voice was bossy, scolding. Like I did it on purpose.

"I'm fine," I struggled to sit up. "I need to

get back . . ."

"You're wrong there, Mister Stage Coach Driver," she said primly with her hands on her hips. "Captain Van Der Horck himself said you are to stay in bed until you feel better — even if it takes all day, that you are to rest and drink this broth. And that's an order."

"We're not done with the barricades."

"There are others to get it done."

She turned and bustled off, muttering something about the Widow Scott. I let my head fall back on the pillow. In truth, I felt terrible, like every nightmare I ever had was coming true. I tried to push down the panic, squeeze back the hysteria by sheer will. But too much had happened for that to be particularly successful.

"Would you like me to keep you company?" Inga handed me an enamel cup of beef broth. I drank the entire cup.

Surely anyone could look at me and see I was as ruined as the team. I'd wept at the graves of both the Larsons and Lewis, and yesterday I shed tears over a team of horses. It must mean I was losing my grip, my cowardly weakness showing through. Worst of all, Inga had been there to see it all.

"How about if I recite as much of the 23rd Psalm as I can remember, and you can help me over the rough spots," she said.

"That would be good." I felt tears again. "I recited the Apostle's Creed and the Lord's Prayer all across Minnesota. It was the only thing that kept me sane."

"My mor taught the 23rd Psalm to me," Inga said, "and when Gunnar died, I recited it over and over again." She picked a bit of lint off the blanket and I could feel the warmth of her hand through the fabric. "I was in the valley of the shadow, as we are now."

She sat beside me in the smothery room, her belly big and rounded beneath her apron, and recited the ancient verse. "The Lord is my shepherd, I shall not want. He maketh me lie down . . ."

Her voice and the words were like fresh water after an afternoon of haying. *Oh, Inga, I thought. If only you were free.* I thought of how it would be, sitting across table from her every meal for the rest of my life with the young ones gathered round. How sweet to leave the trail and its dangers and become a family man. The land didn't seem that important anymore, just Inga. I thought of how her hair would look unbraided, hanging down her back almost to her knees. It was a wondrous dream, even if I wasn't asleep.

"Do you think it was Crooked Lightning?" she asked after the room had been silent for many minutes.

"What?"

"Crooked Lightning. The Widow Scott said one Indian had a face painted half black and half green, like Crooked Lightning."

It was the thought I'd been struggling to push back all day. I felt nauseated, ill. I reached for the basin at my side and retched until my gut was empty.

"You had too much sun yesterday," Inga said. "Too much sun makes a person sick."

# 24

"Battle of New Ulm, Escape to Mankato"
~ St. Paul Journal

Captain Van Der Horck assigned a task to each civilian. I still felt weak in the knees, but every man was needed. The women cooked the meals and molded bullets. The men divided into groups to build fortifications, stand guard, and practice drilling. It seemed ridiculous to practice formation drilling when there was so much work to do with the ramparts. Rasmuss and I chuckled about it as we worked, mocking the stocky farmers trying to march in a row and learn the art of weaponry.

Jack Tarbel had the reputation of being a sharpshooter. He wasn't above bragging a little about his own skills. "The Indians have a name for me. They call me 'Clear Sky' because I can shoot from such a distance that it seems the bullet comes from a clear sky."

Some of the men scoffed and laughed.

"You'll see," he drawled. "Just put me in a high spot where I can rain down fire on the devils. You'll see."

We were assigned to a work detail building barricades from the stacks of firewood the recruits had been cutting all summer.

The fort was poorly situated for defense, brush and cover abundant along the Red River that looped into an irregular border on the east and south side of the buildings.

The flies tormented us as we slaved in the heat. We scooped dirt around the logs as a type of breastwork defense, all the time keeping a vigilant eye for Indians who might be hiding along the river. To supplement the cordwood, we pulled barrels of salt pork and beef to fill the gaps. There were even a few barrels of pickled herring. We pressed dirt around the barrels and logs, forming a solid wall with loopholes at eye level where men kept watch. We felt rushed, unable to do enough to build up the entire perimeter. But we did our best, every man knowing we had little time.

I kept the Danzig at my side. I was jumpy. The least noise startled me.

"I wish they had built a stockade around the buildings," Rasmuss said.

"*Ja*, a stockade would be a help about now," I said. "I'd be glad to hide behind a wall where the Red Indians couldn't see me."

It was hard being forted up. We felt the Indians surrounding us, waiting to attack and destroy. We had no choice but to make a stand, knowing we were not professional soldiers, that we were surely outnumbered. Settlers thought of crops left in the fields and wondered if their houses still stood. Women fussed about children and neighbors. Soldiers worried about the coming battle, whether we would be strong enough to hold. It was an anxious time.

"It's too green to burn, but if we could burn the brush and weeds away from the river it might do some good," Rasmuss said. "As it is, they'll have the best cover."

"After the first frost hits, we could burn it, but not now," I said. "It's been too wet. If the Sioux hold off a while we might get a frost. We're about due."

"Thank God for the firewood," Rasmuss said. "It might be enough to get us by."

"I'd feel better with a stockade."

"But we can hold out until the reinforcements get here."

"*Ja*, we can make it until the reinforcements come." I wondered if they would come, if they even knew of our plight. Messengers didn't always get where they were going.

The Georgetown expedition returned the following evening, and we cheered to have them back. It didn't mean the addition of many men to our defense but at that point every man counted.

Cattle milled and bawled as they crowded into a corral next to the stable. Haystacks by the barns would feed the cattle, and while we had the cattle there was no worry about food for us. Horses were housed in dugouts along the riverbed as well as in the stable. The garrison had three twelve-pound field guns and a few experienced gunners in residence. As long as our ammunition held, we could hold out until reinforcements arrived from Fort Snelling.

It wasn't exactly a celebration but that night we butchered a fresh beef and had a big supper. We needed a boost in morale.

"Cheers to the Georgetown expedition returned to Fort Abercrombie," toasted Captain Van Der Horck with his coffee cup.

We toasted them and feasted on fresh meat. It was a rare treat to eat fresh beef in the summertime. The women had cut and fried all day, making food to last in case of a battle. I watched Inga and Solveig fry down the slabs of meat and layer them in a huge crock. When they poured the melted tallow over the meat, sealing it into the crock, it brought back memories of home.

Mor would make hundreds of tasty meatballs and cook them in a huge cast iron pan. She packed them in a large crock and covered them with melted lard from the hog butchering. The crock sat in the corner, providing food all winter. Another crock would be filled with browned pork chops. It was often my job to scoop out enough meatballs for supper during the dark winter months and bring them into the kitchen. The fat would be melted off and poured back into the crock to keep it sealed.

"What are you thinking about?" Inga washed the frying pan. She pushed back a tendril of hair that escaped from her crown of braids.

"It reminds me of my mor," I said, nodding in the direction of the crock.

I wondered again what Mor would think of the utter brutality of this war with the Dakota. She wouldn't understand the butchering of innocents although in Norway's history the Vikings were violent, always warlike.

"Did your mor want you to come to America?"

"*Nei,* but she knew it was my only chance. She had no idea it would be this dangerous."

"People die in Norway, too," said Inga.

"Five of my six brothers are dead and also my sister. That's a lot of young lives gone to waste."

"It is not all bad here." Inga looked at me with those liquid brown eyes that caused my heart to skip a beat. "There are good people here who make life worthwhile."

"Many good people." I looked at her until she turned away, bustling back to her duties, cheeks red like Solveig's.

That night I awakened to shots and shouts. It was still dark and I struggled to orient myself.

"Indians! They're stealing the horses!"

It was over before I could pull on my pants. Indians crept into the corral behind the stable where the animals were kept and stampeded the cattle and stole some of the horses. More than three hundred animals vanished. The guards, a young private from Renville and a corporal from Sleepy Eye, were found with throats slit and scalps gone.

"They are master horse thieves," I said to Rasmuss as we stood by the empty field. The only horses left were the ones in the barn and one dugout they missed. "When Crooked Lightning almost stole our horses, he walked through the barn, and the horses did not so much as whinny."

"I slept right through it," Rasmuss said. "When I got up in the morning they were gone."

"Rasmuss, my friend." My voice cracked. "Thank God you slept through it unharmed."

He grasped my hand and shook it vigorously, then grabbed and hugged me, pounding me on the back until tears came into my eyes.

"The dreams, Evan," he said. "The dreams were sent by God to make me cautious."

There was no denying it.

We did not return to our beds. No one could have slept anyway, and Captain Van Der Horck ordered a full alert. Instead we silently went to our designated posts and shivered in the dampness, bellies rumbling with hunger, keeping watch for attackers. The season was changing; the morning chill confirmed it. The grass was wet with dew. A thick fog shrouded the riverbed, making visibility difficult and heightening the anxiety of every man in the fort.

Our barricade consisted of firewood and two barrels of pickled herring. It faced the

east side overlooking the river crossing. Rasmuss and I knelt next to each other beside
a private from Pig's Eye, a young man
named Rolf Jorgenson.

"At least we won't starve." I tried to
lighten the mood. "If we get hungry we can
dig out some herring."

"You notice they put Norwegians next to
the herring barrels," Rasmuss said. "They
wanted to be sure it was appreciated."

"Like a fox guarding the henhouse!"

Looking back, it doesn't seem funny, but
at the time it was hilarious. Rasmuss and I
laughed until our sides hurt and there were
tears in our eyes.

"I'd rather be next to a field gun," Rolf
said seriously.

Of course he was right. It was no time for
joking. But we had been through too much
the past few days and needed the release.

It was quiet all day although we saw the
shadows of our enemy from time to time
across the Red River. It may have been my
imagination but it seemed there were more
and more Indians as the day progressed. I
could see them slinking from bush to bush,
just waiting for the exact moment when they
could do the most damage with minimal
danger to themselves. Just out of reach of
our rifles, they set up camp and feasted on

stolen cattle. We were helpless to stop them.

"Damn savages," Rasmuss said. "Look at them eating our beef. Lord knows what we'll eat if this keeps on much longer."

He was right. The Dakota had an ability to gloat over their enemies. I thought of how Crooked Lightning put a stake through Lewis' heart and the agent at the Lower Agency found dead with his mouth stuffed with grass. They managed to get their point across pretty clear without use of pencil or paper. We could see them stuffing beef into their mouths, shaking their fists at us from time to time, dancing around the fire in celebration.

"This scene annoys me beyond toleration," Jack Tarbel said as we watched them. "I think I'll season their meat with lead."

He calmly primed his rifle and packed it with ball and shot. Propping the rifle in the loophole, he coolly tested the air for wind with a spit-dabbed finger. The sounds of the gun and the dropping of a dancing brave were almost instantaneous.

"By God, you got him!" shouted Sven. "Old Clear Sky downed a warrior right in the middle of his supper."

It was an amazing shot. We laughed as the Indians hurriedly moved their feast farther back, out of range. It was plain to see Clear

Sky put a damper on their meal.

The next morning Captain Van Der Horck crept from barricade to barricade, cheering on the men and giving orders.

"I sent Frank Kent and Jack Tarbel out last night, just as it was getting dark," he said to us as we huddled behind our wall of dirt and herring. "We need to be sure Fort Snelling knows our predicament and sends reinforcements."

We nodded in silent agreement and I spit a stream of brown snuff to one side. They would be a loss to our defense, both top-notch fighters.

"If anyone can get through, they can," he said.

Captain Van Der Horck was a wise man and a good one to follow at such a time. Perhaps the messenger sent out earlier didn't make it; better to have another pair going out. I tried not to worry about losing our best sharpshooter. As if reading my mind, the captain spoke.

"We have trained artillerists," Captain Van Der Horck said before he crept to the next barricade. "They'll keep the savages back. That's a promise."

Three twelve-pound field guns guarded the fort. One overlooked the south and west sides of the fortifications. The second was placed in a house near the north side of the fort to protect the north and east sides. The women and children were housed in this log building. The third howitzer stood in the men's quarters and covered the approach to the fort from the river on the east. Experienced gunners from Company D, former German soldiers, were in charge of the guns.

"They think they're really something," Rasmuss said, as he watched the artillerists take charge at their posts.

"*Ja,* they strut and stick out their chests for all to see," I said.

"Best keep their heads down or they'll find themselves on the wrong end of a bullet," Rasmuss said. "The Indians may be better shots than they think."

The women took turns bringing food and coffee to the men on guard. Solveig brought the morning coffee in a big gray enamel pot, padded with folded rags and clutched in her capable hands. On her arm was a pail of empty cups.

"Go back," Rasmuss said. "It's too dangerous."

"I'll be fine," she answered. "I'll stay down low."

She smiled at him and turned red from

her neck to widow's peak.

"Do you miss me?" he asked in a husky voice and leaned forward to kiss her.

"Here's your coffee!" she said and pushed him away. "I need to go round to all the men."

"Dirty Injuns even keep me away from my wife!" Rasmuss said in disgust. "I hope this siege doesn't go on much longer. A man gets used to having his wife beside him at night."

As we drank our cooling coffee, I wondered how it was between a man and his missus. It seemed there was a deeper bond, something that tied them together. Maybe it was love. My parents had it, I knew, and Bror and his new missus. The memory of Inga's brown eyes beneath her sunbonnet came to mind. She didn't love Ericson, I knew for certain.

Inga followed with breakfast. How she crawled around in her condition, I'll never know, but crawl she did, dragging a pail of pancakes rolled with sugar. We grabbed a few out of the bucket and stuffed them into our mouths as fast as we could swallow.

"Save some for the others," she said.

"They're too good to skimp," Rasmuss said with a full mouth.

"My mor's recipe." Inga laughed that low

chuckle. "I made them myself."

"Give the recipe to Solveig," Rasmuss said. "These taste like my mor used to make."

"But don't tell her Rasmuss asked for it," I said. "There'll be trouble if you do."

Inga's eyes crinkled, and we all laughed. The Dakota Nation surrounded us, thirsting for blood and revenge, and yet we laughed. I'm not saying we were anything special, but we were as brave as we could be under the circumstances. When Minnesota held by a thread, we banded together and made a stand. We did the best we could.

I watched Inga crawl on to the next barricade, belly in the way, dragging the pail of pancakes. Rasmuss chuckled and when I looked at him he was mocking Inga's belly, mimicking her clumsy moves.

"Don't be cruel," I said and felt my blood boil. "It's not her fault."

"I didn't mean to be cruel," he said. "I was just making a joke."

"Joke about something else." I reached for another sip of coffee but anger made the cold coffee splash out on the ground. I threw the rest out on the grass and tossed the empty cup to the side.

"Whew!" he said. "That explains it."

"What do you mean?"

"It's plain to see where your interests lie."

"That is none of your business."

Anger welled up inside. I was in love with a married woman and no good could come of it. Lashing out at Rasmuss was unfair and I knew it.

"I'm sorry, Rasmuss." I said. "I'm not myself."

"Don't you think Solveig and I know how it is? If we could do anything to help the situation, we would."

I looked at him blankly. Of course it would be impossible to keep such a thing from Solveig. She managed to get to the heart of every matter, was gifted in wiggling out information. They had been in the stage the day I stopped at her cabin. No wonder they figured it out. It was small comfort.

Then I thought of the summer evening when Lewis asked me why I didn't seek Tilla Spitsberg myself and how I told him I was in love with someone already taken. I remembered the look in his eyes, the look of friendship and compassion.

It was a short jump to the memory of his body dug up from his grave. Hysteria displaced my fury. The fresh blood had smelled like butchering day in Norway. I shook my head, tried to stop the faces from coming at me. It was hopeless. My hands shook and sweat dripped from my face.

"You're ill!" Rasmuss said.

"I must be." What else was there to say.

The next time Captain Van Der Horck made his rounds, Rasmuss reported my illness, and the captain ordered me into the house to rest.

"I'll be fine," I protested. "Too much sun yesterday, that's all."

"I won't chance it. We need every man. Rest today and stand guard tonight when there is no danger from the sun."

It was quiet except for the occasional call of a coyote — or maybe it was an Indian. If you want the truth of the matter, I was scared to death. Rolf Jorgenson and I guarded the south end, and I stayed as close to him as I could without revealing my terror. We stood a short distance apart, within calling distance. I kept thinking of the two guards whose throats were slit. The heft of the Danzig was a comfort in my grasp.

Towards morning Captain Van Der Horck made his rounds. He startled me, whispering my name when he was but a few yards away.

"It's Captain Van Der Horck."

"What are you doing out here?" I asked, too frightened to use good manners.

"I fear an attack at dawn. Keep a close eye on the stables."

He had scarcely crept to the next post when a rifle shot cracked the night. I lifted my rifle but couldn't see a thing. When I crept toward the sound, I found Rolf kneeling beside Captain Van Der Horck.

"I shot him!" said Rolf, near hysteria. "He surprised me, and I shot him before I knew it was him. I seen an Injun slinking by the river a while ago and feared it was him."

The captain cradled his arm. I bound his wound the best I could with his handkerchief and helped him to stand. He was able to walk though shaky and unsteady.

"I'm sorry, Captain." Rolf looked like he was about to cry.

"It was an accident," he answered. "I doubt it's a mortal wound."

"I'll help you to your quarters."

"Keep watch, private," Captain Van Der Horck said. "I fear an attack."

"I'll be right back," I said.

It was only natural I would wake Solveig and Inga to care for him.

"Not the captain!" Inga's dark eyes widened with concern. Her hair hung loose over her shoulders, and she wore an old flannel gown, one that had been washed and rewashed a hundred times from the look of it.

She was beautiful.

"It was an accident," I focused back to the crisis at hand. "He needs his wound dressed."

"Who's second-in-command?" asked Solveig. Once again she had had the most sense of any of us. There was no one better in a crisis than Solveig.

"Fetch the second lieutenant," said the captain from the cot, "and Dr. Brown." Captain Van Der Horck pulled me closer to his face. "Evan, wake the men. There will be an attack — I can feel it."

Before I could leave the room, shots were fired. Men streamed to their posts pulling on britches and dragging their guns with them. It was still dark.

There seemed to be a million of them, but I know now there were only five hundred braves in that morning attack. Almost nude, wearing nothing but a loincloth and war paint, screeching like attacking eagles, they came from the south end and directed their full force against the stables.

Rasmuss and I, ran to the west side of the stables and kept a steady stream of fire on the attackers. Maybe all battles felt like this, the bile in the back of the throat, a coppery taste that parched and gagged, the fear that drove one to kill another human being.

When all was said and done, I had no urge to shoot the Dakota. *Ja,* I had a grudge against them for what they did to innocent people, but in myself I had no desire to kill any of them. I just wanted them to leave us alone and go away.

A Dakota warrior crept up and set a haystack on fire. Indians screamed in triumph when its flames lit the sky. It so outraged a farmer named Riggs that he stormed out in a one-man charge, killing two Indians hiding in the stables and undoubtedly preventing greater damage. He fought like a berserk and came through unscathed.

"It was a beautiful hay stack and took a lot of work to get it that way," he explained later. "I never could abide waste."

We shot until our hands blistered from the heat of the guns. The noise deafened us. Our faces blackened with powder and smoke.

"Will they never quit?" asked Rasmuss at my side, half dressed with suspenders dangling down his sides. His lips were cherry red against the black of his face, and his eyes had a wild look. "They keep coming and coming."

The sound of a bullet plunking into the herring barrel in front of me caught my attention. A leak of pickle juice dribbled out where the bullet pierced the wood.

"Good God! The herring!" Rasmuss stuffed a handkerchief into the hole as a plug. "Dirty devils rob me of my crop, prevent me from sleeping with my wife and now ruin perfectly good herring. They are heathen indeed."

Mostly we were too busy to talk, too busy to think. The sun grew hotter, and we kept fighting. The man across from me wore only his union suit. It might have been funny if the situation was less critical. A wounded soldier lay on the ground about a hundred yards away. Enemy fire made it impossible to retrieve him. He lifted his head a time or two, and I called out to him, "Keep still, help is coming soon." He raised his hand weakly in response.

My throat parched, but there was no time to stop for food or drink. I needed to pass water, felt my bladder bursting but dared not stop the never-ending cycle of loading, firing, loading. Our lives were on the line. If we didn't stop the Dakota, we were dead. Worse yet was the thought of the Dakota getting their hands on the women. I pushed back the thought of Inga at their mercy and kept firing.

Just when it seemed we were being overrun, that we couldn't fire another round, the Indians retreated. I had been firing as fast as I could all day, wondering if I had hit anyone at all. Almost hoping I hadn't. But in the end it was the field guns that made the difference. The Indians could not stand against them, in spite of their massive numbers. They pulled their dead and wounded away and vanished.

The loss to the defenders was slight. Two soldiers, Private Edwin Steele and Corporal Nicholas Hittinger, were wounded. Private Steele was the soldier lying in the sun all day, just out of reach. By the time he was brought to the commander's house, it was too late.

We stood in confusion. *Could it really be over?* The fact we put up a good fight did not surprise us. The fact we prevailed over the Dakota did.

"Three cheers for the artillerists!" someone cried.

"Hip, hip, hooray! Hip, hip, hooray! Hip, hip, hooray for the artillerists!" sounded across the yard. It was a glorious moment, one I will always treasure. How we fought them back though outnumbered four to one.

"The artillerists can strut and gloat all

they want," Rasmuss said. "They've earned it."

"Be on your guard," shouted the lieutenant. "They may come again."

Exhausted privates staggered to each guard post. The rest of us drank water, ate bread and found time to relieve ourselves. It had been a long day.

"Where's the coffee?" asked Sven.

"One of the women in the house had a baby during the battle," Farmer Riggs said. "The baby's dead and the mother not far behind."

I tore out of the yard and into the house, not taking care, not staying behind the barricades as I ought. Either the Indians were too far away or not interested in shooting me for they had their chance. I flung open the door and met Inga carrying a wrapped bundle, weeping.

"He's dead," she said. "He never even took a breath."

"Are you all right?" I held her by both shoulders and looked into her tear-stained face.

"Of course. But this baby is dead and his mother dying."

I let go of her shoulders and slumped against the doorframe. It was pure relief I felt.

# 25

"Stage Attacked and Driver Killed; Station
Keeper Killed at Old Crossing"
~ St. Paul Journal

Routine noises kept me awake when I tried
to sleep that afternoon. I had been assigned
night watch again, but I was exhausted and
keyed up at the same time, not used to
sleeping in the daytime. A pesky fly determined to land on my nose. I swatted and
smashed it flat against the blanket.

Mostly I just lay in bed, thinking about
Inga, thanking God we had survived. I tried
to push down my fears but knew only too
well that one battle wouldn't drive them off.
Had I actually shot anyone with all my
blasting and firing? What would Christina
think about it if she knew? When I finally
drifted off to sleep I dreamed of Lars and
Christina herding goats on the mountain-
side, calling and waving for me to join them.

I awakened with a start. It was dark, and I feared I had overslept. I struggled to my feet and shook the sleep from my eyes. Suddenly I was hungry and wide-awake.

The mess hall buzzed with activity. Solveig and Inga sifted through the contents of a field gun canister with their bare hands. Men pried open the canister covers and then repacking the empty canisters with bits of scrap iron and stones. Others melted lead and molded new bullets at a steady pace.

"What's going on here?" I asked Sven who wrestled with a canister cover at a table. Sweat ran down his forehead in his efforts and his eyes bulged.

"Darn army never gets it right!" He struggled to remove the cover.

"What do you mean?"

"The arsenal holds 40,000 rounds of ammunition."

"Get to the point," I said.

"The men are armed with Harpers Ferry .69-caliber muskets and the ammunition boxes are labeled as .69 caliber." Sven stopped to spit a stream of snuff into a nearby spittoon. "But when we opened the crates, the ammunition is .58 caliber. It don't fit our guns."

"*Nei!*"

"An artillerist remembered the howitzer

canisters were packed with balls as well as scrap iron. We pried one open and found .69-caliber ammunition inside," he said.

"Thank God."

"So now we're prying the canisters apart and digging out the right caliber ammunition and repacking them with the .58 caliber as well as scrap iron and stones." The stubborn canister cover poppped off with a puff of gunpowder. "The women are melting down the .58 caliber and remolding the bullets."

I found a plate of lukewarm stew and a cup of thick coffee and headed for an open spot next to Rasmuss and Solveig. It really wasn't my fault Inga sat there. It was impossible to avoid someone in a fort this small.

"Did you sleep?" Solveig turned a critical eye toward me.

I felt she was examining me, finding fault and hoping to find me sick and incapacitated so she could order me around some more.

"I'm fine," I said. "You worry too much."

"Well, someone needs to worry about you," Solveig said in her bossiest voice.

"Eat your supper," Inga said. "We need help with these canisters."

Her face smudged black and her hands were as black as my friend Gabriel Timmers. I couldn't help but smile.

Looking back I can say it was a wonderful evening, sitting in the mess hall, working together to make the ammunition we needed. It seemed more like a husking bee or a cabin raising rather than a strenuous effort for survival. We forgot the Indians surrounding us, forgot we were waiting for reinforcements from St. Paul, and pushed away the worries of crops and houses and family.

We worked until Captain Van Der Horck came in. His arm was bandaged in a sling and he winced with every movement.

"It's time for bed," he said. Looking around the room he added, "I'm proud to serve with you here at Fort Abercrombie. Good night and God bless you."

We filed out of the room quietly, reminded of the dangers, the laughter over. For all we knew the entire state had fallen, the Chippewa may have joined from the north and the Winnebagos from the south. It may have been our last evening alive on this earth.

"Inga." She turned toward me with tired eyes.

"I thought it was you today," I said. "Someone said a woman was dying."

"Evan," she laughed and said quietly, "My baby isn't due for two months."

"I'm glad to hear it," I said. "I won't have to worry for a while yet."

Her laughter brought Solveig back to the room. It was a normal conversation said in the usual fashion, nothing to remember as special in any way. But I remember every detail to this day, how Inga's eyes sparkled as she spoke and her laugh that brought Solveig back into the room.

After the ladies left, I sought out the captain. "How's your arm, sir?"

"It's fine, nothing serious." He grimaced, and I knew he wasn't being entirely truthful.

"It's good luck finding the .69-caliber rounds."

"Leave it to the army to bungle up even the simplest supplies," he said. "I run a general store when I'm a civilian. My business wouldn't last a week with those kind of mistakes being made."

"It turned out well."

"It did," he said.

"Do you think they'll attack again?" I bit my lip to keep back the stutter and reached into my pocket to finger Christina's hair.

"Maybe or maybe not," he said. "But keep watch as if your life depended on it." He finished drinking the last swallow of coffee and stood up to leave. "Because it does."

Rolf and I were assigned guard duty on the east side. The fog had lifted a little and streams of moonlight shone down on parts of the Red River, making it easier to see anyone trying to sneak into camp.

"Don't shoot any more captains," I said to Rolf in a joking way as we separated to stand at our posts. Immediately I was sorry to have brought it up.

"I didn't mean to do it." His lip quivered.

"Of course you didn't," I said. "Holler if you need me."

The fear rose up within me as soon as I was alone. Every noise was an Indian coming with his knife to scalp me. Every movement was a sneaking warrior.

Jack Tarbel had said it was Little Six leading the Dakota. Others said it was Little Crow. Whoever it was, he did a good job. So far, the Dakota had managed to have it their way. I started reciting the Lord's Prayer to stay calm. "Thy kingdom come, Thy will be done . . ." My thoughts drifted to Inga and how she mourned over the dead baby. She was tender in heart, as Mor used to say.

The weather was changing to autumn. I rubbed my hands together to keep warm with the Danzig propped under my arm. I wondered if it would frost and what affect the weather would have on the crops left in everyone's fields. The crows and raccoons would be having a holiday, feasting on the farmer's labors. A shame to work so hard and have it go to waste.

"Evan!" Rolf whispered. "I see something."

"Where?"

"Right by the crossing in front of you," he said.

Something or someone crawled toward the river, just out of range. Fog swirled over the water. I wished I could pick a target and deliver the ball and shot like Jack Tarbel. Instead I waited, my Danzig primed and loaded, barrel resting in the loophole of the barricade. Eventually he would crawl close enough that I could shoot.

To this day I can't tell you why I hesitated. He was within range, just in the water. I could have shot him and saved myself countless grief. But I hesitated, and he lifted his face from the water just as a cloud broke in front of the moon. It was Ingvald Ericson.

My hands itched with the thought of it. If I'd only fired, he'd be dead and Inga would be free. No man would fault me or question my story. That bastard would never hurt Inga again, boss her around, and ruin her life. We could be together. My finger moved on the trigger. The ancient Danzig would blow him out of the water.

But then I heard a voice, an audible voice so real I turned to see if she was standing beside me. It was the voice of my mor saying, "Thou shalt not kill."

I dropped the gun.

# 26

"Fort Abercrombie Under Siege, Waiting
for Reinforcements"
~ St. Paul Journal

Rolf risked his life crawling to the river to
drag Ericson to safety. I should have helped,
but my legs shook so hard I couldn't have
gone had I tried. Instead, Rolf went alone,
crawling in full view of the Dakota Nation,
risking his neck to help the bastard. I
watched with the Danzig ready and the
watch fob of Christina's hair tucked in my
left hand. I needed to feel the warmth of
her hair, to remember the Commandments
and Mor's voice that prevented me from
committing murder.

Ericson's clothes were tattered, and his
face dirty. Rolf half-carried, half-dragged
him behind my barricade before collapsing
on the ground beside him. Ericson looked
thinner, worn down in the face.

"Are you all right?" asked Rolf between gulps of breath.

"Of course I'm not all right!" Ericson said in his same superior tone. "Get me a cup of hot coffee at once."

"Get your own damn coffee," I said and walked to the next barricade. Someone else could deal with him.

The two messengers, Kent and Tarbel, returned a few days later, sneaking into the fort after darkness had fallen. They'd made the trip Fort Snelling in forty-four hours, an unheard of time, but one that gave credit to their strong mules.

"Fort Snelling sends regards," Frank Kent said to the crowd gathered in the stable. "It'll take them a while to get reinforcements here, but the message is to hold on until they do."

The settlers and soldiers cheered at the much-needed words of hope.

Frank Kent was a slim man, nearing middle age. His receding hairline was the cause of many jokes. Sven was sure the baldness saved Kent from Indian attack. "There's nothing there to scalp," he reasoned. "Why would they go after him?"

"What's the news?"

Frank Kent looked grim. "It's all-out war.

The Sioux have emptied the entire western half of the state."

"Where's Sibley?"

"He reached Fort Ridgley with 1,500 troops." Kent pulled out his tobacco pouch and put a pinch into his lip. "He's whipping the Sioux at every turn. People are running scared from Sioux Falls, Mankato, and Iowa. Raids by St. Cloud and along the Abercrombie Trail. Word has it there's not a soul left in Douglas County, but it's hard to know the truth at this point."

Jack Tarbel added, "The Rebs are so afraid folks will blame them for the mischief they released three hundred prisoners of war to help fight back the Indians."

"The Rebs?" said a soldier in the rear. "That about plants their name on the whole situation, don't it?"

"Well, now," Tarbel drawled, his voice smooth and stretchy, "if the Rebs want to help us fight Little Crow and Little Six and all the other dirty red bastards, why don't they send old Robert E. Lee up here to take charge hisself."

The erupting laughter was a sweet release.

"His white hair would decorate a teepee real nice," he said. "I've seen a picture or two of the old general, and his curls would look real pretty in Little Six's teepee."

"That's just what he deserves!" a private hollered. "Let the Sioux have him!"

"Why if Robert E. Lee would visit us here at Fort Abercrombie, we'd be glad to turn over the keys to the fort and our war with the Indians." Tarbel paused to take a chew of tobacco. "Captain Van Der Horck himself would admit this little spot of God's creation has little strategic value to the Federals. Perhaps a trade could be made — trade Fort Abercrombie and its battle with the Sioux for . . . the state of Virginia."

The entire room whooped with laughter. "It seems a fair trade to me. Those Virginia boys can be a feisty lot. We'll take them and Virginia and let Robert E. Lee take Fort Abercrombie and the Sioux Nation. It's a fine trade."

"I'll post the paper in the mess hall," Frank Kent said after the laughter died down. "Sibley's coming. It'll end soon."

"I demand to know what's taking so long." Ingvald Ericson stepped forward. He had scrounged a suit coat somewhere but it was at least two sizes too small and pulled his shoulders back in a ridiculous pose.

"They're on their way." Kent narrowed his eyes and dropped his voice. "They're a little busy right now with the Sioux Uprising and all."

"It's two hundred and fifty miles," drawled Tarbel. "Marching men take more time than two quick mules and riders of heroic character."

The men roared.

"You made it back sooner. It's possible," continued Ericson in that stubborn way of his. "It's neglect, pure and simple, to leave us at the mercy of the heathen."

"Maybe you need to write a letter to the governor and complain," drawled Jack Tarbel in a sarcastic voice. "I'm sure he'd want to know of this public neglect you're so worried about."

"I will write a letter," Ericson said in his haughtiest tone. "And I will see that Governor Ramsey receives it."

"I'll draw you a map," Tarbel said with a steely glint in his eyes. "You can deliver the letter yourself, leave after dark. Hell, I'll even loan you my mule."

Ericson turned on his heel and walked away amidst jeers and laughter.

"Don't tarry with that letter," Tarbel said. "You can leave tonight."

"Who the hell is he and who brought him here, allowing him to escape a much needed and merciful death?" asked Jack Tarbel after Ericson was out of earshot.

"He crawled in the other night, the Indians put him afoot near Chippewa but he managed to get away and made it to the fort," Rolf Jorgenson said.

"He's a bastard, all right," Riggs said.

"I'd say that one should stand guard duty on the riverbank, away from the barricades," said Tarbel. "Maybe one of Little Six's men would oblige us a favor."

"He's too ornery to die," I said. "He made it here through the middle of the Sioux Nation and didn't mess a hair."

"He ain't got hair," shouted Sven. "That's why both Ericson and Kent made it through without a scratch."

"The Injuns look for those with flowing locks to decorate their teepees," Tarbel said in his easy way. "But I was too quick for 'em, too small a target." He tossed his hair over his shoulder in an exaggerated motion that set the men roaring.

I was reminded of Gabriel's lilting voice and realized Tarbel spoke the same way although his skin was as white as mine. That language must not be limited to Negroes after all.

Ericson's arrival turned my life at Fort Abercrombie to pure misery. He insisted Inga serve him his meals and stand at his side until he finished. His commands never ceased, kept her running all day to please him. If Captain Van Der Horck had allowed it, he would have had Inga take his turn standing guard duty.

No longer did we have the chance to talk over breakfast or converse while doing chores. Her jailer was back. Inga's smile faded, and she no longer laughed. She didn't look at me anymore from across the serving hall. It seemed she had left the fort altogether.

The Dakota played a cat and mouse game with us. If anyone tried to leave the fort, they were fired upon. We could hardly dip water from the river without drawing gunshots. They were always around, slinking and sneaking, driving us crazy with the waiting and watching. We were stuck without news, without reinforcements and without assurance we would get out of Fort Abercrombie alive.

"By God, I'll speak to the governor about this!" sputtered Ericson one day. He was assigned to the next barricade for guard duty one perfect fall afternoon. "The savages will answer to him for the way they are persecuting us. They should all be exterminated, like a pack of wolves."

"For once I agree with you," Rasmuss said at my side. "Don't you, Evan?"

I didn't answer. Instead I spit a stream of snuff through the loophole. Maybe it was because Ericson spoke so freely about his position or because of Crooked Lightning. Whatever the reason, I disagreed. Somehow we needed to work it out and live together in peace.

Solveig brought around a pail of the freshest, lightest doughnuts a man could ever eat. Greedily I stuffed a whole one in my mouth and hooked two more with my fingers.

"These are wonderful," I said. "You make 'em?"

"*Nei,* Inga did this morning."

"I'll take a few more," I said.

"You've had your share." She crawled to the next barricade, and I saw Ericson take the doughnuts and bite into one.

"Damn woman!" he said. "She never fries them long enough. This one is doughy in the middle."

It was all I could do to keep my mouth shut and my hands away from his throat. I should have killed him when I had the chance. Words failed me in my contempt. Instead I jumped over the barricade and snatched the doughnuts, even the one half eaten, and returned to my post.

"I'll take them if you don't want them." I

shoved them in my mouth as fast as possible.

The look on his face was worth it.

As the day dragged on, Ericson started spouting about the need for those of nobility to immigrate to Minnesota and take over the politics of the state.

"Shut your mouth, Ericson, or I'll shut it for you," Rasmuss said. "I've heard enough of your nonsense to last a lifetime,"

"What do you mean?" sputtered Ericson.

"We left the Old Country to get away from pompous bastards like you. Every man has a vote here, not just the upper class." Rasmuss stopped long enough to shoot a perfect stream of snuff at Ericson's feet. "It'll be a cold day in hell before I vote for you or anyone like you."

I agreed with my friend completely.

It was to be expected the men would be getting edgy, kept away from their women for weeks on end. Rasmuss complained about it every single day.

"It's been three weeks since I slept with my woman," he said.

I kept silent. What could I add? My bed was cold and lonely every night of the year, Dakota or no Dakota. I thought of the women I had met in America, thought of Tilla Spitsberg and wondered if she lived. *Nei,* such pondering only led to more hopelessness. Inga was taken. My life would be one of solitude.

At least Ericson couldn't get his hands on Inga — all the men were housed in the bunk house, and the women at the commander's residence. It more than made up for Rasmuss' complaints.

We ran into each other quite by accident. I left my post on the east barricade and met Inga on the pathway to the river. Most men spared their wives this dangerous chore and fetched the water themselves, but not Ericson. Poor Inga, big as a house, an easy target, lugged buckets by herself. It was only human decency to help her. I would have helped any woman in her situation.

*"Mange takk."* She gratefully gave up the buckets and pushed her hair back off her face. Her belly seemed bigger than ever, and she walked with a slow waddle that made me smile. *God, she was beautiful.*

"How are you?" I searched her face for the truth.

"I'm fine." I noticed she bit her lip.

"What's wrong?"

"He's mad. Said I abandoned the animals and ruined our chances of success. Is mad that I took his savings." Here the tears started falling in spite of her efforts. "Said the Indians could have killed me and the money would have been lost forever." She hiccupped a short sob. "Says he'll teach me a lesson — one I'll never forget."

"Damn him! I should have shot him when I had the chance." I was instantly aware I said too much.

"What do you mean?" Inga looked at me with eyes that saw straight through me.

"It was my mor," I said. "She spoke to me, said I shouldn't kill him. I had my gun on him, Inga, the night he crossed over into the fort." The words rushed out in a torrent. I hadn't realized I was saving them for Inga. "At first I thought he was an Indian coming. I could have shot him, knew you'd be free. But I couldn't do it. Couldn't break the commandment and live with myself afterwards."

Her hand touched my face, only a second's touch but it burned my cheek, seared a lasting imprint on my skin.

"You're a good man. Any woman would be proud to stand by you at the altar." She pushed up her chin and tears dripped down her face and neck. "But you need to go on with your life. Look at me. I'm bound to him as long as I live. Nothing will change it." She stopped to push back the strands of hair behind her ears. "I hoped he was dead, even prayed the Indians had killed him. But he's alive and there's nothing we can do about it."

It was a cascade of emotion, raw and painful.

"I love you," I started to say, but she cut me off.

"Evan!" Her eyes blazed. "There are more Commandments."

## 27

"More Murders at New Ulm,
Forest City Attacked"
~ St. Paul Journal

Clear Sky and the artillerists kept the
Dakota from overrunning the fort. Jack Tarbel sat in the second story window of the
commander's house and shot any brave who
dared show his face. The howitzers stood
ready. A burst of deadly fire was sure to
scatter even the most courageous Dakota.

They tried a full-scale attack a time or two
more but we sensed it was half-hearted,
afraid to approach the big guns. The days
dragged into weeks. One day Jack Tarbel
sounded an alarm from his high perch.

"There is a cloud of dust coming our way.
It looks like Indians. To arms! To arms!"

We scurried to our posts, wondering if this
day would be our last, if we could stand
against even more Dakota braves attacking

the fort, if the dwindling ammunition would hold. Inga served stew behind a long table, and our eyes met for a second as I rushed past her. We hadn't spoken in days.

"Wait!" Tarbel called down. "There are four men coming ahead of the others. White men! Soldiers! Soldiers are finally here!"

A hurrah went up from the seventy-five soldiers and eighty civilians in the fort. It was a cheer for the reinforcements but also for us. We'd done it. We'd held off five hundred Dakota warriors for almost six weeks with hardly a loss of life in spite of the poor position of the fort and lack of stockade. Many of us were forted up even longer. It was September 23, 1862, a day I'll never forget as long as I live.

Rolf Jorgenson started "Rally Round the Flag," and soon we were all singing it as loud as we could. German and Scandinavian accents melded with American tones. I'm not sure what you'd call Jack Tarbel's strange speech, but it boomed out in strong melody, "The Union forever, hurrah, boys, hurrah! We'll rally round the flag, boys, we'll rally once again. Sounding the trumpet call of freedom."

We sang while the soldiers marched toward the fort, crossed the river and came into the midst of the campaign grounds.

They were dirty and sweaty, carrying full packs. The civilians in the fort formed two long lines and the reinforcements marched between them. Folks patted them on the back, shook their hands, and thanked them many times. Some of the women kissed them as they strutted down the line, much to the chagrin of fathers and husbands.

I didn't stand in line with the others. I was glad to see them, but shied away from such public display of emotion. The heart beating inside me was numb with grief. It was too soon to hope.

The horses pulling their supply wagons were familiar to me from my days as hostler at Fort Snelling. Instead of gawking over the new soldiers, I went to the stables and greeted for my old friends. They whinnied and stomped their hooves as I petted and combed them. There was water in the trough and enough oats to perk their appetites. They drank and ate their fill while I whispered my story to them in Norwegian, my guilt over ruining the team named after my brothers, the loss of the woman I loved, the panic that came when the faces pressed in. It had been a long haul from Fort Snelling in more ways than one.

"Evan," someone called from the doorway.

A grinning Adam Sullivan greeted me.

Behind him stood his far, Joe Sullivan. Both were dressed in the blue uniforms of federal soldiers. Adam seemed to have filled out, grown taller. Joe was thinner, frailer. His face was lined and his eyes were that of an older man. The Reb prison camp must not have agreed with him.

"By God, it's good to see you, Joe." I shook his hand. "It's been a long time."

"The Rebs let him out of prison to come and fight the Sioux," chimed in Adam. "He came home a couple of weeks ago, surprised the hell out of us."

"Watch your language."

"Ma was so glad to see him she hardly noticed when he gave me permission to enlist," Adam said. "I signed up right away, and they let me come with Pa and the Exterminators."

"Exterminators?" I said.

"That's what we call ourselves," Adam said. "We're here to exterminate the Sioux, just like they deserve."

"Adam," scolded his far. "You're talking too much. Go find some supper and let us visit in peace."

Adam ran out, looking for supper. Joe slumped down on a pile of grain sacks.

"That hike about did me in," said Joe. "I'm still weak from the poor rations at the prison camp."

"It was bad, then."

"Terrible. Weevily corn and rancid bacon, dirty water from a fouled stream, not a doctor to care for the injured or sick. More died from bad food and water than war wounds."

His eyes took on the far-away, detached look I had learned to connect with hardship. "They forted us up, without shelter or clean water, in the hot sun. Almost drove us mad."

"It's hot down there?"

"Hot as hell and the Rebs are worse than the Indians. Our own men became like animals, preyed on each other. Hellish."

It was too much. Anxiety swirled in my chest. I quickly changed the subject.

"How is the war doing?" I asked. "Are the Rebs running yet?"

"No. It'll take a strong effort to defeat 'em." He pulled off his tall boots and rubbed his feet. A strong odor wafted toward me, even stronger than the dirty stalls. I noticed with a wince how he wiped fresh blood and green pus from his foot with his coat sleeve.

"We got beat at the Second Battle of Bull Run and then there was the slaughter at Antietem," he said. "God, will it ever end?"

"I haven't heard news for weeks."

"It's all bad," he said. "We need every man."

Guilt washed over me. Maybe I should join up and be done with it. Who knew if I even had a job waiting for me anymore; the army wouldn't look kindly on me for losing all their horses. There was no hope of Inga. All my dreams were shattered.

"What about your place?" I asked. "Did the Sioux raid that far east?"

"No, not much damage east of St. Cloud though folks were worried and some had livestock stolen. The people banded together and built fortifications, though, to be on the safe side."

He took a filthy rag out of his pocket and began to wind it around his right foot, starting at the toe and wrapping toward his ankle. Just looking at it and smelling the foul odors made me a little light in the head. He flicked maggots off his heel.

"The Sioux massacred every white person they could find. Captured some of the women and children; looking for wives, I guess. Killed some kinfolk I had in New Ulm. Burned, raped and killed all across Minnesota. Hundreds dead and folks leaving the state like rats off a sinking ship. There's talk that it's the worst Indian war in United States history."

"What's happening now?"

"The army stopped them at Fort Ridgley and chased them out of the Minnesota River Valley. They're still raising hell on the fringe areas, further out in the frontier away from the Lower Reservation, out of the army's reach."

"So we are on the fringe of it all?"

"*Ja,* this area saw only scattered raids," he said.

My brain went numb. It was bad enough the way I had seen it.

"Any word of the Chippewa or Winnebago joining in?" I asked.

"Not that I've heard," he said. "But I've hardly had time to read a newspaper. So much of it is gossip and hearsay, it's hard to know the actual truth."

"What did you find on your way out here?" I was annoyed beyond description to hear my voice squeak. "Anyone left?"

"Not many." He looked at me with hollow eyes. "Farms emptied out as if the last trump sounded. Folks left their homes to find safety east of where they were. Other folks further west left their homes and found the vacated houses of those already gone and settled in there."

"How about the Abercrombie Trail?" I asked. "Anyone still alive along the trail?"

"Pomme de Terre is standing," he said. "We spoke to some folks by the name of Estvold." I offered Joe a chew of my snuff plug and he took it with a quick nod of the head. "Turned out I knew their son, Emil, fought with him at Shiloh. And there was a pretty girl and her family staying with them. They traveled west from Douglas County to fortify at Pomme de Terre. Can't remember their name but she's a beauty and the oldest of a big family . . ."

"Spitsberg? Tilla Spitsberg?"

"Yes, that was her name. The man that gets her will be one lucky fellow."

I couldn't help but agree with him. Tilla was a beauty, everything I ever dreamed of in a woman. Gladness surged through me to think they had survived.

"How about Cold Spring? Did you see Bror Brorson?"

"He has an Irish wife and two little ones? The boy talks almost as much as Adam."

"*Ja.* That would be Billy."

A wave of relief washed over me, leaving me weak in the knees. Joe rubbed his legs and finally stood up, stretching up and down, trying to limber his muscles before pulling on his boots again.

"Damn cramps! I wonder if I'll ever get back my strength."

"You need rest." In Norway the low feeling lingered long after food was back on the table.

"I'm ready for supper," Joe said. "My belly button is scraping my backbone."

"I'll join you in a little while. I'm going to finish with the horses."

A few minutes later Solveig found me in the stable where I curried the last horse.

"How are you?"

"Fine." The sunstroke lasted only a few days, there was nothing wrong with me.

"Inga told me about your conversation, how she told you to go your separate way."

I didn't answer but fought back a fresh stab of grief, pushing the flat comb harder against the horse's side.

"She's right, you know," Solveig said. "You need to forget about her and find someone new." Solveig picked at the straw in the manger, pulling out a single, hollow strand and blowing across the top of it, making a small whistling sound.

"It's none of your concern."

"She loves you." Solveig was always butting in where she had no business to be. "But she truly wants you to be happy, not wasting time waiting for her."

"Solveig," I said. "You talk too much."

"Supper is almost over," she said. "You

need to go before everything's gone."

I threw down the currycomb and stomped off to the mess hall. There were times when a man needed solitude. Being forted up prevented any such opportunity.

# 28

"Dispatch from Colonel Sibley,
A Flag of Truce"
∼ St. Paul Journal

We weren't out of danger, that's for sure, but we were a whole lot safer with the reinforcements in place. The first thing they did was to send scouting parties to gather in animals scattered and stolen by the Indians. They found over 150 sheep and a few horses and beef as well.

"The Sioux must not like mutton any more than I do," Jack Tarbel said in his twangy voice. "No sir, the Sioux prefer the taste of beef. They have left the sheep for us to eat as a token of their disrespect."

Betty stood in the scraggly group of horses, covered in cockleburs. She hung her head as if she felt guilty about her capture. She amazed me. In spite of her many stumbles she always managed to come through unscathed. She was thinner and one of her shoes was loose.

"I'll fix it for you, Old Girl." I petted and stroked her back. "You couldn't help it. It wasn't your fault." Betty whinnied in reply and stuck her nose in the oats set before her. It was like meeting an old friend, and I felt tears in my eyes. After having so many of those I cared for killed, it was a satisfying relief to find Betty alive and well.

Other scouting parties foraged surrounding fields for potatoes to supplement the fort's food supply. The fort resumed a peacetime routine. Settlers no longer stood guard at night; Indians were in the vicinity but none were spotted near the fort.

On September 26, messengers rode to St. Cloud to deliver full particulars of the state of affairs at the fort. A patrol guided them a few miles to protect against Indian attack. Later, while the patrol was watering their stock in the river, Indians fired upon them. From the wooded area along the river, twenty shots were fired, killing two teamsters, one horse and one ox. Heavy fire was returned by the patrol, and the soldiers at the fort, hearing the volley, sent out a patrol to assist them. Those of us left at the fort took our defensive positions and waited.

"I see one of the bastards!" called Frank

Tarbel and promptly fired into a tree along the river. A wounded savage fell from the treetop, landing in a fork of the tree. The soldiers cheered.

A few rounds of the field guns routed the remaining Indians and ripped off entire treetops in their way. Men from the cavalry were ordered to mount and pursue them. They took with them one twelve-pounder and chased the Indians without resistance while the rest of us waited at our battle stations. We stood watch all day until the cavalry returned towards suppertime.

"We followed them to their camp," Adam said that night. "It was loaded with plunder. Everything you could think of from cooking pots to silk dresses. We helped ourselves, taking whatever we wanted before setting fire to the camp." He held up a pearl handled knife. "Look."

"Anyone hurt?"

"We didn't even see any Indians," he said. "They ran away."

A couple of days later, three Indians were spotted near the Wild Rice River but they fled when they saw the patrol. Indians skulked around the fort every day but no one was injured.

We were all anxious to leave the fort, to get back to our normal lives. When I heard talk of an expedition of civilians returning to St. Cloud, I volunteered.

"I can transport women and children in the stage," I said to Captain Van Der Horck. "I'll use the team from the army supply wagon."

"It's not a bad idea," he said and leaned back in his chair, stretching his feet in front of him. "There's mail and dispatches." He took his glasses off and wiped his eyes with a clean handkerchief. "We need to get regular communication between forts as soon as possible. I don't know if this is the end of the Indian trouble or not, don't know what's happening in the rebellion in the south. I need to know."

"I'll to need someone to ride shotgun," I said. "Don't dare go it alone."

"I'll send a soldier along. Captain Burger will lead the expedition."

*"Mange takk."* I shook his burly hand. "The survival of the fort rested squarely on your shoulders, and you came through for all of us."

"We did it together," he said.

"It's not safe to go back to your farm," I said.

"I know it's not safe, but I'm sick and tired of being forted up. Maybe the crows haven't eaten it all." Rasmuss paced back and forth in the stable while I hitched the team. "There's potatoes to dig."

"Admit it, Rasmuss," I said. "You just want to get home so you can have Solveig all to yourself. That's the real reason, isn't it?"

He threw his cap at me and tried to wrestle me down to the floor.

"Stop!" I yelled. "The floor's dirty!"

"I'll show you what shit smells like." He proceeded to manhandle me to the barn floor, rubbing my hands in fresh horse manure.

We were tussling and laughing when someone cleared his throat. I threw Rasmuss back and looked up. Ingvald Ericson stood before me.

"I'd like to purchase a ticket to St. Cloud," he said.

I jumped to my feet and brushed the filth and straw from my hands and clothing.

"There will be no tickets sold," I said sternly. "Women and children will ride on the stage to St. Cloud without price."

"But you don't understand," he said. "I need passage to St. Cloud. I have money." He straightened his shoulders and gave a haughty look. "I'm prepared to pay."

It was a terrible temptation and I couldn't

resist. My hand reached out and landed on his shoulder where I proceeded to rub dung on his coat while speaking in a soothing voice. "I'm sure you understand the need for transporting women and children in the stage, Mr. Ericson," I said. "You can march with the men."

The tone bewildered him, I could tell. He wasn't used to folks speaking to him in a kindly manner. But then the smell of fresh dung met his nostrils.

"Get your filthy hands off me!" He stomped out of the barn in a rage.

Rasmuss burst out in laughter, holding his sides in near hysteria. "You got him good!"

Mor had often reminded me that vengeance belonged to the Lord. In my heart I felt no better.

# 29

"White Prisoners in the
Hands of the Indians"
~ St. Paul Journal

We were taking a chance and everyone felt
it. There was no guarantee an expedition,
even though sixty men strong and escorted
by cavalry patrol, would make it to St.
Cloud with Indians still in the vicinity.

It frosted a few weeks before, and the bugs
were gone. Minnesota autumns were breathtakingly beautiful with shades of orange and
gold in the hardwood foliage and the brilliant red of sumac and maple. We had
perfect traveling weather but time was short
before the temperatures dipped too low for
comfort.

The stage was crammed with expectant
women, crying babies, and small children.
Inga wedged between the stage wall and
Gunda Hanson, a large woman with year-

old twin daughters. The other women and children walked with their men. Inga avoided eye contact, and I must admit I kept away from her. It was hopeless, and we both knew it.

Joe Sullivan climbed up on the box beside me. "I'm assigned as your shotgun rider," he said with a grin. "Much easier on the feet than marching all the way back."

"Where's Adam?"

"He's being kept at Abercrombie."

I nodded. It must have been hard for Joe to be separated from Adam when he was so young and green. The young ones seemed to be most zealous, take the most chances.

As if reading my mind, Joe said, "It's better for him to stay close to home rather than being sent to fight Rebs in the South. At least here he'll have a fighting chance, and the weather isn't so damn hot."

The team was rested and in good shape. While they weren't of the caliber of the team named after my brothers, they had a lasting step and a strong endurance. No doubt they would pull us home in spite of the heavy load of human cargo.

Ingvald Ericson rode out on Betty, pulling the reins and kicking her in her flanks. Lazy bastard! No doubt he felt it beneath him to walk with the men. I found out later the army came out on the better end of that deal. Betty was an unreliable mount, and Ingvald paid dearly for her.

Ingvald cursed Betty, pushing through the marchers until he drew up beside the stage. He pulled sharply at the bit, causing Betty to roll her eyes and snort.

"You'll have to ride with the cavalry." My voice icy and stern. I should have killed him — life would have been easier. I never could abide a man who mistreated his animals.

"I'll ride next to the stage with my woman."

"There'll be no horses next to the stage," I said, holding my voice to a civilized tone though anger raged through my body and my racing heart and gulping breathing made it difficult to talk at all. "The trail is too narrow. Move to the rear with the other mounts."

"It's a free country," he said and jerked Betty's reins until she reared back and almost stepped on a woman walking beside the trail. "I'll ride where I want."

I didn't say a word but slowly picked up the ancient Danzig and held it loosely in firing position, not exactly aimed at him but in the general direction. His eyes widened and then narrowed.

"I'll leave," he said. "But rest assured your

superiors will hear of this back at Fort Snelling."

He yanked the reins and charged through a cluster of women and children.

"Watch where you're going!" a woman yelled. "You'll kill somebody!"

"Can you believe that?" Joe snorted at my side. "He's afraid to ride with the other horses, thinks it safer towards the middle of the group."

*"Nei,"* I said when my breath slowed to a regular rhythm and I was able to talk. "He thinks himself too good to ride with the others; he's too arrogant to be afraid."

We traveled east, worried and anxious, searching the horizon for lurking Indians. We arrived at Rasmuss' farm mid-day.

"Bossy!" Rasmuss cried as he ran around back of his soddy. "Come Bossy!"

His face was crestfallen when he returned to the stage. "Damn savages took my cow," he said. "I'll never rest 'til I get back at 'em."

Solveig joined him and awkwardly put her hand on his shoulder and turned cherry red in doing so. "But look, Rasmuss. Our house stands, there's corn in the field, and the potatoes are ready to harvest."

Rasmuss perked up at the encouragement.

"We'll harvest our crop, such as it is," Rasmuss said.

"No, you won't," Captain Burger said. "It's still unsafe. My orders are to take you all to St. Cloud; no exceptions."

Rasmuss shook his fist at Captain Burger's back as he rode back to the cavalry detail. "He's worse than the Red Men to keep me from my crop!"

"It's better to be safe than sorry at such a time," I said. "Let the army deal with the Dakota."

"You think they know what they're doing?" His face was almost as red as Solveig's and his hands trembled. "They'll never put down the Sioux in time for me to harvest my potatoes. I'll have nothing for Bishop Whipple."

We spread out by Rasmuss' house and had a picnic lunch. Solveig dipped cold water from their well and acted as hostess. The women took turns using the outhouse and the men relieved themselves behind the barn.

"We have to keep going," Captain Burger said. "It feels like rain moving in."

The thick bank of clouds to the west reminded me of the gray wool Mor used in her quilts.

"How far to Dayton?" Captain Burger.

"Not too far," I said, "if we keep moving."

We reached Dayton by nightfall, and it

was a weary and footsore bunch that arrived. Children cried and women scolded. Men cussed the Dakota, the army, and life in general. The only good thing was the absence of mosquitoes. Thank God the frost had put an end to them for the year.

I couldn't go into Lewis' cabin. It wasn't superstition or any nonsense like that, but the faces were always just beneath the surface of my thoughts, and I wanted no stirring up of them.

When I opened the door to help the women out of the stage, the stench of sweat and urine wrinkled my nose.

"Thank you," said Gunda, a twin on each generous hip. "It would have been a long walk with such a load." She handed a baby to me and stepped down, large wet areas beneath both arms and her skirts sodden with urine where the babies had sat. The babies were soggy and out of sorts, their sharp screams caused the horses to shy.

*"Mange takk."* I reached for Inga's hand and helped her step out of the stage. Her skirts were wet as well. She undoubtedly had held one of the twins. The trip had been hard on her, I could tell. Her hair was tousled, and her face tinged gray as the clouds to the west. A wedge of grief caught in my throat but I had no words for her. I

merely nodded my head.

I led the horses toward the barn and then thought better of it. Instead I rubbed them down in the yard and let them drink from the outside trough. Too many memories lurked in the buildings. We'd sleep in the yard unless rain drove us in.

Rasmuss built a campfire, and Solveig cooked coffee. The smells and promised comfort revived our struggling company. Someone brought out a pail of eggs and a crock of pickled beef. Solveig fried pancakes on a small griddle, and we ate until we were full, then lounged around the fire with the other civilians. The cavalry had their own fire closer to the trail. Guards stood at their posts, alert for enemy movement.

I don't know who started it but soon the whole encampment was singing the song I had wanted to learn, "The Battle Hymn of the Republic."

". . . Mine eyes have seen the glory of the coming of the Lord, he has loosed his fateful lightning where the grapes of wrath are stored. . . . His truth is marching on."

It might have been the way the stars hid behind the clouds or the absence of the moon, but it seemed real to us, the Lord coming with His wrath for our enemies.

". . . Glory, glory hallelujah. Glory, glory

hallelujah. His truth is marching on . . ."

Emil Estvold had written the words in a letter home to his parents in Pomme de Terre many weeks ago. It took the melody to make it alive.

I dreamed that Lewis had crawled out of his grave and told me something important. His mouth moved, but the words were blown away before I could hear them. I called out to him to say it again.

"Wake up!" A sleepy private shook me awake. "You're yelling — thought it was an Injun."

I roused myself and looked around to see if I had bothered anyone else. "A bad dream." I rolled over and tried to return to sleep. It was useless. The morning lined the eastern sky in pink and orange. An owl hooted, and a light frost covered the ground as I climbed down from the box and walked to the edge of the yard, trying to avoid Lewis' grave.

Inga appeared out of nowhere with an old shawl wrapped around her shoulders and her hair hanging down in a long braid. "It's hard to believe what happened here," she said.

"I keep telling myself it was all a dream."

"But we survived. Crooked Lightning didn't kill us."

"He's a friend. But Lewis was a friend, too. It doesn't fit. Nothing makes sense anymore."

"What are your plans when this is over?"

"I've thought to join the army," I said. "There's nothing to keep me from it now."

"What about your farm?"

"It doesn't matter anymore," I said.

Inga started back for the cabin. I watched her go and thought how hopeless it was for us both. Her life with Ericson would be a nightmare. Mine without her would be empty.

That morning the guards crawled on top of the stage and slept with the baggage. The extra weight for the horses worried me, but I kept quiet. I stood guard myself too many nights and remembered the overwhelming need for sleep. I would take it slower and rest the horses a little more.

My heart pounded when I thought of the settlers along the trail. Would we find anyone left? The faces threatened. I called out to the team in Norwegian, urging them to pull hard and long.

We found more victims just east of Dayton. Two bodies alongside the road. Flies buzzed around them, and we chased a few persistent crows. One man was ripped from naval to throat with his heart and liver torn out. His head was cut off and stuffed inside his chest cavity. Lungs lay on top of his chest. The hands were cut off and placed to one side. The other man was found with his skull smashed in and his brains scattered about, his arm broken by a rifle ball, eighteen stab wounds on his body.

"See how the heads are placed facing the feet," said Captain Burger. "The hands, the head — symbolic gestures telling us a message. I'm not sure exactly what the message is, but it is a message. Corporal, sketch a drawing of the bodies at once. Maybe someone in St. Paul will be able to explain."

"Yes, sir!" The corporal pulled out a sketchbook from his pocket and a stubby pencil. He completed his task quickly. Then I noticed him rush to the bushes nearby and vomit. I didn't blame him, felt myself getting light-headed, the faces pressing in.

"Private, gather a burial detail," said Captain Burger. "We've no time to waste."

Joe Sullivan looked at me when I returned to the stage but didn't say a word. I lowered my head between my knees and sucked in fresh air until my breathing evened and my mind cleared. I concentrated on the Lord's Prayer, how it said, "Thy will be done on earth as it is in heaven," and wondered if it was His will for Inga to remain married to

Ingvald Ericson. It must be. But then a new prayer formed in my mind. A short prayer, "Show me."

Just west of Pomme de Terre, Ericson argued with the captain. "I'll check on my place and stay there if I wish. No one can stop me."

"I have orders to bring this troop to St. Cloud. You will not stay here," said Captain Burger in a stern voice. "I'll arrest you."

"You have no authority over civilians. Arrest me and you'll face court marshal if it's the last thing I do." Ericson's rage colored his face purple. "If I choose to stay, it's none of your business!" He sawed the reins in a vicious manner, causing Betty to squeal with pain and fear. His boots cruelly gouged the horse's flank, and he galloped off toward his house across an open field.

It was like a dream. We watched him gallop off against orders, too surprised to say anything at all. Captain Burger was at a complete loss for words, his jaw open. Betty's hooves caused small puffs of dust with each step, reminding me of the need for rain. As if in a dream we saw Betty break stride and stumble in a gopher hole. Ingvald was thrown from the saddle. He sailed through the air, landing on a pile of rocks. Every movement was slow and deliberate,

like running in a dream and getting nowhere. I wondered if Inga had piled those
rocks. No one moved or said a word. We
watched and gasped in disbelief, remembering the thud of flesh against stone.

Captain Burger rode over to examine
Ericson. He climbed down from his mount
and walked to where Betty was lying. He
pulled a Colt revolver from his holster and
shot her in the head. I hadn't noticed
Betty's screams until they stopped. Then he
walked over to Ericson and knelt beside
him, touching his shoulder.

Finally Captain Burger stood and called
out, "He's dead. Neck broken."

From the corner of my eye I saw Solveig
go to the stage door and heard her telling
Inga about her man's death. Inga left the
stage and walked slowly to where his body
lay. Her face showed no emotion. There was
a whispered conference with Captain Burger
and two privates went out with spades.

Ingvald Ericson was buried in the field
where he died. There was no priest to pray
over his grave. Not a kind word could be
found for eulogy. My throat was thick with
grief, but it was for the loss of Betty. No
one else seemed to mourn her.

"Does anyone have anything to say?"
Captain Burger said.

"I do." Solveig stood at the grave and read loudly from Psalm 37: 1-5. "Fret not thyself because of evildoers, neither be thou envious against the workers of iniquity. For they shall soon be cut down like the grass, and wither as the green herb." Then her voice softened and she turned to Inga and read, "Delight thyself in the Lord; and he shall give thee the desires of thine heart."

It was an unusual funeral message; even I could see that. But leave it to Solveig to hit the nail squarely on the head.

# 30

"Letter from Little Crow to Colonel Sibley;
He Wants to Make Peace"
~ St. Paul Journal

We were almost to Pomme de Terre before it hit me. Inga was free. Strange that something I had longed for, dreamed of would slip by until that moment. In the whirlwind of recent emotions, I'd felt nothing. Nothing at all.

"Thank God you're alive!" Anton Estvold pumped my hand hard.

"How did you make out?"

"Thank God Olaus came to Pomme de Terre. His gun helped push them back without loss of life. Come in!"

"There are too many of us."

"Of course. It's so good to see people again that I'm not thinking. We'll put your horses in the barn and cook food for the entire bunch."

"Remember Joe Sullivan?" I said. "He fought with your son at Shiloh."

"It is a pleasure," Anton said and reached for Anton's hand.

I left them discussing war and politics while I unhitched the horses in the barn. They were dependable beasts, steadfast and true. A man could put his faith in one and never be disappointed.

"Evan!" a voice called from the barn door.

I turned and was surprised to see Tilla Spitsberg. She was breathtakingly beautiful. Her golden hair curled softly around her perfect face. Blue eyes looked at me with gladness. She ran to me and threw both arms around my neck.

"I thought I'd never see you again," she said. She smelled faintly of lavender, reminding me for a second of my mor. How helpless I felt in her presence, overwhelmed by her words and freedom of emotion. I stood stiff and unbending, arms at my side. Behind her the door opened and Inga stood in the doorway. She took one glance and turned around and left, slamming the door behind her.

"Tilla." I pulled away. "Don't."

"I thought you were dead," she said and hugged me again. "I prayed you would be spared. That we could meet again and have a life together."

Her tears were hot on my neck. Things were out of control. "Tilla, you don't understand."

"I prayed for you every day." The look on her face frightened me with its intensity.

"Go back into the house and help your mor."

"She'll understand," Tilla said. "She knows how we feel."

"I'm promised to another," I said bluntly. "Someone else."

Tilla looked at me with surprise and wiped her eyes with an embroidered handkerchief. "Oh," she said. "I didn't know."

Turning on her heel, she walked to the barn door in a dignified manner. As soon as she thought she was out of my sight ran into the house like a little girl. I watched through a crack in the wall, her blonde curls flowing behind her as she ran. It was a wonder Little Six didn't have those strands decorating his teepee.

Later, Inga's face was haggard and drawn. Others may have thought she grieved her man but I knew better. Life had turned complicated, out of control. Solveig almost threw the stew on my plate. Some splashed off the side and burned my fingers.

"Solveig!" I cried, "watch what you're doing!"

"Hmm?" was all she answered.

"What's your problem?" I popped the burned finger in my mouth.

"You ought to know," Solveig said. "Big shot stage driver with a woman at every stop."

It was hard enough to deal with Inga let alone Solveig's big nose sticking into my business. I took my plate to the furthest corner of the yard and sat against a rock. It reminded me of the day I met Gabriel Timmers at Fort Snelling. How I wished Gabriel were there to cheer me up again.

Rasmuss joined me in the corner. He stuffed stew and bread into his mouth and mumbled with his mouth full.

"What did you say?" I asked.

"I said you have gotten yourself into one big mess."

"What are you talking about?" I hadn't done anything.

"Inga saw you courting that Spitsberg girl." He took another bite of stew, blowing on it to cool before swallowing it down whole. "What were you thinking of?"

My temperature started to rise and heat climbed my cheeks.

"If it were any of your business, which it

413

isn't, Tilla embraced me and I didn't hug her back." I was talking too much and knew it. "Furthermore, I might also tell you that I told Tilla in no uncertain terms that I was promised to another." A terrifying thought entered my mind, that I had lost Inga and would never have another chance with her. "After all we've been through together, you'd think a man's friends would stand by him and not jump to conclusions."

"I'm sorry," he said. "Solveig said . . ."

"Solveig!" I snorted. "I rue the day I brought you two together."

"You don't mean it!"

I willed myself to calm down, to let the anger drain out of my body.

"*Nei,* I don't mean it," I said. "Solveig is a steady hand in trouble and a true friend in time of need. I just wish she'd keep her nose out of my business."

"I'll talk to her," Rasmuss said.

Later that evening, Inga walked toward the outhouse behind the barn. Most of the travelers had settled down to sleep, bedrolls filled the house and barn. Some slept in the yard. I had taken to sleeping on top of the stage as the guards did during the day. It was a comfortable spot, off the damp ground. It also gave me a good view of all that went on.

When I spied Inga from my perch, I decided to speak to her about what she'd seen in the barn. I called to her from the side of the path on her return trip.

"Inga," I said. She stifled a scream.

"You scared me, sneaking up on me like that!"

"I'm sorry, I just wanted to talk to you."

"There's nothing to talk about." She sat down on a stump with a weary sigh.

"I think there is," I said. "So much happened today, my mind can't grasp it all."

"I know what you mean," she said. "Too much. I'm holding my breath until something bad happens again."

"Like seeing the Spitsberg girl hugging me in the barn." I broached the subject cautiously, knowing I was on thin ice.

"Something like that." She looked up at me with those melting brown eyes and my heart thumped like a locomotive engine. "Solveig told me what happened. I shouldn't have gotten so mad."

"It's understandable your nerves would be bad."

It was almost dark and I could hardly see her face, but I could hear her weeping. I fished a dirty handkerchief from my pocket. Stained with dried blood from Captain Van

Der Horck's wound.

"Now then," I said. "Here's a dirty hand-kerchief."

She laughed in spite of her tears. "*Nei.* I reek of baby puke and wet diapers, a little more won't hurt this apron."

"Inga." I was cut short by her two fingers across my lips.

"*Nei.* Wait a while. My man is gone, but I need time to think."

# 31

"107 Whites and 162 Mixed-blood
Prisoners Rescued from Sioux
at Camp Release"
~ St. Paul Journal

A young couple hailed us along the trail the next day. They wore tattered clothing and looked emaciated to the point of starvation. The man carried a small child on his back.

"Where are we?" the man asked in Norwegian and collapsed to the ground. Joe jumped down from the stage with a canteen and gave him a drink. The woman was in tears and the small boy wailed a thin lament.

"We're not far from Alexandria Woods," I said. "Who are you?"

"We are Christian and Hannah Omang and our son, Jon."

"What happened?"

"Indians attacked our cabin, we held them

off as long as we could and sneaked away when darkness fell. Haven't had anything to eat but grape leaves and raw potatoes since the attack," he said. "I think it was three weeks ago."

Captain Burger rode up from the other cavalrymen. "What's the trouble?" When he saw the small family, he called for a soldier to bring food. In a short time they were gobbling cold biscuits.

*"Mange takk, mange takk."* They eagerly pushed food and drink into their mouths.

"Where are they from?" Captain Burger asked, and I offered the question to the man in Norwegian.

"Rock Creek," he answered around mouthfuls of bread.

"That's forty miles from here!" I said. "Take it easy on the bread, you need to go slowly so you don't sicken."

"We dared not strike a fire, even if we'd had flint. We searched for a safe haven but everyone fled from the savages," he said in a hushed voice either too weak or too afraid to speak out. "Our two-year-old daughter died a few days ago. We buried her along a riverbank south of here. She couldn't live without cooked food."

The young boy looked close to death, too and the missus was almost naked with only an apron tied around her chest to cover herself.

"We'll noon here," said Captain Burger and rode back to his men.

Solveig brought a blanket. "I'll help you wash up and get a decent meal." Solveig's capable hands wrapped the blanket around Hannah's shoulders.

"We dared not say a word." Hannah's face was ashen, her eyes wild. "We didn't know where the Indians might be, where they might be lying in wait for us." She picked at the blanket and wrapped it tighter around her. "Except Jon would whisper in our ears while we carried him. He'd whisper, 'I'm hungry.' Ingrid grew too weak to cry. She grew quieter and quieter and finally didn't move at all."

Joe picked up the small boy and carried him to the shade. The man collapsed beside him. Solveig led the woman there, too.

"It doesn't make any sense," Solveig said. "No sense at all."

*"Nei,"* I answered. "It doesn't."

It hurt me to do it, but I had to ask the women in the stage to make room for the new family. The Omangs were in no shape to take another step. Inga started to get up, but Gunda pushed her back gently.

"I wouldn't mind the walk if you tend

419

the twins," Gunda said.

"That would be fine with me," said Inga.

Christian and Hannah climbed into the stage and wedged themselves into the seat where Gunda had been. Jon perched on his far's lap and Inga clasped the twins. It was a tight fit but it had to work.

Captain Burger ordered a different pace than my usual one, marching civilians taking more time than a stage with fresh horses. We passed Lars's farm without stopping, the burned-out buildings visible from the trail. I pushed back the thought of Lars with the arrows, the baby nailed to the door. Where were the little girls?

"Know those folks?" Joe said.

"*Ja.*" I swallowed hard. "Good people."

"Did they make it?"

"*Nei.*" I pushed back the faces and smells with all my willpower. I knew I had to redirect the conversation to something else, anything else. My hands shook and my quivering voice asked, "Joe, who is working your harvest with both of you gone?"

I half listened as he told of a second cousin willing to help.

We camped at an unsettled place, merely a flat piece of ground without too much brush. The Sauk River nearby provided water. I felt out of sorts, on edge. There were too many memories, thick and smothering. The ground was covered with a foot of oak leaves, dry and crispy. Every step caused a whisper or a rattle.

"We'll sleep safe here," Captain Burger said. "The leaves will be our watch dog."

The women built a fire and cooked coffee. We fairly inhaled the brew, delicious in the crisp autumn air. One of the civilians shot a young buck and dressed it out. Solveig buried potatoes in the fire. We feasted although there was no salt for the meat or milk for the coffee.

Inga sat with the women and made no effort to meet my eye or speak to me. There wasn't a moment as of late when I wouldn't have jumped at the chance to wed Inga, but suddenly without Ericson, I wasn't so sure. She carried his child. I wondered if the child was destined to be like his far. Madness and criminality ran in families, at least that is what I had been told all my life. What if stubbornness and meanness was inherited? Besides, I had nothing to offer her. There was no guarantee my job waited for me. I didn't have a thing.

"God, this is good," said Rasmuss.

"Do you hunt?"

"Once I shot an elk in my corn patch," Rasmuss said. "You hardly see an elk around

421

Foxhome anymore."

Solveig joined us, her face reddened when she sat next to her man.

"Have you ever eaten buffalo?" I asked.

"*Nei,* though I've seen them west of my place," Rasmuss said. "Have you?"

"My Dakota friend fed me buffalo more than once," I said. "It's good, better than beef."

"Inga told me you ran into Crooked Lightning on the way to the fort," Solveig said. "Said he spared your lives."

"*Ja,* he's a friend," I said. "Nothing changes that, not even the uprising."

I wondered again how Solveig knew everything. Folks poured out their hearts to her at the drop of a hat. On some occasions I had shared my heart with her myself, not too many could say that of me.

"Is Inga still your friend?" Solveig's eyes twinkled, and my anger toward her drained away.

"That, my dear Solveig," I said with all the sarcasm I could muster, "is none of your damn business."

It came to me as I drove the stage the following day that I had asked God if it really was His will for Inga to be married to Ericson. Shortly after the prayer I had seen with my own eyes the death of Ericson. Was it a coincidence or an answer to prayer? I would ask Bishop Whipple.

We made less time every day. Captain Burger ordered the children to ride on top of the stage and Joe to march with the men in the rear for a day or two. Captain Burger rode his horse beside the stage to protect us from attack.

The children clamored up on top of the stage, giggling and laughing, their eyes round with excitement. They liked to watch me spit snuff over the side of the stage and argued how far I could spit, if I could aim at a certain stone or plant. It kept my mind off the Indian raids and the day flew by.

We stopped Carl Evenson's that night. The house was standing but no one was home. Things were as I had found them over a month ago. Dishes still on the table, corn in the field. I wondered where they were, if they had left the country, survived.

Solveig pumped a pail of water, and I fired the cook stove. Coffee soon cooked in a big kettle, filling the room with its fragrance. The whole world seemed brighter with fresh coffee. It was a comfort.

"Do you think I could borrow a dress for Hannah?" Inga entered the cabin. "I'm sure the missus of this place would understand."

"It's not up to me," I said. "But I know the missus, and she has a kind and generous heart."

Inga's brown eyes were dull and her dress soaked from holding the twins all day. It looked like she could use a change of clothes herself.

"Maybe there would be another dress that you could borrow," I said looking at her wet skirt. "I could return it next trip."

"Do you think so?" Her face flushed. "I am sadly in need of a clean dress."

"In truth, you reek to high heaven," I said and laughed. It was the wrong thing to say, I saw at once.

"You try holding twins all day without getting your clothes wet!" To my horror she started to cry.

"Inga," I said. "I meant nothing disrespectful. It was only a little joke."

"Keep your jokes to yourself!" She went to the row of pegs on the side of the room that held the family's clothing. She took down a dress for Hannah and another for herself. She left the cabin with her chin tilted up and her hair falling down from its braided crown.

"Women!" I said after she slammed the cabin door on her way out, "I'll never understand them."

"You shouldn't have said that." Solveig chuckled. "Even if it's true. You hurt her feelings."

"I meant nothing," I said.

"She's been through a lot, and I expect her nerves are a little raw about now, her condition and all."

I poured a cup of coffee. "I'll drink my coffee in the barn. I need to check on the horses. My nerves are a little raw, too."

Solveig fixed biscuits, and Gunda found a bucket of molasses in the pantry to serve with them. After eating, the men sat around the cabin while the women washed dishes and laundered a few small items of clothing. Little children fell asleep anywhere they could find a spot to lie down.

Inga looked nice in the clean dress. Her hair was combed and she had found time to wash her face. She still looked tired. I hoped she would get one of the beds, but it looked like Gunda had claimed one of them for her and the twins and another woman was putting her children in the other one.

One by one the folks said good night and left the cabin. I waited for Inga outside, knowing she would visit the outhouse before going to bed.

"You look nice in that dress." It was what I had rehearsed while I waited.

*"Mange takk,"* she said. "I hope I smell better than before."

"Inga, I'm sorry, I meant no . . ."

Her giggles stopped the apology. "You were right," she said. "I smelled to high heaven and needed a bath and change of clothes."

"You've been through a lot lately," I started lamely.

"I had no reason to jump at you," she said. "I don't know what's wrong with me."

There was no privacy anywhere. People were bedded down in every direction and beyond the yard, soldiers watched and slept. I tipped a bucket upside down and motioned her to sit. Then I plopped down on the cold ground beside her. Her teeth chattered. She pulled her shawl closer around her.

"We need to talk," I said.

"I know."

"Inga . . ."

"*Nei,* let me speak," she said. She paused and the sounds of the night pressed in. The murmur of folks settling to sleep, someone snoring, a baby crying. "When my parents died, I felt I had no choice but to marry Gunnar. I loved him, had loved him all my life, but the choice was taken from me. It was either marry him or hire out as a

426

servant." Her belly rested on her legs and she hugged her knees in the darkness. "When Gunnar died, I had no choice about marrying Mr. Ericson. It was either marry him or return to Norway where I had nothing. In one year, I've lost two husbands. This time I want to think about it and make a good decision, not just marry to survive."

That she might refuse left me hollow and empty. Tears crowded my eyes and I dared not trust my voice. "What will you do?" I finally said after what seemed like an eternity of silence.

"That I don't know," Inga said and tilted her chin upwards. "But I'll find out."

# 32

"Let the Sioux Race be Annihilated"
~ St. Paul Journal

A barking dog greeted us at Bror Brorson's farm the next day.

"Prince!" I called. "Hello, Prince."

Billy ran out of the house. Curtains fluttered in an open window. The fields were harvested and a smug prosperity covered the farm.

"Ma, Pa! It's the stage!" he called. "It's Mr. Evan!"

Bror greeted me with a bear hug when I jumped down from the box.

"Thank God you're alive!"

The public emotion frightened me, and I felt myself pull away, both physically and emotionally. In truth, I was glad to see him but didn't know how to show it.

Sadie joined Solveig in helping folks from the coach. Solveig plopped a twin on each hip, and Inga climbed down. Her legs wobbled, her walk a stiff waddle. Sadie walked by her side, guiding her to the cabin. My eyes watched, though my heart felt dead. I never thought Inga wouldn't want me.

"Fort Abercrombie was besieged for almost six weeks," I said forcing myself to converse with Bror. "We made it through by the grace of God."

"Sit down, sit down. Sadie baked a cake today." Bror found stumps to sit upon. The others sprawled out over the yard while the soldiers made camp by the trail.

"Did you fight the Injuns?" asked Billy at my side. "Did you see any up close? Did they wear war paint? Was anyone scalped? Did you shoot any?"

"Billy," said Bror sharply. "Don't talk so much."

"Are you still an injun-lover?" Billy looked at me with a serious expression.

"*Ja,* we fought the Indians." I had little desire to discuss any of it. "There was a man at the fort called 'Clear Sky' because he could shoot from a great distance. He kept the Indians away."

When I grew tired of talking, I nudged Billy in another direction.

"See that man over there?" I asked.

"The one with the black boots?" Billy said.

"He's a famous war hero, fought in the battle of Shiloh and spent time in a reb prison camp." It was a dirty trick, but I was desperate for a minute of peace.

"He did?" Billy asked, excited. "What's his name?"

"Joe Sullivan."

"Hey, Mr. Sullivan!" Billy called and joined him on the step.

The quiet was a sweet relief.

"I saw how you did that," said Bror.

We laughed and poured another cup of coffee.

"Looks like your crops were harvested after all," I said. "Were they worth all your worry?"

"*Nei,* not worth the agony I spent over them," Bro said. "But I had a fair harvest, was able to sell a little wheat and corn. Had a nice crop of potatoes." He stretched out his feet in front of him, trying to get comfortable on the stump. "I made enough to get us through the winter and put in another crop next spring."

"Not many can say the same," I said.

"*Nei,* I expect not." Bror pulled a blade of green grass and chewed on the end. "The priest organized work teams to harvest the community's crops. Some stood guard while others worked in the fields. The job got done and we all survived."

"Now that was a smart way to do it," I grudgingly admitted, hoping it wasn't an affirmation of popery.

I briefly told him about being forted up, the battles fought and the journey to bring the civilians to St. Cloud. I didn't mention the trip out to the fort, the terror and violence, the faces pressing in. Maybe I would tell him some other time.

We walked out to the barn and found the mare that would drop my foal. In all the commotion, I had forgotten about our deal.

"She survived. Do you know how scarce horses are?"

"*Ja,* she survived by the grace of God, the bark from our good dog and the wise advice from you, our good friend." He paused to clear his throat. "You deserve the foal and more."

"Keep it," I said. "Horses are worth their weight in gold right now."

"*Nei,* I keep my word." Bror laughed a booming laugh. "Except for ham promises."

"Ham?"

"The pig got away. Either the Indians ate it or some wild critter. There will be no ham this year for Christmas."

"Don't worry about it," I said. "A bachelor

like me has little use for a big ham."

"Maybe I can help you find a wife," Bror said with a twinkle. "I owe you, remember?"

I quickly changed the subject to something less personal.

"Is it safe for you to remain on the farm?" I asked.

"We're staying, although there has been a steady stream of people leaving the state. Folks are running scared, giving up."

"They have reason."

"No sign of Indian trouble since you were last here, and it sounds like the army has things well in hand," he said. "It may be a risk, but I'll be watchful and keep Prince close by to warn us. The priest has organized patrols to check on each of us, to warn of danger."

"I wish you the best," I said. "Seeing you is almost like seeing family from home."

He didn't answer. He was completely clean — hands, shoes, clothes, hair. Marriage was a mysterious thing, that's for sure.

As we left Bror's, I thought how Sadie was content to live with him in spite of the dangers. No wonder Inga wanted nothing to do with me; I had nothing to offer.

We straggled into Ole Swenson's place that night with barely enough light to see the trail. A glowing lamp from their window guided us to their door.

One of the older girls answered our knock, her face red from weeping, hair straggled and unkempt. She was too thin.

"What's wrong?" I feared Indians.

"It's Mor," she said. "She's dead."

"Solveig!" I called. "You're needed."

The mister called from somewhere inside the house. "Who is it?"

"It's the stage driver."

Solveig took charge at once, introducing herself and going into the house.

"It's a bad time," I said. "Your daughter says you've lost your missus."

"*Ja.*" His voice choked. "It wasn't time for her sickness yet, she had another month to go. But tonight after supper she lay down on the bed and started jerking and shaking. Then she quit breathing."

"I'm sorry, Mister." Even in my own ears the words sounded feeble. What caused such a thing. Maybe a doctor could have prevented it. Then I thought of Inga facing her own sickness soon.

"I lost them both."

Solveig had a pot of oatmeal cooking on the stove when we went in. The missus lay on the bed with a blanket pulled over her. The smaller children were sleeping on pallets spread on the floor. The two oldest wept in the corner. Everything was neat and clean, though threadbare.

"Do you mind if our party camps in your yard?" I asked. "We will do no damage and will leave in the morning."

"*Nei,* stay as long as you want. The well is in the yard for water."

I explained the situation to Captain Burger and we made camp in the yard. It was hard to sleep knowing the fresh grief inside. I wondered how they would make it without a mor to care for the eight children. The oldest couldn't be more than twelve or thirteen. The youngest was still a baby.

"Where's Solveig?" Rasmuss asked.

"Inside helping out." Rasmuss rolled out the blankets he carried, making a bed for the both of them while I made a small campfire. "She'll join me later."

"There's not much room in the cabin."

"We were here before, on our way back to Foxhome."

"I'd forgotten." It seemed like another life, another time and place.

"Solveig has talked about little Halvor," Rasmuss said. "She was real taken with him."

"I wonder what'll happen to him. Things were hard before. And now this."

"It's a terrible thing for a family to lose

their mor," he said. "And in such hard times."

It wasn't long before Solveig came out from the house. She walked over to where we were and spoke directly to Rasmuss.

"Could we take Halvor? This poor man will never make it with all these children. We would be doing him a favor and giving Halvor a better life."

"Wait a minute, now," Rasmuss said. "Aren't you getting a little carried away with this? Swenson's already lost his wife and baby."

"Could we ask him?" she said.

"Hmm," said Rasmuss. "It wouldn't do any harm to ask."

*"Mange takk!"* Solveig grabbed Rasmuss around the neck and kissed him square on the lips. Suddenly she remembered I was watching and backed away, turning as red as a scarlet tanager in the firelight.

"Don't stop!" Rasmuss attempted to kiss her again. "This is good!"

"You!" She pushed him away. In a serious tone she added quietly, *"Mange takk,* dear husband. *Mange takk."*

The burial was a hasty affair the next morning. Captain Burger read from Proverbs 31:27-28 "She looketh well to the ways of

435

her household and eateth not the bread of idleness. Her children arise up and call her blessed; her husband also, and he praiseth her."

"Blessed be her memory," Captain Burger said and prayed the Lord's Prayer.

Halvor was dressed in a clean shirt and carried a small bundle in his tiny hand. Solemnly each member of the family kissed him good-bye. Then Solveig put him on one hip and perched Fisk on her opposite shoulder and walked with the others. I don't know to this day what Solveig said to make Mr. Swenson grant permission for her to take Halvor, but it didn't surprise me one bit.

Citizens of St. Cloud greeted us like heroes, clapping and cheering when we straggled into town. Jane Grey Swisshelm, editor of the *St. Cloud Democrat,* made a speech and commended us for our patriotic duty in resisting the savages.

"The Sioux need to be exterminated, driven forever from our land," she said in a loud voice while standing on a stump in the center of town. "They are vermin, filthy animals incapable of civilization. Just ask the citizens of Hutchinson, Forest City, New Ulm."

A murmur of approval rippled through

the crowd. I thought of Crooked Lightning's family, the friendship I had experienced as a stranger in the land, the dignity he had extended to me.

"They should be pushed out of our state forever; the blood of the innocents demand it," her voice rose in a fevered pitch. "Thank you, my friends, for doing your best to fight back, to resist the violence of the savages. You are a credit to our state."

She stepped down from the stump amidst a round of applause while the women of the town put together a hurried meal. Miss Swisshelm mingled among our bedraggled band while we ate, asking for bits of information to put into her newspaper.

"You must have stories to tell," she said as she shook my hand. "You're the one who drove the stage ten miles in thirty minutes to get away from attacking Indians, aren't you?"

My English failed me completely. To my horror I could not answer one word that made any sense. I'm not sure if it was the fact she was a female or that my words would be quoted in the newspaper. Either way, I was of no value to her whatsoever. She turned to Joe Sullivan next to me and began asking him questions.

She quickly found out he had been in a

rebel prison camp and began pumping him for information.

It was a relief to flee to the barn with the horses.

A crack in the barn wall allowed me to watch the other members of our group disperse. I saw Solveig and Rasmuss take Halvor by the hand and approach Inga. Together they walked to the only hotel in town. It was reassuring to know Solveig would keep an eye on Inga.

I was shoeing horses the next day when someone called out, "Wagon train coming!"

The streets crowded as a small wagon train, three covered wagons and one flatbed pulled by mules, rode into town. It was mostly women and children escorted by a few soldiers. They were in sorry condition.

"Where you from?" asked Joe Sullivan of a private riding by on a broken-down horse.

"Camp Release," he said and kept riding.

"Where's that?" Joe said.

"You'll find out."

We followed the caravan to the center of town. A captain conferred hurriedly with Captain Burger and jumped up on a wagon to address the gathered citizens.

"We have here a group of unidentified prisoners that were held by the Sioux and exchanged at Camp Release." He wiped his sharp nose on his sleeve. "We think they were captured on the northern frontier but have no way of knowing. Most of them cannot speak English and some of them are in shock, unable to tell us who they are or where they're from."

"Damn savages," someone muttered.

"These people are in bad shape," the captain continued. "We need your help to identify them. Some of the children are too young to give us any information. If you would have an interest in adopting any of them, just speak up."

The soldiers began to unload the covered wagons and flatbed and gather the victims in a small cluster. Children and babies cried. Women stared in stony silence, filthy and ragged, some dressed in the shirts of soldiers who had taken pity on their nakedness.

She stood alone by herself, off to one side. Her dress was a tattered rag that did not quite cover her body. I recognized her and walked over to where she stood.

"Missus Schwarz," I said with hat in hand, "It's me, Evan Jacobson, the stage driver."

Her eyes met mine. Her expression was placid, and her hands hung calmly at her side, but there was a wildness in her eyes.

She looked at me for a long minute. It was a shock when the words came. Never before had I heard her voice.

"I watched them into the yard come." Her voice was high pitched. "The bell I should have rung but instead I gave them bread, hoping Mister Schwarz would not see, that he would in the field remain. Bread I gave them."

Her voice broke slightly and I looked at my boot tops, wishing I could be somewhere else, anywhere else.

"They ate. Always before it was one or two who to the door came. This time in paint and feathers came seven. They stank of grease."

Her voice trailed off. I hoped it was all she would say.

"The house they tore apart. Knocked over the stovepipe until filled with smoke the room. Spread hot coals around the house. On the clean bed and the wood box. Then outside they dragged me."

I couldn't help but lift my eyes to hers.

"As their wife they used me. All of them . . ." her voice cracked, and I expected tears but there were none. "Mister Schulz raging came into the yard. A hatchet in the belly they threw, but dead he wasn't. Forced him they did to see how they used me."

"Missus, you don't have to tell me . . ." The faces pressed in, and I could smell burning flesh. My head started spinning and I feared I would faint. Her voice droned on in a dead tone. An Indian with face painted half black and half green chopped off Mister Schwarz' hands and dragged him back into the burning house.

By sheer will, my head began to clear.

"A beating I risked to feed them but they abused me still," she said. "My help it did not matter."

I reached for her. She backed away in fright and I pulled back. How stupid to think a man's embrace would comfort her after what she had been through.

"I'm sorry, Missus Schwarz," I said lamely. "Do you have family I can reach for you?"

"There's a sister," she said slowly. "Marta in Mankato."

"What's her last name?" I asked.

"Marta," she said and her eyes took on the wild stare again. "Her name is Marta."

Rasmuss and Solveig joined me, hearing the last bit of conversation. Solveig handed Halvor to Rasmuss and held out a gentle hand towards the missus.

"Do you want to see my cat?" Solveig asked.

Silently the woman reached out a hand

and stroked the gray head of the royal cat. Solveig led her to a bench beside a building.

"Rasmuss," I said. "You have one capable woman."

"She is one in a million."

We turned to leave when out of the corner of my eye I spied another familiar face. A cluster of children stood patiently in the square, utter bewilderment on each dirty face.

"Ragna!" I called softly, not wanting to frighten her. "Ragna Larson."

I went to her and knelt on one knee before her. Her clothes were filthy dirty and torn beyond recognition. There were sores on her face and around her mouth and her hair was a tousled tangle. A lump in my throat threatened to choke me when I saw a large bruise the shape of a hand across her cheek.

"Ragna, it's me, Uncle Evan," I said. "I've been looking for you."

Blank eyes filled with tears and remembrance.

"Uncle Evan!" She threw herself into my arms. "I want my mor!"

My eyes searched the remaining children but I saw no sign of Borghilde.

"Shh . . ." I crooned to her, just as I crooned to a frightened horse or calmed a nervous team, "Shh . . . you're with your Godfather now. Everything will be all right."

Her small arms molded around my neck. My love for Lars and his family swept over me with such strength I felt tears in my eyes. I thought of the promises I had made, the ones I had broken and the one I would keep. From that moment on, the faces left me.

# 33

"Sioux Payment Investigative Report
Suppressed; Gotten with Great Difficulty"
~ St. Paul Journal

There was no other way. I took Ragna by
the hand and found Inga. She was in the
lobby of the hotel, Gunda and the twins
nearby. The room was luxurious with velvet
curtains and heavy furniture, ornate and
formal.

"Inga," I said. "I need your help."

"How can I help you?"

She struggled to get up from the divan,
finally pulling herself to her feet. Her belly
was huge, her face drawn and exhausted.

"This is Ragna Larson," I said. "I am her
Godfather, her only family now."

She looked at Ragna and her eyes melted
to brown pools.

"Hello, Ragna," she said. "What a beautiful name. I had a friend in Norway with the

same name." She reached out and touched Ragna's dirty hand. "My name is Inga."

I wondered what Ragna thought. If this gentle Norwegian woman reminded her of her mor, if she was comforted by Inga's presence like I was.

"Of course, you see my predicament," I said in my most businesslike manner. "It would be most improper for me to care for a little girl by myself."

Inga looked at me, waiting for me to speak. I had this wild urge to ask her to marry me, to help parent Ragna, to let me father her unborn child. But it was a foolish thought, too absurd to mention. I had nothing, would probably never have anything to offer.

"Could Ragna stay with you until I can make other arrangements?"

I thought I spotted a quick look of disappointment in Inga's eyes but couldn't be sure. It was comforting just to speak to her, to hear her voice and watch her smile at Ragna.

"Of course." Inga made room for Ragna beside her on the divan. "We have much to talk about, Ragna, and I'm sure you are hungry and tired."

"Uncle Evan!" Ragna's voice rose to a pathetic wail. She clutched my hand in a vise grip and refused to let go. "Don't leave me."

Gunda stood up and picked up the twins. "I'll be going outside for a while to get some air," she said. "You can take my place."

I sat beside Inga on the divan, holding Ragna in my lap. The divan was covered with scratchy horsehide and reminded me of my aunt's house in Norway. A wave of homesickness washed over me, a quick ache that soon left.

Inga was neatly washed and bathed, smelling sweetly of lavender. Ragna was crawling with lice, I noticed to my horror. Not that I was much better. My own clothes were filthy and stiff, hair greasy and unkempt and my beard a red jumbled mass. I couldn't remember my last bath — certainly it was before the Indians took to the warpath. It would not do to ask a favor in such condition.

"I'm sorry, Inga." I stood up so quickly that Ragna would have fallen to the floor if I hadn't reached down and held her to my chest. "It looks like Ragna and I could both use a bath and change of clothes. In truth, Ragna is lousy. I'll come back later after we've cleaned up."

Inga's eyes opened wide and looked at me for a moment. "In truth, you both reek to high heaven," she said, and I felt a quick flame spread up my cheeks.

Before I could answer, I heard the laughter. It poured out of her like water through a broken dam, musical and heartening, leaving her weak and helpless and holding her sides. Another laugh joined hers, and it took me a few seconds to recognize it as my own. It was almost foreign, a sound I hadn't heard in ages. I set Ragna on the divan and she looked at us with round eyes, not comprehending, almost fearful while Inga and I laughed until the tears flowed, a sweet release from the weeks of stress and worry.

Suddenly Inga was in my arms and I was holding her close, her mounded belly tight against me. Her hair was a drawing sweetness, and I buried my nose in it. I wanted to touch it, caress it, and see it flow down her back without pins or braids. But then I felt her baby kick against me and I stepped back in surprise.

"I felt him move," I said.

"*Ja,* he's an active one," Inga answered and her face lit up. "Every day he is stronger." She placed a protective hand on her belly.

"He'll need a *far,*" I said, speaking almost without thinking.

"*Ja,*" she said, "he'll need a *far,*"

We stood looking at each other, the moment ripe and full. Her eyes melted brown, like a doe in the forest. Her face was thin, too thin, but some regular meals would take care of that. Her beauty and pure goodness overwhelmed me, making my legs wobbly.

"Ragna will need a *mor,*" Inga said quietly.

"*Ja,* she'll need a mor," I said and stepped, though the ice was thin and I had no guarantee of the answer. "And I need a wife; someone to love and care for, family in this faraway place, a home of my own."

I didn't exactly ask, and she didn't exactly answer, but a kiss sealed the agreement without words. All my life I had wondered how a man would feel kissing a woman. I had thought it might be awkward or embarrassing, but it wasn't. It was the most natural thing in the world but still I glanced over at Ragna, now sleeping on the divan. It wouldn't be proper to display such affection in front of a child.

"Don't worry," Inga said and placed the palms of her hands on my cheeks, smoothing the wildness of my beard. "She'll get used to it."

# 34

"Sibley Moving Army and Sioux Prisoners
to Lower Agency to Continue Trials"
~ St. Paul Journal

Rasmuss and Solveig were overjoyed.

"I knew it," said Solveig. "The day the stage stopped at her house and you had coffee even though the mister wasn't home."

"But it was perfectly proper," I protested. "We spoke only of our homeland and the troubles in getting established in a new place." I was saying too much but I wouldn't allow Inga's reputation to be damaged in any way. "Nothing improper about it."

"I didn't say anything bad happened that day," Solveig said. "I only said I knew from that first day. The expression on your face when you came out of the house, the grief in your voice. I knew you were in love from that first day."

I should have known she would figure it out.

"Since we can't go west to Foxhome until the Indians are under control," said Rasmuss, changing the subject, "we've decided to winter at Fort Snelling. Maybe Bishop Whipple would take his housekeeper back for the winter months, and I could find work cutting wood."

It all fell into place with that one statement. Rasmuss and Solveig with little Halvor would travel with us to Fort Snelling. Inga and Ragna would stay with them until we could be married. It was decided Bishop Whipple should perform the ceremony. The rest was in the hands of God.

"There's no guarantee my job awaits me," I said looking at Inga.

"*Nei,* there are no guarantees," she said. "But we are young and strong, and there will be work somewhere."

"Will you go back to Inga's farm in the spring?" asked Rasmuss.

My jaw almost fell open. Once such a driving force, the land had not entered my thoughts.

"There's Ragna's land to consider also," said Solveig. "That farm seems a little more prosperous though you'd have to rebuild the house."

It was too much, too soon. Inga rescued me.

"We have all winter to make our plans." She looked at me, and I remembered the brown eyes underneath a sunbonnet that captured my heart. "We'll take it day by day and trust in the Good Lord to lead and guide us as He has done already."

"Amen," said Solveig. "Thanks be to God."

While I agreed with her our need to put our faith in God, I shuddered to think of her confidence in me. What if I failed?

Joe Sullivan had orders to return to Fort Abercrombie. Rasmuss would ride shotgun, and the women and children would ride in the stage. The Widow Schwarz was traveling with us as far as Fort Snelling and would go on to Mankato to search for her sister. She wore a dress donated by Jane Grey Swisshelm, who was sympathetic to her plight. Miss Swisshelm published a story about the widow's search for her Mankato sister in the *St. Cloud Democrat,* her ordeal with the Dakota.

"If anyone contacts me, I'll direct him to Fort Snelling," said Miss Swisshelm as she walked the woman to the stage. "I hope and pray you find your family."

*"Danke,"* Widow Schwarz said in a quiet

451

voice. Her hands were relaxed, but I avoided looking into her eyes. If they looked wild, I didn't want to know about it. Solveig could deal with her.

"Would you give this letter to my wife?" Joe pressed an envelope into my hands.

"*Ja,* I will."

"And tell her we are well?" he asked. "And that I send my love."

"I will tell her," I said.

Captain Burger came out to the stage as we were about to leave "You should be safe enough," he said. "There's been little in the way of Indian raids east of here, and the worst of the lot have been captured. The Indian trials continue at the Lower Agency, they have over 300 cases to hear."

"We'll keep a sharp eye anyway." I wondered if Crooked Lightning was one of the captured Dakota. "I've seen enough bloodshed to be cautious."

"Here are the dispatches," Captain Burger said. "I've taken the liberty to write an explanation of your whereabouts these last weeks — maybe it will secure your job."

"*Tussen takk,* Captain." My voice thickened in spite of my efforts to keep the emotion down. He was an important man, and I was deeply touched he would take the time to try to help me, a poor and ignorant immigrant. "Whatever happened to the Indian gold?"

"It was at Fort Ridgely during the battle."

"At Fort Ridgely?"

"It arrived one day too late."

The news staggered me. One day too late to stop the Indian war. If the gold had arrived one day earlier, there would have been no massacres, no burnings, no rape. Baby Evan could have grown up to be president, Lewis could have met Tilla Spitsberg, Lars would have written home to his mor about his corn crop, Ragna would still have her parents. It was beyond words, beyond explanation.

My voice refused to speak, but I forced myself back to the present. I flicked the reins over the backs of the army team. The horses were sturdy and dependable. It came to my mind how much I was entrusting to them — my new daughter, future wife, and unborn child. *Ja,* they were up to the challenge and would safely carry us to the fort.

The fields were harvested, homes left standing; it was hard to believe the Indian Uprising really happened. Everything seemed normal — except for the many abandoned houses.

No one was at the Sanger farm. The crops had been cut, but the animals were gone and no one lived there. We went into the cabin and made a quick fire to cook some dinner. The Widow Schwarz found a broom and swept away the dust and cobwebs from the wooden table and kitchen area. She rarely spoke but was helpful with any small task Solveig assigned her to do.

"Good thing I have a few potatoes left." Solveig found a cast iron skillet in the pantry and an old pork rind in an empty crock. The pork rind had enough fat to grease the skillet and soon the aroma of fried potatoes filled the air.

"Smells good!" Rasmuss playfully tried to kiss her neck while she chopped onions into the pan.

"Rasmuss!" she said. "I'm busy right now!" Her face turned cherry red, maybe from the heat of the stove. Rasmuss chuckled and picked up Halvor and carried him around the room on his back.

"Ride the horsie, Halvor!" he cried. "Ride the horsey!"

Halvor smiled but made no reply. It came to me I had never heard the boy laugh. Time would help, I knew, but it was hard losing a mor and finding another. It reminded me of Ragna and her great need.

I looked over at Inga, sitting at the table and wondered how it would be to kiss her neck whenever I wanted. My own cheeks turned rosy with the thought, and I quickly stood up and left the room. I'd best tend to business and avoid thinking about such things. It was a precious thought, just the same, to think that soon I could kiss her whenever I wished. I would wish it often.

"I'll check on the horses," I called back over my shoulder. "Come with me, Ragna. Let's go see the horses."

We slept at the home of Anders Johnson.

"Evan!" Anders greeted me. "Thank God you're alive."

"By the grace of God," I said. "Can you put us up?"

"Of course. I'll tell the missus."

Around the table we ate a hurried supper of cream and bread, Halvor and Ragna half asleep already. The women and children bedded down on the floor. I couldn't help but notice Inga awkwardly lying down on her pallet and think of how soon I could lie beside her and not a commandment in the world would forbid it. She looked at me and smiled goodnight. I couldn't help but wonder if she thought the same thing.

Anders, Rasmuss, and I chewed snuff and drank coffee until the women and children were asleep. Then we told Anders our experiences with the Dakota, keeping our voices low so as not to alarm the women or children if one would awaken.

"Were there any raids around here?" I asked.

"*Nei,* we only heard about the troubles when the rider from Cold Spring came by, warning us to gather to defend ourselves. It seemed far-fetched, impossible to believe," said Anders. "We kept watch but never left the farm. It was in the middle of harvest and we would have lost the whole thing had we left."

"You were lucky," said Rasmuss bluntly. "Others weren't so lucky."

We told them about the siege at Fort Abercrombie, the killings, the murder of Hjalmer Thoreson, and the prisoners from Camp Release.

"It was worse down in the Minnesota River Valley," said Rasmuss.

"By God," Anders said. "Something has to be done with those savages."

"The worst of the lot are going to trial for their crimes," Rasmuss said.

"The children will only grow up to avenge their fathers," Anders said. "We can't expect them to think like civilized people."

I thought of the questions Crooked Lightning had asked about the steam engines, the sharp perceptions he expressed about our military system. *Nei,* I did not think him uncivilized. But Lewis' body.

"Some say they should be exterminated," said Rasmuss taking a chew of snuff, "like rats in a corncrib."

"There was wrong on both sides." I spit a brown stream into the spittoon. "Their people were starving. We didn't keep our end of the bargain."

I told them about the gold payment arriving one day too late.

"By God," Anders said. "One day late and all hell broke loose."

"Actually it was months overdue," I said quickly, not willing him to think the army was only twenty-four hours late with the payment. "But the payment came one day short to avoid the uprising."

"If you find a newspaper with the court proceedings," said Anders thoughtfully, "I'd like a copy."

"I'll keep you in mind."

"What's the news from the south?" Rasmuss said.

"We don't hear nuthin' without the stage going by," said Anders. "A man gets to feeling cut off without any regular news every week or so."

I slept on top of the stage that night and chuckled when Rasmuss complained of bedbug bites the next morning.

"Why didn't you warn me?" Rasmuss said as we were on our way. "We could have bunked in the barn had we known."

"It seemed only fair," I said. "When you and Solveig had the barn alone that night on your trip to Foxhome, I suffered from bites for days afterwards."

"You seem like such a gentle soul, and yet here you are paying me back months later."

"Come on, Rasmuss," I said. "You know that night alone in the barn was worth it all."

"You're absolutely right. It was well worth it."

We rode on in silence, everything worth saying already been said. We drove in civilized country, far from the Indian raids. There was no need for a shotgun rider.

"Why don't Inga and me change places?" asked Rasmuss. "I'd like some time with my wife and no doubt you and Inga have much to discuss."

It was a tempting thought.

"It might be hard for her to get up on the

driver's seat," I said.

"We'll help her up."

I stopped the stage in the shade of an oak tree along the trail. Its leaves were brilliant scarlet and red sumac made a splash of color. The wind was chilly, but Inga held her shawl around her and seemed pleased with the plan.

She took my hand, and Rasmuss gave her a boost from behind. Soon we were plodding down the trail, almost alone.

"Tell me about yourself," I said. "I know so little about you."

"There's not much to tell," she said with a laugh. "I grew up in Trondheim, two brothers and myself."

"Two brothers?" I asked. "I only heard you speak of one, the one in the army."

"My oldest brother Roald died in the famine, right after he was confirmed. Trygve and I were younger." Her voice trailed off and it seemed an effort to bring herself to tell the rest of the story. "After Trygve and I were confirmed, Mor and Far both died of smallpox. For some strange reason, neither Trygve nor I got it though we cared for them until they died. Trygve decided to join the military, and I was promised to Gunnar. The farm was worth so little, it was hardly a cottage and garden space, that we decided to trade it for passage to America. It was Trygve's wedding gift to us, his part of the inheritance, as little as it was."

I shot a stream of brown snuff over the side of the stage, making a crackling sound in the fallen leaves along the trail. A red fox with white tip on his tail skirted into the underbrush at our passing and pushed his long nose out of the brush to look at us.

"You know the rest," she said. "There's nothing left to tell."

"Did you ever play 'Hide the Thimble'?"

"*Ja*, of course!" she said. "It kept us busy for hours during the dark winter days."

"And did you ever use the thimble to draw pictures in the frosty windows?"

"*Ja*, beautiful pictures of castles and princesses."

"I did the same. And dreamed big dreams of going to America with Christina and being a rich landowner."

"Christina, the sister who died," she said. "But you have her hair."

"I still hold it sometimes when I'm afraid or lonely." I laid bare my feelings openly and yet somehow without fear. "It comforts me."

"Evan," she said slowly. "I hope I will be a comfort to you."

"Already." I looked at her with all the love

I could put into my expression. "You have done that already."

The horses plodded, and I draped the reins over my legs and held her in my arms, kissing her. No one was there to see or disapprove. "This is how it will be," I thought to myself. "This is how it will be to kiss her whenever I wish." My hands undid the pins in her hair, and I watched it fall and flutter in the breeze.

It was almost a disappointment when we reached our noon stop at Joe Sullivan's. Inga's face turned almost as red as Solveig's when she saw the cabin up ahead and she hurriedly tucked her hair back with the pins. I doubted anyone would notice anyway. In a small bend in the road, I leaned over and kissed her once more.

"Dear Inga," I said, "we cannot be married too soon to suit me."

"Someone will see!" She gently pushed me away.

"Let them look all they want," I said in a husky voice. "Soon you will be my missus and no one can say a word against us."

The stage was almost at the cabin when I spoke again. "Will you ride with me again — up in the box, I mean?"

"*Ja,*" she answered. "If it's safe."

Missus Sullivan was pleased to get the let-

461

ter from her man. She looked over the outside of the letter, even smelled it. I hoped it didn't smell of my sweat from being in my shirt pocket. Then she sat down on a wooden box in the yard and read it.

"Thanks for bringing it," she said looking at me. "At least he's out of that hellhole of Andersonville. I'd rather he took his chances with the savages."

I nodded, remembering the harsh accusations hurled at me during my last visit. If she remembered them, she chose not to bring them up.

"There's soup on the stove," she said. "Come in."

Rasmuss helped Inga down from the stage box, and they both laughed and commented on her awkwardness.

"He'll be a big boy," Inga said. "Big and strong and ready to help on the farm."

"It's a boy all right," said Missus Sullivan. "You can always count on a boy when you carry high and to the front." She positioned herself in front of Inga and boldly placed both hands on either side of her belly. "He's a strong one!" she said. "I can feel him kick."

Missus Sullivan took Inga's arm and guided her into the house. Inga seemed a little wobbly, just a little unsteady, and I cast a worried look at her.

"She shouldn't ride in the box again," Solveig said at my side with Halvor on one hip and Ragna clasping her other hand.

"She shouldn't?" I asked.

"Look how swollen her feet and ankles are — it's from being on that cramped shotgun seat." Solveig eyed Inga with a long glance. "She needs to be in the coach from now on."

"I didn't know you were her doctor, Solveig," I said. "But you might be right, and we can't take a chance."

"Besides," she added with a knowing smirk. "It would not do for her to be in a disheveled condition when she arrives at the bishop's. I have her reputation in mind."

It was a quick nooning then back on the trail. If we pushed it a little harder, we could reach Fort Snelling by dark. Solveig must have spoken to Inga because she went directly to the coach and did not ask about riding with me. Our eyes met when I secured the stage door, and the warmth of hers melted my heart, causing me to weaken and ache.

Rasmuss climbed up beside me and talked about the advantages of farming in western Minnesota where it was flat and free of stumps.

"Look," he said. "Every field is a work of agony to first cut the trees, haul them away and then those blasted stumps to dig out. Every tree is a curse to a farmer."

"Now then, Rasmuss," I said in my most soothing voice. "A tree is a comfort and a shade on a hot day and a windbreak from the cold wind. Not every tree is a curse."

"You've got a point." Rasmuss spit a stream of snuff into the side of the trail. "Some trees are good, but I'm glad Foxhome has none to fight. I want to grow wheat and corn, not trees."

We drove on in silence. I was wondering what it would be like to be married when Rasmuss spoke again. "Will you settle on Inga's place?"

There was no answer. I didn't feel quite right about reaping financial reward from her man's death. It didn't seem right to take his farm.

"You could rebuild the Larson place," he said. "Solveig thinks that might be better for you — it's a beautiful spot. One you've earned by raising Ragna."

I felt foolish admitting to Rasmuss that I feared the faces might come back to haunt me if I lived on the Larson place. So I said nothing, just drove down the trail.

Rasmuss dozed in his seat. It was almost a

relief to have a little quiet to think it all over. In truth, I didn't know what to do. I only knew that I wanted to marry Inga and try to find work again with the army stage. The other plans would have to wait until the Indian problem was solved and normal life returned to the frontier.

"Welcome!" said Bishop Whipple. "Come in, come in. I'll fix something to eat, and you can clean up from your journey."

We straggled in from the stage in the blackness of the autumn evening. It was cold, and I wiped my nose on my sleeve, sniffing loudly. Ragna was crying, and I picked her up and carried her into the house and laid her down on the floor next to the stove where it was warm. Then I returned to help the others.

Solveig handed Halvor to the Widow Schwarz and turned to help Inga into the house.

"She's sick," said Solveig. "Her sickness has started."

*"Nei,"* I burst out. "It's not her time."

"Time or no time," Solveig said, "the baby is coming."

When we got into the lamplight, the look on Inga's face alarmed me. She was white with dark circles around her eyes. She looked at me, almost as if begging for help. I quickly went to her side and put my arm around her. She leaned heavily against me and I feared she would fall to the floor.

Bishop Whipple grasped the situation and directed the women to his room in the back. I stood in shock, not knowing what to do, fighting down an overwhelming panic. Halvor lost his mor during such sickness. It happened all the time. What if Inga didn't survive?

"Get a grip on yourself, man!" said Rasmuss. "It'll be all right. Babies are born every day, and they usually come without problem." His voice sounded shaky and his argument weak.

I had been at enough calvings and lambings to know how it worked. It was hard on the mor, I knew that much. Although I wasn't exactly the far, it was hard on me, too.

"Is there a doctor in the fort?" I asked Bishop Whipple, who was trying to find food for all of us.

"The post surgeon might be willing to come," he said.

"I'll fetch him." Rasmuss seemed eager to leave the house, go far from the worries and sounds of birth. I couldn't blame him.

He left, and Bishop Whipple handed me a

slice of stale bread and an apple. "It's not much but it's all I have in the place."

Ragna was already asleep, but I handed the food to Halvor and as I did so almost jumped out of my skin. A moan pierced the air. It reminded me of the wounded soldiers. When I realized it was Inga suffering, the sweat beaded on my face and my knees weakened so that I grasped a chair and sat down.

"I must go to her," I said. "She needs me."

"It's not proper," said the bishop. "The women will care for her and the doctor will be here soon."

"Why is it acceptable for the doctor to help her?" Fear made me belligerent. "I'm the one who is to marry her," I said. "I should be the one to help her."

The bishop looked at me with a puzzled frown.

"You will marry her?" he asked.

"Her man is dead, and I will marry her," I said.

"You will raise her child as your own?" he asked.

"As my very own."

"Then you should marry her before the child is born," he said. "Then he will bear your name, legally be your son."

Of course, the bishop was right. We should

be married before the baby came.

"Can you marry us tonight then?" I heard my voice creak and break. We would be wed on St. Simon's Day. A day to remember for the rest of our lives.

"If she's willing," he said.

# 35

"Indian Trials Resume at Lower
Agency — Guilty Sentenced to
Hang by the Neck"
~ St. Paul Journal

It was not as I had planned. Rasmuss was
out of breath from running for the doctor,
who was not at the post anyway. Inga's face
was chalk white and her hair sweaty and
disheveled. Solveig had a look of firm
resolve, much needed and appreciated, as I
felt near collapse myself, hardly in a position to encourage my dear Inga in her sickness.

We timed the vows between pains.

"In the sight of God and this company,"
Bishop Whipple said in his most official
voice, "do you take this woman to be your
lawful wife?"

"*Ja,*" I said. "I do."

"Inga Ericson," he said. "do you take this

469

man as your lawful husband, to love, honor and obey all the days of your life?"

"I do," she said and grasped my hand with all of her strength as another pain hit. Solveig pushed me aside. I watched Inga twist and stiffen. Her face reminded me of the mares I had helped foal, their desperation to bring forth a foal.

"You can leave now," Solveig said. "You all can leave now."

"I now pronounce you man and wife," said the Bishop. "May God grant you grace and mercy to meet life's joys and challenges together."

She looked at me briefly between pains and smiled a weak and wilted grimace. "I know it will be a boy," she said. "We will have a son."

"Or maybe a sweet daughter to look like her mor." A boy would be an heir, someone to continue the Jacobson name, to help work for our future and then inherit it.

There was no privacy. A wild fear surged through me that she might die, and I would lose my wife before she was really mine.

I knelt beside the bed and whispered in her ear, "Inga, darling, my wife — Inga Jacobson. The old name forgotten forever."

Another pain consumed her, and I was almost bodily removed from the room.

"She doesn't have time for you right now," Solveig said sternly. "Wait out here, and we'll call you when the baby comes."

"Wait out here?" I asked. "Is there nothing else I can do?"

"Pray," she said and slammed the door tight.

The night stretched on unendingly. At times the women came out to fetch more water or to warm the blankets wrapped around Inga's belly.

"Is something wrong?" I asked Solveig on one such trip.

"The baby is too big," she said and rushed back into the room where I glimpsed Inga writhing on the bed.

"Our Father, who art in heaven," I began again and soon heard the baritone voice of Bishop Whipple joining me, only in English. "Thy will be done on earth as it is in heaven . . ."

"When the Indians were attacking and the violence overwhelmed me," I confessed, "prayer was my only relief."

I had longed for Bishop Whipple's listening ear and found it a great relief. "The faces of the dead kept pressing in on me . . . and the smell of burning flesh. They pressed in again and again, almost driving me to insanity." I struggled to express myself, to

471

put into words what had no words. "I recited the Apostle's Creed and the Lord's Prayer and the Twenty-Third Psalm — it pushed the faces back, kept me sane."

"The Lord is a present help in time of trouble," said the bishop. "A sure foundation when the earth gives way."

We pondered the mysteries of life and faith in an anxious silence, waiting for the birth of Inga's baby — our baby. Suddenly we heard a shriek like the cry of an attacking Dakota brave. The hair on the back of my neck stood up, and I pounded on the door, demanding to know what was wrong.

"I believe in God the Father Almighty," I opened the door to see Inga swooned on the bed, blood covering her splayed legs, a gaping hole from where the baby had come with the severed cord securely tied with a piece of sheet. The smell of fresh blood slapped my face, the smell of butchering day in Norway. A baby lay limp in Solveig's hands and the Widow Schwarz hovered near, slapping and coaxing it to breathe.

"And in Jesus Christ His only Son our Lord . . ."

Something in me rose up strong, I reached for the babe and took it from Solveig's bloody hands, gentle as a lamb yet fierce as a berserk. I had seen foals in like trouble and thought it worth a try, a desperate act. A clinging film covered the baby's face and I pierced it with my fingernail and pulled it away. Nothing happened. I held the baby upside down and saw it was a boy. I swiped my fingers inside its mouth and pulled out a gob of glue-like mucous. I cradled the baby in my hands and took my mouth and covered the wee one's mouth and nose and puffed breath into its lungs. The puffs were small and gentle, as my far had shown me when dealing with a new colt.

The baby choked and coughed a weak sound, then inhaled on his own and let out a howling scream that almost caused me to drop him.

"Your son does not like the scratch of your beard," Solveig said, laughing that the crisis was over.

We watched, eyes glued on the new life screaming out an angry protest to the world. Inga called weakly from the bed, "Is he all right?"

"A big healthy boy screams for his mor."

He had fat rolls around his neck and arms. I guessed his weight close to nine pounds. His hair looked dark and curly, pressed against his pointed scalp in a tight cap, covered with the cream from his mother's body. It was a wonder my tiny Inga could ever have delivered him.

Solveig took him from my hands and swaddled him tightly in a blanket. His screaming continued until she settled him at Inga's breast. My eyes fixed on the nursing child and the breast exposed for the baby. It was impossible to believe it was my wife and child — I could look and touch all I wanted.

"The caul he is born with," said the Widow Schwarz. "This I've never seen."

"The caul?" Solveig said. "What's that?"

"It's a film covering his face," Bishop Whipple said from the doorway. "It would have killed him, but Evan knew to pull it away from his nose and mouth so he could breathe."

"It means he will have good luck all his days," I said. "The caul is a sign of good luck."

Then Inga started to grimace and moan again.

"What's happening?" I asked.

"It's the afterbirth coming," Solveig said. "You must leave the room."

Anger, unreasonable and protective, rose up within me, and I felt myself on the verge of striking Solveig. She was always bossing me, giving me advice when I didn't want it. After all, I had saved the baby from certain death. Didn't I have a right to be in the room with my wife and child?

"I will not leave," I said. "Not now or ever."

Solveig looked at me thoughtfully and must have determined there was no changing my mind. I sat at the head of the bed and cradled Inga's head and shoulders with my left hand, supporting the nursing baby with my right hand, while she pushed once more and delivered a pancake like material that resembled raw liver. The sweat rolled down her face and neck, but Inga did not make a sound. I checked to make sure she was breathing. Exhausted, Inga had fallen asleep.

The Widow Schwarz collected the afterbirth in a wooden bucket, covered it with a cloth and left the room.

"Where is she going?"

"She'll bury it in the garden." Solveig took a wet cloth and swabbed the insides of Inga's legs, cleaning off the accumulated blood and sweat. "There's nothing better for a garden than afterbirth."

Then Solveig took a fist and kneaded Inga's flabby belly, causing her to cry out in pain and awaken from her sleep.

"Ow!" said Inga. "Stop it."

"It's necessary," Solveig said. "It prevents

bleeding."

"It hurts," said Inga. "It's worse than having the baby."

Solveig laughed and said, "You're forgetting already what you went through, just like the Good Book says."

"What does the Good Book say on the subject?" I said.

"That a woman in childbirth suffers but when she holds the child in her arms she forgets all about what she went through for the joy of the new life."

"I haven't quite forgotten," Inga said with a wry grimace.

Inga dozed again and the baby nursed. The women hovered around, checking under the blankets to make sure Inga wasn't bleeding too much, fussing with the baby who was doing fine at the breast, worrying about me being in the birthing room, pressing beef broth by the spoonful between Inga's sleeping lips.

"Enough," I said. "Leave us alone. I'll keep watch."

"You must knead her belly every so often," Solveig said with a stern expression. "She might bleed to death if you don't."

"I'll do it," I said. "Don't worry,"

"And make sure the baby switches sides," Solveig said. "Otherwise she'll get sore and have an uneven milk supply."

"I'll take care of it," I said.

There were questions in their eyes, but Solveig kneaded Inga's belly one more time and reluctantly left. In truth, I hated the smell of blood but I loved Inga more. I kicked off my dirty boots and washed my hands in the basin on the dresser, wiping them on my shirt when I couldn't find a dry towel. Knowing the women would be tiptoeing in soon, I dared not take off my pants and shirt as I wished. Instead I crawled in beside Inga on the bed, careful to keep the padding under her hips and my body away from the fresh blood. I thought her asleep, but when I laid my head on the pillow beside her she roused.

"This is heaven. Not only do I have a new man, but a healthy son."

She drifted off to sleep. Although I was more tired than I ever remembered being, I lay awake beside her, dreaming of the life we would have, stroking her breast while our son nursed. I spread her hair across the pillow and caressed the brown curls with my fingers, kissed her fingertips entwined with mine.

It wasn't at all like the wedding night I had envisioned, but it was fine. It was just fine.

# 36

"One Thousand Innocents Dead at the
Hands of the Sioux"
~ St. Paul Journal

A crying baby woke me in the early dawn.
With a start I remembered I hadn't moved
the baby to the other breast or kneaded Inga's belly. Solveig was in the room. She
flashed me a look of irritation.

"You might as well leave," Solveig said.
"You're good for nothing that needs doing
here."

"Evan," Inga said weakly, "take the baby
so I can clean up a little."

I looked at the screaming baby, blankets
sopping wet and stinking. His mouth was
an open maw, and the volume of his screams
equaled that of a Dakota brave on the
warpath. Maybe he would be marked for
life by the Indian wars. It made sense if an
unborn baby was exposed to great trauma,

he would carry it the rest of his life.

"Here." Solveig handed him to me. "Take him in the other room, nearer to the stove. Here's a dry swaddling cloth."

It was awkward but I managed to change the wet cloths and wrap him in the dry ones. His arms and legs flailed, but he calmed with the dry cloths wrapped tightly around him. I soothed him in Norwegian, bouncing him a little as I paced the floor in front of the stove.

His eyes searched my face. Although it was hard to tell, I thought they would be brown like his mor's. His face carried a serious expression as if he were trying to sort out the problems of the world.

I thought then of the happiness my far and mor would have had over a grandson. Then I thought of Christina being an aunt. My heart almost burst with the joy and sadness of the moment. New life and grief together.

Ragna woke up and the Widow Schwarz took her by the hand as they trudged out into the cold to use the toilet, letting a wave of freezing air into the room. Halvor still slept by the stove.

Bishop Whipple came in from outside, carrying a load of wood to the stove.

"Evan," he greeted in a booming voice.

"How is the bridegroom?"

A smile came to my face, as I remembered my change in marital status.

"Good morning, Bishop," I said quietly so as not to awaken the baby who had just closed his eyes. "We are well, husband, wife, and son."

"Thanks be to God," he answered. "It's cold out there. A blessing the refugees are mostly gone. For a few weeks after the uprising, our yard was filled with them."

Baby Evan crossed my mind, and I thought how senseless his death. A quick stab of grief pierced me, but it was no time to dwell on the past.

"What of the Indian trials, Bishop?" I hoped to change the subject.

"They continue," he said.

"Are the proceedings in the papers?" I was eager to catch up on the news. "I'm so behind since being forted up."

"Yes," he said. "The papers are filled with the news of the trials, if you call them trials." He looked at me with such sadness I felt a choking lump in my throat. "The state demands vengeance. One thousand people killed by the Dakota."

"One thousand?" I asked in disbelief. "You must be mistaken."

"No one knows for sure," he said. "Maybe

more. Innocent men, women, and children for the most part. And no one knows the number of Dakota killed — those numbers will only increase as the whites seek revenge."

Questions flooded my mind, all the questions I had longed to ask the bishop. I stuttered out only one sentence, "Why would they kill the settlers?"

"The Dakota do not see the soldiers as their enemy as much as the settlers," he said. "Crooked Lightning told me that it was the settlers who were destroying their hunting grounds and turning the land into farms. The soldiers have no interest in the land and are less of a threat."

It made sense in an uncivilized way. I held my son close to my body, trying to forget the brutalities I had witnessed, trying to shield him, remembering with a shudder the baby thrown into the hot oven.

"But why no accurate account?" I asked. "Don't they know who's missing and who's accounted for?"

"Immigrants don't speak English well enough to report the deaths. Some families in isolated areas were totally wiped out. Who's left to tell? Minnesota is a huge state — people can get lost in it."

Solveig came from Inga's room, and I

handed her the baby.

"How is she?" I asked.

"She's exhausted and needs to rest," Solveig said.

"I need to speak to her before I return the stage to the fort," I said.

"Hmmph." She motioned me away from the bishop and whispered in a stern voice, "Keep your hands off her. A woman takes a long time to heal after a birth."

I looked back at Solveig almost thinking I hadn't heard correctly. She returned my gaze without flinching. "Don't touch her," she said. "She needs time."

It was a relief to flee into the bedroom away from Solveig's big nose. Inga looked pale against the white sheets. Dark bruises encircled her bloodshot eyes. In truth, she looked spent.

"Inga." I kissed her forehead. She smelled of new soap and fresh blood and that milky smell all new mothers, animal or human, have.

She fluttered her eyes open. "How is he?"

"He's strong and healthy." My voice cracked only slightly. "He may grow up to be president, the first citizen in our family."

"A president."

I knelt down on the floor beside the bed and kissed her gently on her lips, savoring the fact it was no longer a sin, no longer a breach of any commandment. The thought left me giddy as a schoolboy. My hand stroked her milk-swollen breast, and she looked at me with sweet tenderness.

Solveig pushed through the door without knocking and brought the baby to nurse. I held my ground in spite of her scornful glance and in the end she positioned the baby at the breast with me standing there, all eyes and wonder.

"See how he eats," Inga said. "He's like a piglet, pushing and grunting."

The baby pushed his hands and feet trying to make the milk flow faster. Even Solveig laughed at the comparison.

"I need to return to the fort and speak to the commander about my job."

Her eyes showed disappointment, but she quickly said, "Of course."

"I'll be back a little later." I wondered why I felt so guilty. A man had to work, and it wasn't as if I had the money to hang around the house all day with the womenfolk. I kissed the little one and kissed Inga. But I admit it was hard to leave.

Not only was I given my old job back, the commander slapped me on the back and commended me for my actions.

"You're displayed courage and clear think-ing," he said. "You deserve a medal."

I stood in awkward silence remembering my terror and confusion, the loss of two good teams, the dead along the trail.

"I'm in need of a driver to take me and my aides to Mankato to oversee the hang-ings," the commander said.

"The hangings?"

"Yes," he said. "The condemned Sioux are in Mankato waiting to be hanged. We'll leave tomorrow."

It was work, and I couldn't afford to refuse it, although I felt close to tears when I said good-bye to Inga. "It's the last stage run of the season," I said, "and I'm lucky to get it. A quick trip before the snow flies. I'll be home by St. Clement's Day."

"By then," Inga said. "I'll be strong again."

"We'll have the baptism when you get back," Solveig said. "And choose a name."

I looked at Solveig with amazement. Her brain was always thinking.

"It's settled then."

"Can Elsa ride along to search for her sister?" Solveig said.

"The Widow is welcome to ride along if there's room."

It was decided. Bishop Whipple agreed to ride along as shotgun for the chance to visit the condemned Dakota braves.

"Over three hundred condemned." Bishop Whipple said once the stage got underway. "I read it in the paper today."

"I can believe it." I remembered the 500 braves who held Fort Abercrombie under siege for six weeks, the slit throats and mutilated bodies.

"Crooked Lightning's name is on the list of condemned."

I nodded my head, not surprised, but my throat turned to dust. Crooked Lightning gambled and lost. I held no ill will toward him, remembering how he had spared our lives. But then I thought of Lewis, dug from his grave.

"It cost over four hundred dollars," Bishop Whipple said.

"What?"

"Aren't you listening?" he chuckled. "Your mind's on your beautiful bride, and I don't blame you one bit." He repositioned himself on the stage, settling into a more comfortable spot before he answered. "The telegram to President Lincoln naming all the condemned Dakota cost over $400 to send to Washington."

"Whew!" Four hundred dollars was over a year's wages for a workingman. "Why did they bother President Lincoln with it?

Couldn't the army take care of it?"

"The people want justice and the political side of it is too complicated for a simple army general. President Lincoln has to decide."

We rode along in a comfortable silence and soon the Bishop was nodding and snoring. A stab of guilt reminded me how we barged in on him and kept him up most of the night. My face warmed as I remembered our wedding and my first night with Inga. We had plenty of time to make up for it later. It was something to look forward to. I wondered how long it would take.

Away from Solveig, the Widow Schwarz retreated into her shell and the wild look returned to her eyes. At our first stop, the soldiers avoided her completely as if her condition were contagious. I tried to reassure her, but although her arms hung placidly at her sides, her frantic eyes darted side to side without stopping.

At Mankato we asked around but no one knew of her sister. Either her family had moved away or were no longer living — not a crumb of information could be found.

"I'm in need of a housekeeper," Bishop Whipple said. "You can return to Fort Snelling and keep house for me."

She smiled in gratitude but the eyes did not change. The bishop arranged for her to stay with a Methodist minister and his family until the stage returned to Fort Snelling. If all went as planned, we would go back in a few days.

Bishop Whipple convinced me to visit Crooked Lightning. I feared entering the pen where they were kept. Although unarmed and shackled, the braves looked ferocious and untamed. I felt the hair on the back of my neck stand up as we walked through the rows of condemned braves. None of the faces stood out as being familiar yet all of the faces seemed familiar. I found myself wondering which one had nailed Baby Evan to the door, which one had gutted Hjalmer Thoreson and scattered mail across the prairie.

"Crooked Lightning." Bishop Whipple smiled and reached out to shake his hand. "We've come to see you."

Crooked Lightning did not smile or say a word, but his eyes shone brightly as they flitted between us. His hands stayed firmly on his lap and he ignored the handshake.

We sat beside him on the ground as the silence echoed. The other braves looked warily at us, no doubt wondering what we wanted. In truth, Bishop Whipple was interested in Crooked Lightning's eternal soul. It was in my mind to thank him for sparing my life.

The bishop was familiar with the Dakota customs and sat politely in silence. My legs twitched at their unfamiliar position, and I fought the desire to wiggle. Crooked Lightning sat as straight and still as a stone, his eagle feathers hanging proudly in his greased hair.

"Thank you," I said at last, unable to stand the silence a minute longer. "That night in the barn."

His eyes glittered but he didn't speak. I worried I had offended him and looked to Bishop Whipple for advice. He shook his head slightly in my direction and I quit talking. Once again, I had spoken out of turn and made a complete fool of myself. Perhaps Crooked Lightning did not consider me a friend, maybe it was all in my imagination. But I remembered how we sat around his fire talking of fireboats and locomotives. We were friends. Proven by how he spared my life — how I spared his.

I stood to leave. I just couldn't take it anymore — the glares of hatred from the other braves, the smell of bear grease and unwashed bodies, the hopelessness and waste of it all. "Good-bye, Crooked Lightning," I said. "I count you as a friend in spite of everything."

He lifted his chin but said nothing, his eyes glittering and sharp.

"I'll be out in a little while," Bishop Whipple said.

The fresh air smelled good after the confinement of the pen and my breath made short puffs in the cold. I reminded myself what the Indians had done, how they deserved such treatment. It was a relief they were shackled. I had no desire to see them swoop down upon me with upraised hatchets and shrieking wails.

A private guarded the gate and tipped his hat to me as I left the compound. He was young, about the age of Adam Sullivan I guessed. His buttons were polished and his jacket immaculate. A fresh pimple bloomed red on the tip of his nose.

"Won't be long till they're hung. Can't come soon enough to suit me."

"You have reason to hate them?" I spat a stream of brown juice into the bushes.

"They killed my brother at Fort Ridgley," he said. "I hate them all right."

"During the siege?"

"They snuck up on him while he stood guard." His voice quavered and broke. "He was a good brother."

A consuming grief engulfed me. I thought of the waste of houses and farms and young lives. A horrible, senseless waste because the gold was one day too late. Then I corrected myself. It wasn't just because the gold was late; the traders were dishonest, the settlers demanded land and Abe Lincoln was too busy with the Civil War to do justice to the Dakota people.

It was cold outside, but I took refuge on the stage pulled into a barn, sleeping on top as had become my custom. At least there were no bedbugs, no strangers to contend with. The horses stomped and chewed in the shadows, keeping guard while I slept like a baby.

In the morning, I awoke to an unexpected snowstorm. A howling wind had come up and the stable door was wedged shut with blown snow. It was early for bad weather. What if the winter lasted and I couldn't get home to Inga and the baby.

I grabbed a shovel and cleared away the snow. My nose ran and froze icicles on my scraggly beard. I knew I looked like an ancient Viking, but I had no choice but to trudge to the commander's temporary headquarters in the sheriff's office.

The commander sat at the sheriff's desk, scowling over a document in his hand.

"Damn the politicians!" He threw the paper down on the table.

"What's wrong, sir?" I held my hat and felt my beard thawing into drops of snot that dripped to the floor. I tried to wipe it on my sleeve.

"Lincoln has put a stay on the executions," he said. "Wants a commission to review the court proceedings. The way the government works, we can plan on another month or two before they decide anything."

I calculated the months in my head. If I were stuck in Mankato for two more months, I would miss Christmas with my new family. I'd miss two months of being a far to the baby, a husband to my missus. In fact, I might miss all winter with the unpredictable weather and trouble getting the stage through unplowed roads. It wasn't worth it, no matter what they paid me.

"Commander." My voice was firm and without stuttering, "I cannot remain in Mankato more than a few days. If you wish, I can leave the stage here and return on foot. Perhaps you could find another driver when you need one."

"I can't stay in Mankato two months either. I've work to do, and there's still a war on in the south. We'll return to Fort Snelling as soon as this snow melts. It's too early to last."

A great sigh of relief escaped me. I never knew the pull a missus had on a man, the draw that brought him back to her. I felt myself smiling, a lightness in my chest.

# 37

"303 Sioux Sentenced to Hang Unless
Lincoln Interferes"
~ St. Paul Journal

It felt like years but the snow lasted only a few days. The sun came out and dried out the trail over the next week. The sky was clear blue without a cloud and the temperatures returned to normal. Though the trail bogged in spots, I thought it safe to make the journey.

Bishop Whipple came to see me while I cleaned out the stable on the morning of our scheduled departure. "I can't leave the Dakota like this. I just can't do it."

"What do you mean?" I kept sweeping. The stage was ready to go and all my thoughts were on Inga.

"I'm going to stay with them until the execution," he said. "They're hated and alone. Maybe I can do them some good, at least stand by them until the end."

"Do you think Lincoln will pardon them?" I put the broom on its nail on the stable wall.

"I heard a rumor he'll pardon most of them due to lack of evidence although it is not a popular decision," he said. "In fact, it's rumored Lincoln might lose the next election if he pardons any of the Dakota. People demand vengeance."

It was true. The newspapers were filled with accounts of survivors and the need for exterminating the Dakota.

"They have witnesses to name only thirty-eight of the 303 braves," he said. "The others are condemned on hearsay and rumor. Not every Sioux is guilty. Many warned their white neighbors and saved lives.

I looked at him and Bishop Whipple answered my unasked question.

"Crooked Lightning has a witness naming him in both murder and rape."

It was no surprise. I remembered how he desecrated Lewis' body. *Ja,* it was no surprise though it grieved me and sent a cold chill through my body. It could have been Inga. It could have been me.

"Crooked Lightning sends a message to you," he said.

"He does?"

"He says that his family flees to the Killdeer Mountains in Dakota Territory," he said. "That if your paths ever cross, remember your friendship with him."

There was nothing to say. I doubted our paths would cross. My plans were to farm in Minnesota, not go to Dakota Territory.

"What will happen to the rest of them?" I asked. "Will they go free?"

"No one knows," he said. "That's for Lincoln to decide. But I'll stay here until it is over." He picked up a few stray grains of oats and fed them to one of the horses. The horse licked his outstretched hand in appreciation. "The rest of the Dakotas have been herded to Fort Snelling for the winter."

"How can they care for all those people?" I thought of the women and children, whole families.

"It's madness," he said. "Not all Sioux took part in the uprising, but all are blamed. There's talk they'll be banished from Minnesota, every last one of them."

I looked at him in wonder. He was an ordinary man, his head balding and a middle-aged paunch starting in his belly. Yet somehow his life had a quality unknown in my own. He was a real Christian. I had known it all along, but I saw it even more clearly on that day.

My throat choked, and I could not reply, only shook his hand and threw my arms around his neck and hugged him for all I was worth.

"*Mange takk,* Bishop," I said. "*Mange takk* for everything!"

"My house is full anyway," he said with a chuckle. "At least here I'll get away from the cackling womenfolk."

The Widow Schwarz decided to remain with the Methodist minister. The missus was in the family way and could use help with their three small children. I hated to admit it, but it was a relief to leave her behind. Her eyes were a continual torment to me, and Bishop Whipple's house was more than full already.

The officers climbed into the coach. I closed the door and jumped up on the box, calling to the horses in Norwegian, putting a chaw of snuff in my cheek.

The temperature dropped, and I longed for my old buffalo coat still at Fort Snelling. Cold froze the ruts in the trail, making it was a bone-jarring ride all the way. But we made fair time and reached the fort after dark the second day on the trail.

I put the horses up, crooning to them and feeding them bits of snuff along with their oats and hay. They weren't the most beautiful team in the world, but they were steady, had done a good job in such weather. I petted them and kissed their noses but stopped short of naming them. *Nei,* I did not name that team at all.

It was snowing when I walked down the hill to the Episcopal Mission. Lights glowed in the windows. Closer to the cabin, I could see Solveig and Rasmuss dancing in the kitchen. Inga sat at the table, smiling and holding the baby.

An ache gripped me and I felt my knees weaken. It was almost as if the dreams Christina and I had shared in our childhood had come true. "Pull yourself together, man!" I said to myself and pushed open the door. For once, I belonged completely.

"We can't wait until Bishop Whipple gets back for the baptism," Solveig said firmly. "If the baby would sicken and die, he'd be damned, and we'd be to blame."

It was a sobering thought and put an end to all talk of waiting for the bishop to return. The little one looked healthy, but I was ignorant in such things and dared not voice my opinion. Besides there was the question of religion. Bishop Whipple was Episcopalian, after all.

"There is a Lutheran priest at Pig's Eye," Rasmuss said.

It was agreed. Rasmuss bundled up and set out to find him. Solveig's cake baked in the oven, and Inga sat in the rocker and nursed the baby. He lifted a chubby hand and patted his mor's breast. It made me envious — he had such freedom while I had to wait for the privacy of darkness. I wondered how long it took women to recover from childbirth, and I found myself wishing Solveig had gone with Rasmuss to find the minister. Her big nose was in everyone else's business, and I thought to ask Inga directly.

The baby finished with a loud burp and slept in Inga's arms. She rose to lay him on the bed, and I made a mental note to build a cradle. He wouldn't stay put in a regular bed for long.

I followed Inga into the bedroom and closed the door. The room was cool, the stove being in the kitchen, and the north wind howled outside the window. I covered the baby with another blanket. It would not do for him to catch cold.

Inga snuggled into my arms and we stood watching the baby, listening to the wind and the sounds of Ragna and Halvor playing in the kitchen, thankful for the moment of privacy.

"We still haven't settled on a name," said Inga.

"We must decide before the priest gets here."

"I'd like to name him after his real far, if you don't mind."

My head reeled, and I felt the wind knocked out of me. To name a wee baby after Ingvald Ericson was too much to consider. That Inga would even think of such a thing was impossible.

"I have a surprise for you," she said sensing my reaction. "A surprise I have been saving to tell you when we could be alone."

"We haven't been alone much."

"I meant to give it to you as a wedding gift but things were too busy."

I had a flash of memory, her screams in bringing forth the new life, the breath I puffed into his nostrils, the acrid taste of blood on my lips.

Inga smiled a radiant smile, brown eyes flashing. "The baby's father is Gunnar Thormondson. I was already expecting when I married Mr. Ericson, in fact that was the reason I married him at all. I owed it to Gunnar to survive and bring forth his son. I never told Mr. Ericson, fearing he would hate the child and make his life miserable."

It all fell into place, the baby coming early and yet full-sized. I looked at the child, born of love and not of duty, relieved beyond description.

"He's one hundred percent Norwegian," I said with pride. "Not a drop of Swede in him!"

"*Ja,* Gunnar Evan Jacobson is no Swede," she said. "He's an American citizen. He can grow up to be president someday."

My throat constricted and tears filled my eyes. My voice cracked and broke. "Gunnar Evan?"

"He is named for his real fathers," she said. "The one who planted him and the one who raises him. They both gave him life." She reached up and wiped tears from my beard, and for once I didn't try to hide them. "Is it not a lovely name?"

Words were not enough, but after a few minutes she pulled away, straightening her hair and dress.

"They'll be here soon," she said with a sassy grin. "There'll be time for that later."

In honor of the occasion, I shaved off my scraggly beard, leaving me feeling light and youthful. Inga wore a new dress she and Solveig had been working on for days. Gunnar Evan wore a white embroidered baptismal gown from Norway.

"My far and his far and his far all wore this at their baptisms as did all of us children," she said. "It makes me know they are here with us on this happy day, watching over us and smiling."

Solveig laid a white cloth on the table and lit the lamps. A washbasin and pitcher of warmed water stood on the table. The Lutheran priest held Gunnar Evan in his big hands and administered the Sacrament of Holy Baptism. Rasmuss and Solveig stood as Godparents. Inga's face shone brighter than the lamplight, and when I looked into her eyes I saw the joy of my own face reflected back.

It was almost midnight, but I couldn't sleep. Quietly I rummaged in Bishop Whipple's desk and found a quill and ink and a sheet of heavy paper. With only one candle for light, I wrote:

St. Clement's Day, November 28, 1862

Dear Ole,
I take pen in hand to share the news. I have a wife and baby son. The boy was baptized today with the name of Gunnar Evan Jacobson. Our family name continues even in the wilderness. We survived the Indian War by the grace of

501

God. I hope you and your family are well and happy. There is land available in Minnesota, the soil black and rich. West of here is land flat and without trees of any kind that produces bountiful wheat and corn. I hope to settle in the central part of the state where lakes and trees abound. It is hillier and there are stumps to contend with, but it reminds me of my homeland. Best of all, a man is free to vote, own land and is judged on his own merit rather than by class. It is a land where hard labor is rewarded. There is room for you, if you wish to come. Give my regards to your missus and family. Greet Per Hansel if you see him.

Your brother,
Evan

Baby Gunnar whimpered in his sleep, and Inga patted his back and pulled the covers tighter over his shoulders.

"Evan," she said, "what are you doing?"

"I'm writing a letter to my brother," I said, "telling him about my new missus and son."

"Come to bed soon?" Her voice was husky with sleep.

I thought of how old the baby was, how many weeks had passed since his birth. I didn't know about such things, but it seemed it was time to celebrate our wedding vows, to start our life together.

"Why don't you put Gunnar in the clothesbasket beside the bed?" she whispered as I turned back the covers to join her. "We need some time to ourselves."

It seemed we had been waiting forever.

# SOURCES

*Over the Earth I Come: The Great Sioux Uprising of 1862,* Duane Schultz, St. Martin's Press, New York, 1992

*The Sioux Uprising of 1862,* Kenneth Carley, Minnesota Historical Society Press, St. Paul, Minnesota, 1976

*Dakota War Whoop: Indian Massacres and War in Minnesota,* Harriet E. Bishop, Edited by Dale L. Morgan, McConkey 1965.

*The Great Sioux Uprising,* C. M. Oehler, Da Capo Press, New York, 1997

*Through Dakota Eyes,* Edited by Gary Clayton Anderson and Alan R. Woolworth, Minnesota Historical Press, St. Paul, 1988

*Fort Abercrombie 1862,* Supplement of *Richland County Farmer-Globe,* Wahpeton, No.Dak. 1936

*Minnesota Days, Our Heritage in Stories, Art and Photos,* Edited by Michael Dregni,

Voyageur Press, Stillwater, Minnesota, 1999

*Ever the Land, A Homestead Chronicle,* Ruben L. Parson, Adventure Publishing, Staples, Minnesota 1978

Assistance from The Minnesota History Center in St. Paul, The Otter Tail County Historical Museum, The Grant County Historical Museum, Fort Abercrombie Historic Site and Museum, Fort Snelling Historic Site and a Five Wings Art Grant made this book possible.

The headlines at the beginning of each chapter were found in archived Minnesota newspapers from various towns around the state. In an effort to provide a cohesive story line, they are attributed to *The Saint Paul Journal,* a fictional newspaper. The episodes of violence between the two opposing cultures portrayed in *Abercrombie Trail* were actual occurrences although the dates and exact locations were sometimes altered to fit the story.

# ABOUT THE AUTHOR

**Candace Simar** is a poet and writer from Pequot Lakes, Minnesota. As a lifelong Minnesotan and the grandchild of Scandinavian immigrants, Candace enjoys a passion for Minnesota History and how things might have been. Visit her website at www.candacesimar.com.